MW01268248

STAR LIGHT, STAR BRIGHT…

By

Barbara Elliott Carpenter

© 2003 by Barbara Elliott Carpenter. All rights reserved.

No part of this book may be reproduced, stored in a retrieval system,
or transmitted by any means, electronic, mechanical, photocopying,
recording, or otherwise, without written permission from the author.

ISBN: 1-4107-1684-8 (e-book)
ISBN: 1-4107-1685-6 (Paperback)
ISBN: 1-4107-1686-4 (Dust Jacket)

Library of Congress Control Number: 2003090737

This book is printed on acid free paper.

Printed in the United States of America
Bloomington, IN

1stBooks - rev. 06/23/03

DEDICATION

To the Arcola class of fifty-eight, and all those boys and girls who lived it; to my two sisters, Bonnie Mitchell, by birth, and Karen Carpenter, by marriage; to my brother, Bill Elliott; to my mother, Janie Schumacher; to my husband, Glenn, who said that I would never do it; to my children, Rebecca and Michael: hold onto your memories…your past has made you the great people you are; and, in the order of their appearance, to my grandchildren: Nicholas, Jessica, Scott, and Stephanie.

In memory of my dad, Willis (Bill) Elliott, who was gone from us too soon. A special dedication to my mother-in-law, Alice Carpenter, who was my sounding board, my encourager, my second mother, who wanted nothing but happy endings, who left us suddenly and will never get to read the book.

SPECIAL THANKS AND ACKNOWLEDGEMENTS

While writing this book, I enlisted many people as "readers", a diverse group, of all ages and occupations: among them, a PHD in English, a retired Air Force Colonel, a high school English teacher, stockbrokers, many friends, and my fifteen-year-old granddaughter, Jessica. Thank you, all of you, for laughing and crying in the right places.

Thanks to Jo Chitty Stallings, whose friends in Carbondale will remember her as Joyce Smith. A chance remark she made, after reading the first chapter, led me to look for and find, my first friend in grade school, Rebecca Jeffries Simon. My renewed acquaintance and correspondence with "Becky" contributed much to the first chapter. While a large percentage of this book is fiction, the remainder is somewhat autobiographical. Thanks to Ellen Cunningham Fondren, Linda Basham Zuber, Sharon Bennett, Sheila Hicks Norris, Shirley McNary Bennett, Cathy Partlow De Fauw, Doug Mullikin, and

Lowell East, for permission to relate incidents, some fictionalized, that involved them or their relatives.

And a special thanks to the following: Jerry W. Davis, Colonel, USAF (Retired), who has pushed and encouraged, counted commas, and who did, indeed, give me my first black eye and is still my friend. Sharon Bennett, my first friend in "Redbud Grove." Dr. James D. Green, my friend, and Bonnie Mitchell, my sister, who were my grammar consultants. Willis (Bill) Elliott, my brother and computer tech support. Becky Jeffries, who gave me permission to use some of her memories, and the phrase about the dust, that "felt like warm, confectioner's sugar." Betty King, who in her excitement with her own first published book, pushed me over the edge and into publication. Melissa Bouland, Sean Tolley, Marie Cochran, George Lopez and all the Cedarhurst Writer's Roundtable members, and in memory of those who left us: Suzy Virdin, Larry Mann, and our mentor, Betty Dunham. Linda Bryant, my constant, forever friend, who has always been there with support and encouragement. Without all of you, the manuscript would have remained in the drawer.

TABLE OF CONTENTS

PROLOGUE

Two events occurred in December of nineteen forty-one that changed the course of my life.

First: My mother and father, who were expecting their second child in less than eight weeks, moved from southeastern Missouri to southern Illinois, with nothing but their dreams, their clothing and a twenty-two month old baby girl, me.

Second: Japan bombed Pearl Harbor, Hawaii.
Only the latter event changed the course of the world.

My first conscious memory is the sound of my mother's frantic voice close to my ear.

"Hurry, Pearlene! It's coming! Run!" I remember struggling to free my face from the quilt that smothered me, and the jarring bounce of my body against my mother's shoulder as she ran. There was an answering shout from Aunt Pearlene, who clutched my quilt-wrapped baby brother against her chest, as she ran close upon my mother's heels.

"Get under the bridge!" My mother screamed.

"What if it floods?" Aunt Pearlene screamed back. The roar of the wind carried away her words.

"Just hurry! Hurry!"

That April tornado, from which we were running, spared the little country house that was our first home in Illinois; but it demolished a one-roomed school building not far from the bridge, where the two women took shelter. It destroyed several homes before it dissipated. I was two years old, and I don't remember the tornado, itself; but I recall the terror.

Colorful vignettes of memory sometimes appear unbidden, and I can revisit a scene, a sound, catch a scent, even an emotion, that is as fresh as yesterday. In one such instance, I reach into a tiny, white-satin-lined casket, to touch the hand of my new baby brother, who

ix

lived for only three weeks. My dad takes my hand away and lifts me into his arms. There are tears on his face. It is a dreary mid-November day. I am not quite four years old, and my first little brother is less than two.

The following autumn of nineteen forty-four my dad was drafted. On that cold November afternoon, we stood on the brick-paved platform of a train depot and waited for the train that would carry him to Georgia, the first leg of a journey that led all the way to war-torn Sicily. We would see him once during the next eighteen months.

Many such flashes from those early years are still vivid; but it seems as though that time was just a preamble to my real life, a life that did not begin until I started first grade.

I had longed to go to school. I had been told that, when I was six, I could go to school; and my sixth birthday had occurred in February. I was extremely disappointed when I learned that it would be another six months before I could enter first grade.

When the long-awaited day arrived, my mother walked with me to the school, holding my hand and reassuring me all the way. At the door she knelt beside me.

"Are you scared, Sissy?" she asked. Scared? Me? I shook my head.

"No, Mommy, I'm not scared. 'Bye."

Until then, my only playmates had been my cousins and my little brother. In that classroom were children who were not my cousins, and we were drawn to one another with magnetic force.

Some of us stuck together like glue.

#

THE BEGINNING

Of course I took apples from the trees—every chance I got.

So did every other child in the school.

My sense of doing right versus doing wrong was on its way to becoming ingrained, but it had not yet become second nature.

Hawkins' apple orchard bordered two sides of the schoolyard. A crisp, cider-y scent permeated the air, drawing bees and yellow jackets and red wasps to the fallen fruit on the ground. No fences separated the properties.

Every year students were instructed that there would be dire consequences should anyone be caught taking, eating, or looking with longing at the lovely red globes that hung from the trees for several weeks after school started. It was permitted to retrieve a fallen apple, but those usually had worms, wasps, or both crawling over them.

Rule number one was: DO NOT TOUCH, TAKE, OR EAT AN APPLE ON THE TREES. That was the first rule I learned to break.

Two white toilets, which could not be seen from the classrooms, perched within an arm's throw of the orchard. Given that forbidden fruit is always the most desirable, the natural thing for a child to do, when given permission to visit the outhouse, was to make a quick dash to the orchard, grab the most luscious looking apple they could reach, gulp a few delectable bites behind the sheltering entrance wall, and then dispense with the remaining contraband into the nearest hole, thus managing to enjoy a brief snack before taking care of other necessary business. No one seemed to mind the juxtaposition of the dining area to the toilet facilities.

The school building had two levels. The upper story consisted of two rooms, one of which held grades one through four and the other, grades five through eight. The lower story, which was actually a high basement, accommodated a small number of high school students. Four teachers managed the whole student body, and did it quite well.

1

I was one of six girls in the first grade that September of 1946. Becky Jeffries, who became my first best friend, was the tallest in our class. A six-year-old cannot be described as statuesque, but it was clear that one day Becky would be just that.

She had heavy, long blond hair that sometimes tumbled over her shoulders in long curls, but most often hung down her back in fat, shiny braids. Her mother wrapped Becky's hair-ribbons around the hot stove pipe in the kitchen, a quick way to smooth them, before tying them three or four inches from the ends of Becky's braids. Her ribbons always matched the color of her clothing.

Becky lived across Route Thirty-seven (we called it the "hard road") from her uncle's fruit shed and orchards, apple and peach, at the south end of the little village. The Jeffries' house stood on a large lot a good distance from the highway and was surrounded on three sides by orchards.

One hot, dry Saturday afternoon my dad took me to Becky's house to spend the afternoon. Becky was learning to ride a new bicycle without training wheels, and I tried to help her; but all I managed to do was cushion her falls.

In the orchards, spray-rigs' tires had ground the surface of the dirt lanes between the trees into a fine, powdery dust two or three inches deep. Becky and I kicked off our shoes and buried our feet in the dust, making muffled, plopping sounds when we walked. It was like strolling barefoot in warm confectioner's sugar. The dust also made a soft landing for wobbly bicyclers.

Becky showed me how to use the limbs of the trees as steps to reach the most desirable fruit. For a short time in the waning summer, there were late peaches and early apples. We could choose a crisp, crunchy apple, or bite into a sweet, fuzzy peach so juicy that it dripped down our chins and made our fingers sticky, which drew that fine dust like a magnet. Becky and I laughed at each other's dirt-streaked faces and wiped our hands on our clothes. Well, there was just no other alternative.

Beside Becky's house stood a towering, soft maple tree with roots that extended above the ground and formed deep crevices and little cave-like tunnels throughout the root system. With spoons and various utensils from her mother's kitchen, Becky had dug out roads and extended the tunnels for her fairy friends.

2

"They live in these little places, you see, but they won't come out for anyone 'cept me," she explained. "Delilah is the queen. She got that name from a Sunday school story. I know 'cause she told me she did." Becky nodded knowingly. She beckoned me to come closer, and I crawled nearer the trunk of the tree. She pointed to a deep crevice.

"You got to look really close. If you sqeench your eyes real tight, you might see her. But be re-e-e-a-a-l-l-l quiet or you'll scare her," Becky whispered.

I lay on my stomach, nearly touching the root with my nose, and did as she told me. I made my eyes the narrowest slits possible that still allowed me to see. Something moved, and I swear that I caught a glimmer of gauzy wings! I crawled backward and looked up at Becky.

"Did you see her?" she asked. I nodded and crawled backward some more. Triumph shown in Becky's big blue eyes. "I *knew* she was there," she said.

"Can we go play somewhere else?" I asked.

"Sure." Becky stood up and brushed the dirt from her hands. "I got a new coloring book. Let's go color." I walked closely beside Becky all the way to her house, not quite clinging to her, but almost. I cast furtive glances over my shoulder toward the base of the maple, which now seemed to loom over us. It wasn't until we were inside her house that I felt safe from the little creatures that hid in the mystical caverns of Becky's fairy tree.

I suspect that they are still there.

Completing our number in the first grade was a boy with curly blond hair, blue eyes that held a twinkle as bright as any diamond, and a smile as infectious as a virus. He had a deep dimple in one cheek. The giggle that erupted from his mouth when something struck him as funny was delightful to hear and impossible to resist. His name was Jerry Davis, and he made a big impression on me. He literally knocked me off my feet.

One afternoon recess, Jerry and I collided at the corner of the building, each of us running as fast as only six-year-olds can. His head hit my eye, and I fell to the ground. There were bright colors shimmering against the darkness, and then pain. When I opened my eyes, I saw the faces of my friends and my teacher, Mrs. Freeman, looking down at me.

Mrs. Freeman was a short, plump woman with silver curls and the sweetest, kindest smile. Every first-grader should have such a teacher. She gently held a wet handkerchief to my face. I lay still for a moment longer, decided that I was not dead or dying, and sat up. The world spun crazily before it settled down and let me stand.

Back in the classroom, Mrs. Freeman held up a small mirror so that I could see the growing lump below my eye; and we all admired the lovely shade of blue that had begun to spread under my brow and along my temple.

"You really got a wallop," Mrs. Freeman said. She turned to Jerry. He held his right hand up to his head, gingerly rubbing the bump that formed just above his hairline. Mrs. Freeman carefully brushed his blond curls away from his forehead and examined the knot. "It looks like you got the better of this encounter, Jerry; but don't count on it next time." She glanced around the circle of sober faces. "Let this be a lesson." Uh oh. I heard rule number two coming: DON'T RUN SO CLOSELY TO THE BUILDING.

I'm not sure that the collision was the beginning of the scholastic competition between Jerry and me, but it probably was. We both loved learning to read. We absorbed Mrs. Freeman's gentle instruction like sweet lemonade poured down a parched throat, never satisfied and always wanting more.

We skipped through the first reading book, Nip and Tuck, a short little paperback about two black and white dogs. We scurried along the pages of the second reader, which was a blue hardback entitled Bob and Judy. It was about a brother and sister who lived with Nip and Tuck and Mother and Father. (I thought that parents were known only as Mom and Dad.)

Jerry and I took turns reading additional pages to Mrs. Freeman. Neither of us wanted the other to get ahead. We were well into the third book, a green hardback called Good Times Together, further adventures of Bob and Judy, when my dad took a job in a town called Redbud Grove, one hundred miles north of where we lived.

Before the war, Dad had worked in a foundry in Mount Vernon, a much larger town a few miles south of our little village. A new foundry had just begun operations in Redbud Grove; and Dad had been hired as a foreman, which meant higher wages. He came home on Friday evenings and went back to Redbud Grove on Sunday afternoons.

I didn't really miss my dad. He had been gone most of the past two years, the last years of The War. I had never been quite sure what The War was; but one of my uncles came home from it with only one leg, and Dad was very quiet after being there, a stranger that, for a while, I found difficult to know. My baby sister, Elizabeth, who was nicknamed Bethy shortly after her birth, arrived a few weeks after Dad returned from The War. I heard my mom tell one of my aunts that she had considered calling the baby "furlough" but decided that it wasn't a very good name for a girl.

I assumed that we would always live as we were: Mom, my sister, my brother and I, snugly secure in the little apartment behind the post office. I was happy with a weekend daddy who read to me, even though he complained that the books I brought from school were too long and why didn't I pick out shorter ones. He took Buddy and me to Doc's restaurant just down the street and bought us ice cream cones. He always had one of us take a big lick from the cone he brought home to Mom. After she had eaten most of hers, Dad would tell her that one of us had slobbered all over it; and Mom would pretend to be upset. Daddy would laugh. I loved to hear him laugh.

I enjoyed going to school and playing with my friend, Becky. When I came home from school, there was my little brother, to whom I could pretend-read from books too large for me, and a baby sister, who was learning to coo and laugh, a real live baby doll. Life as I knew it was good.

One day my mom announced that Daddy had bought a house in Redbud Grove; and we would move to that house shortly after Christmas. I saw no reason why things could not continue as they were.

All eight grades were practicing a Christmas program, and I was part of a trio of girls that was going to sing and do special motions to <u>Santa Claus is Coming to Town</u>. I was in the rhythm band, and we were going to perform a rousing rendition of <u>Jingle Bells</u>. It didn't matter that I had to play the sticks, when I really wanted to play a tinkling triangle.

5

I couldn't leave my friends and Mrs. Freeman. After Christmas there were other lovely projects in the works, and I absolutely had to be a part of all of them. What did she mean by "move"?

Time is inexorable. Nothing slows or stops or changes it. Christmas came and went, and suddenly it was the last week in January. I could not comprehend the extent to which my life was about to change, but one thing was certain. I would leave with the knowledge that I had read many more pages to Mrs. Freeman than Jerry. It was a cold, sunny afternoon the last time I read to her. I stood beside her desk, and she kept her arm around me as I read.

My mom had left Buddy and the baby with a neighbor while she came to school to walk home with me that last day. Mom and Mrs. Freeman listened patiently as I read. It was only after I had stumbled on unfamiliar words several times that Mrs. Freeman stopped me, and handed a handful of gold stars to me. I licked the backs and attached one to each page I had read—fifteen of them.

My teacher helped me clean out my desk and gather all my handwork pages into a folder. She pulled me to her side and hugged me tightly, and then she pressed a kiss onto my forehead. She had never done *that* before. I looked up at her, and there were tears in her eyes.

"I'm going to miss you, Sissy. You be a good girl and listen to your new teacher. You will do just fine."

"I bet Jerry can't read as many pages as *I* did," I told Mrs. Freeman. She laughed and gave me a quick hug.

"Come on, Honey, we have to go," Mom said. She held my books and papers, while I shrugged into my coat.

"Good luck, Mrs. Bannister."

"Thank you." Mom guided me toward the door. I looked back at Mrs. Freeman. She gave me a sweet smile and an encouraging wave of her hand.

"Bye," I said. I took a step through the door, turned back, and said, "Bye." Another step. "Tell Becky and Jerry and Jackie and Martha Ann…"

"Come *on*, Sissy; we have to pick up Buddy and the baby."

"Tell Jerry I beat him!"

The door closed behind us.

6

I knew that it would be several days before Jerry caught up to me. It had somehow escaped me that my victory was hollow, because I wouldn't see his face or gleefully watch him as he tried to catch me. I didn't understand that I was leaving behind everything and everyone, except my immediate family, that I had ever known.

Five of my dad's brothers and one of his sisters lived in the surrounding rural area. Two of my mother's brothers and their families also resided close-by. Together there were twenty-four first cousins, ranging in age from seventeen to infancy, with whom I had regular contact. I had no idea how isolated and alone I would feel in the days that followed.

It is true that children are resilient. It is also true that children feel the sharp slash of fear when being surrounded by totally unfamiliar faces, looking and searching for just one that is recognizable and not finding it. Sometimes it is true that ignorance is, indeed, bliss. That last afternoon I was more excited than afraid. I had not yet had reason to fear.

Daddy had driven straight from work to our little apartment. Uncle Jim had loaded our furniture onto his two-ton truck early that afternoon and had already left for Redbud Grove. It was dark by the time Daddy came for us. Nothing was left to be done except climb into the car and go. The ride to Redbud Grove seemed interminable. Dad drove while Mom held six-month-old Bethy in the front seat of the nineteen thirty-nine Hudson. Four-year-old Buddy and I shared the back.

"Are we almost there?"

I don't know how often I asked the question, but the answer was always "no." I sang every song I knew, from tunes of unrequited love, which I had learned while listening to The Grand Ole Opry, to choruses we sang in the little Methodist Church Sunday School, just down the street from our apartment. (My mom was a fan of country music when it was not the culturally accepted thing to be.) When I couldn't remember the words, I made up my own.

I counted as high as I could, lost my place several times, and had to start over. Somewhere between the counting and the singing I grew drowsy. My head fit quite nicely on the armrest, and the velvet covering was soft against my cheek. The sound of the engine was soothing, a constant purr in the background that lulled me to sleep and kept me there.

"Sissy, wake up. We're here." I sat up and peered out the steamy car window for the first look at my new home. The house seemed huge to me, and desolate in the dark. It sprang up from the center of the frozen, uneven ground that was to be the yard. The roof rose from three sides to form a peak where the chimney released a slow column of coal smoke. On the front side there was a gable with a single window in the upper story. There were no streetlights, but a full moon illuminated the area.

My mother carried the baby, and Dad lifted my sleeping brother from the back seat. I stood in the open door of the car and watched them walk away from me. Suddenly I was afraid. I called to my dad.

"Daddy, wait!" I scrambled from the car, slammed the door behind me, and ran after him. He stopped, reached for my hand, and together we walked into our new house. The front door opened into the living room, where a huge Circulator coal heater took up one corner. Daddy had built a fire before he came for us, and the room was warm and cozy. I wriggled out of my coat and went exploring. Our furniture was already there. Quilts and boxes were stacked against the walls and on the sofa. Uncle Jim had set up the crib for Bethy.

"Sissy, here's your gown. Get ready for bed." Mom's voice left no room for argument. After she nursed the baby, Mom helped Buddy into his pajamas. Daddy rocked the baby in the chair beside the stove. I needed no help and was soon twirling among the boxes in my long flannel gown.

A blast of frigid air assaulted us when Mom opened the door of what was to be the bedroom my brother and I would share the next few years. A downy feather bed, covered with a layer of quilts, had been spread upon the floor. I drew my perpetually skinned knees to my chest and let my flannel gown wrap around me like a cocoon. Buddy made a comforting warm bundle beside me, as the feathers fluffed around us. I grew steadily drowsier while I listened to the sounds of my parents arrange boxes and bedding.

The firelight, that flickered through the mica window of the stove, cast interesting patterns on the walls and ceiling. With heavy eyelids

I watched the play of light and shadow, and I listened to the occasional snap and pop of coals in the heater until I fell asleep.

I slept without waking one time.

It was not a big house, but it had a lot more room than the little apartment that had been our home. My parents spent the weekend placing the few pieces of furniture they owned, setting up beds in the two bedrooms, and putting the house in order. Each room was accessible from another, so Buddy and I could chase each other in a circle all the way through the house.

Between the two bedrooms was a stairway that led to an attic, which topped the whole structure. The attic stairs were steep and Rule Number One in the new house was: THE ATTIC DOOR WILL REMAIN CLOSED AT ALL TIMES AND NO CHILD IN THIS HOUSE WILL ATTEMPT GOING UP TO THE ATTIC AT ANY TIME DO YOU UNDERSTAND. Since there were only two children who could walk, Buddy and I nodded that we understood. It was spring before I broke rule number one.

Those first Saturday and Sunday afternoons Dad drove me along the route I would walk to school. He took me several times, explaining that I must stop at every street crossing, especially Route One-thirty-three, and look both ways before I crossed. The next trip was a test. I had to give directions to Dad, who turned as I indicated. We ended up nowhere near the school. He scolded me for not paying attention, and a big lump formed in my throat. I did better on the next test, adding only a few blocks to the route. By Sunday evening, some of the houses I must pass began to look somewhat familiar; and I finally got it right.

Monday morning I dressed in a bright yellow dress with little red rosebuds on it, struggled into red snow pants with suspenders that had to be pulled onto my shoulders, shoved the skirt of my dress into the pants—to put the snow pants on first would have caused major disasters while trying to answer nature's call—pulled on my matching red coat and furry bonnet and was ready to face a new school.

My mother stood at the front door, hoping that another little girl would come by and walk with me. There was no one. She was getting ready to send me on my way, when someone did come by, a boy, eleven or twelve years old. Mom called to him from the open door.

"Would you take my little girl to school? This is her first day and she doesn't know where to go. She's in the first grade." Stunned, the boy stared at my mother and then at me. He shrugged and grunted an answer that was probably positive. At any rate, I found myself walking along with a strange boy, clutching my school records and a small sack lunch in gloved fingers, too shy to look up.

At the first street crossing, the dreaded Route One-thirty-three, I would have kept walking.

"Wait!" The boy flung out his arm and struck me across the chest, pushing me back as a car passed close to the curb. I was totally and irrevocably mortified. We walked in utter silence, until more boys joined us. I suspect that the boy was as unhappy as I.

"Who's your girlfriend?" one of the boys asked.

My escort mumbled something about my being a new kid, who didn't know where she was going. Some woman had asked him to take me to school, and he couldn't get out of it. On cue, the lump appeared in my throat again. Something about male authority figures seemed to affect me like that.

It was a nine-block walk to school from my house. My view of my first trip consisted of watching my feet strike the brick-paved sidewalks through puffs of steam that formed when I breathed the frigid prairie air. The boys bantered and laughed and seemed to be having a great time, while I was scared, miserable and cold.

"There's the first bell," one of the boys announced. "We've got fifteen minutes until the last one." I looked up and saw that we had arrived at the big red-bricked schoolhouse. The loud pealing of the bell was a foreign sound to me. At my other school, the teacher had simply appeared in the doorway and waved us inside.

"You wait here." The boy placed his hands on my shoulders and pushed me into the shelter of a tall inset window beside double doors that led into the school. He turned his back and ran. Children of all ages milled in and out the doors and scurried across the schoolyard, laughing and calling to each other. A group of girls played with a long jumping rope, taking turns running in and running out, avoiding the sharp thump of the rope that was unforgiving should one misjudge.

Scared and near tears, I huddled against the window frame. When the bell began to ring a second time, a stampede of boys and girls rushed toward the doors beside my station and pushed them open. Suddenly the boy who had brought me to school appeared, took my arm, and walked me inside the big entry and down a hall that was crowded with children. He stopped at the first classroom and gently pushed me inside.

"You go here," he said. Once more he disappeared. I didn't know his name. It was weeks before I saw him again and even longer before I learned that he lived on the other side of the park, just down the street from us. Evidently he took another route to school after his enforced escort service.

I stood against the wall and watched the room fill up with noisy, laughing children. No one spoke to me so I waited silently, hoping that someone would tell me what to do.

"Hello." The most beautiful woman I had ever seen beckoned me to approach the desk, where she sat in regal splendor. The white blouse she wore had little tucks down the front with shiny pearl buttons, and an oval cameo pin nestled between the collar points. Small pearl earrings matched the buttons on her blouse. Her hair, a light, shiny brown, was pulled back from her face, leaving little curly tendrils near her ears and along her temples. She smiled and held out her hand for the papers I still clutched with cold fingers. "What is your name?" she asked.

"Sissy," I murmured. She glanced at the papers, among them my report card and a note from Mrs. Freeman and one from my mother.

"What is your last name?"

"Bannister," I replied.

"And you want to be called Sissy?" I nodded.

"I don't like my real name." I was feeling braver. "My brother couldn't say my name when he was little, but he could say 'Sissy' so that's what my name is now. Don't tell anyone what my real name is."

"Very well, Sissy. You may call me Miss Kate." Miss Kate stood up and put her arm around my shoulders. She helped me take off my coat and snow pants and showed me where to hang them on a row of hooks along the back of the room, and how to store my lunch sack on the shelf above.

She led me to a row of connected desks, assigned one to me, and gave me a small stack of books, which I looked through quickly, expecting to see the happy faces of Bob and Judy. Instead, I found an unfamiliar paperback book with pictures of three children called Dick, Jane, and Sally. They had a Mother and Father, too. I decided that all school-book children must be reared by Mothers and Fathers, not moms and dads.

A small circle of boys and girls gathered around me. I looked at each child, as curious about them as they were about me. A boy with a toothless smile offered a book to me. I smiled back and leafed through it quickly.

"You have to read that," said a little girl with gorgeous red hair. I had never seen anyone with hair like hers. About shoulder length, it grew in a mass of shiny curls. A big white ribbon bow held it back on the left side. She smiled at me. "That's a liberry book from the shelf over there." She pointed. "You get to pick out a book when you write good papers. My name is Melissa."

Another little girl wore bright blue pants, not a dress. I was fascinated. The only pants I had seen on girls were snow pants, like mine, and always worn with a dress, not a sweater like this girl wore. I decided that I should have some just like them. It made more sense than stuffing a dress inside those bulky pants.

After we sang the first verse of <u>My Country, 'Tis of Thee</u>, Miss Kate conducted something called Teeth and Fingernail Inspection. The students spread a clean handkerchief on their desktops and placed their hands upon the white squares. As Miss Kate walked up and down the aisles, the boys and girls flashed their teeth in wide grimaces. Those who had brushed their teeth and cleaned their fingernails were rewarded with a trip down the slide that stood in front of the row of windows on the west wall.

Since I was unaware of the exercise, I was allowed a free ride. Excitement filled me. I had never slid down a slide. I climbed the steps quickly when it was my turn.

"Be sure to put your feet down when you come to the bottom!" Several little voices instructed me. I looked down at them and grinned, agreeable, but totally ignorant of their meaning. I found out soon enough.

The glide down was wonderful, but over too soon and with a painful, ignominious ending. My feet remained extended, and I landed on the hard rubber mat with such force that the pattern of the mat was imprinted on my white cotton panties. While I sat there blinking, my new classmates burst into delighted laughter.

When order was restored, Miss Kate introduced me to the class. There were as many students in that class as there had been in the combined four grades where I had been so happily unaware, one short week before. And so many names to remember; Sharon, Cathy, Shirley, Joye, Sheila, Linda, Janet, Ellen, Judy, Phil, Melissa, Madelyn, Janice, Georgia, Pat, Randy, Jim, Glen, Roger, Larry, Ronnie, Alden, John, Barbara, Charles, and on and on.

A pretty girl with dark hair and large, hazel/green eyes raised her hand.

"Yes, Sharon." Miss Kate nodded.

"The new girl lives behind me in the house Doc Teel moved in from the country. My dad says her daddy was a soldier." A murmur emanated throughout the room. I glanced carefully around me and caught several expressions of awe. Hmmm. I thought that having a soldier for a daddy must be a good thing. Maybe going to this school was not going to be so bad.

At recess I learned the most wonderful thing about my new school. There were no outhouses! Beneath the staircase that led to the upper story, was a flight of stairs that led down to the girls' basement restroom. One closed stall was for teachers. Six open stalls accommodated the girls of all eight grades. A tall privacy panel extended the width of the stalls, shielding them from view of the window well on the opposite wall.

"You have to jump up real fast," Sharon explained to me as I pulled the upright seat down and climbed aboard. I learned why before she could explain. The moment I stood up, the toilet seat sprang upward; and the stool automatically flushed. I barely avoided a smacked bottom, followed by a spray of icy water. I soon figured out that it was best to hold the seat down with one hand and then jump clear as I let go.

At the opposite end of the main hall was another basement restroom that had BOYS written above the door. I discovered it when we walked down the hall to the gymnasium, at the other end of the building, for something called P.E. I had never been in a gym before or taken a P.E. class. At the other school we just had recesses.

Sharon walked home from school with me that afternoon, since she lived one block behind us. She came into my house with me and met my mother. Sharon Bennett, who was a single child, was fascinated with my baby sister and nice to Buddy; but I wanted to show her my toys and tell her about Becky and Jerry and my friends who were surely missing me at the other school. Sharon was the first friend I found in Redbud Grove, a friend for all times and seasons.

Within a few weeks I knew most of the children in my class and discovered that several of the girls lived in my neighborhood. My feelings of fear and loneliness disappeared. There was always someone to walk with, to and from school.

Miss Kate made birthdays special. At the end of the day, with colored chalk she drew a huge birthday cake on the blackboard, complete with burning candles. The birthday boy or girl then proceeded to "eat" the cake with an eraser, some nibbling with tiny moves, others gobbling with huge swipes that soon annihilated the cake. I knew that my birthday was coming up soon, the last of February. I couldn't wait to eat my blackboard cake.

The day of my birthday, I was filled with anticipation. I waited for class to be over, barely suppressing the grin that threatened to break forth periodically. But there was no cake. Miss Kate dismissed the class. I was devastated. I hung around, waiting for the room to empty, and then approached her desk. She smiled at me.

"What is it, Sweetie?"

I fastened accusatory eyes upon her face, looking as pitiful as I knew how.

"Today is my birthday."

"Oh, Sissy, I'm so sorry!" Miss Kate rummaged around her desk. She picked up a notebook and leafed through it, stopped at a page and ran her finger down a list. "I don't have a record of your birthday in my book," she explained. She drew me around the desk and pulled me onto her lap. "I am *so* sorry! We'll draw a cake for you tomorrow, okay?" I nodded happily. Miss Kate hugged me and I smelled the clean, sweet scent that always followed her. This was wonderful! Not only would the cake be mine, I had received a hug and an apology—from a teacher!

My mom loved our new house. Daddy bought a tall cabinet for the kitchen and told Mom to order some of the pans and utensils she needed. After the war ended, metal was no longer in short supply; and there was money enough for my mom to buy at least some of the things she wanted. She perused the Sears and Montgomery Ward catalogues for days. She was like a child in a toy store, with so many items from which to choose that she could hardly make up her mind.

After much editing, Mom finally sent the order. The big box arrived several days later, and we all gathered around the kitchen table to watch as Mom removed the contents. Dad had to help, of course. Each time he held up something he could not name, he asked the same question.

"What's this for?"

"It's a spatula. You turn pancakes with it."

"And why do you need this? Wasn't the old one good enough?" He held up a new potato masher.

"The old one is rusty, Will."

"Don't we have enough paring knives already?"

"They won't hold a sharp edge, Will."

"Why did you order this?"

My mother had had enough. Without looking up, Mom continued to unwrap a set of mixing bowls.

"If I ordered it, I need it!" she exclaimed and she raised her head to glare at my dad, who stood grinning at her and holding up a bicycle seat.

"Don't you think you need the bicycle first?"

"I didn't order that!"

Even after she sent the bicycle seat back, Dad teased her about it for a long time.

With the arrival of spring, I discovered that living beside the small city park held a lot of promise. Not only was it a great place to run and play, there were picnic tables and squeaky swings that drew lots of children as the weather grew warmer. Again, life was good.

I thought about Becky sometimes. There were several soft maple trees in the park. A few times I examined the high roots and knots, but not too closely. I was sure that Becky's fairies would not have left her, but one never knew if others existed in the root systems of soft maples all over the world. One couldn't be too careful about that magical, mystical stuff.

Occasionally I read from the Bob and Judy books. I had finished the one I was halfway through when we came to Redbud Grove. I wondered how long it took before Jerry passed the point where I had stopped reading to Mrs. Freeman. I suspect that, within days of my leaving, Jerry had not only caught up, he had passed me while I struggled with a new home, new school and new friends. Holding those books in my hands somehow brought my old school and old friends close to me.

When I looked at the starred pages, I could see the faces of Jackie, Martha Ann, Katherine, Donna, Becky, and Jerry, a small but memorable group. They were a part of me, my first friends, and I would never forget them.

Never.

#

A BASKET FULL OF CHRISTMAS

Our house sat on the corner of Pine Street and Alley, which separated us from the park. Dad had also bought the adjoining lot to the north, and that is where he and my mother planted a big garden that first spring. My mother had dreams of canning and preserving her own homegrown vegetables. While Mom and Dad planted and hoed and weeded, Buddy and I played happily in the park, but with restrictions. Play rule number one was: YOU WILL BE WITHIN SIGHT AND HEARING DISTANCE OF MOM AT ALL TIMES.

The city had planted the whole park in a tall grass mixture and let it grow high, so it could re-seed itself. By mid-summer it was tall and lush. My friends and I burrowed through the grass, forming tunnels and trails in which to play hide-and-seek. The grass was so tall that it was impossible to see each other unless we stood up. We pressed down an area large enough to make a hideout, and the trails proceeded from that point. Mom could tell where we were by the wiggling of the grass, as we moved through it.

Summer evenings were long, and neighborhood children played until dark. My brother and I were not allowed out of our own yard as twilight faded, but we could chase lightning bugs and play any games we wanted inside the boundaries. My mother was still a little nervous about living in a "big" town. She held us by a short leash that summer. After all, I was only seven and Buddy was five; and there were older, bigger kids in the neighborhood. Mom was always afraid we were going to be hurt.

"But, Mom, why can't I play on the swings with the big kids? They'll watch me."

"Because you might walk in front of a swing and get hit in the head."

"I wouldn't. Shirley gets to play over there and she's seven, too. Why can't I?"

"Because I said."

There never seemed to be an appeal to that edict.

My friend, Becky, and I had written a few letters to each other over the summer; but it was difficult, if not impossible, for children as young as we were to cultivate a friendship from such a distance. She had moved to Carbondale, a college town almost as far to the south as we had moved to the north. Our connection had been the school and friends we had shared, but now we both had new lives with different friends. The connection was broken.

As September approached and another school year drew steadily nearer, I became a little nervous. Excitement filled me, too, because I was no longer at the lowest end of the totem pole. There would be a class of children younger than I, children who would know less about their surroundings than we superior second-graders.

When school started, my first stop was at Miss Kate's room. It was familiar and comfortable and safe. Miss Kate was polite but distant and firmly pointed me across the hall, a mother bird pushing a reluctant fledgling from the nest. So much for feeling superior to the first-graders. I had heard stories about the second grade teacher, Mrs. Erickson; and my one contact with her last spring had not been a positive one. I dreaded the thought of being under her evil eye for the whole school year.

There were so many rules, one of which was: DO NOT RUN DOWN THE BASEMENT STAIRS TO THE RESTROOM. Well, sometimes a person has to run, because the very nature of the destination demands it. At one such juncture, Mrs. Erickson saw me, called me back to the top of the stairs, turned me around, gave me a smack on the bottom, and ordered me to WALK down the stairs. I did, barely making my deadline. Now I had to see her every day.

It turned out better than I expected. Sharon Bennett sat behind me. Mrs. Erickson started her alphabetical seating on the window side of the room, far away from her desk. That was a plus. Not only did we have the open windows on warm days, we were close to the radiators on cold ones. When winter days turned snowy and freezing, damp wool mittens and scarves were placed upon the radiators to dry after recesses, which created an interesting aroma.

Apparently Mrs. Erickson didn't hold my infraction against me. I did what she said, smiled when she looked at me, and we got along just fine. My fellowship of friends increased. There were some new faces in the second grade. Several families had moved to Redbud Grove the previous summer. Oil had been discovered in Douglas and the surrounding counties, and a refinery was built a few miles north of a nearby town. It took a lot of manpower to construct such a big facility and keep it in operation.

As people moved in, disoriented students appeared at various times of the year. I watched closely when a new boy or girl arrived in our class. I knew exactly how they felt, and I made it a point to smile and talk to them as quickly as I could. It was a lot easier to make new friends when someone helped.

Immediately after the Thanksgiving holiday, students at East Side Grade School began to anticipate Christmas. There was talk of real Christmas trees being set up in the classrooms and of making decorations and exchanging gifts. The previous Christmas seemed long ago and far away, a sweet memory that grew fainter with the excitement of the present.

Except for the school program last year, I had no memories of celebrating Christmas, although I'm sure there were gifts for us from Santa. I still had a doll I had received while my dad was overseas. My mother had told me that Santa Claus brought it, but Santa was a non-entity to me. The doll was small and wore a white dress with blue bows on it. My cousin, Ada, who is the same age as I, got one just like it, except that her doll's dress had red bows on it.

"What do you want for Christmas?" was the question most asked and answered in the second grade. I was caught up into the spirit of the season right away. The thought that there really was a Santa Claus, who brought us our heart's desire, was thrilling to me. It was easy to be excited about it. Some new project developed in the classroom every day.

We made paper chains from bright red and green construction paper and draped them in deep festoons around the room. Snowflakes in all sizes and designs, cut from folded white paper, adorned the windows. A pine tree, as tall as Mrs. Erickson, stood in one corner of the room; and each student made a paper ornament and placed it on the tree. It was the first Christmas tree I touched.

19

The final week of school dwindled down to the last day, and the party we had anticipated became a reality. We ate cookies and drank red Kool-ade supplied by the room mothers. We sang <u>Jingle Bells</u> and <u>Up On the Housetop</u> and <u>Jolly Old Saint Nicholas</u>, and we laughed and giggled and had a glorious time. Mrs. Erickson gave each student a small, black New Testament, red-letter edition.

After early dismissal, my friend, Sheila, and I walked home together as we often did. She lived less than a block north of us. It was very cold. Snow covered the sidewalks and crunched beneath our booted feet, but we were too full of Christmas spirit to let twenty-degree weather bother us. We discussed the possibility that Santa Claus might not be real, as voiced by someone in our class. We dismissed the notion as merely a rumor and eagerly exchanged our Christmas wishes. Both of us had thoroughly perused the Sears, Roebuck Catalog and had developed a long list. Our mouths were full of hard candy, which we shifted through gaps from missing teeth; but we had no trouble communicating.

When we reached Sheila's, she invited me to come in with her. I hesitated, knowing that my mother would be expecting me; but we were early, and I had not yet been inside Sheila's home. I accepted her invitation and we entered the white, two-storied house.

"Mother, Sissy is with me. Can she come in?" Sheila called.

"Of course she may. Take off your boots," Sheila's mother called from somewhere inside. We did, and that was as far as I got for several minutes. While Sheila removed her coat and tossed it onto a chair, I stood staring at the long living room, which was bigger than our living room and kitchen combined.

A soft, off-white carpet covered the floor and extended up the staircase at the far end of the room. Several upholstered chairs and two matching sofas were placed along the white walls. Moss green velvet draperies hung beside white sheer curtains at the tall windows.

Pictures in gold frames adorned the walls, and merry red poinsettias in gold pots provided bright splashes of color on wood tables. Near the trio of windows, stood a shiny, black, grand piano, its gleaming ebony and white keys looking like teeth in a wide, friendly smile.

"Sissy, come look," Sheila's loud whisper drew my attention away from the beckoning ivories. I turned to find her kneeling beside the most beautiful Christmas tree I could have imagined. It loomed beside the staircase, reaching nearly to the second floor landing. Full and bushy, the dark green pine branches were laden with a multitude of fragile glass ornaments and strings of bubble lights.

Speechless, I could only stare as Sheila moved quietly among the pile of gaily-wrapped packages beneath the tree. I had no idea that Christmas trees were actually brought into houses. I thought that they were only for schoolrooms and store displays. But this...this was stuff of which dreams were made. Evidently gifts were allowed to arrive before Santa brought more on Christmas Eve.

"Mother says I am absolutely forbidden to shake the packages," Sheila whispered, "but I think one has a doll in it." She held up a long red box and tipped it forward. Our eyes met happily, as a tiny "ma-ma" wailed from inside. We covered our mouths to suppress the guilty giggles. I stayed only long enough to speak to Sheila's mother before donning my boots and coat and heading home.

Spice-scented aromas greeted me when I opened the front door. The living room was warm and cozy and chased away the remnants of the cold walk from school. Sixteen-month-old Bethy lay sleeping in the crib, which was kept in the living room during the winter months. I tiptoed into the kitchen and found my mom and Buddy placing warm oatmeal cookies on a plate.

From then until suppertime I chattered non-stop about the Christmas party, the treasures abounding in Sheila's house, and the tree and packages that were so spectacular. Mom smiled as I described everything to her, but her expression sobered when I started itemizing the things I wanted for Christmas.

"Santa won't be able to bring a lot of toys this year," she said. "Daddy hasn't been working for several weeks, and we can't give Santa much money." I put my hands on my hips and looked at her for a moment, digesting this new thought that Santa must be paid for gifts.

"Can we put up a Christmas tree?" I demanded. "We need a tall one with lots of presents under it like Sheila's. We need..."

"Honey, wait a minute." Mom sat down at the table beside me. She bit her lower lip, hesitating before she continued. "We don't have room for a Christmas tree."

"But, Mom, we *have* to have a tree to put presents under!"

"No, we don't need a tree to get presents. Santa can leave them on the couch."

I ran to the living room, determined to show her that we really did have room for a tree. One wall was taken up with a studio couch. A chair and the crib effectively covered another. An old brown rocking chair and the huge coal stove filled the remaining space. I looked at the drab linoleum that covered the floor, at the ugly, worn, familiar furniture. My shoulders drooped in defeat. I thought of the lovely big room that held Sheila's Christmas tree and the dozens of packages beneath the pine branches. It wasn't fair. It just was not fair!

"Why is our house so little?" I asked. Envy reared its ugly head. I had forgotten that I had been perfectly content with our new house, until I saw Sheila's. "Sheila's house is big and she has lots of toys and pretty things and..." By this time, my mother was thoroughly tired of hearing about Sheila.

"Honey, Sheila's daddy is a banker, and he makes lots more money than your daddy does. Sheila is an only child, and she doesn't have to share anything with brothers and sisters." Mom made the words "only child" sound like a disease. I looked around at the few furnishings, at my brother who sat on the couch, leafing through the catalog, at my baby sister now playing happily in the crib. At the moment, being an only child seemed to hold a lot of advantages.

I was immediately swept with an enormous wave of guilt. My mother was right. Sheila didn't have a dark-haired, blue-eyed baby girl in her house. She didn't have a little brother to whom she could tell stories, a brother who thought that everything she said was absolutely true. I shrugged away the envy and smiled at my mom. Everything was all right in my world again. I knew that I was loved, warm, and supper smelled delicious as Mom finished preparing it. Santa Claus was going to come whether we had a tree or not.

The next morning was December twenty-second. I had asked my mom how many days until Christmas so many times that she circled the twenty-fifth on the big wall calendar in the kitchen. Each evening she let me draw a red X through that day's number. Now only three nights remained before the arrival of Santa Claus. It seemed like forever!

After supper that night, Mom and Dad announced that there was a surprise in the shed for me, Buddy and Bethy. Mom put Bethy in the crib, where the little tyrant immediately set up a terrible howl. Buddy and I were instructed to entertain her while Mom and Dad went to the shed to prepare THE SURPRISE.

"Maybe it's a puppy," Buddy whispered. I shook my head.

"Bethy's afraid of a d-o-g," I spelled. Even at sixteen months, Bethy screamed in terror at the mention of a dog. I knew it could not possibly be a puppy. At five, Buddy knew how to spell that word.

"I bet it's something really nice," I said. "Maybe it's an early Christmas present, like at Sheila's house." Filled with tingly anticipation, Buddy and I took turns retrieving the toys that Bethy delighted in tossing through the slats of the crib. When she tired of that, Buddy crawled under the crib and played peek-a-boo with her until she was practically hysterical with laughter.

Mom and Dad finally came into the kitchen. They had big smiles on their faces; and my dad carried a pine tree, which was nailed onto a piece of crossed wood. I stared at it in disbelief.

"Look, Sissy, Daddy bought a tree." Mom sounded excited. I didn't see much to cause excitement. The short-needled tree barely reached my dad's shoulder, and it looked nothing like the one in Sheila's house. I caught a whiff of pine scent and sniffed suspiciously. At least it *smelled* like a Christmas tree.

Dad angled the crib across a corner in the living room. He moved the chair to the other corner and placed our little play table in front of the window. He lifted the tree onto the table, where it assumed the dimensions of a real Christmas tree. The top of the tree was above my dad's head. My mother brought a brown bag from the kitchen and withdrew a single strand of lights, which Dad carefully draped among the branches, arranging each bulb to the best advantage.

His job completed, Dad sat down in the rocking chair before the big coal stove and removed his pipe from his shirt pocket. He picked up his red can of Velvet smoking tobacco from the ugly brown smoke-stand beside his chair, and carefully tipped just the right amount into the bowl of his pipe. He lit a match with a flick of his thumbnail and applied the flame to the tobacco. I liked to watch him draw on the pipe. His cheeks sunk in against his teeth as he sucked air through the stem. When the tobacco glowed just right, Dad flipped out the match and tossed it into the ash pan in front of the stove.

23

"Here, Sissy." From the bag Mom handed me a beautiful red glass ball and helped me fasten it to a limb just above my head. There were not many ornaments, but each one was lovely and reflected light from the bulbs. Mom placed a tiny glass angel in Bethy's hand and guided her in placing it just so. Bethy clapped her hands with delight.

"Mine," she announced as she pointed to the angel. "Me." She pointed to her chest and Daddy laughed.

"I think you are more of a squirt than an angel," he said. He often called her Squirt.

We three little Bannisters sat cross-legged on the floor and watched Mom drape tinsel icicles upon all the branches. It was finished. Dad turned out the ceiling light and our beautiful Christmas tree glimmered as brightly as the one in Sheila's house. It was just smaller.

But something was missing.

"Daddy, it doesn't have a star." I don't think that I actually meant to say the words. They just popped out.

"Does it need one?" Daddy asked. Tentatively, I looked at him, afraid that, once again, I had said the wrong thing. I nodded and pointed.

"Right on top."

My dad rocked silently for several minutes, as we all gazed at the shining tree. He went into the kitchen, and we heard him rummaging through the metal cabinet and Mom's big wood cabinet/hutch. He returned to the front room carrying a small, empty Rice Krispies cereal box, a piece of tin foil, and scissors. Fascinated, I watched him draw the outline of a star on one side of the box and carefully cut around it. My eyes were on his face, as much as on his project. There was an intensity about him that was compelling.

His pipe whistled softly as he drew on it through his clenched teeth. He seemed not to notice that it had gone out. I watched his eyes, those steely-blue eyes that always looked back at me from the mirror. I knew the exact moment when he was pleased with his work, for he almost smiled.

He stood up and placed the shadow-box star atop the tree. He had covered the whole box, inside and out, with foil; and it caught every glimmer from the single strand of lights. He centered one of the bulbs inside the box so that the whole piece radiated silvery beams upon the tree.

It was beautiful—more than that, it was magnificent—and my dad had made the star with his own hands, just for me. Satisfied and peaceful, I smiled at Daddy and sat back to enjoy my own special, wonderful Christmas tree with its one-of-a-kind star.

With the morning came the realization that only one more night separated me from Christmas Eve. How could I bear the waiting! The sky was overcast with heavy clouds that had dropped two more inches of snow, and the world outside the windows looked like a scene on a Christmas card. Santa's sleigh would glide like the wind above the glistening streets of Redbud Grove and the marshmallow-soft blanket that covered the surrounding countryside.

Mom bundled us up and took us uptown to see Santa Claus that morning. In spite of the rumors that Santa was not real, I clung to the hope and belief that he *was,* and I was eager to tell him what I wanted for Christmas.

Traffic had been blocked from half of Main Street. In the center of the street stood a small red cottage, with an open door and peppermint striped shutters on the small windows. A short line of supplicants had formed in front of the cottage, and we attached ourselves to the end of it.

Mom took my brother and sister inside together when it was our turn. I took one look at the Santa, and refused to enter. If the man sitting in that chair was Santa Claus, I was queen of the world! On the way back home I listened to Buddy chatter about talking to Santa. Bethy was too young to talk, but her eyes were still very big from the encounter.

Buddy was worried that we had no fireplace. How in the world would Santa Claus manage with a chimney that led down to our big coal stove? Mom told him that it would be fine, because Santa had all kinds of magic and would figure it out satisfactorily. I think I snorted. Mom looked sharply at me and I knew that *she* knew what I was thinking. Silently she laid a finger in front of her lips, and that quickly I became part of the Santa Claus conspiracy.

After lunch, Buddy and I lingered over pictures of toys in our favorite seasonal publications, three catalogues: Sears/Roebuck,

Montgomery Ward, and Alden's. I told him that it was probably too late to make changes on our lists, but one could always hope.

About mid-afternoon there was a knock at the front door. Daddy rose from the rocking chair, where he had been reading a newspaper, which he held in one hand as he opened the door. It occurred to me that he had spent a lot of time in that chair the past few weeks. Something was not right at the foundry, but I didn't know what. Sometimes I heard Mom and Dad talk about a "strike." The only contexts I had to judge that word were an advertisement jingle about Lucky Strike cigarettes, and the knowledge that copperhead snakes and rattlesnakes were always lying in wait to strike in the area of Missouri where I was born.

"Hello, Mr. Bannister." The man at the door was Mr. Hicks, Sheila's daddy, who was president of the only bank in Redbud Grove. He was a big man with a round face and rimless glasses that magnified his dark brown eyes. Mr. Hicks wore a long, black coat over his suit, and his red tie looked very bright against the stark white of his shirt. He stomped the snow from his feet on the front step, shifted the bushel basket he carried, and came inside. Mr. Hicks placed the basket at my dad's feet and offered his hand, which Dad seemed hesitant to grasp.

Mom appeared in the kitchen doorway, drying her hands with a dishtowel. Mr. Hicks removed his gray felt hat and nodded politely to her before he spoke to Dad.

"I understand that the foundry has been shut down for some time now."

"Yes." My dad's voice sounded strangely subdued.

"Well, I hope that the strike is settled soon. Several families have been affected adversely." I didn't know what that word meant, but it didn't sound like a good thing. "The bank wanted to help out during this hard time." Mr. Hicks indicated the basket. He looked at me. "Hi there, Sissy. I hope you and your family enjoy this little basket full of Christmas. Well, I'll be going. We have several stops to make. Good-bye and Merry Christmas." With a wave of his hand, Mr. Hicks departed.

"Thanks, Mr. Hicks." Daddy closed the door. He stood with his hands at his sides, looking down at the basket. He said nothing for a long moment, and his face looked very sad. Suddenly he flung the newspaper onto his chair. He brushed by my mother and grabbed his coat from the wall-peg beside the outside kitchen door.

"Will..." Mom said, but Daddy was already out the door, which he slammed behind him.

I turned my attention to the basket. It was a thing of beauty, a new basket, woven of red and green strips. Cellophane, tied with a big red bow, covered the contents. Beneath the shiny covering I could see large red and yellow apples, oranges, grapefruit, bananas, a shaggy round coconut, unshelled nuts of all kinds, a smaller basket of grapes and items hiding beneath the first layers. I caught a glimpse of a small toy car, some books and a box of wooden alphabet blocks. It really was a basket full of Christmas!

Mom lifted the basket, no little task, and carried it to the kitchen table. Within a short time, she had unpacked and put away the fruits and groceries, staples like flour, sugar, coffee, and oatmeal. She cut one of the large red apples and divided it between Buddy and me. Bethy received a piece of a banana.

Daddy did not come home until long after dark. I heard him and my mom talking, and a little later I heard her crying softly after she went to bed. I never did hear Dad go to bed. He was gone again when morning came, Christmas Eve at last. When he did come home, he took my mother into his arms and hugged her tightly.

"I'm sorry," he whispered against her shiny, light brown hair. "I just feel so..." Mom reached up and placed her fingers on Dad's lips.

"Sh-h-h-h. I know. We'll be all right, Will."

Grown-ups sure acted funny sometimes.

Somehow I got through the night. Christmas Eve had to be the longest night of the year. I must have slept some, but periodically I called out to my mother.

"Mom, is it time to get up yet?"

"Can we get up now?"

"Mom, what time is it?"

"Mom!"

Finally, at six o'clock, she allowed Buddy and me to run into the front room. She and Dad brought cups of coffee with them and sat close together on the couch. I had a fleeting moment of confirmation about my new-found knowledge, because the coffee was steaming hot and could not have perked in the short time Mom and Dad had been up. Oh, well. I turned with Buddy to the toys and packages with our names on them. Bethy woke and sat up in the crib, rubbing her eyes and peering at us in wonder, before she demanded to become a part of the festivity.

My gifts included a beautiful baby doll with brown eyes that closed and had real lashes. Her dress and matching bonnet were made of light blue organdy, trimmed in blue satin ribbons. There was a brightly colored metal chicken that shot out little white eggs when I turned a side crank. I loved the doll, but my favorite gifts were a new box of twelve Crayola crayons and a thick coloring book, which I jealously guarded from my brother and sister.

Mom served a wonderful dinner of roasted chicken, complemented by steaming dishes of her home-canned vegetables. She had made a pecan pie with the nuts from the basket, and there was lots of fresh fruit. She smiled briefly when Daddy announced that he was too full for dessert.

Late in the afternoon, when we were all drowsy from the dinner, there was a knock at the front door. Mom groaned and roused herself from the corner of the couch, where she had been half-asleep. She opened the door; and one of Dad's friends from the foundry, Ray Ashley, came inside. Ray was a soft-spoken man, very thin but wiry. He grinned at my dad and with his slow, southern drawl, said three words.

"Will, they settled." My dad jumped to his feet and a joyous smile lit up his handsome face.

"When?"

"Early last night." They clapped each other on the shoulders and shook hands. It wasn't really a hug, but it came close.

Dad always said that he got the best Christmas present of his life that Christmas Day.

But he ate nothing that came from the basket full of Christmas.

Not one bite.

#

JULIE KITCHEN

The first time I came face-to-face with Julie Kitchen, I stepped off the sidewalk and skittered around her, then stood watching as she lumbered slowly away from me. I knew who she was. I had seen her from a distance. My friends in the third grade had told me about the trash lady, but I was not prepared for the height and breadth of her— nor the smell. She was nearly as tall as my dad and seemed much wider; but that may have been because of the layers of clothing she wore.

Although a soft breeze stirred the warm spring afternoon, the woman wore two sweaters beneath a faded denim jacket, that flapped against her wool skirt, which was a bulky black-watch plaid. An ugly orange and yellow paisley scarf covered her head. The babushka knot cut deeply into her double chin, making her face look as round as a plate.

I stared at the rubber galoshes on her feet. The open metal fasteners rattled with each step, adding to the cacophony of Julie's loud, tuneless humming and the big creaking wheels of the wooden cart she pushed. I watched her for several minutes before I turned and ran home, clutching my books to my chest, eager to tell my mother about the trash lady.

"She looks so funny, Mom," I giggled. "She wears a man's coat and boots and her wagon is filled with stuff. And she smells bad."

"That's enough, Sissy," Mom said. Her voice held the tone that said that I had crossed the invisible manners line—again. "We don't laugh at people because of the way they dress; and we don't make fun of *anyone*—no matter how unusual or different they seem. You smile and say hello to Mrs. Kitchen the next time you see her. You be nice."

There it was again. Be nice—the final instruction I received before I went to Sunday school, to a friend's house, to a birthday party. I was so indoctrinated to *be nice*, that I would probably have said "Thank you" to Jack the Ripper as he cut out my heart.

"Sissy? You hear me?"

"Yes, I hear," I answered.

"Good girl. Now go get your homework done. You won't have time after supper. Daddy has a ballgame tonight."

"Okay, Mom." I hurried through my spelling words and quickly finished a page of arithmetic problems in my red Big Chief tablet.

I liked going to my dad's ballgames. He wore a black shirt with white letters on the back and played center field for the Smokehouse Cats softball team.

If my dad loved anything else as much as he loved baseball, it was pool. He often stopped after work at Clark's Smokehouse, the local pool hall. That's how he became a member of the ball team.

My mom was not happy about Dad's devotion to those two sports, but she grimaced and remarked that it could be worse, she supposed. I heard her tell one of her friends, when I wasn't supposed to be listening, that at least my dad came home for supper and to sleep. She also said that Dad never had to pay to play pool, because he was so good at it. I didn't know what that meant. I just liked to watch him play baseball, especially if the Cats were winning.

But should the game be boring, I talked with my friends on the bleachers, or we played tag or Red Light, Green Light until it was time for my dad to bat. He looked so handsome as he stood at home plate, making little circles in the air with the bat as he waited for the pitch. The loud crack of the bat when he hit the ball was exciting; and when everyone cheered, I was proud to be his daughter.

It was a wonderful evening. Dad's team led throughout the game. My friend, Melissa Franklin, sat with me on the top bleacher, and we cheered loudly for my dad.

"I wish my dad would play ball," Melissa told me. "All he does is work at Petro or work on our house." We played string games, carefully transferring the intricate patterns to each other, played tic-tac-toe on pages of precious school tablets, and then tore up the sheets and threw them away before we were scolded for wasting paper. If the evidence were destroyed, there could be no crime.

When the game was over and we were skipping down the bleachers, I caught a glimpse of Julie Kitchen on the outskirts of the ball field. She was alone, and she made no move toward anyone. She looked very lonely.

A few days later, I met her again as I was coming home from school. Except for the jacket and scarf, she looked the same. My heart beat faster, and I took very small breaths as we drew closer together on the brick walk. *Be nice. Be nice.* I could hear my mother's voice inside my head.

"Hi, Mrs. Kitchen." The words came out of my mouth easily enough. The rattling cart halted, and the big woman stared at me. I stared back, more curious than scared. Gray eyes, the shade of water in a galvanized bucket, peered down at me from her round face. Ruddy cheeks and full, thick lips the color of crushed raspberries seemed incongruous against her otherwise pale skin.

"What are you called?" she asked.

"Sissy," I replied. She hadn't asked my name, only what I was called.

"Where do you live?" Julie Kitchen's voice sounded husky and thick, and her words were strangely accented.

"In the yellow house beside the park," I answered. Her eyes shifted upward, as if in thought; and she mumbled to herself.

"The soldier that bought the house Doc Teel moved in from the country. *Da.*" She nodded her head. "You are his kid."

My dad had been a soldier for a long time before we came to Redbud Grove, and I knew that he had bought our house from Doc Teel; so I nodded. Julie scratched her head, ruffling her faded gray hair with the yellow streaks of what must have once been blonde. Cut straight and not a bit becoming, her hair came to the ends of her ear lobes. She reminded me of a picture my teacher had shown us at school, of people working in a field. Miss Covalt had said that the people were peasants in a country called Russia. For a time, I had confused them with pheasants and was worried that my dad and my uncles, when they went hunting, were shooting farm workers.

"I have to go home," I told Mrs. Kitchen. "'Bye." I walked away when she did not answer. I turned around once and she was still watching me, so I waved. After a moment she raised one hand in a kind of salute. Sometimes being nice was—well, *nice.*

When I told my friends the next day that I had spoken to Julie Kitchen, they were appalled. "Why would you get that close to her?" Melissa asked. "She's so *dirty!*"

"And she smells awful!" Shirley added. "My mother says it looks like Julie could find some scraps of soap in all that trash and take a bath once in a while." So, rather than appear strange to my friends for befriending the trash lady, I avoided Julie the rest of the year, sometimes going a block out of my way when I saw her in the distance. I did not feel good about my actions; there was nothing *nice* about it. My conscience was a living, breathing thing inside me; and guilt hovered over me like a swarm of pesky gnats.

When we moved into our house, the only plumbing consisted of a sink in the kitchen that was not hooked up to a drain. A red pump in the front yard supplied our water, one bucket at a time. A few feet from the kitchen door stood a shed, connected to the house by a new concrete walkway. Inside the little building were a coal bin and a small workbench, where Dad stored his tools; and in the far corner, with a separate door, was the toilet. Most houses in the area had toilets, but more and more people were piping water into their homes and installing bathrooms.

My mother dreamed of having a bathroom and a utility area, where she could use her prized new wringer washing machine and rinse tubs. She had voiced the desire in passing several times, but without really expecting it to happen, I think. Then one day, contractors arrived and started measuring footage on the north side of the house. My mom was speechless, which was a near impossibility. When Dad came home for lunch, Mom greeted him at the door.

"Can we afford this? Are you sure you want to build onto the house right now? The strike hasn't been over very long." Daddy grinned, a big lop-sided, happy grin that lit up his face.

"I can cancel it, if you've decided we don't need a bathroom and wash room."

"Don't you dare!" Mom threw her arms around Daddy's neck and hugged him. He lifted her up and twirled her briefly around the kitchen before he let her go. He winked at me.

"There's more." He paused dramatically. "When the work is finished down here, we're going to make a nice bedroom upstairs, for Sissy. And in a couple of years, we'll make one for Buddy."

"Will, the stairs are so steep," Mom began to protest; and my heart sank. I was going to be banished from that lovely attic forever.

"We'll put up a sturdy handrail, Jackie."

He did. By the middle of that summer, all the work was completed; and I moved into my own bedroom upstairs. I loved the sensation of being above everyone else in the house.

One night a thunderstorm woke me. I lay in my bed beside the attic window, enjoying the cool breeze, and an occasional sprinkle of raindrops on my skin through the screen. I pulled the sheet up to my chin and gazed out the window at the black sky. The storm was not a frightening one. The rain became a drizzle, and the clouds broke to reveal a three-quarter moon that shimmered high above the dark horizon. The sweet smell of rain-washed grass and trees filled the air; and I breathed deeply, filled with a sense of something for which there was no word in my vocabulary. I had nearly drifted back to sleep, when I heard a familiar sound. I sat up and pressed my nose against the window screen. From the darkness of the park, the noise gradually becoming louder, came the wooden cart, pushed by Julie Kitchen.

She looked at our house as she passed by; and I drew back, afraid that she would see me. That conscience thing pricked me, and I knew that I had to do something about it. The moon illuminated Julie quite well. She wore the galoshes, splashing along in the puddles; but the only other garment on her body was a slip with wide built-up shoulders like my great-grandmother wore. Julie wasn't humming. She just plodded along behind the cart with its big, solid wheels. She looked tired.

"It's only Julie Kitchen," I heard my dad tell my mom. His voice came through the open vent in the attic floor. "I heard a funny story about her the other day," he said. The bed creaked as he lay down. Mom's reply was muffled. She sounded more sleepy than interested, but Daddy kept talking.

"A crew of electric linemen was installing a pole on the corner near Julie's house, when they heard her screaming. So they ran inside

33

and found her caught in the wringer of her washing machine." Dad chuckled. "You know that old saying about getting a tit caught in a wringer? Well, that's what Julie had done."

"Oh, the poor woman," my mom murmured in sympathy.

"The bad part was that they couldn't get the wringer to release, so they had to reverse it. When she finally got free, she chased the men from her house, screaming that she was going to kill them in various painful ways."

"You're making that up," Mom accused. Daddy laughed.

"No, I'm not."

I rubbed my hand across my flat chest, trying to imagine what it was like to have something dangling there all the time. I decided that it must feel really strange and a little embarrassing. Sleep closed in on my thoughts, but from far away I heard my dad speaking softly.

"Be careful when you do the wash, Honey. I would hate to see this flattened like a pancake."

"S-h-h-h-h. Sissy will hear you."

"No, she won't. I will be very...very...quiet..."

Throughout that summer, I spoke to Julie every time we met; and the awful guilt thing went away. Sometimes we had short conversations. One day she reached into her cart and pulled out a plastic pinwheel on a stick and gave it to me.

"Thought you would like this," she said. "You are a good girl." Although one of the spokes was broken and the red and white colors faded, I thanked her. She patted my head like most people would pat a dog. "Maybe sometime you will come to my house," she said; and without another word she pushed her cart away, humming her private melody. I decided that I would be friendly to Julie Kitchen forever; and if Melissa and Shirley didn't like it, that was just too bad.

Another day Julie offered me half a donut, carefully breaking it and handing me the unbitten side. It was fresh and sweet and good. "Mr. Cunningham leaves a donut for me behind his office every morning. He wraps it in a paper and puts it on a box beside the trash. I never see him, but I know he means for me to have it. I feel him watching me. *Da.*"

Julie's eyes softened when she spoke of Mr. Cunningham. He was the father of my friend, Ellen. He had always been friendly and kind to me. A slender man with silvery hair and frameless glasses, he owned an insurance office in Redbud Grove. Unlike my dad, Mr. Cunningham always wore a suit and tie to work. I was glad he was good to Julie Kitchen.

Julie and I became friends that summer. One afternoon, when I came down the long flight of steps at the library, she was waiting for me "Hey, come with me. There is a surprise at my house."

I hesitated, remembering all the don't-go-with-strangers admonitions. But Julie was not a stranger now, so I felt that it was all right. My mother wouldn't worry if I were a little late coming home from the library. It took hours to look through all the magazines in the reading room. Sometimes I poured through back issues of National Geographic, looking at the pictures and trying to figure out why it was acceptable for African native women to wear no clothing, while I had to wear a cotton camisole under blouses and dresses in the hot summer.

The front porch of Julie Kitchen's house peeked from behind a vanguard of tall cedar trees. A rusty iron fence surrounded the corner lot. Several maple trees shaded the patchy lawn, and grew tall enough to cast heavy shadows upon the house. A single redbud tree grew near the fence. I expected the gate to creak; but it made no noise as Julie pushed it open, and we stepped inside.

"Come on." She motioned with her hands; and I followed her up the brick steps to the covered porch, which was encompassed by a decorative concrete block railing. The house was a multi-colored hue, having been painted various colors at various times; and chips of green, yellow, white and dark blue paint showed in patches all over the exterior. I thought it looked interesting and creative. Our house was a boring shade of yellow.

Boxes and bags stood atop each other, forming a layer inside the rail and along the front of the house. Julie maneuvered her bulky body into a corner and slowly lifted a flap from a big box that lay on its side. "Look." She pointed inside the box.

"Oh," I breathed. "Oh." A beautiful, longhaired calico cat reclined upon a pile of rags in the corner of the box. Four furry feline balls tugged at her, their little paws working rhythmically at her side. I looked up at Julie. "They are so tiny," I whispered.

Julie gazed at me so strangely that I was a bit disconcerted. She lifted her hand and brushed my hair away from my cheek. Her fingers were rough, but gentle. Sadness filled her gray eyes; and there was such a yearning, hungry something on her countenance that I didn't know how to respond.

"They will grow up," she stated. Her hand dropped to her lap. "They will grow up, and then they will not always be so sweet. They will have claws; and they will bite, if they take a notion." She didn't sound like the woman I had come to know. There was something else different about her. She wore a clean cotton dress, and she smelled like soap. It occurred to me that perhaps the unpleasant odor I associated with her came from the cart. I was glad. My mother was always telling me that cleanliness was next to godliness. I know that she believed it, because she did laundry several times a week. I must have had the godliest underwear in Redbud Grove. Mom insisted that I put on clean underwear every morning, change again if we went somewhere—in case I was in an accident—and another clean pair after my bath every night. I turned my attention back to the kittens.

"Could I hold one?" I asked. Julie shook her head.

"No. Patches does not know you yet. Maybe next time. You go home now. Mothers worry when their young are gone. I remember."

My reading skills improved dramatically that summer. At first I checked out small books that I could read quickly, or picture books that took no time at all. That was about to change. Miss Ghere, the librarian, was also my Sunday school teacher at the First Baptist Church on Main Street; and she took a special interest in my choice of books. She decided that they were not challenging enough for me. She introduced me to Laura Ingalls Wilder; and at the age of nine, I was hooked on the Little House series. Miss Ghere did not allow me to check any of the books out of sequence. She kept a list of the ones I had read; if someone before me had taken the next book in line, I just had to wait.

Miss Ghere then gave me permission to check out the fairy tale collections, and I became quite knowledgeable on the Brothers Grimm and Hans Christian Anderson. I developed a new respect for Becky Jeffries's fairies and wished that I could have another chance to see them. I even squinted my eyes and looked closely at the pictures of fairies; but I never did see one that matched Delilah, whom, by now, I was convinced that I had seen. I loved those books, in fact, all books.

Melissa went to the Catholic Church camp for two weeks, and Ellen went on a long vacation out west with her parents. Shirley's grandparents took her home with them for a month; and Sharon's parents took her to a place called "Nawlins", which I later learned was New Orleans. I had lots of time to play with Julie's kittens.

Patches accepted me. She seemed to wink at me the first time I picked up one of her babies. Julie was not home that day, so I stayed only long enough to cuddle and kiss the hissing little ball of fur. It was not nice to be at someone's house when they were gone.

I was never sure what kind of mood Julie Kitchen would be in when we met. Usually she was short-spoken, but friendly. There were times when she seemed not to see or hear me, as if she were in a place so distant that she could not focus on me. It was then that she dressed in her bizarre manner and wore the ugly paisley scarf knotted under her chin.

Then came the day that Julie invited me into her house. No longer uneasy around her, I was curious about the way she lived. Like the porch, the walls of the front hall were lined with boxes and bags overflowing with various things, mostly rags and clothing. Double doors opened on each side of the hall, revealing rooms filled with wonderful clutter—boxes and tables stacked high with magazines, papers and books. Framed pictures and prints lined the walls; and old photographs covered the fireplace mantels, one in each room.

"Come through here," Julie commanded. I followed her through the room on the left, where another set of double doors opened into a dining room with a three-bay window. Dark green shades covered the glass, but pinprick sized holes and cracks in them let in tiny shards of light. "Come."

Julie led me through the dining room, into the kitchen, which was much brighter than the rest of the house. A row of windows above a blue linoleum-covered counter brought in dappled sunlight, reflecting brightly off dented copper pots filled with red geraniums.

"Sit." Julie indicated one of two chairs at a round table in the center of the room. A space, large enough to accommodate a square cloth on the table, was set with two china plates—one chipped—and two china cups in saucers. She filled a teakettle with water and placed it on the stove.

"These are pretty, Mrs. Kitchen," I said. I touched the cup carefully, enjoying the cool, satiny porcelain.

"I found them," she replied. I looked around the kitchen, as she took something that smelled wonderful from the oven of a big green and cream-colored range. In one corner stood the infamous wringer washing machine and two rinse tubs, much like those in my mother's laundry room.

The counters were covered with dishes, pans, glasses, and books. Bushel baskets on the floor held packaged groceries. Julie measured loose, black tea into the flowered china teapot; and when the kettle whistled, she poured boiling water into the pot.

"Now we will eat." She placed the kettle back onto the stove and up-ended a baking tin of steaming muffins into a shallow platter. I had never tasted hot tea. Julie didn't ask how or if I wanted it. She poured the hot amber liquid into my cup, added a good teaspoon of sugar, and plopped two muffins onto my plate. She dipped a knife into a small crock of butter and slathered the tops of the muffins with it. "Eat."

I did. It was heavenly. The muffins were filled with nuts and raisins, coconut and cinnamon; and the tea tasted grownup and sweet. I ate slowly, partly because the food was so hot, partly because I watched Julie. Unmindful of the temperature of what she ate, she consumed a muffin, dripping with butter, in two bites, and washed it down with gulps of tea. While I nibbled, she emptied the platter and rose once to replenish the pot with more tea and hot water.

"This is really good," I said, mindful of my manners. "Thank you." Julie merely nodded, rose abruptly, and cleared the table of our dishes.

"I have something to show you," she said. I followed her back to the front room. She removed a stack of papers from a faded over-stuffed chair and told me to sit. From the mantle she took several photographs and handed them to me, pointing to the one on top. "This is my mother." I looked at the sepia-toned image of a pretty woman with a round face, dressed in a long, dark skirt and a blouse with big puffy sleeves. "She was a servant in a big house in the country where I was born," Julie continued.

"Who did she work for?" I asked.

"Someone." Julie's eyes shifted, and a closed expression came upon her face. "Someone from long ago. He is dead now." I held up another picture.

"Who is this?"

Julie took the picture from my hand and peered at the tall, stocky figure of a man wearing a heavy coat and round hat. He had a drooping mustache and bushy eyebrows that were knitted into a deep frown above stern-looking dark eyes. A slim, pretty woman, with her hands folded in front of her, stood beside the man. The woman looked very sad.

"Jacob Kitchener. When we were on the boat, people shortened his name to Kitchen; and he kept it like that. He said that would make it harder for his people to find him. He was my husband. He was a butcher. I push his cart." She paused. "He was not a mean man—just hard." She pointed to the woman. "That is me."

"It *is*?" I looked from the picture to Julie, and her lips twitched.

"I look different now." I thought that maybe the polite thing to do was say nothing about how different.

"Do you have any kids?" I asked. There was a long silent moment.

"A long time ago I had a little girl. She had yellow hair and blue eyes like you. She got sick. She died."

I didn't know what to say, so again, I said nothing. I looked at the remaining picture in my hands. It was behind domed glass in an ornate gold frame. A man in a uniform, with a wide sash across his chest, sat beside a beautiful woman, who held a baby dressed in a long, flowing white dress. Two older girls stood, side by side, next to their mother. All were dressed in elaborate, formal clothing.

"Who are these people?" I asked. Julie looked at the picture, then at me. She sat down beside me.

"I will tell you a story," she announced. "No one in this town knows this story—no one in this *country* knows this story. I never told Jacob because it was not safe for him to know." She shrugged. "Now no one cares much. It was a long time ago." She smiled at me. "No one will believe you if you tell it, but I swear that it is true." The distant look washed over her face. When she spoke again, her voice came from a far away place and with a more pronounced accent.

"My mother went to work in the summer house, when she was young and pretty. She learned fast to please the people, and they made her a table server. Others of her family worked in the fields." Julie paused and I thought of the picture of the peasants. "The young master was not yet married and he took a fancy to her."

"What's a fancy?"

Julie focused on me. "You are too young." She stood. "You are too young. You go home now." I stood, too, recognizing dismissal by an adult.

"Thank you for the tea and muffins, Mrs. Kitchen," I said. Julie ushered me out and then beckoned to me from the porch.

"Wait."

I walked back up the steps.

"I have a pretty thing to give you." Julie turned and I followed her back inside the house. She led me into a bedroom, where she opened a drawer of a big dresser, and removed four pieces of linen that had begun to fray around the edges. She swept a stack of magazines from the corner of the bed and placed the squares of linen upon the bed. With her hands, she smoothed away some of the wrinkles from the linen. The pieces were beautiful.

"What are they for?" I asked. Julie shrugged.

"I hauled away some things in my cart for a woman in a big house. She let me choose something from her house for helping her. Look." Julie held up a piece that had a linen collar in a lighter shade stitched to it. The collar was trimmed with handmade lace and intricate embroidery, with many French knots and smooth satin stitch. One of the samplers had dozens of differently shaped buttonholes, all handmade and uniform in detail. Another displayed a series of various patterns woven by hand to fill the cut out squares.

The loveliest one displayed a colorful design, executed in needlepoint and cross-stitch embroidery. All the squares were dated eighteen-eighteen, and bore the signature of the artist, Emily, in tiny stitches that blended into the linen.

"The woman told me that she was going to give them to her grandkids to make doll-clothes, if I didn't take them." With roughened fingers, Julie touched the delicate handwork. "Which one do you want?" she asked.

"You mean I can have one?"

"*Da.* Yes." It was an easy choice. I picked the colorful one. "The woman told me that these were made by one of her husband's people, many years ago. They were for a young girl's dowry. Only sixteen, she was. Poor little girl." Julie shoved the sampler at me. "Now you go home."

I tucked the lovely piece of fabric between the pages of one of my books and hurried down the porch steps.

"My name is Juliana," she called after me "You call me Juliana."

That night, at the supper table, I pushed the meatloaf and mashed potatoes around my plate, pretending to eat. I was still full from the delicious muffins.

"Are you feeling all right?" my mother asked. "Why aren't you eating?" I shrugged. "Did you eat junk this afternoon?" Anything sweet was labeled "junk" by my mother.

"Wel-l-l," I hedged, "it wasn't really junk…" So I told my family about my visit to Julie's house and about the tea party, but I didn't mention the sampler that Julie had given to me. I knew that my mom would make me give it back. "And, Mom, she said that I could have a kitten if it's all right with you." Mom and Dad exchanged raised eyebrow looks.

"I'm not sure I like the idea of your going inside Mrs. Kitchen's house," Dad said.

"And *eating* with her," Mom added. "Is her kitchen clean?" I crossed my fingers under the table and made myself think about the boiling teakettle.

"Clean as hot water, Mom. And she's really nice." I knew that would get her.

"Don't make a pest of yourself," she warned, "and don't stay a long time. You need to be at home."

"OK, Mom. What about the kitten?"

Dad chuckled. "It's up to you, Hon," he told Mom.

"I suppose," she said, but she didn't sound very happy about it. Buddy and I both squealed and clapped our hands, while Bethy banged her spoon on the table. She sat in the high chair, which was pulled up to the table, but without the tray. I could hardly sleep that night for thoughts of the kitten I would soon be bringing home.

The following weekend, Mom and Dad announced that we were going to take a little vacation. Excitement filled Buddy and me, for we had never before been on a vacation. Our parents loaded the trunk of the car with a suitcase and several bags of clothing. Mom covered everything with quilts and pillows, just in case Aunt Edith didn't have plenty. Aunt Edith's farm, somewhere in Iowa, was our destination.

My mother had told me stories about Aunt Edith and Uncle Rolla, but I had no memory of them. Aunt Edith was the younger sister of my mom's mother. My grandmother, who was only twenty-four at the time, had died less than two days after giving birth to her fifth child, my mother. The other four children had been placed in the homes of aunts and uncles willing to care for them. My mother had been taken to the home of her maternal grandmother, who had reared and cared for the little girl for nearly five years. Aunt Edith had still lived in her parents' home at that time, and had helped care for my mother. I could tell that Mom loved Aunt Edith very much.

What Buddy and I did not understand about a vacation, was that it meant long hours in the car. Bethy, now three years old, sat between Buddy and me in the back seat for the first hour.

"Mom, Bethy won't sit still."

"Mom, make Buddy give me back my comic book."

"Mommy, Sissy won't wet me see. Huh won't shawuh huh book!"

"Bethy, give that back! Mom!"

With Dad still driving, Mom reached over the seat and plucked Bethy up and into the front with her and Dad. Buddy and I expanded our territory; and everything was fine until one of us invaded the other's space, either intentionally or otherwise.

"Mom, he's *touching* me!"

"Mom, Sissy keeps putting her foot on my part!"

"Mom, make Buddy quit!"

"If you kids don't behave, I'm going to stop this car and spank both of you!"

When Dad spoke, *everybody* listened. For the next four hours, the back seat was quiet. Our disagreements and disputes were silent ones, conducted with grimaces, finger wagging, and faces drawn into such outrageous contortions that we ended up laughing at each other.

Dad stopped the car at a filling station for gas one time. We parked at the far end of the station's lot to eat the lunch Mom had packed. There were sandwiches and lemonade, which she had poured into a gallon jar, half filled with ice. After a mandatory trip to the rest rooms, we were back on the road and quickly bored again.

It was the longest car ride I had ever taken. The narrow highway stretched for miles through a tunnel of green. Parallel fields of corn undulated along the hilly countryside, occasionally broken by a crossroad. Farmhouses, usually upon the crest of a high sloping hill, were surrounded on three sides by fields of corn. Sometimes a mailbox at the edge of a driveway was the only indication that a house must be nearby.

Aunt Edith and Uncle Rolla lived in such a farmhouse. They must have heard us coming, for both of them stepped from the wide front porch and came to meet us, before Dad stopped the car. I loved them instantly. After she hugged and kissed my mother, Aunt Edith reached for me. I had never had such a hug! She enveloped me against her ample width, which was covered by a calico apron. She smelled like good, homemade cooking and soap, with an underlying, though not unpleasant, hint of honest sweat.

She greeted everyone in the same manner; and then the process was repeated with Uncle Rolla, but without such fervor. He seemed more reserved, a tall, stolid, man of the earth, dressed in overalls and a blue chambray shirt.

Aunt Edith possessed no physical beauty whatsoever. Her face looked like pictures of the young Prince Charles of England. A long nose, small eyes and a mouth that resembled the painted smile of a puppet, held no trace of even the slightest prettiness; but the love that shown from her little brown eyes transcended every physical flaw.

The farm was a place of wonder and delight. Uncle Rolla held me in front of him and showed me how to milk a cow. I was afraid that I would hurt the animal, but Uncle Rolla assured me that I would not. When I finally managed to squeeze a thin stream of milk into the bucket, I felt triumphant. The next morning, when Aunt Edith served biscuits made from buttermilk, and covered with butter drawn from the buttermilk which all came from *my* bucket, I was ready for my dad to buy a cow. Nothing else had ever tasted so good.

During our stay with them, Aunt Edith and Uncle Rolla took us to a rodeo, held in Des Moines. We all had to go in our car, because Uncle Rolla had only an old pickup truck to drive. He called it a "pick-em-up truck." We went to a place called "The Ledges", a beautiful park with streams and high steps, that reached all the way to the tops of the rock formations.

The steps called my name. In the worst way, I wanted to start climbing, winding along the curved path, that disappeared into the tall trees so high above us. I got no higher that the first few steps.

"Sissy, that's high enough! You come back here!" The high pitch of my mom's voice told of her fear.

"But, Mom, I want to climb!"

"No! You'll fall off and break your neck!"

"Jackie, I'll go with her," Aunt Edith said.

"You'll have to watch her every minute, Aunt Edith," Mom warned. "You can't trust her to be careful. She's a dare-devil without any sense of caution at all!" Aunt Edith patted Mom's arm.

"She'll be fine, Honey. Relax." So Aunt Edith held my hand and went up the steps with me, until we were out of my mother's line of vision. Aunt Edith sat down on a stone bench, breathing heavily. "You go on to the top, Sissy. I'll sit here and wait for you."

I couldn't believe it.

"You mean I can go *by myself?*"

"Just be careful. Don't go too fast, and don't go too near the edge. I'm trusting you, Sissy."

A song I sometimes heard in church popped into my mind. I hummed it all the way to the top of the ledges: *Glorious freedom, wonderful freedom!* And it *was* glorious! When I reached the summit, I looked out over the river below, and felt so light that it almost seemed possible to take flight. I wandered among the other visitors, feeling very grown up and capable, all of us ooh-ing and ah-ing at the view.

Aunt Edith stood up, as I descended the rock steps. She smiled at me and put her finger in front of her lips. There was a twinkle of conspiracy in her eyes. "Now I don't hold with keeping secrets from your mama, Sissy; but this one time I think it will be all right."

I didn't have to be told twice.

Uncle Rolla showed Buddy and me how to shell corn with a corn sheller, an ingenious device with a handle and a spout. We took turns cranking the handle and feeding ears of corn into the mouth of it. He showed us how he rolled his own oats, which Aunt Edith cooked. I don't know how she made them taste so good.

The most wonderful result of our vacation on the farm, was the transformation of Bethy, who had always been terrified of dogs. Uncle Rolla owned a border collie, named Laddie, who was gentle and calm, and remained unperturbed at Bethy's screams. Gradually Uncle Rolla was able to convince Bethy to touch the dog, then to pat him once, then twice. Before we went back home, she was comfortable enough with Laddie to stand on the ground beside him and pet him without fear, for which she received applause and cheers.

"Bye, Aunt Edith, 'bye Uncle Rolla!" We waved and called goodbyes until we could no longer see them. Aunt Edith held her apron to her face to wipe away her tears. My mom cried, too.

The only interesting thing that happened on the way home was a hitchhiker. Mom protested when Daddy slowed down to pick the man up.

"Will, I don't want you to stop. He could be a...you know."

"A lot of people picked me up when I was hitching back home from the army," he said. And that was the end of it. The man came running up to our car. "Need a lift?" Dad asked. "We don't have room in here, but you can stand on the running board and hang on to the post. How far are you going?"

"Just to the next town," the man replied.

"Jump on," Dad said. So for several miles I looked at the man's arm, which was wrapped around the post between the back seat and the front seat.

"Thanks a lot," the man called. He jumped off the running board at a stop sign, at the edge of the next town, which he had said was his destination.

"You're welcome." Dad sounded very pleased with himself.

It was good to get home. A vacation was nice, but I could wait quite a long time for the next one. At least I had something to tell my friends when they told me about theirs. I bet none of them got to milk a cow.

The next afternoon I skipped the library and went straight to Juliana's house. I thought that she would be interested in all I had to tell her, but I never had the opportunity to talk to her about our trip.

Juliana opened the door to my knock; but she seemed distracted, muttering to herself about finding an egg. I had no idea how one could lose an egg. She seemed not to be aware that I had been gone for a week.

"I know that it is here," Juliana said. She moved stacks of boxes, one at a time, from one place to another, until she found the one she wanted. "Ah, this is the box." She shoved books from the beat-up cocktail table in front of the sofa and placed the box upon the cleared surface. Juliana opened it, and from mounds of torn newspaper, withdrew another box, a wooden one with a hasp closing. From that one, she took a heavy, gold, metallic container. Fascinated, I held my breath as she opened it.

"Oh, Juliana," I whispered. Julie Kitchen, or Juliana Kitchener, as I would thereafter think of her, held up the most beautiful, fragile, paper-thin, porcelain egg, encrusted with pearls and gems and gold leaf trim. There was a small click; and the egg opened, revealing a brightly colored painting of a Madonna and Child on one side and a painted portrait of a uniformed man on the other. It was the same man in the picture with the beautiful lady and the children, that Juliana had shown me.

"Who is he?" I asked, still whispering.

"My father." She stared at me, directly into my eyes; and her own water-gray ones were clear. "My mother told me that he was my father, but that I must never tell anyone, because the Bolsheviks would kill me. They killed him and the rest of his family, his wife and children. My mother's friends gave me enough money to get to Germany. After Jacob and I were married, we came on a boat to America; and a long time ago we came here, to this place." Her next words were spoken in a language I did not understand. She held up the egg and stared at the portrait, and her whole countenance and demeanor changed. She stood taller somehow, with her head high and her shoulders thrown back. In a loud, majestic voice she announced, "I am Juliana Romanov."

"Roman-off?" I repeated.

"No. R-r-r-r-omanov!" The R's rolled from her lips. I was impressed. I didn't know what she was talking about, but it seemed important to Juliana. "My mother gave this egg to me. My father gave it to her shortly after I was born, before he married Alexandra. Jacob never knew I had it. He would have made me sell it, but it was going to be my daughter's."

"What was your father's name?" I asked, trying to figure out how he could not be married to her mother, and still be Juliana's father, and then be married to someone named Alexandra.

"Nicholas," she replied and there was a sudden spark in her eyes. "Nicholas of the Romanovs." Just as suddenly she looked as weary as death. "You go home. I am tired."

"Could I take a kitten home with me?"

Juliana nodded. "*Da.* Yes. Choose your kitten and go."

I already knew which one I wanted. He was mostly black, with white paws and a white tip on his tail and a perfect white star between his eyes. He was braver than the others and often came mewing to greet me. I picked him up, looked at Juliana, and placed the kitten on the concrete rail.

On an impulse I ran to the big, sad woman and put my arms around as much of her as I could reach, and kissed her cheek. A solitary tear formed and spilled over, running down her face.

"Go now." She smiled, and at that moment Juliana was beautiful. I took the kitten, went down the steps, then turned to ask a question.

"Juliana, what are Bolsheviks?" The smile faded, and it was like looking at the light suddenly going out of the day.

"Someone in the old country. They killed and burned and took what little the people had, so everyone would have the same."

"Do they live here?" I felt a stab of fear at her words.

"*Nyet.* No. Maybe a few. But here there is something bigger than they are."

"What is bigger?"

"Freedom, Sissy. Freedom."

The next afternoon, Juliana Kitchener pushed her cart into the path of the Illinois Central passenger train that streaked through Redbud Grove each day at three-ten. The engineer said that the woman did not look up, or seem to be aware that she was on the tracks. He said that there was a scarf tied around her head, and she was staring into the wooden cart.

Redbud Grove had no radio station. The local newspaper published only on Thursdays, so word of mouth was the most effective system of communication. Someone at the Grab-it-Here grocery told my mother about Julie Kitchen's death that same evening. Mom didn't tell me, until after she had tucked me into bed.

"But Mom—but she has a—but Mom—Mommy-y-y-y." She gathered me into her arms and held me as I wailed. She cradled my head against her breast and crooned to me, like she did my little sister. She brushed my hair from my face and kissed my forehead. "Who will take care of Patches and the kittens?" I sobbed.

"Sh-h-h-h. Everything will be all right, Honey. You'll see."

When I finally quieted, she pulled the sweet smelling sheets around my shoulders and kissed me again. "I'll be back in a few minutes," she said.

I hiccupped a few times and took deep, shuddering breaths. I looked out the window at the black sky filled with millions of stars, familiar yet mysterious. "Star light, star bright, First star I see tonight…" I couldn't finish the rhyme. I didn't know what to wish for if I completed it.

The only thing I knew for certain about death, was that it caused permanent separation. There had been another baby in our house when I was not yet four, and my brother, less than two years old. My other brother lived three weeks and then was gone. Everyone said that he was an angel in heaven.

I tried to picture Juliana in heaven, complete with white robe and wings and a golden halo, without her creaky cart. I couldn't do it. God would just have to do something different with Juliana Kitchener.

There was a sound on the stairs, and my mother came into the bedroom. "I thought you might like a little company tonight."

"Thanks, Mommy." I sat up and took the kitten she held out to me. The tiny creature snuggled under my chin and began to purr.

"Just for tonight, now," Mom cautioned. She brushed her hand over my hair. "Good night, Sweetheart."

"Good night, Mom." Throughout the night, I felt the comforting little ball on or near my body. "I'm going to call you Juliana," I whispered. "I think she would like that."

The next day I made no pretense of going to the library. I had a mission—someone had to take care of Juliana's cats. Patches met me on the porch, meowing and anxious. The food bowl was empty. I went into the house through the side door, which led directly into the kitchen, and found the big bag of cat food on the kitchen floor. I filled the bowl and poured fresh water, then gave the kittens some cream from the icebox. I checked the ice compartment and saw that there was still a big chunk, so I wouldn't have to worry about that for a few days; but someone would have to pay the iceman next time he came. Satisfied that the cats were fine, I went into the house. I knew that Juliana would never come back, but I wanted to be sure that it was just not a big mistake.

I walked slowly from room to room; and although it was crammed with Juliana's things, the house seemed empty. I wandered among the boxes, touching here and there, missing my friend. Standing on tiptoe, I could reach the photographs on the mantel. I took the one of Juliana's mother and the one of her father with the fancy lady and the children. I placed them upon a stack of magazines and looked around some more. The box that held the pretty egg was still on the table.

Unable to resist, I opened it and carefully removed the gold box. I knew that I should not, but I wanted to see it once more. I lifted it from the red velvet lining, placed it atop another box, and bent close to see the sapphires and pearls and emeralds and diamonds, that covered the surface of the egg and cast colorful prisms of light.

"What are you doing in here?"

The man's voice was so unexpected that I jumped. I must have appeared as guilty as I felt. It was Mr. Carter, the vice-president of the gray granite Bank of Redbud Grove. He stood just inside the room, but I had not heard him open the door.

"I—I was feeding Mrs. Kitchen's cats," I stuttered.

"Well, you go on home and don't be nosing around in here again. Someone will take care of the—um—cats. Go on now." He was staring at the egg. I grabbed the pictures and a couple of magazines and fled. At the doorway I looked back, but Mr. Carter seemed to have forgotten about me. He had lifted the egg; and he stood transfixed, turning it round and round. I heard the click when he opened it; and I heard him draw his breath sharply, then say in an awed whisper, "Dear God in heaven!" I left.

There was a funeral for Julie Kitchen, but I didn't attend. My mother thought it would be better for me, not to go. There was talk about Julie for several days, mostly about the strange things that were found in her house. Beneath stacks of newspapers, the discarded organ from the Methodist church was discovered in dismantled pieces. Julie had appropriated and hauled the pieces in her cart, one at a time, until she had the whole instrument inside her house. A broken grandfather clock lay beneath several old blankets, obviously beyond repair, but still with beautiful wood.

When Julie's will was read, there was cause for controversy. That she had a will at all created wonder. No one thought that she possessed anything of value; but she owned the big house, free and clear of any debt. And she left it to Mr. Cunningham.

The will was dated only weeks before her death, duly witnessed and completely legal. The strangest bequest was that of a Fabrege' egg to a girl called Sissy, who was the daughter of a soldier who lived in a yellow house on the northeast corner of the park in Redbud Grove, Illinois. No such item was found. I told Mr. Patterson, the attorney, that I had seen the egg and that Mr. Carter, the banker, had also seen it. However, Mr. Carter had no memory of the egg. The matter was dropped.

It was merely coincidence that Mr. Carter came into a large inheritance shortly after Julie died. No one seemed to remember the wealthy aunt, who left him enough money to build a fine house on the outskirts of Redbud Grove—a house complete with the most modern conveniences available at the time, things like a dishwasher, the newest Amana refrigerator, and the first television set in the county.

For a while I missed Julie, but her memory faded with time. The kitten disappeared, so there was not even that reminder. Mr. Cunningham took possession of the house and turned it into an office. He had the organ rebuilt and took it into his home, where his older daughter learned to play it.

The pictures and the linen sampler became a part of my "stuff", the things that get put into boxes as valued mementos of childhood, then left in closets until college or marriage or moving reveals their contents once again. It was not until I was in college, sitting in a class on European/Asian history, that the memory of Julie Kitchen rushed into my mind with the speed of the train that had killed her.

The professor was lecturing on the downfall of the Czars of Russia. Just about the time he mentioned the murders of Nicholas and Alexandra and their children, I came upon a picture in the textbook that made me gasp. It was a copy of the photograph that I had taken from Julie's house, the day she died.

I stared at the page. No way! It just was not possible! How could so unlikely a person be the child of a king? How could such a mound of flesh house a princess, a descendant of generations of royalty? I looked closely at the children in the picture. Was there just a hint of Julie in the round face of the youngest child? Could it be possible that the gentle eyes of Nicholas held a touch of her gaze, or was I inventing a likeness?

I leafed through the book, looking for dates and historical facts. The professor's voice droned on, while I compiled notes and fragments of sentences. The time frame was correct. Julie had told me that she was born before the marriage of Nicholas and his beloved wife, Alexandra. Her accent was undeniably Russian.

Possible? I would never, could never, know with certainty. But maybe, just maybe, for a short while in my childhood, I knew a princess.

And her name was Juliana.

#

THE GRANDPAS

Grandpa Bannister was the best grandpa in the world. All forty-one of his grandchildren loved him, and looked forward to visits from him. On the other hand, Grandpa Loring knew nothing about being a good father, much less a good grandpa; and none of his twenty grandchildren loved or even liked him.

Shortly after Julie Kitchen died, both of my grandpas came to Redbud Grove to visit us—the same week. Grandpa Bannister arrived first, chauffeured by one of his daughters and her husband, who had driven to southeastern Missouri to bring him north for his annual visit with his Illinois children and grandchildren.

We knew that he was coming. Buddy and I vied for the honor of sacrificing our beds to the comfort of Grandpa. The obvious best solution was that Grandpa sleep in one of the twin beds, in the room Buddy shared with Bethy, since it was close to the bathroom. The decision was made. Bethy would sleep upstairs with me, a treat that thrilled her little three-year-old soul.

The first evening of his visit, Grandpa had Bethy on one of his knees and Buddy on the other, while I stood behind his chair and wrapped my arms around his neck. At nine, I may have thought that I was too old to sit on anyone's lap; but as soon as one of Grandpa's knees was vacated, I perched upon it.

"Well, lookee here," Grandpa said. He had reached into his pants pocket and pulled out a handful of paper-wrapped Double-Bubble bubble gum, a commodity that never seemed to run low with Grandpa. He never chewed it. His dentures and chewing tobacco prevented that. Even so, his grandchildren learned how to blow gum bubbles from Grandpa Bannister.

Grandpa smelled like smoked cigars, chewed-up wet cigars, and Red Man chewing tobacco, which should have made him completely undesirable. But it didn't. We thought he just smelled like Grandpa, and we breathed in his scent with appreciation for his presence. He wore khaki or gray work clothes made of cotton twill that became softer with each washing. When he went out, whether for a long trip or a short stroll around the yard, a brown felt hat with a wide brim and smooth crown covered his head, which was nearly bald. He knew by touch how to position the hat at just the right angle for comfort. His fingers knew where to smooth the hollows at the front tip of the crown, and how to tilt the brim slightly downward to shield his gray-blue eyes.

Grandpa's hat gave him an air of dignity, covering his vulnerable baldness and momentarily erasing a few years from his appearance. He stood tall, well over six feet; and his shoulders were broad, his arms and legs long and big-boned. Besides the bubble gum, Grandpa carried in his pockets a box of matches and a watch, attached to a gold chain, which was hooked through a belt loop.

One of six children, Grandpa Bannister grew up in a farm community, as did most people of his generation in Southeastern Missouri. Education rarely extended past grade school; and in Grandpa's case, schooling didn't progress that far. Reading was not his strong suit. Survival of the family depended upon as many able-bodied sons as his father could keep working in the Black River bottomlands and rocky hillsides.

Grandpa bought his own farm in time, married and fathered ten children. He also developed carpentry skills and passed that on to three of his sons, including my dad. When Grandpa was in his early fifties, his wife died of pneumonia, two days after Christmas in nineteen thirty-four, leaving six children at home. My dad was fourteen at the time, and was recovering from a nasty case of the measles.

Grandpa's best friend became a long-necked bottle. Between that friendship and the lean years of the Great Depression, he lost his farm and the big white farmhouse with the red roof, where five of his children and one granddaughter, called Sissy, were born.

None of that mattered to us, his grandchildren, who loved him. He was like a gentle Saint Bernard, who allowed yapping poodles to crawl and pounce and cuddle, who never scolded or was mean-tempered. Grandpa played checkers with us, took long walks with us, patted our heads, told us stories, and loved us.

We had finished supper and were sitting at the kitchen table the first evening of Grandpa Bannister's visit, when someone knocked at the front door. Expecting it to be a neighborhood child, my dad called out.

"Come on in. We're in the kitchen."

"Am I too late for supper?" A tall, thin man dressed in overalls and carrying a cardboard box with a string tied around it, appeared in the doorway. No one moved at the table for several moments before my dad rose and extended his hand to the man.

"Well, hello, Arthur."

"Howdy, Will." He nodded to my mom and Grandpa Bannister. "Howdy, Jackie, Herb." Grandpa stood up and shook hands with the man. My mother just sat in her chair and stared at him. She did not look pleased. I knew who he was, because I had seen pictures; but this was the first time in my memory that I saw him in person. It was Grandpa Loring, my mom's father.

"How did you get here?" Dad asked him.

"I took a bus. A feller at the station told me where you live. I heard in Doniphan that Herb had come north, so thought I'd come on along." Grandpa Loring's voice was soft and a little gravelly. He looked at me. "Hi, Girlie," he said. He seemed not to see my brother and sister. Mom stood up.

"Sissy, you and Buddy take Bethy outside and play." She gathered up our plates and motioned with her head that we should go right now. I watched her from the kitchen door. She placed a clean plate and utensils at the place where she had been sitting, filled a glass with water, and indicated that Grandpa Loring should sit. "Sit down and eat, Poppy," she said. Mom looked up and saw me in the doorway. "Go, Sissy." I went.

Sleeping arrangements remained as planned, except that Buddy gave up his bed to Grandpa Loring. Buddy didn't mind. The new sofa with its plush, brown velvety cushions made a comfortable bed. The only one who seemed out of sorts was my mother. When she came upstairs to tuck Bethy and me in, she sat upon the bed and talked to us.

"It's nice that Grandpa Bannister could come visit us," she said.

"And Gwandpa Lowing," Bethy added.

"Say Gr-r-r-randpa Lor-r-r-ring, Bethy," I instructed.

"Gw-w-w-w-andpa Low-w-wing," Bethy dutifully repeated. Mom and I laughed and Bethy giggled with us. At three, she just could not pronounce certain letters. Her speech was charming; and, secretly, I hoped that it would be a long time before she spoke like everyone else.

"Girls, I want you to listen to me, now." Mom sounded very serious. She smoothed my hair back from my forehead and did the same with Bethy. "You know how you always sit on Grandpa Bannister's lap, and he plays checkers with you and takes you for walks in the park?" We nodded. "I don't want you to sit on your other grandpa's lap or go on walks with him. I don't want you to go *anywhere* with him, unless Grandpa Bannister goes, or Daddy or I am with you. Do you understand?" We nodded.

"But, why, Mom?" I asked.

"Because he's not a nice man."

"But, Mom, he's your dad, isn't he?" Mom nodded.

"Yes, Honey, he is my dad; but he wasn't a *good* dad. He was mean to my brothers and sisters and me. I will not let him hurt you. So you remember what I'm telling you. Okay?" We nodded. Bethy's eyes were very big.

Mom kissed us goodnight and went downstairs. Bethy cuddled against me.

"Sissy, I'm sca-wed."

"Don't be scared," I said. I put my arm around her and drew her close to me. "We're as snug as a bug in a rug. Look out the window, Bethy. Just look at all those stars. God is out there somewhere and He's taking care of us, too." I thought that I sounded very grown-up and knowledgeable. I wasn't sure where God was, but at Sunday school they kept telling me that He was *there*; and I thought that my teacher was surely smarter about those things than I was.

So I breathed a little prayer. *God, please protect us from Grandpa Loring. Amen.* Something about that sounded really weird. Grandpas were supposed to love us, not hurt us. Bethy went to sleep, but I lay awake. The house had been quiet for a long time. Quiet, except for the two grandpas snoring. They sounded like a duet of growling bears.

"I don't want him here, Will." Mom's soft voice came up the vent. "I don't want him around the girls. We'll just have to make him go back home."

"How are you going to do that?" Dad asked. "Don't you think he'll be all right, especially with my dad here?"

"You know what he did!"

"But, Honey, that was a long time ago. He's an old man now."

"He's sixty-six, Will. That's not exactly ancient, and I don't trust him. If he touches one of my girls, I'll kill him!" Mom's voice was low, but she sounded really mad.

"Shh, Jackie, calm down. I'll talk to Dad about it, and he can keep an eye on Arthur. Don't worry. He'll be gone in a couple of days."

It was a long time before I went to sleep.

The sun was high when I woke the next morning. My little sister had already left my room, and I could hear her laughing downstairs. I looked out my window and saw Grandpa Loring headed north, toward the center of town. Quickly I dressed and went down to the kitchen where Bethy and Buddy were having cereal, while Grandpa Bannister sat at the table and clicked his false teeth at them. I poured milk into a glass for myself and joined them.

Mom filled a cup with coffee and set it in front of Grandpa. She stirred cream into her own cup before sitting down next to him. He patted Mom's arm and smiled at her.

"Don't worry," he said. "Will and I had a talk early this morning. Just leave everything to me." Mom smiled at Grandpa Bannister and nodded her head. "Hurry up, Kids, and we'll go looking for money in the park." We finished in record time, washed our hands and followed Grandpa, like the children in The Pied Piper.

He had taken us "money looking" the last time he visited us, but he was the only one who had found a coin, a shiny half-dollar. We found nothing. Grandpa had three shadows as he walked. We looked for a long time, covering the park thoroughly, without finding a penny.

"Well, I guess we'd better go back to the house," Grandpa said. He took his hands out of his pockets and suddenly stopped. "Lookee here," he said. With his toe he kicked at the grass just in front of his right foot, and there was another half-dollar. He bent and picked it up, turned it over and over in his fingers, and put it in his pocket.

"Grandpa, can't we look some more?" Buddy asked.

"No, I'm tired," Grandpa replied. "Maybe we'll look again tomorrow." He chuckled softly as we trudged back home.

Grandpa Loring had returned. He sat at the table in the kitchen, while Mom angrily made lunch. I had never seen her in such a state. Her lips were tight, and two vertical lines had appeared between her eyes, which flashed blue fire.

"Just put your shirt on the bed, and I'll sew up the tear," she was saying when we opened the kitchen door.

"Hi, Arthur." Grandpa Bannister took off his hat and hooked it on a wall peg beside the door. "Find what you needed?"

"No. They want four dollars for a shirt in that store uptown. In Doniphan I can get one for two dollars, and I ain't payin' any more than that. Jackie can stitch up the rip in the sleeve." Grandpa Loring smiled at me. He didn't *look* mean. His hair was a beautiful white and very thick. Blue eyes, unencumbered with glasses, were just like my mom's. He had a great smile that revealed white, even teeth. *The better to eat you with, my dear!* I glided closer to Grandpa Bannister. I wasn't taking any chances.

There was lots of banging and clanging of pots and pans and dishes, as Mom made lunch. I couldn't remember ever hearing that much noise in our kitchen.

"Sissy, set the table! If the rest of you would go out of here, I'd get finished quicker!"

Grandpa Loring reached for Bethy's hand.

"Come on, Little Girlie. We'll take a little walkie while your mommy fixes dinner."

"Elizabeth, you come here to me!" Everyone froze. Mom *never* called Bethy "Elizabeth." Bethy ran into Mom's arms, and Grandpa Loring shrugged his shoulders. He grinned at Mom before he went into the living room.

That afternoon, while Bethy took her usual nap, Grandpa Bannister asked Buddy and me to go uptown with him to get some things he said he needed. In Arrol's Drug Store, he bought several items and then ordered ice cream cones for us, while he had a cup of coffee.

"What are all those mugs on the wall behind you?" he asked the clerk.

"Those belong to regular customers. Their names are on the mugs, and we serve their coffee in them whenever they ask for it. Would you like to put your name on a mug?"

"No, thanks. I'm just visitin'." Grandpa stared at the mugs in their little cubbyholes, as he sipped his coffee. "Would you happen to have a mug with 'Arthur' on it?"

"We have just about every name you can imagine," the clerk boasted.

"Good." Grandpa wrote on the receipt and gave it to the clerk. "Do you have all these names?" The clerk looked at the list.

"All but this one." He pointed and I could see that the name was mine. I was glad he didn't have it.

"Grandpa, my middle name is Carol."

"We have that one," the clerk said.

"Then package them up," Grandpa ordered.

After supper that night, Grandpa Bannister asked Mom if she would make some hot cocoa for all of us at bedtime.

"Isn't it awfully hot for cocoa, Herb?" she asked. "Wouldn't you rather have some iced tea or lemonade?"

"No, I think cocoa would really hit the spot—make us all sleep better."

Mom shrugged. "Okay."

While Buddy, Bethy and I got into our plisse crepe pajamas, Mom made hot cocoa. The sweet aroma drifted upstairs as I brushed Bethy's dark curls. We hurried down to the kitchen.

"Honey, I think I'll pass on the cocoa," Dad said.

"Me, too," added Grandpa Loring.

"Oh, come now," Grandpa Bannister scolded. "Jackie has made it, and we're all gonna' have some. I bought special mugs today, and that's what we're gonna' use tonight." Grandpa was adamant.

"Let me help you, Jackie," he said. He took two mugs, his and the other grandpa's, and stirred them with a spoon, while Mom carried the other mugs, on a tray, to the living room. After a few seconds, he followed her, and offered a mug to Grandpa Loring. "Here you go, Arthur."

So we sat together, on a steamy August night, sipping hot cocoa. It was surprisingly comforting.

"Seems like a lot of chocolate," Grandpa Loring complained; but he drained his mug and then declared that he was going to bed.

"Sleep well, Arthur." Grandpa Bannister smiled benignly.

The sun had not yet cleared the horizon next morning, when the sound of the bathroom stool's flushing woke me. My sister was still asleep beside the window. A cool breeze blew across the bed, and Bethy's little body curled in a fetal position, seeking warmth. I pulled the sheet over her and lay back down. It was much too early to get up. I dozed.

Someone flushed again. I heard muttering downstairs and the grandpas' bedroom door shut, hard. I sat up and looked out the window. It was only a little lighter, but the birds had begun to sing. There were sounds of Mom making coffee downstairs, so I crawled out of bed and joined her in the kitchen.

"Why are you awake so early?" she asked. "Daddy isn't even up yet."

"Someone in the bathroom woke me up," I replied. Just then we heard the bathroom door slam shut and more muttering inside. Daddy appeared from the back hall, yawning and stretching, still in his undershirt and boxer shorts.

"Hi, Sissy. How come you're not in bed?"

"I couldn't sleep. Too much noise down here."

"What's going on, Jackie? Somebody sick?" Dad asked.

"I don't know. There seems to be lots of activity in the bathroom."

Grandpa Loring stormed out of the bathroom and into the kitchen. He looked really mad.

"What did you put in that cocoa?" he demanded. He glared at Mom.

"Milk and sugar and cocoa," she answered, "like I always make it."

"Well, *I* think you've poisoned me!"

"Hold on, Arthur, Jackie didn't put anything in your cocoa. We all drank from the same pot." Dad's eyes could flash, too.

"Well, *something's* give me the shits and I think it was that damned cocoa!"

"Watch your language, Arthur!" Now Dad was mad.

"Sissy, go upstairs." Mom's voice meant business. I turned and ran upstairs, then quietly slipped back down, so I could hear.

"You never was any kind of a cook! You still ain't!" Grandpa yelled at Mom. Gee, I thought Mom was a terrific cook.

"That's enough, Arthur." Uh-oh. Dad's voice had become very quiet. That meant he was really, really angry. "You pack your bag or your box or whatever you brought with you, and get out of our house. Go to the bus station, and take the next bus south or wherever; but I want you to leave."

Grandpa didn't answer. He just hurried to the bathroom; and in a little while, we heard the stool flush again. I ran back to my room and listened from the top of the stairs. Grandpa Bannister came out of his bedroom, looked up at me, winked and smiled, and went into the kitchen.

"What's all the commotion?" he asked. "Um, Jackie, that coffee smells good. Think I'll just help myself, if you don't mind. Believe I'll rinse out my name-mug and have my coffee in it." He didn't seem the least concerned about the noise.

"Dad, I've told Arthur he has to leave. He's not going to talk to Jackie, ever again, like he just did," my dad told Grandpa.

"That was nothing, Will," Mom said. "You should have heard him when I was a kid. You have no idea. He used to whip my brothers with a six-foot long black snake whip—for nothing. He always called me and my sister 'Girlie', never by our names, like we were just females whose names he couldn't remember. He used to…" I heard Mom sob.

"Ah, Jackie, Honey, don't cry," Daddy said. Her sobs became muffled; and I knew that Daddy had put his arms around her. "I should have made him leave when he first got here." The bathroom door opened, and Grandpa Loring stomped into the bedroom. Within minutes he came storming out, carrying his string-wrapped box and his old gray hat. I slipped back down the stairs and peeked around the corner.

"I'm leavin'," he said, "and I know you tried to poison me!" He pointed a long finger at Mom. "Don't you ever expect anything in my will! If I leave you anything, it'll be a penny! I'm goin' and I won't ever come back here!" He reached for the back doorknob, then stiffened and stopped. "Oh *shit*!" he exclaimed and ran back to the bathroom. I barely had time to scoot up the stairs.

After Grandpa Loring left, I sat at the table with my mom and dad and Grandpa Bannister. It was almost time for Dad to get ready for work.

"I wonder what made Arthur so sick," Dad said. "Everyone else is fine."

"I don't know," Grandpa answered. He took a small packet from his pocket and put it on the table. It was blue and had dark letters on it that said: EX-LAX, Chocolate Flavored. "Must have been something he ate." Grandpa crumpled the box and grinned at my daddy.

"Dad! *The whole box*?!"

Grandpa just grinned and sipped his coffee. "Jackie, there's a cup in the sink with Arthur's name on it. I don't think he'll be back, so maybe you should just throw it away."

I suppose Grandpa Loring went back to Missouri. We didn't hear from him. Mom washed the sheets from the bed where he had slept, and Buddy moved back into his own room. Mom relaxed, and we enjoyed our good grandpa's company for the rest of the week. On the morning of his last day, Grandpa suggested one more money-look in the park, before we drove him back to my aunt's house, down where we used to live.

As before, Grandpa walked with his hands in his pockets, looking at the ground with us. We hadn't walked long until Grandpa freed his hands. From the corner of my eye, I saw a shiny flash from his hand, just before he stopped. "Well, lookee here, Kids." He kicked the grass again, and once more uncovered a fifty-cent piece. Bethy stooped down, picked it up, and gave it to Grandpa.

I stared up at him. "Grandpa!" I put my hands on my hips and glared at him. He grinned down at me. He knew that I had caught him, silver-handed, so to speak. He glanced briefly at Buddy and Bethy, and held his forefinger against his mouth. I nodded and grinned back at him.

61

"Well, Kiddees, we'd best get back to the house. It's time for you to take this old grandpa to see some of your cousins."

It was a great trip. Grandpa sat in the back seat between my brother and me, and Bethy sat on his lap during the whole two-and-a-half hour ride. We missed Grandpa after we came back home. We wished he lived closer to us and that we could see him more often.

Grandpa Loring never came back to our house. When he died, at the age of ninety-five, he left my mother exactly what he had told her he would leave her in his will.

One penny.

#

MRS. MURPHY'S LAW

I really wanted to go to West Side for the fifth grade. At East Side the fifth grade teacher was a *man.* I was used to women teachers, and the enemy we know is much less scary than the one we don't. Besides, West Side was more like a real junior high school, with classes of one fifth grade, two sixth grade classes and one seventh.

My assignment, predictably, was to East Side, while my friend, Sharon, was sent to the West Side. The first day of school, I found myself sitting in the first seat of the second row from the door, which placed me at the corner of Mr. Robert Brehm's desk. I soon discovered that there was nothing to fear from Mr. Brehm.

Literally tall, dark and handsome, he was one of the best teachers I ever had. Except for oral book reports, which I hated, I enjoyed the whole school year in his class.

New friendships were formed among boys and girls who had not shared classrooms since second grade, although we had shared the same school and playground for four years. Until fifth grade, my friends in Redbud Grove had all been girls. That year I discovered that it was perfectly okay to number boys among my friends, too.

For the first time, we had a teacher who didn't seat the class in alphabetical order, which gave me a break from Joe Bob Brady. Mr. Brehm put Joe Bob in the row beside the windows, instead of right behind me.

Doug Mullikin, who was assigned the desk behind mine, was a funny, friendly boy with thick, dark hair and brown eyes and a smile that showed off perfectly straight, white teeth. Doug's great-aunt, Dorothea Mullikin, owned Mullikin's Café, everyone's favorite restaurant in Redbud Grove. Mr. Brehm had a great appreciation for Doug's quick wit, and the friendly banter between them often sent the class into peals of laughter.

During a discussion of vocabulary words, one of which was "compromise", Mr. Brehm called on Doug.

"Doug, if you asked your mother for permission to go to Pat Monahan's house, and she said that you couldn't go, and then you asked your dad's permission and he said that you *could* go, they would have to reach an agreement. What would you call that?"

"I don't know," Doug shrugged.

"It starts with the letter C," Mr. Brehm hinted. Without blinking an eye, Doug answered,

"Communism."

The fifth grade was full of good boys: Pat, Bert, Jimmy, Larry, Karl, Norman, Johnny, Frank, and many more. And then there were two or three who were bullies, who delighted in tormenting the timid, and those smaller than themselves.

Every society, even classrooms, seems to have that element in their midst. Bullies have to be dealt with in some manner: tolerated, ostracized, or jailed. In the fifth grade, toleration was the method of choice. I ignored them, and they, wisely, for the most part, left me alone. Even most bullies are not completely stupid, except in packs.

Occasionally, my friends and I were pelted with buckeyes as we walked home from school. They didn't do any real damage, because the bully-boys throwing them rarely hit their targets. It was just part of growing up in a small town. When I complained to my mom about it, she only chuckled.

"Those same boys will be wanting to date you in a few years," she told me.

"Mo-o-o-m-m-m-m! That's just disgusting!"

Most people in Redbud Grove were good, friendly, salt-of-the-earth citizens, who loved their town, their families and friends. If neighbors could not be loved, or even liked, at least they could be tolerated. I liked speaking to people, who sat on their porches, on my way to and from school. It made me feel grown up when they answered me with, "Good morning" or "Good afternoon."

Sometimes new friends were discovered in the most un-auspicious circumstances. One autumn afternoon, on the way home from school, Sheila and I discovered two pear trees behind Mrs. Munson's house on Main Street. The season was past for good fruit. Many leaves had already fallen, covering the ground with large, yellow and orange maple leaves, which protected pears on the ground from early frosts.

It was with a great sense of triumph that I uncovered a good, solid pear beneath the leaves, that chilly October afternoon. The first bite out of the cold, crisp fruit hurt my teeth and sent juice running down my chin. Trying to wipe it away with the sleeve of my sweater merely spread the stickiness across my face, without soaking up any of it.

I had just taken the second bite, when I looked up and saw Mrs. Munson, whose pear I was eating, looking at us from her kitchen window. I froze, not knowing whether I should chew, spit or run. She was one of the women to whom I had spoken, but I didn't really know her. Mrs. Munson smiled. Seconds later she opened the back door and stepped onto the small porch.

"Did you find a good one?" she asked. I looked at Sheila, who was trying, without success, to hide a big pear in her small hand. "I'm glad you found some," Mrs. Munson continued. "I have rheumatism in my back, and I don't feel like bending over to pick up the fallen ones. You girls stop any time and get what you want." She went back into her house.

"Boy, she was *nice!*" Sheila exclaimed. I chewed, and swallowed gratefully, since the juice was about to strangle me. "Not like Mrs. Murphy," Sheila added. I nodded in agreement. There was no other woman in Redbud Grove like Mrs. Murphy. We held our books in our left arms, and grasped the contraband-turned-legal fruit in our right hands, and munched happily on our way home. Sheila, unfortunately, lived next door to Mrs. Murphy. To get to my home, I had to walk right past the Murphy house, which I did, very carefully.

There was no indication that the house had ever been painted. Weathered and porous, the boards had acquired a dark grayed-brown hue. Rising well above the ground, the one-story dwelling's lower half received no sunlight, shaded as it was by the six-foot-high growth of various flowering bushes that reached high enough to cover the bottom panes of the windows. Although the shrubbery was dense, no weeds marred the beauty of the bridal wreath, the hydrangea, the snowball bush and the hollyhocks.

Every summer, grass as uniform and thick as plush green carpet grew to the edge of the sidewalk; but not a blade touched the concrete. No other house stood in need of paint or repair as Mrs. Murphy's did, but neither did any other lawn equal the pristine condition of that owned and groomed by Mrs. Murphy.

At seventy-nine, Mrs. Murphy stood a mere five feet tall and weighed no more than ninety pounds. Tiny tremors shook her head, a palsy condition that had afflicted her for several years. It made her look as if she were constantly shaking her head over some terrible event, too awful to be endured. She cut her own hair short, in no particular style, and wisps of thin gray strands grew in various lengths around her face. She often wrapped a faded scarf, turban style, around her head.

Mrs. Murphy wore baggy cotton dresses in the same condition as her house—a faded color that always managed to look brown. She was toothless, and her lips disappeared somewhere between her nose and chin. Skin browned by years of exposure to the sun stretched tautly across her face, clearly defining the bone structure.

Mrs. Murphy, tiny and apparently defenseless, was an old woman; and every child in Redbud Grove was terrified of her. Anyone who walked by her house, child or adult, passed precisely in the center of the pavement. There was an unwritten law, decreed and enforced by Mrs. Murphy, recognized and respected by the town's residents.

Her law was simple: KEEP OFF THE GRASS! She had posted no signs; but to the children of the town, each blade of grass in Mrs. Murphy's lawn flashed a green neon warning: TOUCH ME AND DIE.

She lived less than a block from our house. During school months, I walked past her property twice a day. Much of the time I crossed the brick-paved street before I neared her place; but I became braver as I grew older. By the time I was eleven, I had even spoken to her several times, but always from the center of the sidewalk.

In the spring and autumn, Mrs. Murphy worked in her yard every afternoon. When I and other neighborhood children came home from school, she held some lawn tool, a rake, a hoe, a shovel or broom, as she watched us go by her house. She was patrolling her grounds, and the tools were her weapons, potentially dangerous or even lethal.

"I'm gonna ride my bike across Old Lady Murphy's yard today."

As one body, Sheila, Cathy, and I turned to look at Travis Kent, who rode his bicycle a few feet behind us. We didn't like Travis. He was the smallest boy in fifth grade, and he was the most obnoxious kid in the whole school. His orange-red hair had the texture of straw, and a three-spike cowlick stood up at the crown. Lashes the color of his hair framed light blue eyes. His skin, mottled with all sizes of freckles, was unmercifully sunburned from spring to fall.

"No, you won't," Cathy replied. "You're too chicken."

"You dare me?"

"Sure, I dare you."

"You just watch!"

We crossed the street two houses north of Mrs. Murphy's corner. Travis remained on the sidewalk, riding slowly until he passed the spot where Mrs. Murphy stood, about ten feet from the pavement, leaning on a garden rake and glaring balefully at him. Suddenly Travis pedaled forward quickly and angled his bicycle across the corner of the lawn. He rode in sweeping curves and finally exited onto the intersecting street, where he stopped and looked back.

At first, Mrs. Murphy stood as though in shock. Then she moved more quickly than any of us could have imagined. The high-pitched screams and squawks that emanated from her toothless mouth could have been nothing but profanity. We recognized a few words— "bassard" and "dad-durned snot-nose blat" among them. She brandished the rake, as she chased Travis. He allowed her to reach the edge of her lawn before he pedaled away. We heard his mocking giggle as he disappeared.

It was the beginning of a feud that lasted for several weeks. After school closed in June, Travis made forays across Mrs. Murphy's grass at various times and on different days. At first I admired his courage, although I didn't like him; but as summer neared mid-July, I began to feel sorry for Mrs. Murphy. I dreaded the sound of her fury that reached our house each time Travis made an appearance. I wished that he would just go away and leave her alone.

I had discovered that bullies are not necessarily larger than the object of their abuse, for Travis Kent was bullying Mrs. Murphy.

There is a fine line between confidence and cockiness, and one hot summer afternoon, Travis crossed it. We heard his voice above Mrs. Murphy's shouts.

"What in the world—?" My mother followed Buddy, Bethy and me out the door, and we walked the half block to the corner of Pine and Highway One-thirty-three. Mrs. Murphy's house was across the highway on the opposite corner. We arrived in time to see Mrs. Murphy swing her broom at Travis, who backed away from his downed bicycle.

"Get away, you dad-burned bad boy! Get away!" Mrs. Murphy shrieked.

"Just give me back my bike!" Travis shouted.

Swish! She swung the broom again, and then Mrs. Murphy sat down on the front wheel of the bicycle. Each time Travis came close, she brandished the broom; and he stepped away.

"Get off my bike, you crazy old woman!" Travis' voice became as shrill as Mrs. Murphy's.

It wasn't long before other neighbors gathered, and a wide circle formed around the combatants.

"We'd better call Pat," someone said. Within a few minutes the town's solitary policeman arrived in the town's solitary patrol car.

The officer opened the car door and just sat in the seat with one arm draped over the steering wheel. For several moments he observed the confrontation on Mrs. Murphy's beautiful green lawn. The man sighed audibly, then shook his head and slowly emerged from the vehicle.

Pat Murphy was a short, stocky man with curly dark hair and a pug nose. His round face held warm brown eyes framed with wrinkles, caused by years of sun and the quick smiles that came so readily to his countenance.

He ambled slowly along the path that opened for him through the crowd, until he stood looking down at the militant little woman, who glared up at him. Pat placed his hands loosely on his hips, shifted his substantial weight to one leg, and cleared his throat with a sound that resembled smothered laughter.

"Don't you think you should get off the bicycle, Grandma?" he asked. Mrs. Murphy pointed her broom toward Travis.

"He won't stay off my grass!" Mrs. Murphy's lips snapped together in an audible smack. "And now these people are trampling all over it. Make them go away, Patty."

Pat Murphy ran his hand through his hair, as he squatted beside his grandmother.

"Grandma, you have got to give the bicycle back to the boy."

"No."

"Grandma—"

"No! He keeps riding on my grass, and he's not getting it back!" Mrs. Murphy gave the bicycle a sharp whack with the broom. Travis groaned. Pat pursed his lips. He stood up and put his arm around Travis' shoulders.

"Come over here, Son." He led Travis a short distance away. "So you're the bad boy who's been driving my grandma crazy this summer." Travis bowed his head.

"I was just having a little fun," he muttered. "I didn't know she could be so scary." Pat chuckled.

"She's been scaring the hell out of me all my life," he said. "Tell you what. You promise not to ride across her yard ever again, and maybe we can settle this."

"I promise." Travis sounded sincere to me. It was quite nice to see him humbled. Pat went back to Mrs. Murphy, steering Travis to stand closer to her than Travis really wanted.

"Grandma, Travis wants to say something to you." Pat shifted Travis even closer to the old woman and her threatening broom.

"I promise not to ride on your grass again," Travis mumbled.

"Louder," Pat ordered.

"I won't ever ride on your grass again!"

"And you're sorry."

"I'm sorry."

"Louder."

"I'm sorry!"

"Okay. Grandma, let him have his bike and he'll go away." Pat took the broom from her wrinkled hand, gently brought the little woman to her feet, and led her toward her house.

"I don't like boys," Mrs. Murphy muttered.

"I know, Grandma."

"He's just like you always were, Patty, no good. Boys are no good a'tall."

"I know, Grandma." Pat Murphy looked back at us and gave a broad wave of his hand. We knew what he meant: GET OFF THE GRASS.

Travis rode his bicycle away. He never crossed Mrs. Murphy's lawn again; and to my knowledge, no other boy tormented her for the remaining two years of her life.

After she died, we kind of missed her.

Funny.

#

THE GYPSY WITCH

I didn't know that Cora Parker was a witch, the first time I saw her. She was in the grocery store at the meat counter where my mother and I were next in line. In those days, meat was cut to order. Chops and steaks were not prepackaged in shiny plastic wrap, or arranged according to cut in display counters.

The grocery store in Redbud Grove was larger than the small mom and pop market we had left in southern Illinois. I stood close to my mother, not quite holding to her coat, but able to should the need arise. Curious as any seven year old, I stared at the other customers.

The lady in front of us fascinated me. She was tall and had an abundance of long, curly black hair that tumbled down the back of her glossy fur coat. Shiny gold hoop earrings glistened when she moved her head.

She saw me staring at her; and she smiled, revealing the most perfect set of white teeth, except for one just off center, which was gold. Her eyes were black, also, fringed with long, curly black lashes. She wore bright red lipstick that matched the red scarf tucked into the neckline of her coat. The woman was very beautiful. I smiled back. That was before I knew she was a witch.

"Will that be all, Mrs. Parker?" the butcher asked. He didn't sound very friendly. He switched the toothpick from the left side of his mouth to the right, and folded his arms across the wide expanse of white apron that stretched across his protruding belly.

"Yes, for now," the woman answered. She smiled at the butcher, who did not return the courtesy, picked up the parcels of meat, and went to the checkout counter.

"And what can I get for you, Ma'am?" The butcher beamed at my mother. She told him what she wanted.

"Who is that pretty lady?" Mom asked him. He snorted.

"Wouldn't exactly call her a lady," he said. "She's no better than she oughta be, if you get my drift. Name's Cora Parker. She came here with her husband a few years back; then he took off. Word is, she's a gypsy. Don't know why she hangs around here. There's a few womenfolk in town who'd be glad to see the last of her." The butcher winked at my mom. "If you get my drift," he added.

My mother cleared her throat and pointed to the bread rack. "Sissy, go get two loaves of white bread and one of the dark." She gave me a small shove and then spoke tersely to the butcher, telling him what she wanted, how she wanted it cut and then didn't say another thing to him as he worked. He kept up a running monologue, asking questions that did not receive answers, giving opinions about the weather, which was cold, Mr. Truman, who was okay as a president, although of the wrong political persuasion, and would there be anything else?

"No, thank you." Just those three words, and ice encased each one. The butcher didn't seen to notice that he had just been frosted. That's what my dad called it when Mom spoke that way to him. I learned early on that frostbite was one of my mother's most effective weapons in her arsenal against bad manners, unruly children, and/or an insensitive husband.

"Yes, ma'am, you're welcome. Anything you want, you just ask ole Ollie." He pointed to the name on his shirt pocket. "Short for Oliver," he explained. "Anything at all, Ma'am." He shifted the toothpick again and looked at my mother, from her head all the way to her feet and back again. "Just anything at all." Mom's lips tightened, and her cheeks turned pink. She put the meat parcels in the grocery basket.

"Come on, Sissy." I looked back at Mr. Ollie, feeling sorry for him, because he didn't know how awful it was to be frosted by my mom. He didn't look upset. He was watching Mom walk, and he had a lop-sided grin on his face that made him look silly.

From that day on, my mother never bought another piece of meat in that store.

The summer following my fourth grade year, my dad tore down the shed with the toilet in it, and built a garage big enough to hold our car and a bigger workshop. He also brought home a small puppy with a tail that curled over its back and big patches of light tan on its white coat. Someone at the foundry had brought a whole litter to work with him, and had found homes for them that very day. We couldn't decide on a name for the dog, so we simply called him Pup.

Dad attached a high pen for Pup onto one end of the garage. He installed a doggie door so the little fellow could get into the garage when it rained, and later, when it snowed. Bethy was a little hesitant at first; but in a short time, she was comfortable rolling in the grass and playing with "her" dog.

Pup was not very happy with me that summer. On days that I rode my bicycle, he had to stay in the pen. My friends, Shirley, Sharon, Cathy and I spent most days riding our bikes around Redbud Grove, first to one house or another, finding the most compatible mother who would tolerate our giggling and noise.

We were ten years old, a little cocky, full of energy and wonder at the world around us. Our mothers made us promise never to go anywhere alone, to always remain in a group and not do anything foolish or dangerous. Of course, we promised, each mentally crossing our fingers to allow for necessary breaches, just in case circumstances hindered our good intentions.

Those summer days were perfect: long sun-filled mornings and afternoons, that seemed to be encompassed with a hazy, golden aura. We wore sleeveless shirts and pedal pushers or shorts. No one worried about sunburns, and there was no sunscreen, just a heavy lotion called Coppertone, which none of us used. I don't remember getting sunburned one time.

Sometimes we spent an afternoon in the gray granite library, where the rooms were cooler and held the wonderful smell of old books. We looked at back issues of National Geographic, the same ones I had examined the summer before, smothering our giggles as we looked at pictures of naked native women. The men always seemed to be facing away from the camera.

On our way into and out of the library, we sneaked peeks at the nearly nude statue of the young David, which stood on a pedestal in the vestibule near the entrance. The figure held a great fascination for us. Not only did he hold the head of the vanquished Goliath in one hand, and a sword in the other, there was a big leaf of some kind sprouting between his legs.

73

We were very discreet. We didn't want the librarian, who was also our Sunday school teacher, to catch us staring at "that part" of David. Whatever would she think of us? And more importantly, what would she tell our parents? We finally decided that David was deformed.

We rode our bicycles up and down every street in Redbud Grove. We had orders to stay on the east side of Route 45 and not to go near the river, but there were no other restrictions. However, there was just no way that we could avoid the river. It called our names, loudly.

Redbud trees and river birches lined the west bank, and there were wonderful places for wading over and around the long roots that extended into the water. None of us could swim, but we were not afraid to try.

One hot afternoon, the four of us stripped down to our underwear, daring each other so that we all had to take the dare; and we waded into waist-high water and dog-paddled, until we were convinced that we were swimming. We broke little twigs into cigarette size pieces and pretended that we were smoking like the glamorous women we saw in the Saturday matinees. We laughed and squealed and splashed in the warm river, until the trees began to cast longer shadows onto the sun-dappled surface.

Reality hit us when we climbed onto the grassy bank and looked at our mud-stained underwear. How were we going to explain to our mothers?

"Let's go to my house and crawl around on my dad's sand and dirt pile," Shirley suggested. "We can get as dirty as we want, and they won't know that any of it came from the river." So that's what we did. Shirley's dad had dug out a foundation for a garage, and dirt was piled all around the site.

"Where on earth have you been to get so dirty?" my mom demanded when I got home.

"Playing on the dirt piles at Shirley's house," I answered. It worked like a charm. The next time we went into the river, we took off all our clothes. All four of us had been banished from the dirt pile, so there just was no other option.

My dad named us the Redbud Rovers. Safety was taken for granted. Mothers all over town kept an eye out for stray children.

For the first time, my mother relaxed her eagle-eye vigilance. She would have tied me to a tree in our yard, had she known everything we did and everywhere we went.

It was inevitable that one of us would suggest that we ride by Cora Parker's house. I don't remember who first mentioned it. I know that I did not. My witch alarm pinged at the sound of Cora Parker's name, but I would never admit that I was afraid of her. We had all heard our mothers talk about the spells Cora cast on men. We thought that maybe she turned them into frogs or worse, for some of them had actually disappeared after being with her.

Adults' witch recognition is practically zero, but we actually learned from our mothers that Cora was a witch. Of course, we were not supposed to be listening to grown-up conversations, but what better way to learn about grown-up stuff?

"I heard Mom say that Cora Parker is a witch with a B," said Shirley. "I never heard of a B-witch before, have you?" None of us had.

"Maybe an A-witch has more power. Maybe Cora isn't as bad a witch as we thought." Sharon made sense to me. But any kind of witch was one I would rather leave alone.

"I also heard Mom tell Aunt Mona that there are three other women living in that house with Cora, and that they're all sisters under the skin," Shirley continued.

"I didn't know witches had sisters."

"Well, wouldn't that make them all witches?" I asked. My spine tingled at the thought of four witches living in that house.

"Wouldn't that make their magic stronger?" I wondered. I liked this conversation less and less.

"Let's ride by the Parker house, and maybe we can see them," Shirley said. She sounded excited and a whole lot braver than I felt. I pedaled along with the three of them. Maybe some of their courage would rub off on me.

On Hanover Street, the Parker house had once been magnificent, a two-storied Victorian with a turret and many gables and dormers. Tall, spreading oak and maple trees, as well as a buckeye tree, shaded the peeling white house with its deep porches. It sat back from the street. Shades covered the windows and the oval glass in the front door.

75

"We can't see anything now, but I bet we could tonight," Shirley said. She became excited. "I know! Let's have a slumber party! Then we can come back late tonight!"

"That won't work," I replied. "None of our moms would let us go out at night."

"Look, I'll tell my mom the party is at your house. You tell your mom it's at Sharon's. Sharon, you tell your mom it's at Cathy's. Cathy, you tell your mom it's at Shirley's; and no one will know where we are."

"But where will we sleep?" I asked.

"When we're done, we'll go to one house and say we just decided to change houses. It'll work!"

I was afraid that she was right. At seven o'clock, while it was still daylight, we met at Shirley's, ostensibly to pick her up.

"Have fun, girls," her mother called as we rode away. I felt a pang of guilt, but only a tiny one. A delicious excitement spread throughout my body, making my fingers and toes tingle. We became giddy and giggly with our daring.

"Let's get some ice cream first," Cathy suggested. "I have a quarter." So we went to the Sweet Shoppe and got ice cream cones, which cost a nickel each, leaving Cathy with five cents change. We sat in a booth up front and watched the teenagers in the back dance to the music of a jukebox, admiring the ease with which they did the jitterbug and foxtrot and the romantic slow dance, which made parents very uneasy.

We took as long as possible to eat. Twilight was fast becoming darkness when we left the Sweet Shoppe. Purple skies in the west showed golden streaks that swiftly faded and disappeared, leaving an evening illuminated only by the few streetlights in the middle of town.

It was very dark by the time we approached Hanover Street. Light shone from windows of houses along the street; but the trees shaded much of it, casting even darker shadows upon the brick sidewalks. A dog barked in the darkness. I had goose bumps.

"There it is," Shirley whispered. "Let's leave our bikes behind that bush and sneak up to the house." Carefully we lowered the bicycles to the grass. I hated to let go of mine. Everything in me said

76

that this was a mistake. It just was not smart to mess with witches—A, B, or any other type.

The front of the Parker house was dark. Silently we crept along the big porch, stopping when we saw a sliver of light coming from beneath the shade on a back window.

"It's too high to see in," Cathy said. "Maybe we should go." I thought so, too.

"No, I want to look inside," Shirley insisted. "We need something to stand on." We bent low and searched along the side of the house. There was nothing. "Over there," Shirley said, and pointed to a shed a few feet behind the house. Unluckily, we found a five-gallon bucket beside the outdoor water faucet. We carried it back to the window, turned it upside down, and Shirley stood on it. She stretched as tall as possible, but could not see inside. She stepped down and pointed to me.

"You're the tallest. You try."

Too scared to breathe, but too cowardly to defy her, I climbed onto the bucket. Through the two-inch sliver of window, I looked into what appeared to be a bedroom—but *what* a bedroom! There was a huge bed with high posters and a red silk canopy above it. Gold tassels swung from the high ruffles around the canopy; and the red coverlet was turned down, exposing mounds of red and gold pillows. Groups of candles of all sizes and heights stood on a dresser and little tables, providing a soft glow.

"What do you see?" whispered Sharon.

"Sh-h-h-h-h," I answered.

I almost lost my balance when Cora Parker came into the room. She wore a black lace halter and black lace panties. Over the panties was a black garter belt holding up black lace stockings, and on her feet were the highest high heels I ever saw. No woman in Redbud Grove wore shoes like those. She wasn't dressed like any witch I ever imagined. She was beautiful, like a movie star.

"Are you ready?" Cora's voice was muffled through the glass; and I ducked, thinking that she had seen me. An answering reply reassured me, and I raised my head just enough to see into the room. Coming into the bedroom was a man. I gasped. It was Mr. Oliver, the butcher who had made my mother so angry at the grocery store.

Mr. Oliver was a big man with a big belly and beefy arms. There was the strangest expression on his face, almost as if he were in pain. His mouth was half-open, and he was breathing hard. All he wore was a pair of black and white striped boxer shorts, exposing surprisingly skinny legs.

"I'm always ready," he panted. Fascinated, I watched him reach for Cora, the witch. Now, I thought, she will turn him into a frog. My fingers grew numb from holding onto the window ledge, but I wasn't about to let go. I wanted to see the transformation.

Cora moved between Mr. Oliver and my view of him. I felt a momentary pang of fear for him, but then he really wasn't a very likable man; so I decided that he deserved whatever horrible fate lay in wait for him. Cora seemed to be reaching around him and then down, and I waited for him to become something green and slimy. Cora stepped back and led Mr. Oliver toward the bed. My mouth dropped open, and I let go of the ledge. I tottered for a moment and then came crashing down to the ground. The bucket crashed into the side of the house and made an ear-splitting clatter.

"Run!" I whispered loudly, frantically scrambling to my feet. The muttered oaths that came from the house were not reassuring. We ran for our bikes, not daring to look back. We heard a door slam and feet pound on the sidewalk as we rode away, but no one could have seen who we were in the darkness. Riding as if our lives depended on it, we didn't stop until we reached Main Street. Gasping for air, we rested beside a light post.

"What did you see?" Shirley demanded.

"Was she casting some horrible spell?" asked Sharon.

"Did she kill someone?" from Cathy.

I looked at them, wondering how to explain what I had seen, wondering if I had really seen what I thought I saw, and wondering what it all meant. There was no doubt that Cora Parker was a witch to have caused such a disfigurement to Mr. Oliver. Shirley stamped her foot.

"Did you see anything at all?"

"Tell us!"

"You won't believe it," I announced. The importance of my discovery rushed to my head. I suddenly remembered snatches of whispered conversations, filled with words and phrases I didn't

78

understand, between older girls in the restroom at school. *Could what I had seen be connected to the subject those girls were talking about? Was it possible that Mr. Oliver's "transformation" was not the result of witchcraft, used by Cora Parker? Could it be that <u>all</u> men were made like that? I certainly hoped not, but I would have to think about that later.* Maybe I needed to ask my mom a lot of questions.

"Let's go to Sharon's and I'll tell you all about it. But I'll tell you one thing right now." I paused dramatically.

"That leaf between David's legs is a lie—a *big* lie!"

#

BUDDY AND BETHY AND GRANDMA CHINN

One of Buddy's prized possessions was a genuine Hopalong Cassidy pocketknife, complete with a textured plastic handle. A silver-colored image of the beloved cowboy, astride his rearing horse, was glued to the plastic. Buddy managed to hold on to the knife for several months after the Christmas he received it. Unfortunately, he lost it in the park. He was only nine, but he stoically took his scolding for being careless with his possessions.

One Sunday afternoon, Bethy, who was determined to learn how to play "jacks", had somehow coerced Buddy into playing the game with her on the broad front step, at the front of our house. Bob Walters, a boy about a year older and a lot bigger than Buddy, stopped his bicycle on the sidewalk, and called to Buddy.

"Hey, I just found a knife in the park."

"It's mine," Buddy announced. He left Bethy on the step and walked up to Bob, who stood on the sidewalk, with his bicycle balanced between his legs.

"How do you know it's yours?" Bob demanded.

"Because I lost mine over there," Buddy told him. Five-year-old Bethy joined her brother. She looked from one to the other, as the conversation progressed. The rest of us could hear the discussion quite well. Dad got up from the couch and stood beside the window, where he could watch the situation unfold. My mother held some embroidery in her lap, and I continued to read my library book.

"That doesn't mean it's your knife," Bob stated. "When did you lose yours?"

"This summer. It's been awhile, sometime after school was out." Buddy nonchalantly put his hands in his pockets. He was a negotiator.

Bethy, on the other hand, was a combatant. Both of them usually worked out confrontations to their own advantage, but Bethy's was more direct and much quicker. Dad chuckled as he watched.

"Jackie, come watch this," he whispered. Mom and I joined Dad at the window.

"Oh yeah?" Bob challenged. "What did your knife look like?"

"It's a Hopalong Cassidy knife with a silver picture on the side," Buddy described. Bob looked at the sidewalk and shifted his bicycle.

"That don't mean nothin'," Bob countered. "What color is the handle?"

"Black. It has little ridges in it." Buddy sounded very calm. Bob kept one hand on the handlebar of his bike and withdrew the knife in question from his pocket. "That's my knife," Buddy told him.

"You can't prove it," Bob taunted. "You can't prove it's yours, and I'm gonna' keep it." He started to replace it in his pocket.

"You give my bwothuh back his knife!" Bethy flew at Bob Walters with the fury of the just. She attacked him with both hands, pushing the much bigger boy, and nearly toppling him over onto the sidewalk. Bob dropped the knife, which clattered onto the pavement. He grabbed the handlebar with both hands to keep from falling, while Bethy continued to hit him with doubled fists. Buddy picked up the knife.

"Keep the old knife!" Bob shouted, and Bethy backed away from him. He found his balance and pedaled away.

"It's broke," Buddy said. Bethy stared at the knife in his hand, and then looked up at her big brother's face. She put her hands on her hips, stepped away from him, and glared after Bob Walters, who was already half a block away. "The silver piece came off when he dropped it, and the blade is all rusty," Buddy continued.

"Maybe Daddy can fix it," Bethy suggested.

Daddy, in the meantime, was quietly laughing with delight at the hotheaded little girl, who was so much like him. We all sat down and continued with our individual projects, deceitfully ignorant of the battle. When my brother and sister came in to tell of the triumphant outcome of the skirmish, Dad was appropriately sympathetic and proud. He led the way to his tool shop in the garage, where he restored the silver Hopalong to its rightful place on the knife.

Only days later, we received word that Aunt Edith and Uncle Rolla were bringing Grandma Chinn to stay with us for a short time. Grandma was leaving her home in Missouri and would live out the remainder of her life with Aunt Edith. It had been two years since our little vacation with my mother's aunt and uncle in Iowa, and we all looked forward to their coming. Living so far away from our relatives made visits from them a grand occasion.

Sleeping arrangements had to be determined. Since none of the three guests could safely climb the steep stairs to the upper bedrooms, only one of us would be sleeping in a downstairs bed. I was chosen to take one of the twin beds in Bethy's room, and Grandma Chinn would sleep in the other. Buddy got the couch in the living room, and Dad would take Buddy's room. Mom and Bethy would share mine.

My mother cleaned our little house with the fervor reserved for really important occasions. She assigned tasks to each of us, and I thought that my dad was lucky that he only worked in a foundry. Mom baked cakes and pies and bread, then wrapped and stored them in the icebox. Menus were planned for the days her aunt and uncle would be with us, before they went back to Iowa. Grandma Chinn would stay for three weeks.

One of my jobs was to peel what looked like a mountain of potatoes for Mom's special potato salad. Unfortunately, I had not yet learned how to take off the peeling in a thin, fine strip like my mother did.

"Sissy, I'm going to have to peel your peelings! Just look how much potato you're leaving with the skin! Pay attention to what you're doing." In the process of trying to do a better job, I cut my finger, and was immediately band-aided and demoted to dusting the furniture. I considered it a good move. My finger had bled just enough to send me out of the kitchen. It must have been a Freudian slip of the knife.

I thought about Grandma Chinn as I dusted. It didn't take all the fingers on one hand to count the times I had seen her, but my mom spoke of her so often that Grandma Chinn was a living legend in our family. We were not certain what year she was born, but it was told that Grandma remembered hearing her parents talk about the assassination of President Abraham Lincoln, when Grandma was a small child.

My first memories of Grandma were as clear as yesterday. I was four years old; and my mom took Buddy and me by train to a tiny little place called Oxley, Missouri, where Grandma lived. While my dad was in Italy, during World War II, my mom took my brother and me on several trips to see far-off relatives.

It was the summer of nineteen forty-four. I recalled the acrid stench of coal smoke from the steam engine and the clickity-clack of the wheels on the rails, as we rode the two hundred miles to Grandma's house. I remembered the softness of my mother's body and the clean, starched scent of her dress, as I snuggled against her side and sneaked quick peeks at the man who sat across the aisle.

He wore a brimmed felt hat, as most men did in those days; and it was not unusual that he wore a blue chambray shirt beneath blue and white striped overalls, common day-wear for men in Ripley County, Missouri.

What fascinated me about him was his head. The side that was visible to me had no ear. Where his ear should have been, was a small black hole. He turned and caught me staring at him. He grinned, which made the hole move and also exposed brown, broken teeth. I retreated into Mom's side, probably leaving the imprint of my forehead.

When the uniformed conductor swayed through the coach calling, "Oxley. Oxley. Next stop, Oxley," I thought of the game my cousins played, shouting, "Olly-olly-ox-in-free!" My mother took Buddy's hand while I held his other; and with one suitcase and two small children in tow, Mom left the train.

There was no depot, only a wood platform with a couple of weathered benches beneath a roof, held up by four rough-hewn poles. "Hold Buddy's hand tight, Sissy. Don't let go of him." I tightened my grip on my little brother's hand, feeling older and protective.

It was a short walk to Grandma Chinn's house from the platform. My mother pointed to a white house, surrounded by many kinds of flowers. It rested on a high slope, like many of the houses in the tiny hill-town. Concrete steps led up the incline to the front porch, where a short woman in a dark calico dress stood waving to us.

"There she is!" Mom exclaimed. "There's Grandma Chinn!"

I was prepared to love her. My mother had told so many stories about her, and described her so vividly, that I felt as if I already knew her. As my short legs took one step at a time, Mom lifted Buddy and hurried up to the porch. I stopped and watched, as my mother, still holding Buddy, embraced her grandmother. Tears ran down Grandma Chinn's face. She kissed Mom's cheeks repeatedly, kissed Buddy's head and face wherever possible, then clutched them close and kissed them again.

"Oh, Baby, I thought I'd never see you again! But you brought your little babies back!" Grandma kissed Buddy's cheek once more.

"*Down!*" he demanded. Grandma laughed through her tears, and then she saw me.

"Oh," she said. There was something in her voice that, I now know, was wonder. "Oh, Honey, come to your grandma." She came down the porch steps and opened her arms. I looked into her face, as I climbed the remaining stairs to the grassy landing. It was my mother's face, only much older. Blue eyes peered from a face whose skin looked like a piece of parchment that had been crumpled and then smoothed out, leaving tracings of lines and creases, a road map of her life.

I went into her arms as naturally as if I remembered all the times she had held me, the first two years of my life. Grandma brought me close to her chest and rocked gently to and fro. She sat down on the first porch step and pulled me onto her lap.

"Oh, oh, oh," she crooned softly. She cupped my face with her hands. Her blue eyes squinted, trying to focus without the glasses that did no good whatsoever pushed atop her head, where they rested. She kissed my mouth, a common practice for close relatives, before society decreed it unhealthy, and then rained kisses all over my face.

"You don't look like your mommy," Grandma said, "but her hair was yellow, like yours, when she was a little girl. You're just about the size she was, when I had to give her up." I didn't know then what all her words meant. They flitted through my ears and lodged somewhere inside my head, to be remembered and understood as I grew older; but the unconditional love she poured over me soaked into my skin and became a part of me.

I remembered fragments of that visit, as I dusted the furniture in our living room in preparation for Grandma's visit. I recalled the sweet sensation of waking to the aroma of home-cured bacon, and listening to the sizzle as it cooked in an iron skillet atop Grandma's wood cook-stove. Coffee bubbled in a big blue enamel percolator and sent fragrant steam wafting throughout the house.

I thought about the pallet of her handmade quilts that Grandma had made for me, and of the mosquito netting that she had draped across chairs that were arranged around my floor-bed. From there I could see my mother sitting at the round kitchen table, while Grandma worked happily at the stove. Their soft voices and gauzy images lulled me back to sleep.

I recalled sitting cross-legged between Mom and Grandma in the porch swing, while Buddy napped inside with Grandma's husband. I wasn't old enough then to understand the meaning of security. But in a world where baby brothers went to sleep and did not awake, and where daddies and uncles dressed up in something called uniforms, and went away to participate in something called a war, I felt safe, wedged between two women who loved me.

They talked over each other's words, asking and answering questions, sometimes holding or patting my hands and one another's hands. I still remembered the perfume of sweet peas, hollyhocks, and garden phlox; and the lazy drone of honeybees, that seemed like background music to the duet of female voices in a symphony of conversation. I rested my head against a soft arm, I don't remember whose, and dozed.

One evening there was music. John Ashcraft, Grandma's new husband, played a fiddle. He could play only while sitting down and tapping one foot to the beat of the tune. I was delighted with the music. My dad played a guitar and a mandolin and harmonica. There had been no music in our house since the baby died, and Dad had to go overseas.

When Grandma stood up and began to dance, I was enchanted. She seemed transformed, no longer an old woman, but somehow agile and younger. There was such a sober, intent expression on her face as she moved nothing except her feet, tapping and pounding in a beautiful dance she called a jig.

I didn't remember the train ride home from Grandma's house.

Thinking about that trip as I worked made me all the more eager to see my great-grandmother again. I hurried through the chore and asked my mom what else I could do to help. She looked at me as if she wondered who I was.

85

"I divorced the old fart because he was mean to me." Grandma Chinn pointed a shaky finger at Bethy and me. "Don't you ever think that you have to live with someone that's mean to you, I don't care *what* some preacher says. I only married John 'cause I hated livin' by myself. Then I hated bein' married to him *more* than I hated livin' by myself."

My brother, sister and I sat at Grandma's feet, where she held court from an easy chair in the living room. Supper over and the dishes washed, the adults sat in the chairs and the sofa, while we three gathered as close to Grandma as we could. Her merry eyes twinkled as she told of her divorce from her husband, only months after she had married him, eight years previously.

"The only thing I liked about John was his fiddle, and then he up and sold *that!*" Grandma actually cackled. I looked from her face to my mother's, and saw what my mom would look like when she was old.

"Gwandma, tehwus about Mommy when she was wittow," Bethy begged. I knew what she was thinking. None of the three of us could imagine our mom being a child, but being a child without a mother was incomprehensible. I glanced at Aunt Edith, whose homely face was suddenly sad.

"Two days after your mommy was born, *her* mommy died. My poor little girl was only twenty-four years old, and she'd just birthed her fifth baby. That awful flu killed her; and it's a wonder it didn't kill her baby, too. Your great-uncle Everett took that little baby in his arms and carried her across the field to my house, and I kept her 'til she was pert near as old as you. The other four little mites went to different kinfolk."

"The baby was Mommy?" Bethy asked, although she knew the story.

"That's right," Grandma said. She touched Bethy's nose. "She was a sweet little thing and smart, too. Her hair was so pale it was just about white. Your Aunt Edith took care of her, too; 'cause your Uncle Rolla there hadn't come along yet.

"Then your Grandpa Loring up and got married again and brought all five of the younguns' back to his house. Pert near broke our hearts. He wern't worth shootin' then neither, but someone oughta' done that before he took all them poor little things back into that house. When I think about him, I don't swear; but if I'da spit on the ground, the grass would'a died!" Grandma spit into the coffee can she held in her lap.

"How come you chew tobacco?" Bethy asked. Buddy and I looked at each other, expecting the ax of Mom's disapproval of the question to fall on our little sister's head.

"Well, I'll just tell you. When I was 'bout eight years old, I sneaked some of my daddy's 'baccy from his pouch and hid under the porch and chewed like I saw him do. I was careful not to swaller it, 'cause I knew it'd make me sick. I liked it.

"My mommy found me and switched me good and tied me to the bed post under her high bed and told me I had to stay there 'til I promised never to chew 'baccy again." Grandma laughed and spit into the can. "I wouldn't promise. She finally had to let me go, and I've been chewin' ever since." She pointed at us again. "But don't you ever start."

I shuddered. She didn't have to worry about that.

"Did you know that old Jake Bishop died this spring, Will?" Grandma asked Dad.

"No, we hadn't heard about that, Grandma."

"Well, he died in his bed one night; and no one found him for a day or so. He was stone-cold." Grandma became quite graphic in her description of "Old Jake's" demise and body. Bethy's eyes grew round. She left our little circle and climbed into Dad's lap.

"Just about all the old-timers are gone now. I was the only one left, and now I'm movin' in with Edie and Rolla. Won't be none of our kin in Ripley County. A lot of the old houses are gone, too." A momentary touch of nostalgia wavered in Grandma's voice before she continued. "Jackie, I'm plum tuckered out. If you'll point me to a bedroom, I'll take my phy-sick and go to bed."

A short time later, I entered the room I would share with Grandma, thinking to find her already asleep; but she was sitting on the side of her bed. I couldn't help but stare at her. She had taken down her hair. It hung in long, thin white strands over her shoulders. She held a tangled, flannel nightgown in her lap; and she was trying to find the bottom of it.

"Sissy, straighten this thing out for me," Grandma ordered. I took it from her hands and opened the gown for her. I stared at her chest. It took me a moment to realize that the folds of loose skin that hung on her chest, were her breasts. For the first time in my life, I knew that I would not always be a child, that my body would not always be young and firm and strong, and that the sore buds on my chest that promised the appearance of a real bosom, would one day be empty, sagging skin. "Slip that over my head." Grandma held up her arms, and I dropped the gown over her head in the same manner that I had helped my little sister. "Thank'ye."

Grandma sighed and swung her legs into bed. She pulled the light sheet up to her chin and told me to get her some more covers, because she "slept cold." I took two quilts, stored in the cedar chest beneath the window, and spread them over her. She caught my hand and pressed it against her cheek.

"You're a good girl, Sissy," she told me, "and you're going to be a fine woman. I brought some quilt tops to give to you and your mommy. In the morning I want you to pick out one you like."

"You mean I get first choice?" I asked. Grandma nodded.

I felt as if she had blessed me.

Sometime in the night, Bethy climbed out of my bed upstairs, which she was sharing with Mom. She quietly crawled into Buddy's room, where Dad was sound asleep. In the faint light, she moved to the bed and stared at him for several minutes. Only inches from his face, she could not determine whether or not he was breathing.

Carefully, Bethy placed her little hand against Dad's chest, upon which Dad opened his eyes; and in the darkness, seeing a face above his and feeling a pressure on his chest, he reacted as any normal man would.

"AUG-H-H-H-H-H!" Dad screamed and sat straight up. He caught a fleeting glance of Bethy's little behind, as she crawled as quickly as she could from the room. She hopped back into bed with Mom, who immediately jumped up to see what was wrong with Dad.

"Will! What's wrong? Are you sick?" She turned on the light in Buddy's room. Dad was sitting up in the bed, breathing hard and holding one hand against his chest.

"She nearly gave me a heart attack!"

"Who?" Mom demanded.

"That little demon in your bed!" Dad pointed at the mound beneath the covers in the room across the hall, and then he started to laugh. By that time, everyone else in the house was awake, and wondering what had happened upstairs. "Bethy, come here," Dad ordered. Bethy peeked from beneath her sheet and slowly emerged from the safety of the covers. "Come on, Honey."

Deciding that she was not going to be spanked, Bethy approached Dad, who lifted her onto the bed beside him.

"What were you doing?" he asked.

"I was afwaid you might be dead wike the man Gwandma tode us about. I don't want you be dead, Daddy. I just wanted to touch yowuh hauwt," Bethy said. Dad pulled Bethy close.

"You wanted to touch my heart?" Dad hugged Bethy tightly against his chest. "You did that, Sweetheart. You certainly did that." He kissed her forehead and set her on the floor. "Now get back to bed. Goodnight, everyone!"

I think Grandma was the only one not wakened by Dad's scream. Blissfully unaware, she slept peacefully through the night and woke early, loudly demanding when breakfast was going to be ready.

Aunt Edith and Uncle Rolla left two days later, and the real visit with Grandma Chinn began. She was a gentle tyrant, whose minions vied with one another to be the first to do her bidding. We loved her.

Buddy enrolled in a wood workshop, held that summer by the high school shop teacher for nine to eleven year old boys. Buddy was quite gifted with his hands and could make just about anything he wanted. He had made several plaques, some of which were embellished with word-burned designs, nail-head pictures, and simple carving. He loved the class.

One afternoon, while Grandma Chinn was still with us, he brought home an unusual item. He approached the kitchen table where Mom and Grandma and I sat, side by side, looking at old family pictures. Buddy seemed very subdued and serious.

"Mom, there was an accident at the shop today," he said.

"Oh, that's too bad, Buddy. Did someone get hurt?" Mom asked.

"Well, yeah, they did."

"What happened?"

Buddy sat down and put his hands on the table. He held a small matchbox, which he looked at for several seconds before he spoke. His voice was very quiet.

"One of the boys got a finger cut off," he said.

"Oh, no, Buddy! Oh, how awful!" Mom was horrified.

"Yeah, Mom, it was pretty awful. The teacher thought that we all needed a lesson on being more careful around the saws and stuff..." Buddy slowly opened the little matchbox and extended it toward Mom. "...so he let me bring this home; and tomorrow another boy will take it."

"Oh, my God! Oh, Buddy, no!" Mom screamed and put her hands on her cheeks. Inside the box, lying on a bloody tissue, was the middle finger of a hand. "Oh, Buddy, whose finger is it?" Mom was almost in tears.

"Mine," Buddy replied.

"What?" Mom nearly fainted.

"It's mine," Buddy repeated, and calmly withdrew his finger, through the hole in the bottom of the box, and wiggled his whole hand in front of Mom's face. "It's a joke, Mom. See?" He opened the box and showed Mom the hole and how he had inserted his red-paint-stained finger into the box. "It's only a joke, Mom."

Grandma started to laugh. She actually chortled and cackled.

"Hee-hee-hee-hee! Oh, pshaw-hah-hah-hee-hee!" She laughed until she had to wipe the tears from her eyes. Mom, on the other hand, did not think it was funny; and Buddy made a hasty exit. We heard him laughing all the way to the park.

"Oh, Jackie, what a boy!"

"That's for sure," Mom grumbled. "He took ten years off my life!"

"Naw, he didn't. He was just funnin' with you. He's a good boy, that Buddy is."

"I know, Grandma. I'm proud of all my kids."

"You *are*?" I asked. Mom grinned at me.

"Don't get big-headed, Sissy. There's nothing worse than a big-headed kid."

Grandma grinned at me. The humor and joy in her eyes told me more than Mom's scant and rare words of praise. The days that Grandma spent with us passed quickly. Uncle Dan, one of my mother's brothers, came to take her to Iowa; and we really missed her after she left.

Grandma lived the rest of her life on Aunt Edith's farm, and died at the age of ninety-one. Grandma Chinn was a remarkable lady, who endured hardship and tragic loss with an indomitable spirit and love of life.

Many years after that wonderful visit, while watching a professional Irish dance troupe, I recognized the steps that Grandma had danced, what she had called a jig; and I wondered if, somewhere down the ancestral line, there was a connection. Grandma danced until she could no longer walk; and every time I thought about her during my life, I smiled.

I still do.

#

FRANK

The red stallion's powerful muscles bunched and rippled, as he reared up on his hind legs and pawed the air with lethal front hooves. I cringed beneath the green picnic table in the park, where my dog, Pup, and I had sought shelter from a sudden summer shower. I had fallen asleep on the cushiony grass, Pup curled against my stomach.

"Pup, come back!" I screamed at the frenzied little dog, who darted around and between the horse's legs, barking and snapping at the monstrous animal. I made a frantic grab at my pet when he circled near me, and grabbed enough hair and hide to pull him close and hold his wriggling body tightly in my arms. He whined and panted and tried to get free of me, desperate to defend his space against the intruder. I held on, terrified that the slashing hooves would strike him, if he freed himself.

"Whoa, Rusty. Easy, easy now." The rider's soothing voice and strong hands on the reins quickly subdued the startled horse, and Pup's yapping quieted to a disgruntled growl. I peeked from beneath the table. I had recognized the horse immediately, but had never hoped to see him and his rider at such close range. My line of vision showed a scuffed leather boot at the end of a long, denim-clad leg that clung to the horse's heaving side. The animal sidestepped away from the table, and I saw the whole man astride the powerful stallion.

And he saw me. We stared at each other for several seconds. Fascinated, I peered up at him. In a time when men's hairstyles were very short, Frank Thompson's black hair grew to his shoulders. A full mustache, as dark as his hair, hid his upper lip; and implacable black eyes gazed at me and at the dog, still struggling in my arms.

A faded denim shirt clung to his wide shoulders. The rain had dampened all his clothing; but instead of appearing wet and bedraggled, he looked refreshed and comfortable. He pushed up the brim of the black cowboy hat he wore, and I thought there was a hint of a smile on his handsome face.

My eyes fell and fastened on the pistol that was strapped at his waist. The black handle protruded above the leather holster attached to his belt. A bolt of alarm shot through me, and I thought of the scary stories that my friends and I had heard from older kids, and the speculations about the Thompson boys we had overheard from our parents.

I raised my eyes to his face once more; and I knew that, in spite of the stories, Frank Thompson was not a threat to me. His voice was deep and calm when he spoke.

"Take care of your dog. He'll always be your friend, probably the best you'll ever have." With two fingers, he touched the brim of his hat in a brief salute and pulled it down to shield his eyes. Frank nudged his horse forward and rode slowly across the park. I watched until he disappeared down the road that led to the outskirts of town, only then releasing Pup, who continued to growl as he sniffed the grass where his enemy's scent lingered. With a final "hurmph" he lifted his leg and covered the spot with his own special mark.

Frank Thompson's horseback ride through the park was not unusual, nor was Pup's reaction to the red stallion. As a rule, the princely animal ignored the little dog's yapping. It must have been the sudden confrontation that had spooked the horse.

I had expected verbal abuse, at the very least, and possibly much worse at the hands of Frank Thompson, the sinister gun-toting loner of Redbud Grove. But his voice had been kind, and he had almost smiled at me.

I crawled from beneath the table and lay down on the bench. The damp wood was cool. Pup continued to patrol the area, periodically giving vent to a half-hearted growl. Above me spread boughs and branches of oak and maple trees that connected to form a canopy of green, dappled here and there with shafts of sunlight that broke through the dispersing clouds.

I thought about the strange Thompson family, who lived a little over a mile outside the boundaries of Redbud Grove. The neighborhood children were threatened with tales of unspeakable things that could happen, should they carelessly wander too close to the heavy wire fence that surrounded the Thompson place.

The Thompson place. Too small to be considered a farm, in an area where farms were comprised of hundreds of acres and often tended by tenant farmers, the Thompson's owned enough land to support a few dairy cows, two horses, some chickens and a brood sow and one boar. The old house stood within a grove of trees that overshadowed both the house and outbuildings. Everything was painted a dark gray that seemed to blend into the foliage. A small wooded area curved around the back of the property. Barbed wire topped the high fence, successfully keeping intruders out and residents in. There was an air of mystery about the place.

An open porch stretched across the front of the house. The elder Mr. Thompson sat there every day, during the months of spring, summer and autumn. Someone had said that he must have been glued to his chair, because he never seemed to move. Even when his two big black chow dogs ran the length of the fenced property, barking viciously at passers-by, the old man remained motionless and quiet.

I had never heard him referred to by a name other than Mr. Thompson; and the wiry little woman, who flitted from the house to the barn, was simply Mrs. Thompson. I have no idea what her face looked like; for the times I had bicycled past their house, I had caught only glimpses of her busy body.

She walked slightly stooped and angled forward, as if she were in a hurry to reach whatever building was her destination. She rarely, if ever, left the fenced yard. The only members of the Thompson family seen around town and the countryside were the two sons, Frank and Jesse. They each rode a horse wherever they went, sometimes together, but more often singly.

I left the picnic table and ambled toward the two sets of swings on the far south side of the park. The wet grass was cool and squishy beneath my bare feet. Pup trotted beside me, sniffing and bristling as we crossed the horse-scent. I had barely seated myself on a swing before I heard my mother's voice call my name, as only she could. I knew that the neighbors, on all four sides of the little city park, had also heard the summons. With a resigned sigh, I turned and trudged toward home, Pup at my heels.

Summers passed slowly in those days. Hours stretched as long and languorously as a satiated cat, lazy and unhurried. Neighborhood children gathered in the park two or three times a week, sometimes more, to play games and use the squeaky swings. Living beside the park held distinct advantages, for I was seldom without a playmate.

Although I kept a steady vigil, I didn't see Frank Thompson ride the red stallion along our street again for weeks. Sometimes at night, as I gazed out my window, I thought about that day in the park. I watched the big dipper, twinkling against a black sky, and wondered about so many mysterious things, not the least of which was Frank Thompson. I was eleven years old and caught in the throes of a full-blown crush.

I fantasized that the shaggy-haired, darkly handsome horseman would wait until I grew up, at which time he would become my Prince Charming. I imagined damsel-in-distress scenarios, garnered from the Saturday movie matinees and fairy tales. In every fantasy, my hero, riding his swift, powerful horse, sped to my rescue and plucked me from the midst of extreme danger; and I rode away with him, the wind rushing against my face, as the movie screen in my mind faded slowly to black.

As often as I could, I persuaded Shirley, who lived a couple of blocks east of my house, and Sharon, who lived a block west, to ride their bicycles with me to the south edge of town. An oiled road, running north and south at the crossroads, led to the Thompson farm. The east/west road was all that stood between Redbud Grove and acres and acres of farm ground.

It didn't take long to reach the farm by bicycle. Fascinated as I was, I was not yet brave enough to venture past the vicious dogs and staring eyes of old Mr. Thompson by myself.

One afternoon the three of us saw the younger Thompson boy, Jesse, drag something from the woods behind their house. Jesse straightened and took his hands from whatever it was, when he saw us. I stared at him, recognizing similarities to his older brother. At seventeen, Jesse was not as tall as Frank, and was smaller framed. He seemed much younger than Frank, although only three years separated them in age. Twenty-year-old Frank looked like a man.

Jesse's hair grew long and black, but he was clean-shaven. He had dropped out of school, after the eighth grade, and seemed to have no friends, besides his brother. The two made a striking scene galloping together, Frank on the red and Jesse astride a smaller chestnut.

Jesse stood with his hands on his hips, silently watching us as we pedaled slowly on the side of the road farthest away from the barking dogs.

"Let's get out of here," murmured Shirley.

"Not yet," I answered. I was hoping that Frank would materialize.

"Come on! It's spooky here," whispered Sharon.

"In a minute," I replied, glancing from barn to shed to house.

"Ohmigosh, look!" Shirley squeaked. I turned my attention back to Jesse, and my heart jumped into my throat. Jesse held a silver-barreled pistol, waving it loosely in our direction. Of course! If Frank wore a gun, it stood to reason that Jesse would, also.

In a flurry of loose gravel, at the edge of the oiled road, we turned and pedaled away as fast as we could. Every few minutes, we looked back, to be certain that Jesse was not about to shoot us as we fled. We rode to the park and collapsed on the grass, panting and frightened.

"I'm not ever going back there!" Sharon's dark, curly hair bounced as she emphatically shook her head.

"He wouldn't really shoot us, would he?" Shirley asked.

"Nah," I stated. "He just wanted to scare us." I was feeling much braver.

"Well, he did; and I'm not ever going back there, either." Shirley folded her arms around her knees. Neither of them would even talk to me about riding out that way again.

I saw Frank once more that summer, just before school started. Up earlier than usual, I had taken a book to the park, assuring my mother that I would stay within hearing distance. Of course, with her remarkable voice, I could have gone two blocks away and still have been obedient; but, discreet girl that I was, I didn't share that with her.

Engrossed in my book, I sat cross-legged atop the picnic table. I looked up only when Pup, who lay beside me, growled. Frank Thompson, sitting loosely in the saddle, rode his horse along the far side of the park. Unmoving, I watched him.

The sun danced off the silver trappings on his saddle and bridle, creating blinding shafts of light where it touched the metal. Without conscious thought, I raised my hand and waved. Shocked at my audacity, I quickly dropped my clenched fist into my lap, wishing I could withdraw the gesture. My face burned with embarrassment, and I started to look away.

Elation followed the warmest sense of acceptance I had ever experienced, for Frank Thompson lifted his left arm and waved back to me. Unable to move, I stared in utter adoration until he was out of sight. Fuel for my fantasies had been replenished.

School started, and the old routine began with a new teacher. With two classes of each elementary grade, our circle of friends shifted every year, which gave us the opportunity to form new attachments. Sharon and I were united again, after being separated during the fourth and fifth grades.

I found a new friend in school that fall. Leah and I had not previously shared a classroom, but we quickly became friends. Leah was simply delightful. We were the same height, and we both had sun-streaked strawberry blond hair; but Leah had the most beautiful, big brown eyes and a warm, husky voice. Her laughter was a joyous thing to hear.

I may have had a crush on Frank Thompson, but I still enjoyed playing on the see-saw with Leah. We laughed at and with each other the whole year.

Leah lived on a farm, so the only time we had together was at school. Most households owned one car, which was reserved for the breadwinner. Transportation was not available for country kids to come to town, or for town kids to visit country friends. We didn't like it. That's just the way it was.

The route to the West Side Grade School, which housed the junior high classes, included crossing two highways and the double tracks of the Illinois Central railroad. For the first time, I was allowed to ride my bike across busy Route Forty-five. My lunch bucket, with the Cinderella motif, fit nicely on the handlebars of my bicycle, where it rattled cheerfully morning and afternoon, leaving no doubt as to when I arrived at school and at home.

Caught up in the academics and activities at school, I seldom had time to think about Frank Thompson; but occasionally he crossed my mind. One snowy winter day I imagined him, dressed in a fur-lined leather parka like the cowboys in the movies, riding his horse across the white fields. All my romantic fantasies came from the movies.

That autumn, a series of burglaries and break-ins occurred in Redbud Grove and the outlying farms. They continued sporadically throughout the winter.

Our one law enforcement officer, Pat Murphy, suddenly found himself with more official complaints than he could handle. There was no pattern or similarity of locations burglarized, and not one piece of evidence suggested the thief's identity.

One night the residence of the mayor was hit. Not only were expensive items lost, such as a mink jacket, an AM/FM radio, and one hundred fifty dollars; a teakettle, the mayor's house slippers, two bed pillows and a lace doily were taken. The theft was especially brazen, since the mayor lived on Main Street. No one saw anything out of the ordinary that evening.

A few nights later, the target was a farmhouse three miles from town. From that residence some pillows, several old quilts, and the farmer's clean underwear, taken from a bureau drawer, disappeared.

Speculation abounded. Some thought that pranksters were responsible, because of the wide variety of things stolen. Others suggested that itinerate broomcorn workers had to be the guilty parties, but the broomcorn season was long past. What really scared me was the theory held by my dad and most of the men in our neighborhood. They were convinced that the thieves were the good-for-nothing Thompson boys. My heart sank to my toes when I heard Mr. Norris talking to my mom and dad about it. They thought I was upstairs in my room, but I was on the bottom step, listening.

"They have no reason to steal," my mother rationalized; and I silently blessed her. "I heard that the oldest boy works the night shift at Petro. Mrs. Thompson gardens and cans fruits and vegetables all summer, so I know that they have food."

"Well, I think someone should search that house and barn and all those old sheds on the Thompson place," Hal Norris insisted. My dad chuckled, and I risked a peek around the corner, that led from Bethy's room into the living room.

"Do you want to be the one, Hal?" Dad asked, and I heard the teasing laughter in his voice. "I bet you could just walk right past those dogs and the two gunfighters, without any problem at all."

"Well, they sure are named right," Mr. Norris sputtered. "Frank and Jesse! I guess they think they're the James boys, toting those guns and wearing their hair like that! And riding those silly horses all over the country!" He shook his finger at my dad. "I tell you, they're *guilty*!"

I slipped back upstairs. I was supposed to be asleep, and I wished that I had been. I wished that I hadn't heard the conversation, for I didn't want anyone to believe that Frank Thompson could be guilty of anything bad. But before I went to sleep, I had a nagging memory picture of Jesse Thompson, dragging something heavy through the woods, and pointing his silver pistol toward me.

Winter continued to blast the little prairie town with fresh barrages of snow and frigid temperatures throughout January and well into February. The mysterious burglaries ended as suddenly as they began; and the sheriff, with a wry grin and twinkling brown eyes, bragged in the two local cafes, that his dogged detective work had scared the perpetrators out of the country. My dad said that he suspected that the cold and snow had more to do with it, than good-natured Pat Murphy's efforts. No thief, worthy of the name, would leave a trail in new snow.

My twelfth birthday came and went, leaving me with only one more year, before attaining the promised land of the magical teen years. I maintained the image fantasy that I would appear much more grown up, when Frank Thompson rode my way again.

Meanwhile I continued to live my real life mid-way between childhood and adolescence. I looked at my dolls with disdain in front of witnesses; but privately I sneaked in reassuring hugs to each one. I didn't want to hurt their feelings. My friends and I raided our mothers' cosmetics drawers and experimented with rouge and lipstick, trying to duplicate the look of Elizabeth Taylor or Lana Turner or Natalie Wood. We failed miserably, but we enjoyed the attempt.

Suddenly it was March, and a week of warm, southern winds brought the promise of spring. "Mom, I think I'll ride my bike over to Shirley's before supper. OK?" I held my breath, fingers crossed, waiting for her answer.

"Homework done?" she asked.

"All finished."

"Don't stay long and wear a coat. This warm spell won't last and it gets cold quickly."

"OK, Mom." I grabbed a light jacket from the hall closet and ran to the garage to get my bicycle. I really intended to go to Shirley's house, but I could make a quick run out past the Thompson place first, and then circle back by my friend's home, therefore not actually lying to my mother—not that she would understand my rationale. Pup whined from the garage, after I shut him inside. I was afraid he might get hurt if the Thompson's chows got to him.

As soon as I was a block from home, my bicycle seemed to turn of it's own volition, away from town and toward the outlying fields that surrounded the Thompson farm. It was not a long ride, but shadows lengthen quickly in late winter. The sun dimmed without warning; and I slowed to a stop, thinking that I should probably turn around and go back home. But what could it hurt if I made a really fast trip out and back? Frank might be there, and it had been a long time since I had seen him. Determined, I buttoned my jacket against a sudden, chilly blast and resumed my journey, which set in motion a series of events that affected my life, as well as others, for a long time.

By the time I approached the Thompson property, clouds had thickened and hung low in a graying sky. I shivered inside my light jacket. I wished that I had worn the coat my mother had told me to wear. I pedaled slowly past the fence. The dogs were not in sight. Nothing stirred in the yard. The absence of the dogs automatically made me more daring.

I stopped at the far edge of the property, where a dense clump of brush and sassafras hid me from view of the house. The air was suddenly filled with snowflakes, small at first, but increasingly larger, until there was a veil of white that softened the edges of the buildings. I started to push away on my bike, but a movement outside the nearest shed stopped me. I thought I recognized the dark haired figure of my hero through the falling snow. I hesitated.

The cold, the snow, and a healthy respect for my mother's wrath, all said to me, "Go home!" But curiosity and a burning desire to see Frank, for just a moment, was my undoing. I propped the bicycle against a small tree, in case I needed to make a fast get-away, and slipped along the fence that connected to the shed. I would take a quick peek through the window and then hurry home, before the falling snow became a blizzard—and before my mother sent my dad after me. My last window-peeping experience flashed through my mind, but I pushed it aside. This was entirely different from spying on a witch.

The window was so high that I had to stand on the tips of my toes and stretch as tall as I could. Even then I could barely see above the sill. Years of dirt and scum covered the inside of the glass. I could just make out the form of a man inside. The flashlight he held struck beams off several items on a wall of rugged shelves. When the light suddenly moved across my eyes, I dropped to my knees and made myself as small as possible. Carefully I crawled along the fence for several yards before I stood to run.

"You nosy little brat!" The low growl of fury sent more chills down my back than the snow and rising wind, and I ran faster than I dreamed that I could. The sound of Jesse Thompson's pounding feet followed the rattle of the chain fence and I knew that he had leaped over it. Even as he chased me, I wondered how he cleared the barbed wire.

I reached my bicycle, straddled it and pedaled as soon as it was upright. I think that I could have escaped, had it not been for the snow on the slippery oiled road. The bike skidded and threw me sideways; and Jesse Thompson hit me broadside with his heavy, angry body. There was a sense of being air-borne just before I landed in the road ditch, and then there was only darkness...

Angry voices hovered just beyond total comprehension, as I regained consciousness. Snatches of sentences penetrated my aching head, but I was too tired to open my eyes. I lay quietly on a musty smelling something that was dry and relatively soft. I tried to concentrate on the voices.

"...shouldn't have brought her in here."

"She saw the stuff. I couldn't let her go blabbing all over town."

"You didn't have to hurt her."

A warm hand touched my forehead.

"I wish I'd killed the little sneak."

"You may have, Jesse. If we're lucky, she'll be all right; but I think she should be awake by now."

I opened my eyes a slit and looked directly into the face of Frank Thompson. He winked at me and placed a finger across his mouth, indicating that I should remain quiet. I closed my eyes and lay perfectly still.

"I don't want her to wake up. I think we should take her out to Amish country and dump her. By morning the brat won't be able to bother anyone again."

"Don't be stupid, Jesse. Things are bad enough without killing a kid." Frank stood up. I heard his boots on the wood floor and felt the vibration as he walked away from me. Jesse's words were frightening, but I knew that Frank would keep me safe. That's what heroes do.

"Have you taken anything else?" Frank demanded.

"No. I told you I wouldn't." Jesse's voice sounded sullen.

"Go saddle Rusty."

"What for?"

"So I can clean up your mess, like I always do."

"But—"

"Dammit, Jesse, go saddle my horse! I've already missed my ride to work, and this kid's folks will have a search party out looking for her! Do you want them to find her here?"

I could feel the stare between the two brothers. Seconds later the door opened and slammed closed behind Jesse.

"Can you walk?" Frank knelt beside me.

"I don't know." My voice sounded strange, like the squeaky gate at my Aunt Rachel's house. I sat up slowly. A lantern swung from a nail on the far wall and cast deep shadows inside the shed. A menacing growl emanated from a dark corner.

"Stay, Bruno!" Frank grasped my upper arms and helped me stand. "Ow!" A searing pain shot upward from my right ankle, and I crumpled against Frank. The dog growled again.

Frank lifted me in his arms and set me back on the wooden tool chest, where I had been lying. He pushed my baggy, rolled up jeans to my knee and looked at my swollen ankle. He gently drew my sock down, and we could see the red and purple steaks already running up my leg.

"I can't tell if it's broken, but it may be," Frank said. "Sit still." He took a long slat from a shelf and broke it across his knee. He tore two strips from a ragged shirt, and within minutes he had secured my ankle and leg with makeshift splints. The door flew open.

"Here's your horse." Jesse glared at me, and I shrank behind Frank's shoulder. "If you know what's good for you, you'll keep your mouth shut," Jesse warned me. "Come, Bruno." He turned and stalked into the snowy darkness, and the big black chow followed him. I shivered.

Frank shrugged out of his coat and put it around my shoulders. He pulled a stretchy wool hat, much too big for me, over my head. He grabbed another coat from a nail on the wall, shoved his arms into it, and turned down the brim of his hat to protect his face against the cold.

"Button up," he told me. "The snow's really coming down, and it's cold out there. Ready?" I nodded.

Frank lifted me up again, and in no time I found myself in my own fantasy. I was in Frank Thompson's arms astride the red stallion, and we were riding away together. The sunset had become a snowstorm; and he was taking me to my parents, not to happily-ever-after.

The wind was fierce. I hid my face against Frank's chest. His coat and his arms shielded me from the worst of the storm. His warmth radiated into my cheek, and I could feel his heart beat through the jacket.

"I wish you would forget what you heard and saw back there." The words were calm, with no hint of a threat at all. "I can control Jesse, and I promise he won't steal again. Jesse just wants too much, and he doesn't really know what he's doing."

"I won't tell. I promise."

"Thanks." I heard the smile in Frank's voice.

By the time we drew near the park, my leg throbbed with every heartbeat. Through a haze of pain, I saw a dozen or more cars parked along the street in front of my house, and in the alley between our house and the park. A group of men huddled together on the sidewalk, their shoulders hunched against the cold.

"Looks like the posse is gathering," Frank murmured. It was several moments before they saw us.

"What's he doing here?"

103

"Shut up, Hal. Maybe he can help find Sissy." I recognized my dad's voice.

"Daddy, I'm up here," I called. The men seemed frozen to the ground, until Hal Norris rushed forward.

"You *bastard*! What have you done to that little girl!" The horse snorted and skittered sideways. Frank spoke soothingly to him, patting the big strong neck.

"Hal, get back! You're spooking the horse!" my dad ordered. Mr. Norris turned away, muttering threats. Frank slid down from the horse, keeping one hand on my arm to steady me, then carefully helped me from the saddle and carried me to my dad.

"I found your little girl along the road not far from our place. Looked like she wrecked her bike. I think her ankle might be broken."

Dad took me into his arms and held me tightly against his chest. He pressed a quick kiss onto my forehead. I felt safe and so very precious.

"Honey, are you all right? Did he—did anyone hurt you?"

"No, Daddy. Frank didn't hurt me. He found me and fixed my foot so it wouldn't get hurt more. He gave me his coat to keep me warm. He's my friend."

The group of men grew quiet. I looked from my dad's face to Frank. They stared at each other for a long moment. Frank touched the brim of his hat. He leaped effortlessly into the saddle, and turned his horse.

"Thompson!" Dad called. Frank looked back over his shoulder at my dad. "Thanks."

Frank nodded, smiled at me, clicked to the red stallion and rode away into the snowy darkness.

"Let's get you inside, Young Lady," Dad said, and I knew that the relief he felt was quickly being adulterated with anger. I sighed and resigned myself to whatever punishment I had coming. At least it would be in a warm place.

My ankle was broken, and it took the rest of spring to heal. I was deprived of listening to my favorite radio programs for two weeks and was not allowed company, except on Sundays. I really didn't mind. My brother brought my school assignments home, as well as library books that Miss Ghere chose for me. I had always been a pretty good student, but all my grades went up, due to enforced home study.

Several weeks after my encounter with the Thompson boys, Frank was drafted and went to Fort Benning, Georgia, for basic training. Less than a month later, Pat Murphy arrested Jesse for burglary; and he was sent to a boy's detention center, where he had to stay until he was eighteen. Hal Norris was ecstatic with "I told you so".

By mid August, I was walking with a slight limp, but improving daily. My parents had forgiven me, and life resumed the usual routine. I replayed my romantic, dramatic rescue over and over in my mind, usually after I went to bed, gazing at the constant stars through my window.

One afternoon in the little grocery store a half block from our house, a stranger, in a soldier's khaki uniform, asked me how I was doing. Schooled never to talk to strange men, I walked away; but something about his voice was familiar. I turned back and looked closely at the soldier. He was clean-shaven and not particularly handsome, by movie standards. His head had the bristly look of an army haircut, but his face held the black eyes of Frank Thompson.

Suddenly shy, I could hardly look at him. For months I had carried the memory of riding the red stallion with Frank, and this ordinary-looking soldier had nothing to do with that memory.

"How's your dog?" he continued.

"Fine."

"Did you get your bike fixed?"

"Dad bought me a new one."

"That's good." Frank put his hands in his pockets. "I'm going to Korea when my furlough is over. Would you ride out and say hi to my horse once in awhile?"

"Sure," I said, but I knew that I wouldn't. "Bye." I walked away, wanting to be gone from this stranger.

"Take care of your dog," he called. I kept walking.

A postcard from Frank came to me a few weeks later, and I was a bit of a celebrity; no other twelve-year-old got mail from Korea. Then word came that Frank Thompson was missing in action somewhere in North Korea. He was presumed to be a prisoner of war, which, it turned out, he was.

A year later, Frank was released, along with hundreds of other prisoners. After an extended rehabilitation, he returned to Redbud Grove. His hair grew long again, and his moustache flourished. He rode the red stallion around the countryside, as before. But the light was gone from his black eyes, and he never waved or spoke to anyone. He didn't ride across the park or acknowledge me in any way when we saw each other, which was rare.

Frank Thompson never regained the part of himself that was destroyed in a North Korean prison camp. After Jesse was released from prison, he took over the care of their parents and the farm; and he and Frank rode together as they had done since they were big enough to sit a horse.

But that wasn't *my* Frank. My Frank was the man who had held me on the big red stallion one cold, horrible night when I was twelve. The man who had saved my life.

My hero.

#

THE COURTSHIP OF MISS KATE

"My mom says that Miss Kate is going to have a baby."

A bomb dropped into the center of Redbud Grove could not have caused more earth-shattering news.

"You're joking," I answered Melissa.

"No, I'm not. I heard her tell my dad last night. That's exactly what she said, and she sounded really disgusted."

"But Miss Kate is *old!* She must be thirty-eight or forty!" I was appalled.

"Actually, she's forty-one. Anyway, that's what my mom says. I think they went to school together or something." Melissa reached for a cookie from the plate my mother had brought to my room, rather, Bethy's room, where I was recuperating from a broken ankle. The two-week grounding period was over, and I could have visitors again; but I couldn't climb the stairs to my bedroom or go to school. I craved company like my little sister craved chocolate stars.

"I wonder why they're having a baby now," I said.

"I don't know. I thought she was too old. She got married just before I went into the first grade, I think. So that's been about six years. Um, these are really good." Melissa took another cookie. "Your mom sure makes good snicker-doodles." I grinned. Melissa was a pretty girl with naturally curly auburn-red hair, green eyes, and a sweet tooth. Her happy, freckled face was a little round, just charmingly so; and her body had the soft contours that would eventually become voluptuous. At twelve, she and I hovered on the edge of adolescence, hoping that something would eventually give us a shove.

"That was just before we came to Redbud Grove," I said. "Why does everyone call her Miss Kate, since she's been married all that time?"

107

"Oh, she's always been 'Miss Kate.' I can't imagine ever calling her anything else, can you?"

I thought about it. "No, I can't." I giggled. "Do you suppose her baby will call her that when it can talk?"

"Did anyone ever tell you about her? I mean how she got married and all that?"

I shook my head. Melissa kicked off her shoes and climbed onto the bed. She folded her legs beneath her and reached for another cookie. "Miss Kate's been teaching first grade ever since she got out of teacher's college. And you know that big yellow house with the slate roof, where she lives?"

"Where we get pieces of slate for hopscotch rocks?"

"Yep. The Madisons built that house, and Miss Kate has lived there forever. I bet that's why her husband moved in there with her. I bet she wouldn't live anywhere else!"

"How did she get together with him?"

Melissa grinned. "It would really be romantic, if they weren't so old. Anyway, this is what my mother told me…"

Although Mr. Clayton King had been superintendent of the East Side Grade School for thirteen years, some of the older folk in Redbud Grove still considered him the young upstart, who had replaced Mr. Howard Simon. At the age of sixty-seven, Mr. Simon had been at East Side for a total of thirty-seven years, first as principal and then superintendent. During those years, he enforced the codes and teaching methods he had learned, some held over from the turn of the century. He was not the beloved of the faculty, or the student body.

One afternoon, hearing laughter emanating from the boys' restroom, located in the dark basement of the old building, Mr. Simon slipped silently down the stairs. It was midway through the half-hour recess, and the boys should have been outdoors with the other children. Mr. Simon tolerated no infractions of his rules, schedules, or traditions.

He stopped at the bottom of the stairs, listening to the high-pitched giggles and laughter of boys whose voices had not yet begun to change. He slid one eye around the corner and saw five little boys playing "Simon Says", in a most disgusting manner, against the urinal wall.

"Simon says write your name."

"I can't," answered blond, blue-eyed Jonathan. "I'll run out."

"Then write Jon." More giggles.

"Simon says make an X."

"Wish I could piss on old Mr. Simon," Jonathan announced.

"Yeah! I dare you!"

"Well, if he was here, I would!" Jonathan declared.

With a roar of indignation, Mr. Simon charged toward the boys, fury in his eyes and murder in his heart. The boys scattered like quail, around, under and through Mr. Simon, leaping up the stairs as fast as young legs and fear could take them—except Jonathan, who struggled in vain to escape from the clutches of an enraged Mr. Simon, who would be, Jonathan was certain, the instrument of Jonathan's demise.

Mr. Simon was not a large man; but he looked huge to the boy who was being shaken back and forth, like a weightless puppet. The man's hands dug into the boy's upper arms, and his distorted face had turned a purplish red. The veins in his neck stood out like thick cords.

"You like to play Simon Says, you evil, disgusting, nasty little delinquent? You are about to learn exactly what Simon says!"

Jonathan cringed and tried to make himself as small as possible. He had heard, firsthand, how Mr. Simon dealt out punishment. He braced himself and closed his eyes.

"Simon says—Simon—says—Si-m-o-o-on..."

Jonathan never knew what Mr. Simon was going to say. Mr. Simon gasped, released the boy, collapsed, and died on the concrete floor of the boys' restroom in the basement of East Side Grade School.

Scared mindless, Jonathan ran from the building and found his friends, gathered under a tree on the playground. When he told them what had happened, they all agreed that it was safer to keep the knowledge a secret; and the four who fled were convinced that Jonathan had killed old Mr. Simon in some mysterious way. They regarded him with a new respect and just a little fear.

The community accorded Mr. Simon the respectful eulogy due one of his position, breathed a sigh of relief that the old tyrant was gone, and hired Clayton King as superintendent. Mr. King brought new ideas and methods of teaching.

With the discovery of an oil field in Douglas and Cole Counties a few years later, new families with lots of children moved into the school district, bringing even more changes.

Oil field workers from several states settled in the community. A small foundry opened. World War II had just ended, bringing home local servicemen. With the booming oil industry came a new refinery, located a few miles north of Redbud Grove. The little prairie farm town thrived.

In nineteen forty-eight, Mr. King reorganized the grade school facilities to house an increasing student body. East Side had originally held grades one through eight. It was changed to one class each of first and second, and two classes each of third through fifth. The West Side Grade School, unused for many years, was opened. Two classes each of sixth and seventh transferred there, and the eighth graders were assigned space in the high school. It was the next best thing to new schools, which was not an option at that time.

Mr. King liked children. It was not uncommon to see him comfort a child with a skinned knee, or to find him playing catch at recess with little boys who had been excluded from the older boys' games. School events accounted for most of his social life. He had no family in the area.

Clayton King's wife had died when his daughter, Leanna, was five years old. From that time, his life had consisted of caring for the little girl, teaching wherever he could, and attaining a masters degree in education. He had successfully reared Leanna, who completed college, promptly married, and moved to Minneapolis. At forty-two, except for an occasional twinge of loneliness, Clayton King lived a life that suited him immensely.

Many mothers of eligible daughters had coached them on ways and wiles to capture the heart of Clayton King. Single ladies, some younger, some older than Mr. King, had set their sights on him, but unsuccessfully. He would have been dismayed had he known how many female hearts he had broken with his polite unresponsiveness to both active and passive pursuit.

He was quite striking in appearance. Tall and broad-shouldered, Clayton looked like the dependable man he was. His dark blond hair, prematurely streaked with silver at the temples, grew thick and glossy. His square chin and firm jaw-line were softened by blue eyes, framed with lashes long enough to make women envious. A wide mouth, full lower lip, and slightly crooked white teeth added to his charm, of which he was totally unaware.

Clayton King was very proud of the changes he had wrought in the schools. Some of the older residents thought it unnecessary; but the system worked well and turned out graduates who could, at least, read.

Six new teachers joined the staff, two men and four women, all of them married. Some of the tenured teachers held themselves aloof from the newcomers for a few months; but Miss Kate Madison, first grade teacher, was gracious to old and new alike.

Miss Kate Madison, a gentle, well-bred descendant of one of the town's founding settlers, was the epitome of what Redbud Grove's population thought that a first-grade teacher should be. Of medium height, she carried her slender frame with a grace and dignity that whispered of lessons learned early from a mother who thought those qualities important to a young lady's upbringing.

Her students called her Miss Kate and remembered her fondly all their lives, for she introduced them, with kindness, to the new world of school. She established routines that became rituals, beginning with the pledge of allegiance to the flag, which held a position of honor in the right front corner of the room. She held a teeth and fingernail inspection every morning, passing up and down the rows of children, who bared their teeth in a broad smile and spread their fingers on a clean handkerchief. Those who passed, and they always did, were allowed to take a turn on the bright green and silver slide that stood along the windows at the back of the classroom.

Children enjoyed being near Miss Kate, as well as looking at her, for the lightest scent of jasmine formed a delicious aura around her. Little girls shyly touched her soft, brown hair, which she wore in a loose knot at the back of her neck. Tiny tendrils curled at her forehead and temples, sometimes forming near her ears to tease the small pearl earrings she wore daily. Her eyes were a true hazel color, with golden flecks; and her mouth curved in a natural smile, touched with just a hint of added color. Good skin, always protected from the sun, and even, white teeth completed an overall extremely pleasing appearance.

Miss Kate loved her young charges; but she kept strict order in her classroom, which remained as neat and disciplined as the rest of her life. Born in the master bedroom of the three-storied house her father built, Miss Kate continued to live in the dwelling that had been her home all her life, except for the brief years she had attended college. Since her parents' deaths, she had lived alone. At the age of thirty-five, her life was just as she wanted it.

Located three blocks from the school, the pale yellow house, with white gingerbread trim and gray slate roof, stood in the center of a large lawn, filled with old maple and redbud trees. In the spring, the redbuds became a mass of heavy, purple-pink branches that turned the grass to a carpet of pink when the blooms fell. A tall decorative concrete fence, topped with iron spikes, enclosed the property. The enclosure looked restrictive, but the heavy gate was never locked. Other houses, similar in size and design but not as ornate, lined the brick-paved streets and exuded an air of comfortable gentility.

Miss Kate owned a car, but seldom drove it. Parked inside the converted carriage house, the nineteen-forty Packard was driven only when the weather decreed. Most days she walked to school, her head held high and her bearing as regal as royalty. If the changes at school upset her, there was no indication. Her calm acceptance and graciousness to the new teachers and additional janitorial staff was simply her manner. It proved what everyone knew about Miss Kate—she was unflappable.

A staff meeting that included the new teachers was held the first week of September. Mr. King introduced each one, encouraging them to give a brief summary of their teaching career and personal history. Near the close of the session, he asked the janitorial team to join the group. Previously, Roscoe Smith, who had been at East Side for close to thirty years, had been the sole custodian. Three men were added to the staff, of which two would work at West Side.

Mr. King introduced them to the teachers, and gave a short welcome, knowing that the men were in the middle of cleaning and preparing classrooms. Two of the newcomers seemed ill at ease, shifting their feet, eager to be gone from the presence of so many scholars. The fourth man appeared comfortable with himself and his surroundings. He nodded to the men and smiled jauntily at the women, as each was introduced.

His name was Jedediah Newman. "Just call me Jed," he said. His voice was deep, a little raspy, sensual. Every woman's eyes swung toward him as one, except Miss Kate's. "I'm not one for formality. Battle kind of takes that out of a man."

"Thank you, Jed." There was dismissal in Mr. King's words. The men turned and walked toward the door, Jedediah last in line. Just before he exited, he looked over his shoulder and directly into the eyes of Miss Kate Madison.

Startled, Miss Kate returned his gaze for a moment. She was surprised; but when he winked at her, she was stunned. She dropped her eyes. Aside from a heightened tint of color in her cheeks, Miss Kate appeared perfectly calm, as always; but in spite of herself, she glanced at the door after she heard it softly close. Although she experienced a sensation of strange warmth, her demeanor conveyed nothing unusual.

The meeting adjourned, and the teachers congregated briefly in the hall, before going to individual classrooms. Miss Kate shifted the small stack of books and folders she carried, freeing one hand to open the heavy door of the first grade room, where she had reigned supremely for fourteen years.

She loved the aroma of learning; the slightly acrid smell of white chalk dust that clung to the walls, the musty odor emanating from old books, and the fresh, sharp tang of newly sharpened pencils. Miss Kate placed the supplies on her big desk, bought for her the first year she started teaching, and still considered new. She sat in the comfortable leather chair that squeaked every time it swiveled. She made a mental note to ask Roscoe to oil away the squeak.

Her gentle eyes surveyed the room, as she thought of individual children among the hundreds who had occupied the rows of connected small desks. She smiled at the memory of Bonnie, the little girl who had printed a big "k" under the picture of a dog, explaining that it stood for cocker spaniel. The child was one of the first of Miss Kate's students to become a teacher.

She remembered Billy, the sweet little boy who had refused to come back inside, following recess one afternoon. With quiet determination, he had remained seated on the ground under a tree until school was dismissed. When Miss Kate had knelt beside him, and asked again why he would not come back to the classroom, he had looked up at her with tear-filled eyes.

"I tore my pants," he had whispered. "I didn't want anyone to see my underwear."

Miss Kate had taken his hand and led him inside, where she had told him to go to the cloakroom, remove his pants and hand them to her. While he had waited, safely hidden from view, she sewed the rip in the seat of his pants and then sent a happy little boy home.

She smiled, content in the knowledge that she had made some lasting impressions on her children, that education and learning remained important to many of her students, long after they outgrew the small desks. She felt very gratified.

The door to her room opened. Miss Kate turned in her chair and met the disconcerting gaze of golden brown eyes set in the confidant, handsome face of Jedediah Newman.

"Can I help you, Mr. Newman?" There was not a hint that she was surprised to see him. The man leaned against the doorframe, arms folded loosely across his chest. Something about his stance irritated Miss Kate. Accustomed to deference and respect from both younger and older generations of the male species, she sensed a lack of both in Jedediah Newman's bearing.

"No, Ma'am. I thought there might be something I could do for *you.*" His voice disturbed her. Pleasantly deep, it held an appealing resonance that had touched something inside her when Jedediah had first spoken at the staff meeting. Miss Kate sat straighter in her chair and folded her hands atop the desk, her come-to-order posture. A sudden shaft of sunlight from the window struck Jedediah's hair, and the warm color made her think of a glossy brown crayon, fresh from the box.

Jedediah dropped his arms and moved into the room. Miss Kate watched him, her hazel eyes direct, but guarded. He carried himself with pride, even dressed as he was in the gray twill janitor's uniform. It was obvious from his bearing, as well as his remark at the meeting, that he was one of the returning veterans. She wondered what his employment before the war had been, then caught herself; he was probably no more than twenty-five or six, so he may not have been previously employed, at least not long-term.

"I haven't inspected the room completely, Mr. Newman; but I'm sure that everything is fine. Roscoe Smith has always taken care of anything I need done." There was a definite tone of dismissal in her words and tone. Ignoring both, Jedediah walked in front of her desk toward the windows on the west wall.

"It smells musty in here," he stated. Effortlessly he raised the heavy, pulley-held frames. Fresh prairie air filled the room with the essence of late summer and stirred tendrils of Miss Kate's hair. Jedediah brushed his hands together. "The sills are dusty. I guess Roscoe hasn't cleaned this room yet." Miss Kate watched silently, as he turned from the windows and stopped in front of her desk.

He braced his arms on the surface, leaned forward and looked into Miss Kate's eyes. She retreated against her chair, feeling as if the air in the room had become very heavy. Jedediah Newman was not a small man, and he seemed even larger at such close range. He was so near that she could see the tiny lines around his eyes, eyes that seemed much older than his face; and she could discern the beginnings of new beard growth, although it was apparent that he had shaved that day. The scent of his aftershave lotion teased her, made her uncomfortable.

"Miss Kate Madison." It was not a question. He merely said her name. He glanced at her hands resting loosely in her lap. In a single fluid motion he reached across the desk and lightly stroked the bare ring finger of her left hand. "No Mr. Madison. I wonder why."

Shocked, motionless, Miss Kate dropped her gaze to the big hand that continued to caress so gently. She barely felt his touch, but the effect was as strong as if he had struck her. Regaining her senses, she pushed her chair away from the desk, rose briskly to her feet, and plucked her hand-tooled, genuine leather bag from the stack of books, where she had placed it. Looking just over the top of Jedediah's left shoulder, she spoke in her usual pleasant voice, hoping that the tremor she felt was not apparent.

"Please close the windows before you leave, Mr. Newman."

Miss Kate did not see the tiny, knowing grin on Jedediah's face, or witness the slightly mocking salute he awarded her back.

Less than a month after classes began, the teaching staff's favorite speculation was that the new janitor was flirting with Miss Kate. Jedediah made no effort to hide his interest. Miss Kate was pristinely polite, when she could not avoid him. If she knew about the gossip, she did not dignify it with acknowledgement.

Gloria Hayes, second-grade teacher and friend of Miss Kate, felt it her duty to enlighten Mr. King about the situation. He listened quietly, asked no questions nor offered an opinion, until Mrs. Hayes was finished. He played with a pencil, tapping it end over end, and chose his words carefully.

"I think that it would be a good idea if no more were said about this. I am sure that neither Miss Kate, nor Mr. Newman, would appreciate being the subject of such gossip." He paused and stared unsmilingly at Mrs. Hayes. "Do I make myself clear?"

"Oh, oh, yes sir!" She made a hasty retreat. She didn't mention the juicy story to Mr. King again, but others on staff weren't so discriminating about hearing good tidbits of rumors.

Mr. King did not repeat the story to anyone; but he watched the janitor and he watched Miss Kate.

When the first perfect scarlet rose appeared on Miss Kate's desk, everyone knew who had sent it. And everyone knew when a fresh one arrived mysteriously every Monday morning. Miss Kate ignored the roses and never mentioned them to her fellow teachers. No one was brave enough to ask. Jedediah was never seen leaving the roses on her desk, but everyone *knew* that he put them there. And everybody knew that he was watching her like a cat waiting for the first drop of cream to fall from the bottle.

Of course, Jedediah watched a *lot* of women; but Miss Kate was the only one receiving roses. Since the whole town knew how privately she lived and how disinterested in men Miss Kate was, a stranger was the only candidate as a suitor. No one else would risk the humiliation of rejection.

Some eyebrows peaked at the difference in their ages, for it was apparent that Miss Kate was a good ten years older than Jedediah Newman. Still, there was no accounting for taste; and Miss Kate's face and figure were undeniably lovely, for a woman of any age.

October waned; and the school's annual Halloween party, planned and supervised by the teachers, created excitement and anticipation for the children. Every person who attended dressed for the occasion, including all the teachers, the janitors, the principal and the superintendent. However, Mr. King had an all day seminar in Chicago the day of the party, and would not be able to attend. He was the envy of the other men on staff.

The harvest moon appeared full and luminous on Halloween night. Heavy frosts had colored the town's trees in brilliant hues of reds, golds, yellows and even purples. A thick cover of leaves rustled on the brick sidewalks as ghosts, goblins, witches, clowns and hoboes kicked their way through the crispy piles along the avenues toward East Side. The air was filled with the happy sounds of children going to a party.

Festive with orange and black crepe paper streamers, the school gymnasium looked warm and welcoming. Bales of straw, placed along the walls in stacks of various heights, offered comfortable, if scratchy, seating. Pumpkins, carved into jack-o-lanterns, smiled and frowned with the flickering of candles placed inside them. Kerosene lanterns hung from the walls, safely away from flowing costumes and rowdy children.

The gymnasium seemed full to bursting with children, and laughter, and creepy fellows bent on scaring each other silly. At one end stood a long expanse of buffet tables, laden with dishes of homemade food provided by mothers and grandmothers in the community. The aroma of freshly brewed coffee and the heady scent of cider, both hot and cold, tempted thirsty revelers; but the meal would not be served until after the judging and unmasking.

Miss Kate arrived at the party dressed in a formal, dignified gown of dark green satin. Once worn by one of her ancestors, it spoke of an era long gone; and Miss Kate looked as if she had stepped from the pages of history. A tight bodice rose from the full skirt, which fell in soft folds that were caught up into scallops that revealed an underskirt, comprised of rows of tiny cream-colored ruffles. Matching creamy lace filled in the top of the bodice and touched the wrists of the long sleeves.

Capricious curls escaped from Miss Kate's upswept hair, held with silver combs at the sides. A silver eye mask completed her

117

costume. There was something not quite Miss-Kate-like about her, but her dignified stature remained the same. She moved gracefully toward the refreshment table, speaking to excited children and parents alike. As she reached for a glass of cold cider, a gloved hand took it before her fingertips could touch it.

"Allow me." The voice seemed familiar, yet not identifiable. Miss Kate turned slightly to confront the tall figure, standing uncomfortably close to her. The man presented the glass of cider to her and bowed slightly. He was covered from head to toe in black: long-sleeved shirt, trousers, tall shiny boots and gloves. A black cape made of rustling satin, a wide-brimmed black hat, and black full-face mask completed his costume.

"Thank you." Miss Kate took a sip from the glass and turned away to speak to someone on her other side; but when she looked back, the man in black had disappeared. She wondered which of the men would dress so dramatically, dismissed the notion that it would be anyone on staff, and decided that it must be a parent. She caught glimpses of him throughout the evening, but he made no attempt to speak to her again. She looked for him when costumes were judged, thinking that he would surely win a prize; but the man had disappeared.

Miss Kate considered again how closely the man had pressed against her when he gave her the glass of cider, and her mouth tightened. Jedediah Newman! It had to be Jedediah! No one else would have been so bold. Anger made her cheeks rosy.

Since Mr. King had not returned from the seminar, the principal awarded prizes to the winners of best, worst, and scariest costumes. Roscoe Smith stole the evening. No one suspected that the tall Bo Peep, who had pranced and minced and simpered all night, was the sixty-nine year old janitor.

The party ended with parents collecting children who were reluctant to leave the festivities. Only the clean-up crew remained in the gymnasium. Miss Kate pushed up her lace-tipped sleeves and helped clear tables, until the job was finished. As she worked, she thought about Jedediah and wondered what she could do to make him understand that his advances were not welcome. Evidently, her polite coolness was not working. She was grateful that it was Friday, and she had the weekend to consider what action she would take.

"Well, it was a pretty good party, Miss Kate." Roscoe Smith smiled at her. "You go on home now, and I'll finish this up tomorrow."

"I need to pick up some things from my room, Roscoe; and then I'll be leaving."

"Take your time, Miss Kate. I'll lock up after you're gone."

The hallway was dark, after the brightness of the gymnasium. It took a few moments for Miss Kate's eyes to adjust. She felt her way along the wall. Her steps rang with a hollow sound in the deserted corridor, but the small circle of light that shone from the transom of her room gave a comforting glow.

She sensed movement in the dark shadows, a rustling of fabric just beyond her vision. She turned toward the sound. Before she could utter a word, long arms drew Miss Kate into an empty classroom, where the darkness was complete. She was pulled against a tall, hard body and held tightly. A gloved hand cupped her chin and pressed lightly upon her mouth, just enough to stop the words of outrage Miss Kate began to sputter.

"Sh-h-h-h-h." The whispered admonition sounded like an endearment, breathed closely to her ear. Between the long skirts of her gown and the enveloping fabric of a satin cape, Miss Kate was virtually unable to move. She held herself rigidly straight, furious at the audacity of the man. Was there no limit to the nerve of Jedediah Newman? She felt no fear, only anger. She would have him fired, at the very least!

Miss Kate endured the whispered sounds in her ear, the feel of his hands moving across her back. Her hands clenched into fists at her sides, where his arms held them. She was enraged at the liberties he took.

But sometime during the ordeal, another sensation crept into Miss Kate's awareness. A distinctly pleasurable shiver chased itself down her spine, and she trembled with the force of it. When the man's mouth touched hers, she felt as if she were sinking into a warm pool of unfamiliar sensations. In spite of herself and the anger she felt toward Jedediah Newman, a tiny sound of longing escaped her throat; and she surrendered to the kiss.

"I knew that kissing you would be sweet," the man whispered against her cheek, "but I had no idea *how* sweet." Kate stiffened, fury at him and disgust with herself flooding her whole being. Embarrassment and anger exploded within her. She pushed away from him and struck out blindly in the darkness, wincing when her right hand connected with the left side of his face. She felt a rush of satisfaction when he gasped with pain.

Miss Kate fled the room as quickly as possible, holding her cumbersome skirts high above the floor. Breathless and flustered, she ran into her own classroom and closed the door. Reflected in the dark windows across the room was an unfamiliar image. Miss Kate stared at the picture of the agitated woman who leaned against the door. She raised a trembling hand to smooth escaping strands of her hair; but on an impulse, she pulled out the combs and pins that held it, allowing the curls to tumble in disarray over her shoulders.

Miss Kate, the teacher, stood face to face with Kate Madison, the woman. The confrontation was devastating for both of them.

The first November weekend seemed interminable to Miss Kate. The previous evening's balmy weather had turned cold with the promise of another frigid winter to come, but she was restless and could not stay indoors. Early Saturday morning, Miss Kate dressed in a heavy jacket and warm wool slacks, a concession to the new trend in women's wear, since the war. She raked away the new covering of leaves from her mother's flower garden, working hard and fast so she didn't have to think. The bright sunshine was deceptive, for the air was crisp and cold with brisk breezes.

Sunday morning, Miss Kate attended services as usual at the big gray-stoned Presbyterian Church, where she had been a member all her life. Although the round, stained glass window radiated brilliant beams of light, and the music was lovely, and the sermon enlightening, Miss Kate's morose spirit could not be uplifted. She knew that Monday morning would come, and that she must confront Jedediah Newman. It was difficult enough for her to try to deal with the disgusting way she had responded to the man's outrageous caresses. How could she endure seeing the intimacy reflected in his eyes when he looked at her? Well, she would just have to rise above it, somehow.

Resolved to get the unpleasant confrontation over as soon as possible, Miss Kate arrived at the school much earlier than usual on

Monday morning. She pushed the classroom door open, and the first thing she saw was a crystal vase full of red roses sitting on her desk.

"Oh, dear." The words escaped from her in a breathless murmur of disbelief. She had never seen so many roses in one bouquet. Her thoughts tumbled over each other in a mass of confusion. In spite of her anger and indignation, she could not prevent a rush of tender feelings toward the sender of such magnificent flowers. How could he afford such an extravagance on his salary?

Miss Kate pulled one bud from the bouquet and sat down in the swivel chair. Her face softened as she inhaled the fragrance. A montage of events, from the first day Jedediah had appeared in her doorway, to the unexpected pleasure she had experienced in his arms, played havoc with her composure. A tint that rivaled the rose flooded her cheeks. She wondered if Jedediah's feelings for her could actually be serious ones, that he was not simply conducting an outrageous flirtation. If that were true, she had been less than kind. Perhaps she had been hasty in her judgment of him.

"Kate, you're not going to believe what's happened!" Gloria Hayes rushed into the room with such force that the door banged against the wall. "We thought he was chasing you, but—! Well, I just can't believe it!"

"Calm down, Gloria. What's wrong?"

"It's Jedediah Newman! We were all so sure that *you* were the one he wanted! He sent you those roses and—oh, my goodness! He sent more? What is he *thinking*?" Gloria stared at the vase of scarlet roses on Kate's desk.

"Gloria, what are you trying to say? What is this about Jedediah?" Just saying his name made Miss Kate blush.

"Kate! He eloped with Susanna Forrester Friday night, while her parents were here at the party! Her mother found a note on the bed Saturday morning, and a suitcase and some of Susanna's clothes are missing. And no one has seen Jedediah. They actually *eloped! Isn't it romantic?* He must have been sending you roses, so no one would suspect he was after Susanna. She's still a senior in high school! Can you believe it?"

Miss Kate sat very still. She swallowed and smiled at her friend.

"We should wish them well, Gloria. I think that the young lady needs a lot of good wishes."

"Well, I'll see you later." Gloria hurried from the room. Miss Kate suspected that there were many to whom Gloria wished to convey the news.

Miss Kate felt like such a fool. She stared at the roses. Nothing made sense. She replayed the incidents initiated by Jedediah: the way he had touched her hand that first day; how he had followed her in the corridor humming a silly tune only she could hear; the mocking bow he had performed when he opened a door for her; insolent little smiles he had given her when they had met in the hall; Jedediah in the black cape...

Panic threatened to choke Miss Kate. It could not have been Jedediah in the black cape! He was not at the party! Who was it? Who was the man who had held her, kissed her, destroyed her perfectly lovely, satisfying life in one evening? Miss Kate threw the rose onto the floor and pushed away from her desk. She stumbled blindly toward the door and ran into a tall figure just entering her classroom.

"Oh, Mr. King, I'm sorry. I—I wasn't expecting you," she stuttered. "I—I—I need to go out for a few minutes. Could I speak with you a little later?"

"No, I need to talk to you now, Kate." Mr. King closed the door. He cradled her arm and led her to the chair. "You seem upset, Kate. Is something wrong?" Miss Kate sat down. She took a deep breath and struggled to keep her face composed. Mr. King picked up the discarded rose. He sat upon the end of the desk, facing Miss Kate.

"What's the matter, Kate?" Mr. King's voice was very gentle, as if he were speaking to one of the children. Miss Kate took another deep breath and reluctantly raised her eyes to look at Mr. King. Even in her distress, she was struck by his unusual behavior. He had never closed a door while conferring with a female teacher, he had never sat upon a desktop in her presence, he had called her "Kate" twice, and he was wearing sunglasses. It certainly was a strange morning.

"Nothing is wrong, Mr. King. I just received some unexpected news, and I'm not handling it very well." She attempted a small smile.

"I'm sorry about the party."

"Yes, I'm sorry you missed it, too," Miss Kate replied. "It was really quite nice."

"Was it, Kate? Was it nice?"

"Yes, it was. I'm sorry you missed it." Mr. King twirled the rose in his hand for a moment, then reached out and softly stroked her cheek with the petals. Confusion furrowed her forehead.

"I was here, Kate. I got back early and came to the party." Slowly Mr. King removed his sunglasses and watched the range of expressions play upon her face, as she looked at him. Her eyes widened.

"What happened to your face?" she exclaimed. He smiled and gingerly touched a classic black eye, which had already turned to shades of purple and green and blue.

"You delivered quite a punch," he said. The grin on his face took years off his dignity.

"That was *you? You manhandled me? You sent the roses? You kissed me?"* Kate stood up quickly, sending the chair crashing into the wall behind her. Mr. King grasped her upper arm and pulled her, gently but firmly, to stand before him where he sat, bringing her eye level with him.

"Kate, Kate, listen. I apologize for scaring you at the party, but not for the roses and certainly not for kissing you. I intended to make myself known to you that night, but you ran away so quickly; and I was dealing with watering eyes, one that was beginning to swell from your right hook."

Reluctantly, Kate felt a stab of remorse. She softened, just a little; besides, there was something stirring about standing so close to him. Somehow, he had gathered her close enough that his hands were on her back.

"Then all this time, it was you? Why didn't you just tell me?"

"Oh, I couldn't do that, Kate. I was courting you." Mr. King smiled; and when his face came nearer and nearer, Miss Kate closed her eyes and gave in to the rush of sensations his mouth created against her skin. It was like coming home.

"Oh, Mr. King," she breathed.

"Do you think that you could call me Clayton?" Mr. King chuckled with delight at her blushing cheeks and promptly kissed her again.

"Kate, have you seen—oh, my!" Gloria Hayes, wide-eyed and open-mouthed stood transfixed in the doorway. "Oh, excuse me!" She slammed the door behind her and fled down the hall.

"Oh, no," Miss Kate groaned.

"My dear, you are severely compromised. I think that you will just have to marry me." Mr. King's glorious blue eyes sobered. "Marry me, Kate. 'Come live with me, and be my love.' I have loved you for such a long time. It just took Jedediah to show me what a fool I was for waiting to show you." He touched his forehead to Kate's. "Marry me, Kate."

Miss Kate Madison smiled, a totally un-Miss-Kate-like-smile. She raised her arms and twined her fingers behind his neck. She boldly kissed him, in a way she did not know she knew. Mr. King gathered her closer and kissed her hungrily, as a thirsty man drinks cool, spring water. Reluctantly, he moved her a little distance away.

"Ah, Kate, sweet Kate. Marry me *soon!*"

"I certainly will give your proposal some thought," she said.

"For how long?"

Miss Kate considered the question. "I don't know how long it would take to get to know you."

"*Know me?* Kate, you've known me for thirteen years!"

"I didn't know that you were capable of such extravagance." She pointed to the roses. "And I didn't know that you could be so underhanded."

"I was just being...determined."

"And I didn't know..." Clayton King stopped Kate Madison's words with a determined kiss, then another and another.

"What else do you need to know?"

"How long will it take your eye to heal?"

"Not very long, Sweet Kate."

"That sounds about right," Miss Kate sighed. It was amazing to her how perfectly her head rested against his chest, just above his heart.

Miss Kate and Mr. King were married in the Presbyterian Church, during the first week of Christmas vacation. A large number of Redbud Grove's population attended the ceremony and the reception, which was held in the school gymnasium. The general consensus was that they made a perfect couple and would, no doubt, live happily ever after.

"So it was Mr. King all along?" I asked.

"Sure was," Melissa replied.

"It really was romantic, wasn't it, even if they were old? Do you suppose anything like that will ever happen to us?"

"You mean like in the movies?"

"Well, yeah, but for real."

Melissa thought for a moment.

"Well, actually, I can't imagine kissing anyone as old as Mr. King. Can you?"

I could not.

I could not imagine kissing anyone. Period.

#

THE WIDOWS

From our home on the corner of Pine and Alley, we could see the houses of nine widows. Diagonally north of us were two more widow's dwellings that we could not see. We lived surrounded by widows, and none of them were under the age of fifty-five.

By mid-summer of our first year in Redbud Grove, most of the widows had come calling on my mother. Most brought something, usually a homemade delicacy or a start of a plant; and some simply paid a neighborly visit. One widow was a crusty, out-spoken, opinionated individual who did not hesitate to voice her opinion. Her name was Dorothea Mullikin; and she owned and operated Mullikin's Café, located a block north and a little over a block east of us on Highway One-thirty-three.

Eating out was not something we did often, no more that a few times a year and only on very special occasions. I liked eating at Mullikin's for numerous reasons. The food, prepared and cooked by Dorothea, was wonderful. She had a way of roasting a whole haunch of beef like no one else. The meat was succulent, with juices that seeped and flavored everything else on the plate. Her mashed potatoes were fluffy and swam in butter.

Dorothea made five or six different kinds of pie early every morning, and they were all gone by nightfall. Grown men moaned over her cherry pie, and sometimes ordered a second piece and ate it right there. Pineapple cream pie, coconut and lemon meringue, chocolate pie with a thick topping of real whipped cream, old-fashioned raisin and raisin cream, apple crumb pie, and her scrumptious cherry pie were on the menu every day.

She made her own bar-b-que from yesterday's roast beef, and chicken and dumplings from the prior day's fried chicken, should there be some left. Dorothea's cooking skills were known county wide. People who just happened to stop there while driving through, often managed to find their way back. The clientele kept the two waitresses busy, and Dorothea filled orders quicker than the girls could carry them to the tables.

"Whadda ya know, Joe?" followed by her barking laugh, was Dorothea's stock greeting to her regulars, the farmers and local business men who came in for early morning coffee, breakfast, mid-morning coffee, lunch, and mid-afternoon coffee. When asked how she was doing, her reply was always the same: "Fine and dandy."

Dorothea Mullikin was not a big woman. She stood no more than five foot three and weighed maybe one hundred thirty pounds. At fifty-nine, she was the mother of one daughter, had been divorced and remarried, and subsequently widowed five years ago. Her once-reddish-blond hair, now mostly gray, still had sandy blond streaks. Dorothea was very fair skinned, and faint freckles covered her face and arms. Behind her glasses, her pale eyes could pin a careless waitress to the wall, or twinkle with appreciation at a racy story.

Although lunchtime brought the biggest crowd, several families ate their evening meals at Dorothea's. On the occasions that we ate there, I enjoyed watching and listening to her, almost as much as I enjoyed her food.

"...and I told her that if she found herself sittin' on a blister, get off of it! Life's too durned short to spend it sittin' on a blister!"

Dad coughed and took a drink from his glass of iced tea. Mom frowned.

"Sissy, pay attention to your plate," she told me. "And don't stare at Mrs. Mullikin."

"I'm not staring," I answered, but I surely was listening. Mrs. Mullikin, as Mom insisted that I call her, was talking to a man and woman who sat against the wall across the restaurant from us. I couldn't hear everything that they said, but what I could hear was very interesting.

"...said she didn't *have* to get married, she *wanted* to, so there wasn't much I could say to stop her. Oh, well, my first time 'round didn't take either, so what can I say? If it works out, that's just fine and dandy. If it don't, she can always come back to mom."

"Sissy, eat!" Mom whispered. "And stop staring!"

"Mom, why would someone have to get married?"

"How about some pie, kids?" Dad asked. He motioned for the waitress. "What kind of pie do you have tonight?"

"Still have some apple, raisin and cherry," she said. "Would you like a little piece?" Smothered laughter emanated from the surrounding tables, and a loud guffaw erupted from Mrs. Mullikin. The waitress, who was no older than sixteen, looked at Dorothea. "What did I say?" she asked, obviously bewildered.

"Nothing," Dorothea replied. She grinned broadly at my dad, who grinned back, then brushed his hand across his mouth. I looked at my mom. She was not smiling.

Sidetracked, I ordered cherry pie; but later I wondered again why anyone would have to get married. I thought that men and women got married because they wanted to be together, and hug and kiss and stuff, like we saw in the movies, like Gary Cooper and June Allyson, Spencer Tracy and Katherine Hepburn. Sometimes, life was a mystery.

#

Mrs. Davis lived diagonally across the street from us. During the summer, Mrs. Davis sat in a metal chair on her front porch several hours a day, usually with her arms crossed upon her apron-covered abdomen, clasping her elbows with her hands. She was a large woman with white hair, which she drew into a bun at the back of her head.

Mrs. Davis's unmarried son, Everett, lived with her. Everett was a tall man with muscular arms and a broad chest, about fifty years of age. He combed his thick, auburn hair back from his forehead; but he could not straighten the tight curls that sprang forth naturally. Everett Davis wore dark plaid shirts and denim overalls daily, from which numerous tools could be seen hanging from tabs and pockets.

In the summer he planted a garden behind their house and tended a small grape arbor, which grew between the house and a shed. When school started, Everett drove a school bus. On rainy days, if Buddy and I could get on his bus without the second grade teacher, Mrs. Erickson, catching us, Everett would let us ride the whole route with him, and drop us off at our house before he parked the bus at his mother's.

128

In order to ride the bus, students were required to live a certain distance from the school. We missed the requirement by a couple of blocks. Teachers took turns monitoring; so in order to ride with Everett, Buddy and I had to slip onto the bus before the monitors got there. We rode only when it was raining, or so cold that frost formed on the ends of our noses.

One afternoon, Buddy and I were safely hidden at the very back of the bus, crouched on the floor behind a seat. I couldn't resist peeking over the seat in front of me, and it was at exactly the wrong time. I met the unsmiling green eyes of Mrs. Erickson, the dreaded second grade teacher.

"Sissy Bannister, you don't belong on this bus! You get off this minute!" Everett watched us from the big mirror above his head, as we trudged toward the front of the bus. He shrugged his shoulders, and I understood that he didn't want to tangle with Mrs. Erickson either. Buddy should have kept his head down; but he got off with me, and we were soaked when we got home. Mrs. Erickson was just not a compassionate person. I don't know how she endured looking at herself in a mirror.

Occasionally I sat on the porch with Mrs. Davis and listened to her tell stories about people and events in Redbud Grove. She had lived all her life in the area. She knew where many of the bodies were buried, and she didn't mind digging up some of them. My age didn't bother Mrs. Davis. She talked to me as an equal, although I was only twelve when she told me the story about a woman she knew, and how the woman's dream broke up two marriages and defrocked a preacher.

"You know that old Ruby Jenkins that lives down at the end of the road?" Mrs. Davis asked me. I shook my head. "Lives in that gray house with the black shutters that's hangin' crooked all the time." I thought about it for a minute.

"That little house with the white tire full of flowers in the front yard?" I asked. Mrs. Davis nodded.

"That's the one. Ruby Jenkins has lived in that house for close to twenty years. Her man lived with her, till she had that crazy dream." Mrs. Davis chuckled. "I guess it wasn't the dream was the problem. It was Ruby believin' it." I pulled my feet up and folded my legs in the chair. It sounded like a story was coming.

"Ruby and Ed Jenkins was married a long time, probably close to fifteen or twenty years; and they never had a child. Ed wanted a boy to carry on his name, and he made life about as miserable for Ruby as a man could make it. Called her 'barren' and 'not a real woman.' Even talked of puttin' her away, like the old geezers in the Bible did, when their women didn't give them sons." I nodded like I knew what Mrs. Davis was talking about.

"Well, Ruby got to talkin' with the preacher that traveled on a circuit, through a lot of the little towns around here. He was a sorry sort, had some queer notions about how folks should live. I only heard him once, and that was enough. I thought he preached a gospel accordin' to Caleb Brown and no one else. That was his name, Caleb Brown. The preacher told Ruby that she just had to try harder to be a good wife to Ed, that it was her duty to please her husband. So that's what Ruby did. She gussied herself up, frizzed her hair, even got one of them flapper dresses.

"Didn't do no good. Ed kept doin' his part, but there just wasn't any babies comin' along; and Ed got to lookin' around at the younger girls. Then Ruby had this dream. She took it to the preacher and convinced him that the dream came straight from the Lord; so the preacher undertook to help Ruby make the dream come true." Mrs. Davis pointed to an empty glass on the porch rail.

"Take that glass to the kitchen for me and fill it up from the pitcher in the icebox," she ordered. "And get yourself a cookie from the jar in the cabinet." I did as she told me and climbed back into the chair. After she had drunk the water, Mrs. Davis wiped her mouth with her apron and picked up the story as if she had never stopped.

"There was a farmer and his wife, lived a few miles across the river back then, that went to the meetins' that Preacher Brown held here and yon. I don't recall their names. Anyway, this farmer's wife was awful religious, and she wouldn't miss a meetin' for nothin'. Made her man go with her.

"Well, as I said, Ruby Jenkins had a dream; and it was about this farmer. Ruby made that preacher talk to the farmer about her dream, kind of feel him out about it." Mrs. Davis laughed. "Seemed the farmer kind of took to the notion."

"What was the dream about?" I asked.

Mrs. Davis looked at me and blinked a couple of times. She pursed her lips and cocked her head sideways.

"How old are you?" she asked.

"Twelve and a half. I'll be thirteen in February."

"Your mama told you about the birds and the bees yet?"

"Um, kind of. Mostly I've learned stuff from my friends, and one of our teachers at school always answers our questions. And you know what I saw at Cora Parker's house a couple of summers ago? I saw..." I whispered in Mrs. Davis's ear what I had seen through the window of the witch's house.

"Naw!" Mrs. Davis seemed delighted. "You were a mite young for all that stuff to be floatin' around in your head, but you seem all right with it now."

"It just all seems silly to me." I shrugged. "I asked my mom about it after I had been at the Parker house, and she told me that I was too young to discuss it. So my friends and I asked some older girls at school, and they didn't think we were too young." Mrs. Davis patted my hand.

"It will all come right for you some day," she said. "Don't worry about it."

"I don't."

"Well, anyway, Ruby dreamed that if she got together with this farmer, that the Lord was goin' to give her a baby. I don't know how she convinced Preacher Brown, but one was about as crazy as the other; so the preacher set up a meetin' between the two. His take on it was that it had to happen in a holy place, if the Lord was goin' to have a hand in it; and what better place than a little old church way out in the country?

"So they all got together at that church one afternoon, Preacher Brown witnessin' the union, so to speak. They was all so taken up with themselves that they didn't hear the Watson sisters come in to clean the church." Mrs. Davis chuckled at the ludicrous scenario she described.

"There was a terrible hue and cry," she continued. "The farmer's wife kicked him out, and Ed Jenkins left Ruby to do the best she could. He divorced her and found himself a young gal that ended up givin' him three boys and two girls. Ruby went to live with an old woman that didn't have anybody to care for her. When the old woman died, she left her house and all her belongin's to Ruby. And that's where Ruby still lives today."

Mrs. Davis crossed her arms and leaned back in the green metal lawn chair. She seemed very pleased with herself, as if the telling of the story had given her immense satisfaction. She rocked her chair slightly.

"Mrs. Davis?"

"What, Child?"

"What happened to Preacher Brown?"

Mrs. Davis laughed and laughed. When she finally stopped, she used her apron to wipe the tears from her eyes.

"Sissy, did you ever hear anybody talk about someone bein' tarred and feathered and run out of town on a rail?"

"No."

"Well, that's what happened to Preacher Caleb Brown. The folks that went to that little church in the woods didn't take very kindly toward his brand of gospel and his use of their buildin'. They daubed him down with molasses, ripped open a couple of feather pillows and dumped the feathers on him; and then a bunch of the men set the preacher astraddle a railroad tie and carried him down the road a piece. He never did come back around here.

"Fetch me another glass of water from the icebox." I did as she told me. When I brought it back to her, she nodded her thanks; and we sat on the porch together in silence, looking at the park and rocking in the green metal lawn chairs.

#

Mrs. Morgan lived in a small white house with a green roof and green shutters on Locust Street, a block behind us. Tall Rose-of-Sharon bushes grew on each side of the narrow concrete path that led from the brick sidewalk to her front door. The pink, lavender, and white blooms, some as large as saucers, filled the air with fragrance all summer.

Mrs. Morgan was a pretty lady. Like a lot of grandmothers in the nineteen forties, she was plump in a pleasing manner, with a pillow-y softness that could cushion and comfort a hurting child or adult. Her hair was truly silver, with lovely strands of pure white at her temples.

Even the tight "beauty parlor" waves didn't detract from its beauty. Mrs. Morgan wore frameless glasses, which slightly magnified her blue eyes.

I thought that Mrs. Morgan was a "widow woman", like the other older ladies who lived alone in my circle of acquaintances; but that was not the case. She was a divorcee, the first one I ever knew.

I was nine years old when I learned about Mr. Morgan. I don't know why they were divorced. I never asked, for which I'm sure my mother was very grateful. One unusual thing about Mr. Morgan was that he had moved into a small building behind the house of Mrs. Morgan. Another was that she was taking care of him, because Mr. Morgan was dying of a hideous form of cancer.

My mother told me about his condition one afternoon, as she was preparing to take a cake to Mrs. Morgan. Mom was a great "cake-taker" to anyone she felt needed a lift, a funeral dish, or just a visit.

"Can I go with you?" I asked.

"Are you sure you want to?"

Morbidly curious, I assured her that I really wanted to go help cheer them up. Mom gave me an enigmatic smile and agreed to let me accompany her, while Dad stayed with my brother and little sister. Mrs. Morgan greeted us with her usual warmth, graciously thanking my mother for the chocolate layer cake.

"We'll cut it and have cake and milk in the back yard, where it's nice and shady." Mrs. Morgan hugged me and planted a kiss on the top of my head. She filled a pitcher with milk and placed four pieces of cake, glasses, and forks upon a big tray. We carried everything outdoors to a square flagstone patio, where a round table and four wicker chairs waited in the shade of a tall maple tree.

Mrs. Morgan set the tray on the table and poured milk into the glasses. She took a plate and a glass and placed them on an upturned milk crate, just outside the door of a small shed-like building. She knocked on the shed's door.

"We have company, Fred," she called. "Mrs. Bannister and Sissy have brought us a lovely chocolate cake." Mrs. Morgan came back to the table and sat down. "Mr. Morgan doesn't like to be too near people," she explained. "Oh, my, Jackie, this cake is delicious." We were nearly finished before the door of the shed opened and Mr. Morgan emerged.

He was a very small man, dressed in overalls and a long-sleeved white shirt. A fringe of reddish gray hair circled his balding head. He moved slowly, painfully toward the milk crate. I shuddered involuntarily when I saw Mr. Morgan's face. Gaunt and lined, pain had etched deep grooves down his cheeks; and the skin sagged loosely along his jaw line.

Where his nose should have been were two holes and a gaping, red rawness that spread across the center of his face. He looked at us, nodded politely, and took the cake and milk back to his private retreat. I was stunned.

I don't remember the rest of the afternoon. Although I liked Mrs. Morgan, I didn't go back to her house until months later—not until after Mr. Morgan died in a fire that destroyed the shed, where he had been sleeping.

There was an investigation and much speculation about the cause of the fire. Mr. Morgan didn't smoke. There was a small kerosene heater in the shed; but the weather was warm, and no fire had been lit. A single, uncovered bulb was the only source of electricity in the building; and it was finally decided that there must have been a short in the wiring. Mr. Morgan had taken heavy pain medication, and the theory was that he did not smell the smoke or hear the fire in his narcotic induced stupor.

Mrs. Morgan never lost the calm, pleasant demeanor I found so comforting; but I wondered about the far-away look that sometimes touched her eyes.

I wondered what she was thinking.

#

Mrs. Lula was Bethy's favorite widow. Her name was Lula Davidson, and she lived behind Mrs. Davis, which presented a problem. We were always mixing them up, saying one name when we meant the other. When Bethy learned Mrs. Davidson's first name, she dubbed her Mrs. Lula; and that's what we all called her. Mrs. Lula seemed to like it. Bethy was very pleased with herself for solving that little bit of confusion.

Inside the covered front porch of Mrs. Lula's house was a porch swing, suspended from the ceiling. I had never before seen a swing inside a house. It presented the opportunity to enjoy a lovely summer shower without getting wet. There was the added attraction of a litter of kittens on the porch. We hadn't owned a kitten since the one Julie Kitchen gave me disappeared, three years previously.

We missed our little dog, Pup, too. He had finally caught one of the cars he loved to chase, but he hadn't survived the encounter. Dad had buried him at the edge of our back yard, and Mom had planted some perennials to mark the site. The pen stood empty, and we talked about getting another puppy; but it just didn't seem that the time was ever right.

When Mrs. Lula told Bethy she could pick out a kitten, my little sister was ecstatic. She chose a yellow and white one and called him Toasty, because he was the color of toast. Mrs. Lula said that it was a fine name. My pick of the kittens was a longhaired black and white one that looked a lot like the one Julie Kitchen had given to me.

"That one's a female," Mrs. Lula told me. "You can tell by the colors. A three-colored cat is always female, and that one is black and white and gray. I doubt that your mama will let you have her. You'd have to get her fixed or you'd have two litters of kittens a year." Mrs. Lula laughed. "Like I do," she added. Mrs. Lula *did* have a lot of cats.

Bethy and I took the two kittens home with us. Unbelievable as it seemed, Mom fell in love with the black and white kitty and agreed to let us keep both of them. I named mine Juliet, partly in memory of Julie Kitchen, mostly because I liked the romantic name. We turned a cardboard box on its side and lined it with old towels. Dad filled a shallow box with dirt from the garden for a litter box, and Juliet and Toasty took up residence in the garage.

In no time our pets were nearly grown. They stayed close to the house, even came inside when Mom was feeling charitable. Dad stood a brick on end in the garage door opening, leaving a space for them to come and go at night.

One morning Dad came back into the house, only minutes after he had left for work.

"What did you forget?" Mom asked.

"We've had an accident," he answered. He looked at me. "Sissy, Juliet was in the motor of the car when I started it. I'm sorry, Honey."

"Is she dead?" I asked. I was stricken.

"No, but her leg is badly hurt. The lower part is practically torn off." We all ran out to see, and there my cat stood on three legs, holding up the injured one and meowing pitifully.

"Will, we'll just have to take her to the vet in Mattoon," Mom said. Dad pursed his lips.

"Won't that be awfully expensive?" he asked. Mom just looked at him. "Okay, I guess you can drop me off at work and take her to the vet."

So we all piled into the car, took Dad to work and drove twelve miles to Mattoon, the nearest town that offered the services of a veterinarian. Juliet reclined inside a box on the front seat, between my mother and me. She seemed to realize that we were trying to help her.

Dr. Sprague took Juliet from us and told us that he would do his best to save her leg. As he opened the door to his inner office, Mom called to him.

"Doctor, can you also spay her while you have her in there?"

"Actually, I can. It would be a good time to do that, since she is going to be laid up for a while anyway. Are you going to wait?"

Mom raised her eyebrows in a silent question. All three of us nodded. "I suppose so," she said. We waited and waited and waited. After a long, long time, Dr. Sprague came out to talk to us. He looked perplexed.

"Mrs. Bannister, I have set Juliet's leg, but we have a problem."

"Oh, no," Mom said. "Was she already going to have kittens?" Dr. Sprague smiled.

"Well, no," he replied. "Actually, Juliet..." he paused dramatically, "is a boy." There was total silence for the space of five seconds before my mother began to laugh.

"So much for the three-colored cat theory," she said.

Dr. Sprague chuckled. "Do you want me to perform the same procedure on him?"

"Absolutely," Mom replied. "What's good for Juliet is good for Romeo."

"I suppose you could call him "Jules", instead of Juliet," Dr. Sprague tossed over his shoulder as he left the waiting room. "It won't take very long to finish with him."

Juliet recovered quite well from his ordeal. Dad was not happy with Mom's decision. "There was no reason to put him through that," he complained. "He wouldn't have given us more kittens."

"No, but he would have sprinkled them generously throughout the neighborhood," she told Dad.

"Yes, but..."

"But, nothing," Mom said. "You're just empathizing with him."

Juliet lived to a ripe old age in his altered state, which kept him happy, healthy, and at home.

#

Of all the widows and older ladies who lived in our neighborhood, without a doubt the most beloved was Mrs. East. She lived across the park from us, one block south, which made it difficult for me learn directions. My friend, Patty West, lived east of town; so when I was trying to decide which way was west, I automatically pointed toward Patty's house—east. Deciding where east lay, I pointed toward Mrs. East's house—south. I finally got it, but I still have a tendency to point east when I mean west.

Mrs. East was not a widow when we moved to Redbud Grove. At that time, her family consisted of her husband and three sons, two boys in their teens and an eleven year old. The youngest boy was the one my mother had enlisted to take me to school my first day at East Side. He had walked a wide circle around our house, until I was well established on the route to school. He was already in high school when the school system was changed, so our paths never crossed.

The first time she called on my mother, Mrs. East brought a brown bag full of fresh rhubarb with her. It was a Saturday morning. She came to the back door and would not come in, because she had been working in her spring garden and her shoes were sticky with the moist, black soil. Her dress was dark blue and she wore a blue scarf, turban style, around her head.

"I'll bring you a start of the rhubarb, if you'd like to grow some," Mrs. East told my mom. Her voice was soft and gentle. "I'm hard of hearing, so you'll have to speak up." She grinned at me, a wide grin from a generous mouth, that showed a narrow gap between her two front teeth. She wore glasses and her eyes were blue, a twinkling blue that spoke of a sense of humor and love of laughter. Mrs. East, whose name was Lena, and my mom formed a friendship that was to last a lifetime; but they never called each other by their given names.

Since Mrs. East literally could not hear it thunder, she was deathly frightened of storms. Mom devised a warning system with the ice card, the big square cardboard sign, that she put in the kitchen window to let the ice man know how many pounds of ice she wanted on ice route days. The card had four colors: red, white, black and green.

Mrs. East could see our front room window from her kitchen. When the ice card, with the red portion up, was in that window, she knew that a storm was coming; and she could seek shelter. Mom and Mrs. East used that system for years, long after we got a refrigerator. Mrs. East had a telephone, but could not hear over it.

The East house held a fascination for me that I never outgrew. It was a tall white house with a wrought iron fence, completely surrounding it. There was a large garden beyond the back yard. Hollyhocks and various other perennials surrounded the outbuildings and garden.

I visited Mrs. East as often as my mom would let me. There was something about a house where boys lived that was just different. In a kitchen corner, close to the wall phone, stood a huge crock full of marbles. A tall stool in that corner usually held a stack of comic books. I knelt beside the marble crock many times and plunged my arms into the contents up to my elbows, bringing handfuls up to examine. I loved the blue ones and the clear ones with ribbons of color that caught the light.

"You can take some of those home with you," Mrs. East told me one time. "The boys never play with them anymore." It was tempting, but I thought about that youngest boy and how unhappy he had been in my company, and I dropped the marbles back into the crock. But I read his comic books without a sense of guilt.

I loved listening to the stories Mrs. East told me about her life. She conjured up for me pictures of a time long gone. Her first husband had been killed in an accident, when she was pregnant with her fourth child. Life for her had been very hard, but she never lost her joy of living. She remarried and bore four more children, one girl and three boys. She had grandchildren my age and children older than my mother. In essence, Mrs. East replaced the grandmothers I had never known.

One day, when I was about eleven and tall for my age, Mrs. East dressed me in some of the boys' clothes, plopped a wide-brimmed felt hat upon my head and sent me home. She told me to go to the back door and pretend to be a hobo. I did as she told me. I went around the park, coming in from the back, so Mom would not see me. I knocked on the back door and kept my head tilted down.

"What do you want?" My mom's voice was not friendly. I kept my head down. "Do you want something to eat?" I nodded, still not looking up at her. Many railroad hobos came to the back door asking for food, and Mom always gave them something. I heard her rummaging around in the cabinet.

"This is all I have right now," she said, and opened the door a crack. She extended a piece of bread with peanut butter and homemade blackberry jelly on it.

"Yum," I said. "Thanks, Lady." I lifted my head and grinned at my mother. I wished that Mrs. East could have seen the expression on my mom's face, which was not a happy one.

"What do you think you're doing? And where are your clothes?"

"At Mrs. East's. She put these on..."

"You go right back down there and get your clothes and come straight home!"

Mrs. East was delighted when I told her Mom's reaction. She laughed that rich, throaty laugh and clapped her hands. I hurriedly got out of the clothes and put on my own.

"Here, you take these. The boys will never miss them." She handed me a whole stack of comic books and sent me home. She was still chuckling when I opened the back gate of her fence.

I came home from the library one day in the summer of nineteen fifty, to find my mother and Mrs. East in the center of the front room. Mom had her arms around Mrs. East, and they were both crying.

"What's wrong?" I asked. Mom shook her head at me.

"Sissy, you go play in the park. Right now." Her voice had that "do as I say!" sound, so I went outside; but I didn't go to the park. I crawled along the wall and sat down under the window, so I could hear them. I was almost sorry I did. The sobs that came from my friend brought tears to my own eyes.

"He'll be all right," my mom said. "He's alive. You just have to believe that he's alive."

"They said that he's missing in action, Mrs. Bannister. My boy is missing in action!" There was such agony in her voice. "They don't know where he is or if he's a prisoner or even if he's alive!" I crawled away. I didn't want to hear another word.

That evening Mom told us that Mrs. East's oldest son, Ralph, from her first marriage, had been listed as missing in action, somewhere in Korea. It was not known whether he was alive or a prisoner of the North Koreans. Thereafter, even when she was telling me a funny story, showing me pictures in her family album, or feeding me some delicious tidbit from her kitchen, Mrs. East's blue eyes held a sadness that never quite went away.

Her son, Ralph Moyer, survived a North Korean prison camp for three years. His name was on the last list of prisoners released from those camps in nineteen fifty-three. The atrocities he described were beyond belief, and I learned about them from listening to conversations I was not supposed to hear.

When her youngest son was in the Marines, Mrs. East's husband was killed in a car/train accident. Mr. East's brother died in the same accident. Throughout the tragedies that dogged her life, Mrs. East's spirit and love of life never dimmed. She remained positive and hopeful, even in situations that seemed hopeless.

Lena East loved to tell and hear bawdy tales that made her shake with laughter, and sometimes have to wipe the tears from her eyes. She knew how to hug me, listen to me, laugh with me, and she loved me. She loved me for as long as she knew me.

And that was a long, long time.

#

REBECCA

"Daddy, can we go for a r-r-ride?" Bethy crawled onto Dad's lap and made her usual summer evening request. She had acquired the ability to pronounce the letter R, and she made the most of every opportunity. Dad tousled her hair.

"Aw, Wiz-bet, I'm too tired tonight."

"Please, Daddy? It's so hot."

I knew he wouldn't deny her. He never did.

"Okay. Go tell Mom. Where's your brother?"

"He's upstairs wor-r-r-king on his model câr-r-r," Bethy told Dad.

"Bud, do you want to go for a ride with us?" Dad called.

"Sure, Dad. Be right down."

I'm not sure if the attraction of going for a ride was the cool air coming into the open car windows, or the car, itself. Dad had recently bought the nineteen fifty-one Pontiac, and we had gone for a drive in it every evening since.

It was mid-August, nineteen fifty-two, and I was twelve years old. My ankle had completely healed. Except for some residual stiffness, which the doctor said would go away, it was as good as new. I was looking forward to the seventh grade, which would start after Labor Day. I felt much more grown-up.

"Which way?" Dad asked.

"Out by the Amish," Buddy answered.

"The river road," I suggested.

"Both." Bethy settled it. Dad headed east, toward the river. Just over the bridge he turned north and followed a winding, tree-lined graveled road that followed the course of the Embarras River. The sound of locusts spoke of impending autumn.

It seemed degrees cooler along the river. The scent, embedded in the river and along the banks, escaped into the atmosphere and hinted of eons of time and decay, ancient, yet part of the present and the future; for in the river, they are all the same. The first time I inhaled that scent, it triggered some sense of déjà vu, perhaps some genetic, or actual, memory from the place of my birth. I never found it to be unpleasant.

"Daddy, how come I always have to sit in the middle? Buddy and Sissy always get a window side," Bethy complained.

"Climb over," Dad told her. Buddy and I ducked her flailing legs as she vaulted into the front seat. We looked at each other, and I gave him a thumbs up, which he returned. Simultaneously, we stretched our legs toward the center of the floor.

A few miles up river, we crossed back over the stream via a rickety wooden bridge that popped and creaked, and sounded as if it would collapse at any moment. Dad always stopped in the middle of the bridge, to make us nervous; then slowly he drove, inch by inch, until we were a mass of squealing Bannister offspring. By now, I knew that the bridge was not going to fall into the water; but still, in spite of my advancing sophistication, I couldn't quell the little uneasy quiver in my stomach.

We crossed Route Forty-five, and the terrain immediately changed to prairie. Many of the roads between the fields were paved on one side, oiled and graveled on the other. Dad said that the concrete side was to accommodate Amish buggies and to keep the narrow wheels from digging into the oiled portions.

The Amish community owned thousands of acres of the rich, black loam, and farmed every acre with horse-drawn implements. They raised all their food and maintained a lifestyle that afforded very little contact with the outside world and the English, as they called all who were not a part of their circle.

"Mom, did you know that the Amish speak German in their homes and in their schools?" I asked.

"Who told you that, Sissy?"

"Melissa Franklin. Her mom hired an Amish girl to help clean their house this summer. Melissa says that the girl was kind of scared at first, but she's friendly now and talks to Melissa a lot. Her name is Rebecca Yoder. She told Melissa about the German stuff."

"How old is Rebecca?" Mom asked.

"Sixteen. Melissa says that Jeff is kind of stuck on her. I don't know why. I think the Amish look weird."

"Isn't Jeff in college?"

"Yeah, but he's home for the summer. He's nineteen and thinks he's too good to even talk to Melissa and me. Going to college doesn't make him any better than anybody else. He's still just old Jeff Franklin to me."

"Do I detect a little sour grapes?" Dad murmured to Mom.

"Could be," Mom answered.

I snorted. "Who cares about dumb old Jeff Franklin?" I asked, not needing or wanting a reply. So what if Jeff *was* tall and smart and had played quarterback for the Purple Riders all through high school? And so what if Jeff *was* the star center on the basketball team and got a basketball scholarship to the University of Illinois last year? So what if Jeff *was* the most handsome boy in Redbud Grove? So what if Jeff *was* six-feet-two-inches tall, had thick, auburn hair, amber brown eyes, broad shoulders and a smile that could melt any female heart within a hundred miles?

Who cares? Certainly not I, a twelve-year-old soon-to-be-seventh-grader, with hair that would not behave, braces on my teeth, and no bosom to speak of yet. I had not seen Rebecca Yoder, but I knew that in any comparison between the two of us, the Amish girl was the winner, hands down, white cap and all. I folded my arms and sank farther down into the back seat. I was sorry that I had even mentioned Rebecca.

As we drove by, I looked at the rambling Amish farmhouses, with the many additions and wings built on, to accommodate elderly parents, or young married daughters and sons. Herds of dairy cattle stood in the large barn lots, either waiting to be milked, or already drained, waiting to be turned into surrounding pastures for the night.

Twilight had fallen in Douglas County. Through the windows of the houses could be seen dim lantern light, for the Amish did not have electricity or telephones in their homes. They thought that wires connected them to the outside world, and they wanted no part of the world that existed past their fences.

A plan formed in my head as Dad headed the car back toward town. I had not met Rebecca Yoder, but I would arrange to do so, and soon. I wasn't actually jealous of her and Jeff Franklin. Although I had a penchant for older men, my little escapade with Frank Thompson had taught me that some relationships were far beyond my emotional, physical, and chronological ability to attain. It rankled a bit that Jeff Franklin, who used to tease me when I was with Melissa, now barely acknowledged my presence.

I didn't see how it could be possible for Jeff or any other Redbud Grove boy to be interested in an Amish girl. He couldn't even tell if she had nice hair under those little white caps that she and all the girls and women wore. Now I had another mission: I would find out just what was the attraction.

Melissa became a willing participant in my plan to discover all I could about Rebecca Yoder and her people. Like all unknown entities, there was a sense of mystery attached to Rebecca, a mystery I intended to solve. Mrs. Franklin drove to the country two days a week to pick up the girl, since the Amish did not drive cars or any other gasoline powered vehicles. I couldn't understand why it was all right for them to ride in a car owned by the "English", and not be allowed to possess one. I think it had something to do with their religion. I decided that a religious belief could be a curious thing.

The Franklins owned a huge, three-storied Victorian house that they had completely refurbished. It had taken years to complete the task, but it certainly was a beautiful dwelling. Melissa's parents had furnished their home with many items they had discovered, and subsequently restored, in the attic and in the long carriage house, which had been converted into a spacious garage.

They had purchased additional pieces from private sales and auctions; and the result was a lovely, eclectic combination of breakfronts, buffets, hutches, tables, and wardrobes, whose various finishes shone with the patina of years of careful waxing, and the loving touch of many hands. Comfortable sofas and chairs and loveseats formed cozy groupings in front of the numerous fireplaces throughout the house.

Melissa's room was every girl's dream. On the second floor, the main focal point of the room was a three-bayed window with a built-in cushioned seat, which was upholstered in the same fabric as the curtains and bedspread. The chintz was just a bit too flowery for my taste, although the greens and blues and lavenders were lovely colors. Glimpses of the river could be seen from the window, but the best view was during the winter when the trees were bare.

"Why don't you come stay all night with me Monday night and you can be here when Mother brings Rebecca?" Melissa suggested, when I told her my plan. "We can talk to her while she works. Mother goes to the country club after she brings Rebecca here on Tuesdays and Fridays, so Rebecca makes lunch for us on those days."

"What about Jeff?" I asked. "Will he be there, too?"

"Dad makes Jeff go with him to the refineries every Monday, and they don't come home until Thursday or Friday night. I think they're going to Oklahoma next week."

"I'll ask my mom if I can come Monday," I said. It was almost too easy. My mom gave her permission, and I was all a-tingle with anticipation. I would meet Rebecca, and Jeff would not be there to complicate matters.

The following Monday evening I placed a paper bag, which held my pajamas and toothbrush, in my bicycle basket and pedaled to Melissa's house. Mr. Franklin had bought the whole block of property that surrounded the big house and had torn down all other buildings upon it. He had enclosed the grounds with a high wrought iron fence that opened only on the carriage house side, west of the big house itself.

A long paved driveway, lined with poplar trees, curved through the grounds to the front of the house and circled a landscaped area, where a fountain stood, encompassed by rosebushes. The Franklins were the only people in Redbud Grove who hired a fulltime gardener, and the only people, except Mrs. Murphy, with grass that looked like a plush green carpet. It was almost a sacrilege to walk on it.

I parked my bike beside the carriage house. Melissa came running to meet me before I got close enough to the side door to ring the bell.

"Guess what," she whispered. I shrugged. "Dad didn't leave today."

"How come?" I demanded. It was Melissa's turn to shrug.

"Something about Petro."

"So is Jeff going to be here all day tomorrow?"

"Probably not all day, but I betcha he'll be here for lunch, since *Rebecca* is making it," she said. I pursed my lips. Hmm. So now I could observe Jeff as he observed the Amish girl. The situation could prove to be even more interesting than I had thought.

I lay awake long after Melissa went to sleep that night. Her bed was not positioned so that I could see the stars, but a cross-breeze filled the room with cool air from the river. An abundance of material comforts was available in the Franklin house. A private bathroom, complete with a big, claw-footed bathtub, opened off Melissa's room. Two of the bedrooms on this floor shared a bathroom; the fourth bedroom, which had belonged to Melissa's older sister, Sonia, who was married and lived in Chicago, boasted a private bath, like Melissa's.

Jeff, the only Franklin son, was also the only boy in Redbud Grove who had his own private loft, which consisted of the whole third story. I could imagine that he hated to leave such a luxurious apartment, especially when he had to trade it for a tiny dorm room at the University of Illinois, no more than forty miles north of Redbud Grove. Jeff drove his own car, a graduation gift from his dad, Paul J. Franklin, the president of Petro, Inc.

It wasn't strange to me that Melissa's family had so much more, materially, than any other family in Redbud Grove. Melissa had just always been my friend. I had seen this magnificent house when it had not been so magnificent, and through all the stages of bringing it back to its original glory. I was as comfortable here as I was in my own bed. I closed my eyes and drifted off to sleep, beneath sheets that matched the curtains and covers and pillows.

"Hi, Sissy, how are you?"

"Fine," I answered Jeff. Great conversationalist that I was, the sight of Jeff Franklin, sitting in the breakfast nook, sipping coffee from a thick mug, destroyed any casual repartee I might have produced. Jeff wore only jeans. The morning sun streamed through the windows that surrounded the gazebo-like nook and turned his bare bronzed chest to gold. My twelve-year-old heart turned to jelly. I actually felt something quiver inside my chest.

"For pete's sake, put your shirt on!" Melissa commanded. "We don't want to look at your old hairy chest while we eat breakfast!" *Speak for yourself,* I thought. "Where's Mother?"

"She drove out to pick up Rebecca," Jeff answered. Melissa looked at me. She raised her eyebrows and twisted her mouth to one side.

"Why didn't you go get her?"

"I offered, but you know they wouldn't let one of their girls ride in a car with a man."

"I don't see a 'man'," Melissa taunted. "All I see is a silly, naked boy."

"I'm not *naked,* am I, Sissy?" Jeff caught me staring at his chest and I felt my face begin to get warm. He laughed. "Am I naked, Sissy?" All I could do was silently shake my head back and forth.

"Well, you'd better get dressed before *she* gets here! One look at you, and Rebecca will run back to the farm," Melissa ordered.

"Oh, dry up, Infant." Jeff stood up, stretched his arms over his head, and casually placed his mug in the sink. "I'll be upstairs for awhile." In the doorway, he stopped and looked at us over his shoulder. A wicked grin spread across his handsome face. "Tell Rebecca that she can start with my room." He winked at me before he disappeared up the back staircase. It looked as if Jeff had not completely given up teasing me; but at that moment, the chasm of seven years age difference yawned before me as deep and wide as the Grand Canyon.

Rebecca Yoder was stunning.

No other word would describe her. She was tall, almost as tall as Jeff; and she was very slender. The plain, dark blue shirtwaist dress could not camouflage her figure. Her waist was tiny, which only emphasized her full breasts and slender hips.

Rebecca had the face of an angel. Perfectly formed dark eyebrows framed her wide-set blue eyes, and all her features worked together to portray an exquisite example of God's handiwork. I was immediately green with envy. Rebecca's skin looked like translucent porcelain, with a delicate hint of pink in her cheeks and upon her full, voluptuous mouth. I hated her. Beneath the white organdy cap, her hair was very dark, almost black. Only wisps of it showed around her face and it was drawn into a large knot in the back and covered by the cap.

"Rebecca, this is Melissa's friend, Sissy Bannister," Mrs. Franklin introduced me.

"I am very pleased to meet you," Rebecca said, and she smiled at me. Even her teeth were perfect! There was a clatter on the back stairs; and suddenly Jeff filled the kitchen, where Mrs. Franklin and Rebecca had just entered. Melissa and I still sat in the breakfast nook with our bowls of Rice Krispies.

Jeff smiled at Rebecca, who looked flustered and smoothed the front of her skirt with her hands. Dressed now in slacks and an ironed button-down collared shirt, Jeff looked as if he had just stepped out of an ad for an ivy-league college. He put his hands in his pockets.

"You can start in the east parlor this morning, Rebecca," Mrs. Franklin said. "Jeff, your father expects you at Petro by ten o'clock. Melissa, you and Sissy do what you want, but stay out of Rebecca's way. She has lots of area to cover today."

"Okay, Mother," answered Melissa.

"Yes, Ma'm," Rebecca nodded her understanding. Mrs. Franklin looked at her watch.

"You go now, Jeff, so you won't keep your father waiting."

"Sure thing, Mother. I've got to get my keys from upstairs." With a brief look at Rebecca, Jeff hurried upstairs, as his mother blew a kiss at Melissa and tucked her purse under her arm. The scent of Chanel Number Five lingered in the air after she left the kitchen. We heard the sound of her car going down the driveway. The kitchen seemed suddenly very quiet.

"So what do you think?" Melissa asked me.

"She's really pretty," I answered. That was the understatement of the year. "Can we talk to her while she works?"

"Sure, as soon as Jeff leaves."

Evidently, Jeff was in no hurry. He had come down the front staircase, and we could hear him talking to Rebecca. Melissa put her finger across her lips. We silently slipped from the nook, crept through the dining room, and into the hall that connected the two front parlors. We slid along the wall, until we could hear them clearly.

"I've been thinking about you all week-end." Jeff's voice seemed very husky. "Didn't you think about me, too?"

"N-no." Rebecca sounded nervous.

"Not even a little?"

"I can't think about you. You are not one of us."

"Why should that matter, Rebecca? No, wait. Don't pull away from me."

"Don't!" Rebecca seemed really distressed.

"Just let me hold you for a second," Jeff was nearly whispering, but we could hear the urgency in his voice. "See? There's nothing wrong with putting my arms around you. I won't hurt you, Rebecca, ever."

Melissa and I looked at each other. She rolled her eyes, and I almost giggled. She pointed toward the sliding parlor doors, which were not completely closed. Carefully we moved farther along the wall, until we could see Jeff and Rebecca through the open space. He was holding her against him, but her arms were braced against his chest. As we watched, Jeff lowered his head slowly toward hers; and then he actually kissed her!

Rebecca made a little sound in her throat; and her arms crept upward, until they were wrapped around Jeff's neck. Melissa and I put our hands over our mouths to stifle her delight and my angst.

"No! I can't do this! I will be shunned!" Rebecca pushed away from Jeff and would have fled from him, had he not grabbed her arm.

"Sh-h-h, Rebecca, it was just a little kiss," he murmured. "I'm sorry. I didn't mean to upset you. Sh-h-h, sh-h-h-h." He held her hand, but she stayed her arm's distance away from him.

"You don't understand," she said. Poor Rebecca. She sounded really miserable. "I am promised. This November I will marry Ethan Martin. It is all arranged. I can have nothing to do with you, even if I were not going to be married. It is not permitted."

"But, Rebecca..."

"Please! Please, just go away! *So much vork I haf here to do!*" Rebecca's distress was evident in the sudden German Amish idioms in her speech. She pulled her hand from Jeff's grasp.

"We'll talk again," he said to her retreating back.

"There is nothing more to say." Rebecca hurried up the front stairs. Melissa grabbed my hand, and we ran on tiptoe back to the kitchen. We barely made it to the breakfast nook, before Jeff stormed through the kitchen and out the back door.

"Bye, Jeff," Melissa called. He didn't answer. "Wow!" she exclaimed. "I wonder if he's kissed her before."

"Probably," I muttered. "I bet that's why she's so upset. Can you believe she's going to get married already? She's only sixteen!"

"What else is there for them to do? They can't go to high school, or even to grade school with kids who aren't Amish. All they do is work and—I guess all they do is *work.*"

The challenge of finding out about Rebecca had dimmed somewhat. I didn't want to talk to her so soon after witnessing such a private thing. I think I felt a little guilty. Melissa didn't seem to share my sentiments.

"My mother would have a cow if she knew about Jeff and Rebecca! Maybe I should tell her." Melissa grinned.

"No, don't tell her, Melissa. Let's just wait and watch and see what happens." I should have encouraged her to tell her mother. Hindsight is such a perfectly honed sense.

For the next two weeks, I went to Melissa's house on either Tuesdays or Fridays, sometimes both. If Rebecca were really busy, Melissa and I didn't bother her. There were afternoons when we helped her fold laundry, and she answered any question we asked her. We learned a lot about the Amish.

"Why do you always wear that little white cap, with the strings hanging down?" I asked.

"Because the Bible tells us that women should have their heads covered," Rebecca replied.

"Can't you take it off?"

"No."

"Would you take the cap off so we can see it?" Rebecca laughed at my question.

"See what?" she asked me. "My cap or my hair?"

"Both."

"I really shouldn't," she told us.

"Oh, please!" Melissa begged. Rebecca pursed her lips and looked from Melissa, to me, and back to Melissa.

"Just for a minute," she warned, and slowly removed the white cap. "We only take our caps off to wash our hair."

"You mean you have to wear this cap to bed?"

"Yes."

Rebecca drew a long, thick hairpin from the back of her hair; and her black tresses tumbled over her shoulders and down her back. She really was lovely. "Look," she said. She held her cap in her hands and pointed out the delicate white embroidery surrounding the tiny pleats that formed the back section.

"We make our own caps," she explained. "None are exactly alike." I looked at the tiny stitches and marveled at the intricacy of the design.

"Why are they white?" I asked. "Why can't you wear colored ones?"

"Because that is our way. We wear only plain colors in our clothes." Rebecca indicated the dark purple of her dress she wore that day. "I must put the cap back on now."

"That would be a shame."

None of us had heard Jeff come in; but there he stood in the doorway, staring at Rebecca, whose face paled. She pulled up her hair, twisted it into a knot, quickly inserted the pin and grabbed her cap from my hands. She turned her back to us, pulled the cap onto her head, and adjusted it to its normal position.

"Thanks for your help folding these towels," Rebecca told us. "Now I will take them upstairs." She picked up the towel-laden cane basket and went, with dignity, up the back stairs. Melissa and I exchanged a knowing glance, and as one, turned to Jeff, who looked as if he had taken a blow to the stomach.

"God, she's beautiful." The way he said it actually sounded like a prayer.

"Come on, Sissy. Let's go for a bike ride. My mother won't be home until it's time for dinner, and Rebecca won't talk to us any more today. Let's go to the park."

"Okay," I replied. I followed her out the kitchen door, but I looked back as I pulled it toward me. Jeff was standing at the bottom of the back stairs, looking up. Before I closed the door completely, I could see him walking slowly up those stairs. I was very young, and very nosy, but I wasn't stupid. I joined Melissa and we rode to the park, where we stayed until my mom told us it was time for Melissa to go home and for me to come in to supper.

With only a very short period of summer left, I spent as much time at Melissa's house as I could. There was so much I wanted to know about Rebecca and the Amish way of life. She seemed more quiet, almost withdrawn sometimes; but she readily answered my questions.

I learned that only married Amish men grow beards, but no mustaches, because mustaches are of the world. Single men are clean-shaven. Young Amish men are allowed to enjoy the pleasures of the world for one year, after they come of age; but at the end of that year, they are expected to marry and take their places of responsibility in the community. At that time, Amish girls were not allowed an excursion into worldliness.

Rebecca told us that the bishops have total power over the people, and their word is law. It is the bishops who decide if an infraction of a rule deserves punishment, and what kind, and for how long. The most severe form of chastisement is something called "shunning"; and it is to be avoided, at all costs.

"When someone is shunned, it is as if they are dead," Rebecca explained. "No one will speak to them, eat with them, touch them, look at them, take food from them, or have anything to do with them at all, until a bishop declares that the period of shunning is over."

"What causes shunning?" I asked.

"Different things," Rebecca replied. "We have a set of rules that must not be broken. Breaking any of them can be punished by shunning." A smile came over her face. "Sometimes, even the suspicion of a rule being broken can cause someone to be called before the bishops. There was a man who did not have good luck growing a nice beard after he was married, and he was called to explain to the bishops why he had such few whiskers. It wasn't his fault. He just could not grow a heavy beard.

"That same man and his wife had no babies for two years after they were married, and they were called before the bishops to explain why. We are supposed to have babies right away."

"Really?" I asked. "My mom and dad would have been good Amish people. I was born just ten months after they got married." Rebecca laughed.

"Where do you go to church?" Melissa asked.

"We have services in our homes," Rebecca explained. "We take turns. We don't have meetings every Sunday, just once or twice a month; and it takes all day because we always eat together.

"Weddings take all day, too. Our weddings are very beautiful."

"When are you getting married, Rebecca?" I asked. She didn't answer for a moment.

"In November."

"Are you glad?" Melissa pressed.

"Ethan Martin is a good man, a kind man," Rebecca said. "I am lucky to marry him. He has a large farm and a big dairy herd, and his house is not far from ours. His wife died a year ago, and he asked my papa for me this summer. Ethan has two sons. One is four and the other is six."

"You mean you will be a stepmother? At sixteen?" It was incredible. Rebecca was only ten years older than one of the Martin boys. "Is it true that you speak German in your homes and schools?" I continued.

"Yes, and in our worship, too."

"Why?"

Rebecca shrugged. "It is our way. We stay with the old ways and avoid the near occasion of sin."

"The what?" I asked.

"The near occasion of sin. If we are not tempted, we will avoid 'the near occasion of sin'." Rebecca dropped her head and smoothed the towel she had just folded. "Sometimes we are tempted and not strong enough to avoid the sin."

"What happens then?" I asked.

"If we are found out, there is chastisement. If we confess, there is also chastisement."

"Did you ever sin, Rebecca?" Melissa asked. Rebecca's ivory skin acquired a pink tint. She placed the towel into the basket.

"That is enough talk for today," Rebecca said. "Mrs. Franklin will be here to take me home in a little while." Rebecca went upstairs.

I became involved in the exciting preparation for school, and I didn't go to Melissa's house for awhile. New notebooks, pencils, ruler, a new box of beautiful, waxy-smelling Crayolas, and all the trappings for the approaching school year made an intriguing stack atop the little desk in my bedroom.

In the evenings I called my friends, comparing new acquisitions and preferences we had for teachers and classrooms. When I called Melissa, she asked me to come to her house the next day.

153

"Tomorrow will be Rebecca's last day. Mother's very unhappy about that, because Rebecca is the best housekeeper we ever had; and she was supposed to work until she got married in November. I don't know why she's not going to work here anymore. She just told Mother that she would have to quit right away."

So at ten o'clock I rode my bicycle up to the Franklin mansion. Jeff's car was in the driveway, but Mrs. Franklin's was not. She had so many club meetings and Catholic Church charity work that she was gone just about every day. Melissa met me at the back door and motioned me to be quiet.

"What's up?" I whispered. Melissa pointed toward the back stairs and we started up them very quietly.

"Jeff and Rebecca are in Jeff's room, and I want to hear what they're talking about," she whispered back. Reluctance to spy vied with my overwhelming curiosity, and reluctance lost. We floated like ghosts up the three flights of stairs, avoiding the steps that were prone to squeak, until we stood on the landing outside the closed door of Jeff Franklin's domain.

The area formed a sitting room, lined with book-filled shelves. A low round table, that held a reading lamp, stood between two large wing-backed chairs. They were covered in a rich, dark red tapestry, which picked up the color from the toile wallpaper on the walls. Melissa motioned that I should crouch behind one of the chairs, and she knelt behind the other. We were hidden from anyone who came up or went down the stairs. We hugged the wall with our ears. Although their voices were faint, we could hear Jeff and Rebecca.

"I don't understand why you have to quit working here."

"Because I cannot be with you," Rebecca answered, and she sounded adamant.

"But, why?" Jeff pleaded.

"Because I am going to be married. I have already sinned against Ethan and my family and God. I am going to be a good wife to Ethan. I can't ever see you again."

"Rebecca, you *can't* marry that man! You love *me*! I *know* you do!" Jeff sounded frantic. "You can leave them, all of them! You can marry me and live here, right here in my rooms with me. I'll leave the dorm and drive back and forth to school, and we can live together here."

"You mean forsake my family? My home? Jeff, I could never do that. You are one of the English. I am Amish. I would be dead to my mama and papa and the rest of the community. They would never mention me again." Rebecca sounded sad, but determined.

"No, I won't let you go! You don't have to go back there! Tonight I'll tell my parents that you're going to stay here, that we're going to get married. They can't stop us, Rebecca; none of them can stop us!"

"Jeff, don't..." Rebecca's voice was suddenly muffled and there was silence for a long moment. "Jeff, no, I can't! Never again!"

"Rebecca, wait!"

The door flew open, and Rebecca ran across the landing to the stairs. Seconds later Jeff followed her, leaving Melissa and me to stare at each other in dismay. We had made an important discovery: eavesdroppers sometimes learn truths they would rather not know. We waited until we were sure that Rebecca and Jeff had cleared the second landing before we crept down to Melissa's room, where we remained behind the closed door until Mrs. Franklin arrived to drive Rebecca back to the Amish community.

"I can't believe Jeff told her he loved her," Melissa shook her head in disbelief. "He must be crazy."

"Yeah, Melissa, crazy in love," I answered. "It's really romantic, you know. Do you think she might change her mind and marry Jeff?"

"Now you're the crazy one," Melissa told me. "My dad has plans for Jeff, and it sure doesn't include his getting married to an Amish girl! And my mom would just die!"

"But what if she decides not to marry that old man with the kids? What if she decides she wants to marry Jeff?" I asked. Melissa looked at me as if I had completely lost my mind.

"Sissy, Jeff is as tied to my dad's laws as Rebecca is to hers. Neither one of them can break away." I knew that she was probably right, but I also knew that Jeff really wanted Rebecca. What good were laws and rules and religion, if they kept people apart who really loved each other? I couldn't see the sense in it; but when we're only twelve, black and white are easily discernible. It's the many shades of gray that escape our comprehension.

A few days later Melissa called and told me to meet her in the park. School had started and we were in separate classes, so I hadn't spoken with her since the day Rebecca stopped working at the Franklins.

I waited for Melissa atop my favorite picnic table in the park. I saw her coming on her bicycle before she neared the highway. She looked both ways, but didn't slow down when she reached it. Her long auburn curls streamed behind her like a banner. She saw me and rode straight to the picnic table, dropped her bike to the ground, and climbed up beside me.

"There's big trouble at our house," Melissa panted. "My dad is sending Jeff to some college in California tomorrow."

"Why? Doesn't he like Illinois University?" I asked.

"Oh, Sissy, it's not that. Jeff doesn't want to go away, but Dad is making him go. Jeff did a stupid thing. You know how crazy he is about Rebecca?" I nodded. "Well, he really *is* crazy! He drove out to Rebecca's house, the day before yesterday, and yelled for her to come out and talk to him. She wouldn't come out of the house, so Jeff tried to go inside; and her dad and two of her brothers stopped him. They made him leave." I stared at Melissa in disbelief. I think my mouth fell open.

"Why'd he do that?" I asked.

"That's not all," Melissa continued. "That night Mr. Yoder came up our driveway in his buggy and asked to talk to my dad. They were in Dad's study for a long time. When Mr. Yoder left, my dad was really mad. He went back into his study and slammed the door, hard, and he was on the telephone for a long time after that."

"Was Jeff there?"

"No. Jeff didn't come home till really late, but Dad was waiting for him. I could hear Dad yelling from my room, but I couldn't tell what he said."

"Where was your mother?" I asked. Melissa rolled her big green eyes, her favorite expression of disgust.

"In her room, avoiding a scene, as usual. She doesn't like *unpleasantness*, you know. Anyway, last night I heard Dad tell Jeff that the transfer from IU was already being sent, and that Jeff would be leaving tomorrow. He told Jeff that he was ashamed of him, that he had disgraced the family and made a fool of himself over a little Amish girl.

"Jeff said that he wouldn't leave, but Dad told him he didn't have a choice. Jeff started to argue with Dad, but Dad told him something that stopped Jeff cold."

"What?" I demanded. Melissa paused, whether for effect or because she was out of breath, I couldn't tell which.

"Dad said that Rebecca Yoder is getting married today."

"But she was going to be married in November. This is only September," I reminded her.

"Well, I think Jeff's going out to their farm scared them. I bet they were afraid that he would change Rebecca's mind, so they're having a quick wedding." Melissa's eyes widened. "You know what *that* usually means, don't you? Do you think she could be *expecting?*"

"I don't think so, Melissa," I said. "It sounds to me like the Amish are awfully strict, and Rebecca hasn't had time to see anyone else except..." I stopped. We stared at each other.

"Jeff." We said his name simultaneously and then both of us looked away. We sat there quietly for a few minutes, before Melissa stepped down from the table and picked up her bike.

"I'd better go," she said.

"Bye, Melissa." Melissa didn't answer me.

Melissa and I didn't see each other for several weeks. We attended different churches and different classes, and neither of us called the other. At the homecoming football game in mid-October, we sat together and soon we were catching up and laughing just like we always had.

"How does Jeff like his new college?" I asked.

"He really likes it," Melissa said. "The school has given him a partial basketball scholarship and he's playing on the team quite a bit. He has a girlfriend named Debbie, and he's planning to bring her home with him at Christmas."

I was disappointed and disillusioned. Jeff could not have cared as much about Rebecca as it seemed, if he already had another girlfriend.

"What about Rebecca?" I asked, before I could stop myself.

"We were wrong about that. I asked Mother, and she said that Jeff would never degrade himself in that manner." For a moment Melissa sounded just like her mother. "She said that it was all just a misunderstanding, and that everything was just fine."

Her tone said, *"And that's that."*

Life just kept happening, as it always does. Rebecca Yoder, now Martin, crossed my mind occasionally; but I really didn't think about her. As I was coming out of the one small department store in Redbud Grove, just before Christmas the following year, I saw an Amish woman climbing down from her buggy. Two little boys jumped down behind her; and her husband placed a baby, heavily bundled, into her outstretched arms.

The woman was dressed in the usual black, brimmed bonnet that tied under the chin. A heavy black cloak enveloped her from shoulder to mid-calf. A gust of winter wind caught the baby's blanket, as well as the woman's cloak; and in one encompassing moment, I knew that the woman was Rebecca and that she was pregnant, possibly five or six months. She recognized me in the same instant.

I looked from her tired countenance to her baby, but Rebecca quickly covered the little face against the cold wind. I started to speak to her, but she nodded her head politely and swept past me toward the store, followed by the two boys and her husband. Ethan Martin was one of the biggest men I had ever seen, and certainly not the most pleasant appearing. He looked very stern and hard, to me.

I stood looking after them. Mr. Martin opened the door for his family; and I caught a glimpse of the eight-month-old baby, peeking from beneath the blanket. My heart jumped. I couldn't tell if it was a boy or a girl, but one thing I knew.

That baby had the beautiful auburn hair and the amber brown eyes of Jeff Franklin. I thought of Melissa, and her mother and father. Should I tell them about Rebecca's baby? Would they want to know, or even care?

I decided not.

They might find it to be a disgrace, a scandal for the family.

Definitely—*unpleasant.*

#

THE WAR BRIDE

Elizabeth Susan Bannister entered first grade the same autumn I entered seventh grade. Mom walked to school with Bethy the first day, to reassure herself that her baby would not be afraid, just as she had walked with me.

I knew that Bethy was going to be fine. I had told her about the first grade room with the slide and how much she was going to like Miss Kate. Unfortunately, I had forgotten that Miss Kate, who was married to Mr. King, the superintendent, was going to have a baby. She retired just before school was scheduled to begin. The new teacher, Sarah Matthews, arrived in Redbud Grove only days before school started. The ink had barely dried on her teacher's certificate.

"You know what? You were *wrong*, Sissy," Bethy told me that first evening at supper. "My teacher's name is Miss Matthews, and she's short and funny."

"Just like you, huh, Wis-bet?" Dad teased. She grinned at Dad, showing the big space where her bottom front teeth had been. Dad had called her Wis-bet since the first time Bethy had tried to say Elizabeth, and it had come out "Wis-bet."

No one else called her that except Buddy, when he was teasing her. He changed it to "Whiz-butt", but only when Mom and Dad couldn't hear him. Of course, Bethy always flew into a rage and attacked Buddy every time he did it.

Bethy was a beautiful little girl with naturally curly dark hair that formed ringlets in damp weather. Her eyes were a bright blue, with a darker ring of blue around the outer edge of the irises. She was a precocious child, totally unafraid of anything, since she had conquered her fear of dogs.

"But I'm gonna grow, Daddy. Miss Matthews won't get bigger, 'cause she's all grown up. You know what? There are *twins* in my class. One's a boy and one's a girl and they both have blond hair and blue eyes and freckles just alike; but you can tell 'em apart. They don't have the same faces."

"What are the twins' names?" I asked.

"Um-m-m, I'm not real sure about the boy." Bethy frowned. "His name is really funny...Grunter or something like that." Mom and Dad laughed.

"Do you mean 'Gunther'?" Mom asked.

"Yeah, that's it! The girl's name is kind of pretty. It's Gretchen. You know what? They can talk two ways." Bethy took a drink of milk from her glass, leaving a heavy white mustache.

"I can, too," Buddy said. "Up like this." He spoke in a high falsetto. "And down like this." He lowered his voice a couple of octaves.

"Not like that, Buddy!" Bethy was clearly disgusted. "They can talk like we do, but they talk to each other another way."

"I think you mean another language, Honey." Mom wiped Bethy's mouth with a napkin. "I think they speak German, like their mother."

"Do you know who they are?" Dad asked. Mom nodded.

"I'll tell you about it later." I caught THE LOOK that passed between them. That meant there was something in the story she wouldn't tell, in front of us. I resented being classed with my younger brother and sister. I was in the seventh grade and would be thirteen in six months, for cryin'out loud. I resolved to listen carefully through the upstairs vent tonight. I had a feeling a good story was going to pass between my parents.

Mom put Bethy to bed early that night. Buddy went to his room earlier, too. He was building a tiny transistor radio in a penny matchbox. He had an advanced knowledge of anything electronic and was always conducting some kind of experiment. At least he hadn't blown himself, or anybody else, up yet.

By nine-thirty, I was in my bed. The nights were still warm, but a nice breeze filtered through the screened window. As I had done so many nights, I watched the stars, wondering what really lay beyond them. There had to be something. It made no sense that everything was just a circumstantial series of events, an accident.

My heavy thoughts became too burdensome, and I grew drowsy. I hadn't meant to go to sleep; but when I opened my eyes, the house was dark except for the faint glow from the nightlight Mom left on in the bathroom downstairs. I had just about given up hearing a juicy story, when I heard the murmur of my mother's voice.

"You really haven't heard about Andy Stratton's war bride?"

"Nope."

"Mrs. East told me about the Strattons, not long after she and I became acquainted. It's quite a story. Are you sure you want to hear it tonight? Are you tired?"

"No more than usual." Dad chuckled. "You could rub my back while you tell me," he suggested.

"Or you could rub mine," Mom countered. "Well, this is the way it happened, according to Mrs. East..."

One of the happiest days in Carrie Stratton's life occurred when she received word that her only son was finally coming home, after two long and arduous years in Europe. It was the fourth of June, nineteen forty-six.

A draftee at the age of thirty-one, in March of nineteen forty-three, Andrew Stratton held the dubious distinction of being the oldest private from Douglas County. For a time, it looked as if he were not going to be shipped overseas, and that the only action he was going to see was a drunken soldier fall from a barstool.

Casualties mounted, however; and Andy was sent to Europe, where he saw more of France and Germany than he would have wished. Aside from a short furlough following basic training, Andy had not been home since he was drafted.

Andrew, lovingly called Andy by his mother and older sister, Viola, had no other living relatives. The three of them lived in the big, white farmhouse where Carrie Stratton had come, as the bride of Harold Stratton, over forty years ago. The only thing that had changed when Harold died was the management of the farm.

Andy had bought new equipment, two steel-tired tractors, a plow, a disk, a cultivator, and a planter, the newest things on the market. Harold Stratton had favored horses, like the ones used by the nearby Amish community; but Andy was more forward thinking. Since there were no other family members to help with the farming, the Strattons had always kept two hired men. Andy had plowed with one tractor, while one of the hired help pulled the disk behind the other.

At harvest time, they had employed traveling crews of threshers to cut the wheat and haul it in wagons to the threshing machine. When the corn was ready, they had hired as many pickers as possible; for the black loam delivered heavy yields. What they had not sold was left standing in shocks to feed their own few head of cattle. Carrie Stratton and Viola fed their workers well, and the Stratton farm was never short of help.

The Strattons owned six hundred acres of the richest, black farmland in Douglas County. With his new equipment, Andy had been able to lease some acreage from neighboring farms, thus increasing his family's income. During farming season, he had risen at four o'clock and had seldom come in from the fields until dark. The routine had been grueling, but rewarding.

Because of the large acreage of his farming operation and his age, Andy had been deferred from the draft twice. Gas rationing had cut down on the use of his tractors, and much of the work had to be done with the big draft horses, as it had been for so many years.

The shock of the actual letter, that began with, "Greetings" from the United States Government in March of nineteen forty-three, caused Carrie Stratton to take to her bed. It was several days after Andy's departure before she gained stamina enough to resume her daily routine. Her hatred for the war narrowed to a fierce intensity that centered on Germany and anything that could possibly be connected to Germany. The Nazi Germans were responsible for taking away her beloved Andy, and she would never forgive them or their descendants.

That first year of Andy's absence the land was tilled by willing neighbors, who used their own horses and equipment, as well as Andy's. Much of the land lay fallow. Redbud Grove had given up most of its able-bodied young men. The older farmers were more comfortable using horses than tractors. Most of the younger farming crews had also been drafted. Many did not return home alive.

The bulk of the regular chores fell upon Viola Stratton. While her mother languished in bed, Viola managed the household duties, as well as the twice-daily task of milking their Holstein cow. One job she enjoyed consisted of gathering eggs from the nests of her prized Rhode Island Red hens.

Long resigned to her single state, Viola seemed content with her life on the farm where she was born. A tall, rawboned woman of forty, Viola possessed a peculiar kind of beauty, more handsome than pretty. Except for her heavy, dark hair, she bore a marked resemblance to her younger brother, who had sandy hair and light blue eyes.

When Carrie decided that she could not bring Andy home by lying in her bed, her strength rapidly returned. Every spring and summer Carrie had planted a huge garden, and this year would be no different. She threw herself into the task of planting and hoeing with a vengeance. Like most women who had access to a plot of ground, she harvested and preserved and canned as much produce as she could. Homegrown fruits and vegetables enhanced meals that were often meatless, or nearly so, as a result of rationing.

Carrie and Viola endured the two years without Andy, waiting impatiently for his letters. Both wrote to him weekly. When the letter arrived announcing that Andy had been discharged, Carrie could not contain her joy.

"Viola, he's coming home! Our Andy is coming home!" She removed her glasses and wiped her eyes before continuing to read the letter. "Three weeks. He'll be here in three weeks! He says he's bringing souvenirs, Viola. He says he found something special and knows that we'll love his surprise." Carrie looked around the kitchen with bright eyes. "We have to clean this house," she said.

Carrie and Viola scrubbed and scoured the big farmhouse from attic to basement. Together they wrestled the heavy rugs onto the clothesline and took turns beating them, until not a speck of dust remained. Viola washed windows, inside and out, with ammonia, then polished them with crumpled newspaper. The women swept down the walls, washed woodwork, cleaned cabinets and washed all the bedding. Carrie had not been as fastidious with the spring-cleaning after Andy left, but she more than made up for it. The old house had never before been so immaculate.

On the third Tuesday of every month, Carrie and Viola attended the all-day meeting of the Methodist Ladies' Sewing Circle in Redbud Grove. The women knew as much about each other as they did about their own families. They had shared recipes and gossip and tragedies for many years.

Not one woman in the group had escaped the horrors of the war unscathed. Each had lost someone—a brother, a cousin, a husband, a son, a grandson—or witnessed the return of a loved one, wounded in body or soul. When one of their own came home in good health and whole, the entire group rejoiced, none more wholeheartedly than those who had lost someone.

Happy faces received Carrie's good news, when she made her joyous announcement at the June meeting. Speculation about the promised souvenirs ran rampant.

"Didn't Andy give you a hint, Carrie?" asked Martha Stevens, the oldest lady in the group. She peered at Carrie over rimless glasses, and her eyes were as bright with excitement as the youngest member's.

"No. He just said that he was sure we'd like what he's bringing." Carrie clasped her hands in her lap. "I'm kind of hoping he's found some of that fancy lace they make somewhere over there. Or a piece of glass, the crystal things someone in Austria makes."

"Now, Carrie, you know that a man with hands as big as Andy's couldn't get a glass souvenir home without breaking it!" Laughter accompanied the nods of agreement.

"What do you think Andy is bringing, Viola?"

Carrie's daughter pondered for a moment. "I really don't have any idea," she answered. "We know that Andy was stationed in Austria for awhile, but he could be bringing something from anywhere in Europe. The censors cut out so much of his letters. It doesn't matter what he brings. I'm just glad that he's coming home."

The days crawled by like a one-legged turtle. Hardly a mote of dust could be seen in the Stratton farmhouse. Wood floors shone from fresh wax and the smell of Old English furniture polish permeated the air. Touch-ups were done daily.

One of the red hens was sacrificed the day before Andy's scheduled arrival. The aroma of Carrie Stratton's homemade chicken and dumplings, combined with the fragrant scent of freshly baked bread and coconut pound cake, wafted through the high-ceilinged rooms. All was done, that could conceivably be done, to enhance one man's homecoming.

Dawn broke on a day as clear and bright as Carrie's windows. The two women dressed carefully, donning their very best for Andy. Viola brought the big, black nineteen forty Pontiac from the shed. She had washed and polished it, until it rivaled the silver in the house. She helped her mother into the car, and they were off to greet their loved one.

They spoke very little on the way into Redbud Grove. The three miles to town seemed long. There were more cars than usual on the highway; and Viola drove carefully, her hands wrapped tightly around the steering wheel. Several cars and a few old farm trucks were parked at the depot. A small welcoming committee had already gathered beneath the extended eaves of the orange brick building.

Carrie and Viola sat down on one of the green benches and someone shoved glasses of lemonade into their hands. It promised to be a very warm day. Carrie fanned herself lightly with her handkerchief.

"Here she comes!"

The cluster of people peered up the double tracks, where a column of black smoke could be seen rising from the approaching train. The mournful sound of a steam engine's whistle reached them, and hearts beat faster as the locomotive raced nearer. Suddenly it was upon them.

The loud chugging and hissing steam made conversation impossible. Carrie remained seated on the bench, her hands pressed against her chest. Viola stood beside her mother. Except for a faint flush on her cheeks, Viola seemed perfectly calm.

A uniformed conductor dropped a set of boarding steps to the brick platform and disembarked. He turned to assist his passengers. Carrie gasped as her son stepped down. He seemed taller than she remembered. The khaki uniform fit him well, and it looked as if Andy had gained some weight—actually quite a bit of weight. Carrie stood, reached for Viola's arm, and together they walked toward Andrew Stratton.

A greeting filled with all her love was on Carrie's lips, when Andy turned back to the train and assisted another passenger down the steps. The very pregnant young woman smiled at Andy, and Carrie's heart sang with pride at the courteous behavior of her son.

165

"Andy!" Carrie could restrain herself no longer. With a glad cry she hurried to him and wound her arms tightly around his waist.

"Mother!" he cried and lifted Carrie from the platform with a great bear hug. Tears coursed down Carrie's wrinkled cheeks. When she felt her feet touch the ground, she placed her hands on each side of Andy's face and gazed at him with utter adoration.

It was the same face, but different. Andy looked older, more solid; and his sandy hair had thinned alarmingly. Still, he was her Andy; and he had come home.

"Hello, Vi." Andy released his mother and gave his sister a brisk hug. Not given to expressing her feelings easily, Viola returned the caress briefly and stepped back.

"Welcome home, Andy!" Friends pressed forward, each with a hearty handshake and a welcoming smile. Carrie never removed her eyes from her son; and she managed to stay within touching distance of his uniformed person, even as others caught his attention. Finally she could stand it no longer.

"Andy, where is your suitcase? Let's get your things and go home. This heat is going to give me sunstroke." Carrie patted her face with a lace-edged handkerchief.

"Sounds like a good idea, Mother." He glanced at several pieces of luggage the conductor had placed nearby. Instead of reaching for them, Andy placed his arm around the shoulders of the pregnant woman, who had stood quietly beside the bags since stepping from the train.

Carrie's mouth dropped open when Andy drew the woman forward, and her heart nearly stopped when he spoke.

"Mother, Vi, this is my surprise, a very special war souvenir, my wife, Elsa."

Stunned silence preceded pandemonium. Carrie stared in disbelief from the proud face of her son to the shy, round countenance of her daughter-in-law. Daughter-in-law! It was not possible, Carrie thought. It must be Andy's idea of a joke, a cruel joke!

Carrie's mouth tightened, as her eyes swept the bulging length of the young woman's round body. She was so—so—pregnant! Her long, full peasant skirt hiked up in front in a most unbecoming and distressful manner.

Somehow Carrie managed to gather her family together; and with as much dignity as she could create, given the circumstances, she allowed Viola to help her into the front seat of the car. Andy maintained a steady monologue all the way home, remarking how tall the corn was, how expansive the fields seemed after being away from them so long. He sat in the rear seat with his wife, allowing Viola to drive, which he had never done before.

At the noon meal, so carefully prepared with such anticipation, Carrie hardly spoke. Viola answered Andy's questions, trying to make up for the lack of participation by their unhappy mother. Elsa ate heartily, smiling at her husband when she caught his eye.

"Is goot, goot," she murmured, through a mouthful of delectable chicken and dumplings; and even Carrie understood the compliment to her cooking.

"Elsa is learning more English every day," Andy announced proudly. "When I met her, she knew only a few words; and I was just beginning to catch on to some German phrases."

Carrie cleared her throat.

"How did you meet her?" she asked, not glancing at the object of their conversation.

"Elsa lived in a little village no one ever heard of," Andy replied. "Some of my buddies and I found it, by accident, on a scouting mission, after a skirmish with some retreating Nazis. The fighting had stopped, and our occupation troops had moved in. We were stationed in another town a few miles away, and every day or so we scouted widening circles around the area. Our patrol stumbled across a path that led into some hilly terrain, so three of us followed it." Andy took a long drink from his glass of icy amber tea.

"From the top of a rocky hill, we could see a small valley village that looked like a picture painted by one of Viola's Dutch painters she likes so much. We slipped into the town, expecting sniper fire any minute; but no one was hostile. One of our men spoke fluent German and did all the talking. The people were curious about us Americans and very friendly—very friendly." Andy gazed at his wife, and a slow smile curved his mouth. Adoration emanated from him.

Viola fixed her attention onto the plate before her. A faint flush of embarrassment tinted her cheeks, and a worrisome touch of envy flitted through her heart. No man had ever looked at her the way her brother beamed at the woman who continued to devour the good food spread upon the table. Viola suddenly felt very lonely.

A variety of emotions played in rapid succession across Carrie Stratton's furrowed brow: dismay, disapproval, petulance, anger, and finally, determination. She stared at the intruder, trying to see in the girl what her son admired.

Sturdy, wholesome, healthy, obviously in possession of a hearty appetite, the girl was completely foreign to Carrie in appearance and demeanor. The coronet of braids that circled Elsa's head could only be described as flaxen. The clear, pink-cheeked complexion of Elsa's round face exuded the very essence of a nationality Carried looked upon with hatred and distrust.

Carrie's mouth tightened with disdain as she examined Elsa's clothing. The white peasant blouse, embroidered with a floral design across the yoke, pulled tightly across her ample breasts, in spite of the generous shirring of the fabric. Her dark blue, gathered skirt amply covered her bulging abdomen. Carrie cleared her throat again.

"When is the—the—when is she expecting?"

"By the end of the month," Andy answered. "I'll take her to see Doc Fishel tomorrow. No one has examined her, except the mid-wife in the village where I found Elsa. She's never been to a real doctor. I wanted her to see one at our base, but she was afraid." Elsa placed her fork on the table and smiled at her mother-in-law. In spite of herself, Carrie felt a touch of sympathy for the young woman.

"Food is goot," Elsa declared. She indicated that she wanted to rise, and Andy rushed to assist her. She whispered her need and leaned on Andy's arm, as he led her to the bathroom in the back hall. Andy had installed the plumbing and fixtures into a corner of the washroom, which held Carrie's washing machine, both conveniences that the Stratton women dearly appreciated.

"Viola, what are we going to do?" Carrie whispered.

"*Do*, Mother? We are going to take care of Andy's young wife—and she *is* young, Mother. I doubt that she's a day over twenty, maybe not even that. In two or three weeks, there is going to be a baby in this house, for the first time since Andy was born. We're going to take care of Elsa and help raise Andy's child. That's what we're going to do, Mother; so you had best start making some baby clothes."

Carrie stared at Viola, as if her daughter had suddenly gone insane. The younger woman actually sounded as if she accepted this awful situation, even welcomed it. She had *never* used that tone of voice when speaking to her mother. Never!

The next few weeks were the most difficult Carrie Stratton had experienced in more than recent memory. It was bad enough that all her friends had to be introduced to a *German* in Carrie's own house. It was worse that she could sense their avid curiosity about the girl's advanced pregnancy and Andy's sickening devotion to his wife. The unprecedented heat wave only made a bad situation worse, and Carrie's nerves quickly approached the breaking point.

The momentous day arrived on Monday, three weeks after the arrival of Andy and Elsa Stratton. As usual, the weekly washing was done early in the morning, sheets first, followed by white underwear and towels. Colored cottons preceded the final dark clothes and overalls. Viola completed the actual task, carrying out heavy woven baskets of wet laundry to the long rows of clothesline. Elsa, unable to lift anything in the final days of her pregnancy, volunteered to hang the wet items on the line.

"You shouldn't lift your arms over your head, Elsa. You'll wrap the cord around the baby's neck." Carrie added one more bit to the homilies she had heaped upon Elsa since the girl had come to the Stratton farm. Elsa smiled sweetly at her mother-in-law.

"I alvays do dis," Elsa explained. "Clothesline is goot, not like spreading tings on rocks." Carrie threw up her hands and retreated to the house, while Viola helped Elsa pin the heavy sheets, folded corner to corner and not simply draped across the line, mind you. That accomplished, Viola returned to the house, leaving a happy Elsa to hang the lighter items.

Unannounced, the Baptist minister arrived to call upon the Strattons. They were not members of his congregation, but word had leaked that they had not been attending services at their own Methodist church. He had no way of knowing that it was Carrie's embarrassment over Elsa that kept her from church. The Reverend Mr. Claude Vest had met Carrie and Viola, but had not yet been introduced to Andy and his new wife. The minister had accepted the call to the Redbud Grove First Baptist Church shortly after Andy was

169

drafted. The pastor was anxious to encourage and uplift, and he found nothing wrong with doing a little proselytizing, whenever possible. Grabbing the Strattons from the Methodists would certainly be a plus.

Always ready to entertain guests, Carrie invited the uninvited visitor to come inside for coffee and homemade sweet rolls. She seated Mr. Vest in the high-ceilinged parlor and served him coffee in one of the china cups reserved for company.

"It certainly is early for the air to be so hot," he observed.

"Yes, it is. I hope we don't get a bad storm. The air is damp, and the wind has come up." Carrie did not give him much help.

"Ahem." The minister cleared his throat, a nervous habit that appeared when he was ill at ease. "I understand that you folk may be, ahem, thinking of possibly, ahem, perhaps attending, ahem, another church?"

"Oh, my," Carrie laughed. "Whatever gave you that idea?"

"Well, someone said that, ahem, you have not been in services for, ahem, several weeks?"

"That is true. You see, my, uh, daughter-in-law isn't feeling well these days; and we thought it best that she not go out in public needlessly, not to say that church isn't important."

"Yes, I had heard that she is, ahem, in the family way?" Mr. Vest had a disconcerting manner of turning most of his observations into questions.

"She is."

The minister placed his empty cup on the glass-topped serving table that had belonged to Carrie's mother. "Could I meet the young lady? I would be most honored. And perhaps I could help her in some way?"

Carrie took three big breaths and resigned herself to the fact that she must introduce this man to the German girl. "Very well. She is helping Viola with the wash." Carrie stood and led the way through her house to the back door, across the wide porch and down the wood steps.

"Elsa," she called. There was no answer, but she could see the girl's feet beneath a row of sheets that billowed out like sails in the hot breeze. She ushered Mr. Vest around the line of whipping linens, to meet the girl her Andy had chosen to bear his children.

"Oh! Oh, my Dear Lord in Heaven!" A gasp and beseeching words of horror escaped from Carrie's lips at the sight of the unfortunate girl. Miserable in the oppressive heat, Elsa had gathered her long, full skirt from behind, pulled it forward between her legs and tucked it into the waistband, forming a pair of gigantic bloomers.

Seeking further respite, she had untied the string that held the gathers of her peasant blouse up, slipped it from her arms, and allowed it to hang from her middle, thus exposing her huge, ponderous, milk-laden breasts. She stood between the two rows of sheets, savoring the cool touch of the wet cotton against her sweltering skin.

At the sound of Carrie's voice, Elsa turned and found that she was facing the outraged presence of her mother-in-law and the gaping visage of a strange man, whose eyes seemed in imminent danger of popping from his head. Elsa seemed not the least embarrassed.

"Iss so hot," Elsa said and calmly raised her blouse to cover the massive white mounds that had become such a heavy burden to her.

"Oh-h-h-h." Carrie's eyes rolled backwards, her knees buckled slowly, and she fell to the ground in a complete, merciful faint.

"Mrs. Stratton!" The Baptist minister recovered his breath and his eyes, and knelt on the grass beside his hostess. "Miss Stratton! Come help your mother!" he screamed. Viola came running down the steps. Quickly surveying the situation, she took a wet cloth from the clothesline and gently smoothed it over her mother's face. Shortly, the older woman revived enough to sit up, with assistance from her daughter and the unwelcome Baptist preacher. She raised a trembling hand to her forehead. Her eyes focused on the figure of the German girl.

"Viola, help her!" Carrie cried. Her voice was surprisingly strong, for one who had just recovered consciousness from a total swoon. Viola and the minister whirled to see Elsa, who stood bent slightly forward. Elsa grasped her expansive abdomen with both hands, and her face was drawn into an expression of pained surprise. When she could speak, she smiled and said softly,

"I tink da bebe comes."

Sometime near midnight, Doc Fishel and Carrie Stratton emerged from one of the first floor bedrooms, where Elsa had spent hours of agonizing labor. Andy, haggard and in need of a shave, rushed to his mother, the question in his eyes, his heart somewhere near the floor with fear.

"Mother?" he said. Tears streamed down Carrie's face, as she took her son's hands. Andy's throat closed and threatened to choke him. "Elsa?"

"Andy, you have a big, healthy son; and Elsa is fine, just very tired."

Andrew Stratton whooped with glee and relief. Carrie put her hand on Andy's arm. "Andy, you also have a beautiful little girl." Andy's mouth dropped open. Carrie opened the bedroom door and stepped aside, allowing her son his first glimpse of his children. Elsa's face seemed luminous on the pillows. She held a swaddled bundle in each arm, nursing two babies at her magnificent breasts.

Carrie stepped briskly up to her daughter. Viola could not seem to control the grin on her tired face. "Well, don't just stand there, Viola. We have to come up with another crib, and start another layette, and help Andy raise these children. And we'll have to get them in church as soon as possible—no telling what kind of heathen nonsense that poor girl was taught." She scurried down the hall to the linen closet, muttering and planning as she went.

Viola watched her mother and said a silent prayer of thanks. It looked like everything was going to be all right, after all, even if Andy's children had a German mother.

Carrie Stratton never said another derogatory word about things Germanic in name, nature, or nationality. And woe unto anyone who did so in her presence...

"And those are the twins who are in Bethy's class?"
Dad sounded sleepy.

"Um-hum. Mrs. East says that Mrs. Stratton dotes on those children. Well, good night, Sweetie. I know you're tired. So am I."

"Oh, I don't know. I'm not *that* tired." Dad was using his "flirty" voice, as Mom called it. I had learned a lot, listening to them through the vent the past few years. If Mom ever realized how sound carried to my room, I was a cooked goose, a gone gosling!

"Aren't you kind of lonesome with Bethy in school?" Dad asked.

"Lonesome? Who has time to be lonesome?"

"Well, I thought maybe...would you like to try for our own set of twins? Ow-w-w-w! That hurt!"

"Good," Mom said and I heard her turning over in the bed. "Go to sleep, Romeo."

Dad chuckled. "Just thought I'd ask," he said.

Gross! I thought. *How simply gross!*

#

LUCINDA BARNES

Proximity and loneliness, as well as gratitude, develop friendships, I think. All three factors contributed to the friendship between Lucinda Barnes and me—gratitude on my part, certainly, and loneliness, on hers. I have wondered if her life might have turned out differently, had she been enrolled in the other class; but that probably had no bearing on the events that unfolded. Mine would have been less impacted, because I would not have been so close to her, perhaps would not have become her friend.

Lucinda Barnes moved to Redbud Grove from Oklahoma, in January of nineteen fifty-three, and entered Mrs. Sylvester's seventh grade class at West Side Grade School, where my gratitude to Lucinda sprang forth in full bloom. From the first grade on, teachers seated us alphabetically; and Joe Bob (Joseph Robert) Brady had been sitting behind me since the third grade, which he was repeating that year. Joe Bob had also repeated the second grade, which made him two years older than the rest of us.

I had been so grateful to Mr. Brehm for giving me a respite from Joe Bob in the fifth grade. But during the sixth grade, and now in the seventh, Joe Bob was behind me again. He was the one element in my life that kept it from being perfect.

Lucinda changed that. Her last name put her in the desk between Joe Bob and me. I would probably have loved her for that reason alone. Joe Bob transferred his obsession/tormenting/hair-twisting/pencil-poking from me to Lucinda, who endured his attentions with indulgent smiles and tolerance. Joe Bob responded to her kindness and her beauty with total devotion and an occasional fingering of her hair when it brushed across his desk.

For Lucinda Barnes *was* beautiful. Her blond hair shone with silvery strands that gleamed like platinum in sunlight and fell like a satiny length of pale yellow silk below her shoulders. Her green-blue

174

eyes, fringed with long dark lashes, tilted up at the outside corners. At the age of thirteen, her body had developed a slender shapeliness that turned boys' heads. Sometimes, men stared at her, too.

I liked her anyway, and Lucinda liked me. Although most of us had spent the past six years together, in my case five-and-a-half, and knew each other inside out, Lucinda was accepted and included in our fellowship right away. No one excluded her, but there was some hesitancy, a holding back on her part—except with me. She seemed most comfortable when it was just the two of us.

If Lucinda had been conceited or hateful, it would have been easy to dislike her. But she was sweet natured and kind, even to Joe Bob, a boy that most of my friends and I barely tolerated.

"How can you stand him?" I asked her one spring morning recess. Lucinda and I lolled lazily in the swings, while Joe Bob did pull-ups on the monkey bars, not far away.

"He's not so bad," Lucinda answered. "I think he's kind of cute."

I looked at Joe Bob. At fifteen, Joe Bob was taller than everyone else in our class, all of whom were twelve or thirteen. His hair fell across his forehead in a thick thatch of straw-streaked dark blond. His light blue eyes had squint lines around them, because he was very near-sighted. The school had notified his parents every year that Joe Bob needed glasses, but none were ever forthcoming.

Joe Bob's nose had a definite twist to one side, the result of being broken during a ball game. His voice had deepened, and he already had a prominent Adam's apple that was the envy of the other boys. His family had come from Kentucky when oil was discovered in the area. Mr. Brady worked on a drilling rig. Joe Bob still spoke with a heavy Southern drawl that made him sound slow-witted sometimes. Cute? Not by my standards.

"You are out of your mind," I stated. "There's nothing 'cute' about him."

Lucinda smiled and gave me an enigmatic look.

"He has potential," she said. "He will be a handsome man."

I snorted. "You're crazy."

Lucinda never talked about her family. She asked about mine as soon as we became acquainted, and I told her everything she wanted to know, probably more than she wanted to know; but she seemed genuinely interested.

"Do you have brothers or sisters?" I asked.

"No."

"Then it's just you and your mom and dad? Do you have grandparents?" I envied my friends who had grandmas and grandpas in their lives. Both my grandmothers had died young. My grandfathers lived in southern Missouri and only one of them was welcome in our house.

"I have a grandma in Oklahoma and two uncles somewhere. There are some cousins, but I don't know them. There's just Mom and me."

"Oh. Did your dad die?" Tactful to the core I was.

"No. Well, maybe. We don't know where he is."

I didn't know what to say.

I met Lucinda's mother after the school's spring concert in May. My family had found Lucinda and me in the crowd; and as we were receiving prejudiced compliments, a pretty blond woman joined us.

"Hi, Hon. Your music was real nice."

"Uh, hi, Mom," Lucinda answered. "I'm ready to go." Lucinda started to walk away.

"Wait, Honey. Ain't you gonna introduce me to your friends?" Lucinda hesitated. My mother held out her hand.

"Hello. I'm Jackie Bannister; and this is my husband, Will. It's nice to meet you."

Mrs. Barnes shook hands with my mother and then my dad, and the bracelets on her wrist jangled like wind chimes. She wore red nail polish and redder lipstick that matched her tight sweater. Her hair, only a little darker than Lucinda's, cascaded down her back in tight waves and curls.

"Come on, Mom. I have homework, and I need to get home." Lucinda tugged at her mother's arm. She looked at me briefly. She seemed uneasy. Mrs. Barnes laughed, a high tinkling sound.

"Well, I guess we'll go," she said. "Bye." She wiggled her fingers and walked away, her hips swaying slightly in the black skirt with the high back slit.

"You can put your eyes back in your head, Will," my mom muttered. I glanced at my Dad. His eyes looked fine to me.

Lucinda and I spent a lot of time together, after school dismissed that summer. My other friends liked Lucinda, but she never seemed to want to be part of a group. Occasionally I went to a birthday party without her, or joined the others for a Saturday afternoon matinee at the only theater in town; but I was not going to give up my friendship with Lucinda. She had rescued me from Joe Bob, and she had my loyalty.

A couple of afternoons a week Lucinda and I got together, usually in the park beside our house or at my house, where Lucinda liked to play with my little sister, who was only six. I thought my sister was a bit of a pest when I had friends over, but Lucinda liked to include her in our games and was always considerate of her. My mother thought Lucinda was special, too. I think she hoped that some of Lucinda's innate kindness would somehow transfer to me.

The only complaint I had about our time together was the hovering presence of Joe Bob Brady. When we went to the park, Joe Bob would be sitting against a tree, or playing on the swings, or pushing the small merry-go-round. He seemed to possess radar fixed on Lucinda, or intuition, or something. Perhaps he simply followed her.

"Why can't he just go away?" I whined.

"Oh, Sissy, forget about him. He's not hurting a thing!" Lucinda always waved to him, and he always waved back. I ignored him.

I hated it when Martha Lewis came to visit my mother. I don't think Mom was thrilled about it either; but she was nice, no matter who came to our house. Mrs. Lewis had the knack of setting my teeth on edge. It wasn't what she said; it was the way she said it. She had an opinion, usually negative, about every one and every thing in Redbud Grove.

Mrs. Lewis was a member of the First Baptist Church on Main Street, the same church where I attended Sunday school, most Sundays. She wore her thinning gray hair pulled so tightly back from her face that the outer edges of her eyebrows were tilted upward. A flat bun, held in place with ugly tortoise shell pins, covered the back of her head.

Mrs. Lewis favored polka-dot dresses and had several in dark colors, all with large round white dots. She also wore dark striped dresses in the same shirtwaist style, buttoned bodice attached to a full, boxy skirt. Short in stature, Martha Lewis was wide enough to cover nearly half of a sofa when she sat. Her flesh was soft and jiggled when she moved, but her ankles were remarkably thin and delicate looking for one carrying so much weight. I wondered how they held her up. I avoided her when I could; but there were times when she made her Sunday school calls unannounced, and I was trapped.

One afternoon I came home from my piano lesson to find her car parked in front of the house, so I quietly let myself in through the back door and slipped upstairs to my room. I could hear her voice, which carried well, coming up the vent. I stepped out of my shoes and carefully climbed onto my bed, hoping the springs would not creak.

Buddy peeked at me from his room across the hall and laid his finger across his lips. He didn't want to see Mrs. Lewis either. He had moved into his new room, summer before last, barely waiting for the paint to dry. It was actually kind of comforting to know that someone else lived in the attic with me. He grinned and soundlessly closed his door.

"I'm telling you, someone should do something about that situation." Mrs. Lewis sniffed. "That awful Parker woman and her nasty 'girls' finally left town, and now we have this other floozy move in." Sniff. "She wasn't here any time at all before she moved that man in—and with her daughter right there in the house, too." Sniff. "That girl will turn out just like her mother, you mark my words!" Sniff, sniff.

"Have some more tea, Martha," Mom said. There was the sound of ice clinking in glasses. I would have liked a glass of iced tea, but I could wait until Mrs. Lewis left. Besides, it would taste better for the waiting. "You know, things are not always what they seem, Martha. Maybe Mrs. Barnes is renting a room to someone."

"Not likely." Sniff. "Doesn't Sissy run around with that girl? If I were you, I would keep my daughter away from that situation." Sniff.

"They're friends," Mom said. "Lucinda's a very nice girl."

Martha Lewis was talking about Lucinda and her mother! I couldn't stand it. I bounced off the bed and went downstairs barefooted, not being careful about the noise, and filled a glass with ice from our new refrigerator in the kitchen. It was wonderful not to have to chip slivers of ice off the big block in the old icebox.

"Sissy? I didn't hear you come in," my mother called. She sounded relieved.

"I came in the back." I went into the living room and poured tea into my glass from the pitcher on the coffee table. "Hi, Mrs. Lewis."

"Hello, Sissy. My, aren't you getting to be a *big* girl!" She looked me up and down, staring pointedly at my chest, which was finally beginning to blossom. I knew what she meant. She made me want to cross my arms and hide.

"Mom, I asked Lucinda over for supper. Is that ok?" I looked into my mother's face, hoping she would forgive the lie. Mom's eyes narrowed; and her lips twitched, just a little.

"Of course, it is, Honey. Lucinda is always welcome here."

Mrs. Lewis sniffed once more and pulled her heavy body, which was stuffed into a dark blue dotted dress at least one size too small, off the couch.

"I'll be going, Mrs. Bannister. You heed my words, now. If we good Christians don't stand up against them, people like that will take over the town." Sniff. My mother walked Mrs. Lewis to the front door. I couldn't resist making a face at Martha Lewis's retreating back.

"Lucinda isn't coming for supper, Mom."

"I guessed that, Honey." Mom smiled and put her arm around my shoulders. "Why don't you make a salad, while I put a meatloaf together." Usually I would have groaned at the suggestion, but Mom had stood up for my friend and I owed her.

At supper that night my dad made a startling announcement.

"Sam Dulaney asked me to join the country club today." My mother's fork stopped in mid-air.

"Whatever for?" she asked. Dad shrugged.

"They have two openings, and he invited me and Tom Marks to join."

"We're not exactly part of the country club set, Will. I certainly don't have the time or the desire to play cards with a bunch of women in a smoky room all day. You don't play golf, so what would be the point?" Mom was not impressed. Dad laughed at her indignation.

"Could we go to the pool, Daddy?" my brother asked.

"Sure, Bud. We'd all be able to swim in the pool, play golf, have birthday parties there, whatever they have available."

"Yay-y-y-y!" Bud cheered. He was only eleven. I was thrilled at the possibilities; but at thirteen, I was a little more dignified.

"Will, I'm not sure about this. What about the cost?"

"Not as much as you'd think, Honey. Sam has a set of clubs he wants to sell, and he'll let me have them at a fraction of the cost of new ones."

"You've never played golf in your life! What makes you think you'd like it?" Mom was not going to make this easy.

"If I don't like it or can't learn, I'll just sell the clubs." He considered for a moment. "Or maybe one of the kids would like to play."

"I'm not crazy about them being at *any* swimming pool, Will, not with so many kids getting polio. They say there's a possibility it's coming from the public pools." There was the dreaded "they" again. I didn't know who "they" were, but "they" interfered with a lot of activities I enjoyed.

"I'm going to join, Jackie." Dad was determined. "If I don't like it after a year, I'll drop the membership. Tom is bringing the clubs to me at work tomorrow." Mom's mouth tightened, but she didn't say another word about it. In fact, she was quiet during the rest of supper; and she hardly spoke to Dad all evening. I think Dad was getting frosted.

Any time I had suggested that we go to her house, Lucinda had brushed me aside with one excuse after another.

"Oh, it's much nicer here," she said, or, "My mom has to sleep during the day, because she works at night," or "Our house is not as nice as yours." But one day I insisted. Mrs. Lewis's remarks about Lucinda's mother and some man, a man Lucinda had never mentioned, had piqued my curiosity. I was shamelessly determined.

"I would really like to go to your house," I said. "What time does your mom go to work?" Lucinda hesitated.

"She works the swing shift this week, and she has to leave the house by two-thirty."

"Then she's been gone for half an hour. I'll tell my mom."

"Well, I suppose it would be all right," Mom said, but she was hesitant. She looked at Lucinda and back at me. "You come home in an hour." She was very firm.

"OK, Mom."

We rode our bikes, and I followed Lucinda's lead. I was surprised when we rode to the far southeastern side of town, where the houses were very small, and some not very well kept. There was a section of old, rundown houses close to the river; and it was in front of one of them that Lucinda stopped her bike. The house was a dilapidated, one-story bungalow, with a rickety front porch and a small overgrown lawn.

"Well, this is it." Her voice was flat, and she didn't look at me. I followed her to the porch, where she sat down. "It's cooler here than inside." It was a hot day, and I couldn't argue with her. She obviously didn't want to take me into the house.

We sat on the porch and talked for a while. I could tell that Lucinda felt uncomfortable; and I was going to suggest that we go back to the park, when the front door opened. Lucinda jumped up. I turned, expecting to see her mother, thinking that something had made her late for work. I was mistaken.

A man stood just inside the closed screened door. He wore gray work pants and a ribbed-knit undershirt with straps, like my father wore; but this man didn't remind me of my dad. A cigarette dangled loosely from his thin lips. His eyes squinted against the smoke, and I couldn't determine their color. Dark stubble covered his square jaw, disappearing into long sideburns that were streaked with gray. Black, silver-streaked hair tumbled in disarray across his forehead. He was tall and muscular, and I was afraid of him.

At least as old as my dad, who was thirty-five, the man didn't look or act like any older man I knew. There was something frightening about him, something that emanated from him as tangible as an odor. After an assessing glance at me, which made my skin feel tingly, he focused half-open eyes on Lucinda.

"Hi, Cindy-baby." The man's voice rumbled in his throat; and the way he stared at Lucinda made me feel queasy. "Who's your friend?" He blew a stream of smoke from his mouth.

"What're you doing here?" Lucinda demanded. She glared at him, ignoring his greeting. The man chuckled. He pushed the screened door open and stepped onto the porch, where the afternoon sun struck him fully.

Coarse black hair curled above the low neck of his undershirt and grew thickly on his heavy arms, all the way down to his hands and the backs of his fingers. It made his skin look very pale. I shuddered with revulsion. I recognized the sour odor of beer as he drew closer. Sometimes my dad smelled faintly of beer, after coming home from a ball game; but this man reeked of the stuff.

"Now is that any way to greet your old Uncle Al? Here I am all alone, and no pretty girl to talk to till you come home."

"You're supposed to be at work." Lucinda's voice was angry and high-pitched. The man came closer. I backed up.

"There was a little explosion at Petro this morning, so I got to come home early, thinking we could spend a little time together; and you were gone." His voice caused unpleasant chills down my back, just like fingernails drawn across a blackboard. I shuddered again. He might be Lucinda's uncle, but I didn't like him. Another low chuckle slithered out of his mouth. Lucinda looked away.

In two quick steps, he stood between Lucinda and me. I watched as he lowered one hand to grasp a strand of Lucinda's lovely hair, and curl it loosely around his tobacco stained fingers. She jerked away from his touch, and a fine tendril caught on the ring he wore. The ring was an ugly thing, heavy gold with a tiny, coiled snake in the center. The snake's red stone eyes caught the sunlight. Uncle Al laughed as he loosened her hair from the ring.

"Let's go." Lucinda ran to her bike, and I followed on her heels.

"Run, Little Rabbit, run," he called, "but one day I'll put you in a pie and eat you, all the way down to the bone." Uncle Al's chuckle followed us as we rode away.

I had to pedal hard to keep up with Lucinda. She rode as if her worst nightmare pursued her. I didn't blame her for not liking her uncle. He was really weird. I couldn't imagine any one of my eight uncles talking to me like that.

We rode to the park and collapsed on the grass, breathing hard. After a bit, I sat up and folded my arms around my knees. Lucinda remained still, one arm resting across her eyes.

"How long is your Uncle Al going to stay with you?" I asked.

"He's not my uncle." Lucinda kept her eyes covered.

"But he said he's your Uncle Al."

Lucinda sat up and glared at me.

"He's not my uncle! He's just some guy my mom..." She bit her lip and looked down, then reached out and grasped my wrist. "You have to promise, cross your heart and hope to die, that you won't tell anyone! Not *anyone!*" I winced as Lucinda's fingernails dug into my skin. She dropped my hand. "Sorry," she murmured.

"I promise. Whatever you tell me, I promise not to tell."

Lucinda took a deep breath and cleared her throat, but it was several moments before she spoke. "Al is sort of my mom's boyfriend right now. He's been living with us for several weeks."

"You mean he's renting a room?"

"No, I mean he's living with us." She looked down, and her voice got very soft, almost a whisper. "He sleeps with my mom—you know—*sleeps* with her. He pays her every week, but not for a room. *I hate it! I hate him! Sometimes I hate her, too!*" Anger made her cheeks red, and her beautiful turquoise eyes filled with tears.

"But, Lucinda, they aren't married," I reasoned. Lucinda looked at me with disbelief and the hint of a smile.

"You really are a baby sometimes, aren't you?" She shook her head. "My mom sleeps with guys, Sissy, lots of guys, for the money. Do you understand? Don't you know anything?"

"Oh," I whispered, and I blushed with embarrassment at my ignorance. The memory of what I had seen through Cora Parker's window, a few years back, rushed into my mind; and I finally understood.

"My mom makes me call the men 'uncle', but no one's fooled. I see how people look at her and the way they look at me. I'm going to leave as soon as I'm sixteen. My life's going to be different when I grow up."

"Is Al mean to you?" I asked. Lucinda hesitated.

"I suppose he isn't really mean," she said, "but he looks at me funny; and he's always trying to touch me, when my mom isn't there.

He makes my skin crawl. It wasn't so bad when Mom was working days, but all this week she's been gone until nearly midnight. So I stay out somewhere, until just before it's time for her come home."

"Where do you go?"

"Oh, just around. I ride my bike all over town. I stayed in the library one night until it closed. Last night I went to the Sweet Shoppe, and Joe Bob was there. He bought us milkshakes, and we took a long time to finish them."

"You were at the Sweet Shoppe with *Joe Bob Brady*?"

"Yes, I was. He's a nice boy, Sissy."

I shook my head. Lucinda's situation just kept getting harder and harder to comprehend. As I looked at her, she seemed much older and wiser than anyone our age should be. I felt so dumb.

"You could stay overnight with me," I offered.

"Would your mom let me?"

"Sure, she would. I heard her tell Mrs. Lewis that you're always welcome in our house."

"Why would your mom tell her that?"

I shrugged.

"I guess because she really likes you, Lucinda."

"She wouldn't let you be my friend, if she knew about my mom." Lucinda lay back on the grass and folded both arms across her eyes. She looked so sad.

"Your mom is really pretty," I offered, "and she's nice, and funny sometimes."

"I wish she looked and dressed like *your* mother," Lucinda said. "Your mom always smells clean, not like heavy perfume; and she wears nice clothes." I blinked and thought about my mother. There was nothing unusual about her. She was average height, not skinny, not fat, with light brown hair and blue eyes. The only make-up she wore was a little face powder and a soft rose lipstick, on special occasions. She just looked like—Mom. A warm sense of security enveloped me. I couldn't have put it into words, but I knew that in my mother I possessed something that Lucinda had never known; and I was humbled.

Several days passed; and Lucinda seemed her old self, funny and relaxed and easy to be with again. She and I had two or three days with no hint of the presence of Joe Bob. One Sunday afternoon, we met in the park, where we turned cartwheels and summersaults and did splits, like the cheerleaders from our school.

"You're really good at this, Lucinda. I bet you could make cheerleader, if you'd try out."

"No, I couldn't. There's no use trying."

"But there is! You're much better at cartwheels and flips than anyone on the squad now. Why don't you try out?"

"Sissy, grow up! The teachers would never let me be a part of that. I'm still the new girl, the Okie they really don't want in their nice little group. And I don't want to be a silly, stupid cheerleader. What good do they do anyway? Just jump up and down and yell and look really dumb. No, thank you." In spite of her denials, I had the feeling that Lucinda would have been overjoyed to be a cheerleader for the eighth grade football and basketball teams. She pulled a handful of grass and tossed it at me. She giggled as I sputtered and brushed it away.

"What on earth is that?"

I looked where she pointed. A battered gray bus, covered with patches of rust, limped along the edge of the park and came to a wheezing halt. Steam rose from beneath the hood. We watched as the side door opened, and a big Negro man climbed wearily down the steps and threw open the hood of the bus. Billows of steam gushed from the engine, and the man drew back. He removed the brown felt hat he wore, pulled a handkerchief from his back pocket, and wiped his face.

"What's wrong with it, Daddy?" A little girl hopped down the bus steps, followed by three more girls, stair-steps themselves in size and age, and all with spiky little braids ending in different colored ribbons.

"It's prob'ly the water pump." The man waved at the billowing steam with his handkerchief. A tall, brown-skinned woman stepped laboriously from the bus. Obviously in the latter stage of pregnancy, she looked as if the slightest movement was a great effort for her.

Lucinda and I stared openly, as others came from the bus: two teen-aged boys, tall and lanky, wearing tee shirts and cut-off jeans with long dangling threads; a young woman, who led a little boy, about three years old, followed by a young man I assumed was the little boy's father; an older couple with gray hair and bent shoulders, who leaned heavily on each other; and the last person off the bus was a girl, who looked close to our age.

The girl stood on the bottom step and gazed at her surroundings, her dark eyes lingering on us for several moments before she stepped down. She wore a white tee shirt and red pedal pushers, and her hair was short and very curly. She moved among the others, not talking to anyone, and finally strolled toward the water fountain, not far from us. She stopped, and without looking at us, asked a question.

"Is it alright if I git a drink here?"

Lucinda and I looked at each other. Why wouldn't it be all right?

"Sure." I answered when Lucinda did not. We watched as the girl bent and drank for a long time from the fountain.

"Thanks," she said. I didn't understand. Why would she thank us?

"What's wrong with the bus?" Lucinda asked. The girl shook her head.

"I don't know. It just started sputterin', so Daddy turned off the highway back there," she waved; "and then all that steam started comin' up, and he turned in the park here." She shifted from one bare foot to the other. "We're goin' to Chicago to a funeral."

"Where are you from?" Lucinda stood up and strolled toward the girl. I followed.

"Alabama. We left home late last night. Had to stop a lot cause a' Granny. She ain't feelin' too good."

Lucinda sat down on top of the picnic table, beside the fountain. I sat on the bench below her and patted the board.

"Come sit down," I said. "I'm Sissy and this is Lucinda."

"My name is Mary Grace. Mary Grace Foster." She waved her hand toward the bus. "That's all my family."

"Mary Grace, don't you be botherin' them girls, now." The driver called to her. "You mind yourself and who you am."

"Yessuh. That's my daddy," said Mary Grace. "He sure is tired. I better see to the young'uns. My mama is expectin' again, and she don't feel good. I cain't sit down, but I thank you for bein' so nice."

Lucinda and I watched, while Mary Grace Foster gathered the three little girls and sat down with them on the grass. She started a clapping game, and the sounds of "Peas porridge hot, peas porridge cold, Peas porridge in the pot, nine days old" rang through the park along with the happy giggles of small children.

The driver took a wallet from his back pocket and counted carefully through it. He withdrew some bills and handed them to the two older boys. They talked quietly together for a moment; and then Mary Grace's father turned, and looked at Lucinda and me. He held his hat in front of him with both hands and approached us slowly, hesitantly.

"Howdy, young misses," he said. "I'm right sorry to bother you, but we was wonderin' if they's a store open anywhere close by. We need to git some milk for the young'uns and another thing or two."

"There's a little grocery store on the highway, about a block that way." I pointed.

"Thank you, Ma'am." He turned away.

"What's wrong with your bus?"

"It looks like a water hose done busted. I doubt that there's a garage open today, bein' Sunday and all."

"What will you do if you can't get it fixed?" Lucinda asked.

"Well, I 'spec we'll just stay right here in the park. Don't rightly know what else we kin do." He pointed to the two toilets on the south side of the park. "You s'pose we kin use them?" Lucinda and I looked at each other.

"It's a public park," I answered. "Anybody can use them." It would have to be a last resort, I thought. I wouldn't go near them. He inclined his head in a polite nod.

"I thank you." There was a quiet dignity about Mr. Foster. His chest was thick and his shoulders broad, but "gentle" was the word that came to mind, as I watched him. His hair, glossy black and combed back in deep waves from his forehead, had wings of gray at the temples. His black eyes were heavy-lidded and puffy underneath, as if he had had little sleep. He gave a scrap of paper to the two boys and sent them toward Lyon's market, the only store open on Sunday afternoon in Redbud Grove.

"Don't dawdle," he called to them and went back to the bus.

"Come on." I tapped Lucinda's arm, and she followed me.

It was the usual, uneventful Sunday afternoon at my house. Dad lay half-asleep on the couch, but he could hear every play of the baseball game on the radio. Bethy slept on the living room floor, coloring book at her head and a crayon still held loosely in her hand. Buddy had gone to a friend's house and would not come home until suppertime. Mom sat at the kitchen table, leafing through magazines and clipping recipes.

Lucinda and I told her about the people with the broken-down bus. I knew what she would do. Before we finished our story, Mom began squeezing lemons and measuring sugar; and within a short time, she had made enough lemonade to fill her big three-gallon soup pot. We emptied the ice trays into the lemonade. Lucinda and I carried the big pot to the park and set it upon a picnic table. I approached the group of hot, weary people, unsure just how to invite them to take the cold drink my mother had prepared.

Mary Grace made it easy. She met me halfway, and I issued the invitation to her. She smiled, a big, warm grin that revealed beautiful teeth.

"Daddy, Sissy's mama made a big ole pot a' lemonade for us. Bring the cups."

Soon the whole group stood or sat around the table, while Lucinda and I filled cup after cup for them. The children were polite and the adults, appreciative. When the two boys arrived carrying small bags of items from Lyons store, they took the lemonade, murmuring quiet thanks without looking at Lucinda or me.

"Daddy, look." The words were spoken so quietly that I barely heard them. One of the boys briefly inclined his head toward the street. I looked, too. Sheriff Pat Murphy had driven up in the police car and parked a short distance from the bus. He ambled slowly toward us, examining the bus as he came.

"Hi, Sheriff," I called. "Come have some lemonade. There's still plenty."

"Hi, Sissy, Lucinda." Pat took off his hat and scratched his cheek near his mouth. "What seems to be the trouble?" he asked Mary Grace's father.

"Well, suh, I think the water hose is busted," he said. "Don't seem to be any place open where we can git one 'til mornin'. Looks like we'll havta stay here in the park 'til then, if it's alright with y'all." Pat looked at the ground and then up at the dark faces surrounding him.

"That won't be necessary," he said. "I'll find someone to help you. Sissy, you and Lucinda go on back to your house now."

"We're still pouring lemonade," I said. "My mom made this big pot full and..."

"Sissy, take the pot and go home. Now." I looked at him. He didn't sound like the Pat Murphy I knew. He sounded like a grown-up, who had to be obeyed. I looked at him and opened my mouth to argue; but his eyes narrowed, and he put his hands on his hips. Sullenly, I spoke to Lucinda.

"Come on, Lucinda." Defiantly, I stopped long enough to refill cups, as we passed those nearest to us. I risked one accusatory glance over my shoulder at the sheriff, who stared back at me with no change of expression. "Who does he think he is?" I whispered.

"He thinks he's the sheriff, Sissy." Lucinda whispered back.

Within an hour the sheriff came back to the park, followed by Leroy Burton in his tow truck. Leroy owned Burton's Garage, which was never open on Sundays; but apparently he opened it for the sheriff. Leroy climbed onto the front bumper of the bus, and in no time had installed a new hose and water pump. We watched from the kitchen window, as Mary Grace and her family got back on the bus. It started without hesitation, and slowly pulled onto the street and disappeared toward the highway.

Sheriff Murphy got into his car, but he left the door open. He sat with one foot resting on the grass for a long time before he pulled his leg inside and closed the door. He folded his arms across the steering wheel and rested his head upon his arms.

"What do you suppose is wrong with him?" I asked Lucinda, who shrugged and dipped a glass into the remaining lemonade.

"Who knows? Who cares? He wasn't very friendly to those people, and he sure wasn't nice to you." I joined her at the kitchen table.

"But he usually is. I've always liked Sheriff Murphy."

"Maybe he's just tired." My mother filled a glass and sat down with us. "Someone must have called him. I'm sure this is his day off, and he likes to listen to the baseball games, almost as much as your dad. Maybe Pat's listening to the game in the car." We could hear the radio in the living room, but now my dad was sound asleep. We heard the sheriff's car door slam; and a few seconds later, there was a knock at the back door.

"Still got some of that lemonade?" The sheriff called through the screen.

"Come in, Pat," Mom called. Lucinda and I exchanged glances, and I was sure that I was in trouble for being less than respectful to the sheriff in the park. Mom filled another glass with ice and invited Pat to sit down. Dad snoozed on in the living room.

Pat took a long drink, before he turned his soft brown eyes upon me.

"I'm sorry I was short with you, Sissy, and you, Lucinda. But you girls really shouldn't have been in the park with those people."

"Wait a minute, Pat. I knew they were there, and I was watching. I sent them back with the lemonade, and they weren't in danger." Mom sounded a little irate. Pat took another drink.

"It wasn't the girls I was worried about, Jackie. I have no doubt that they were safe."

"Then what?" My mother demanded. Pat took a deep breath.

"You've lived here for, what, six or seven years?" he asked. Mom nodded.

"I got a phone call from one of your neighbors that a busload of coloreds were camped in the park, and that two white girls were with them. I was also told that it was my duty to enforce the 'sundown ordinance', or someone was going to get hurt." Mom looked confused.

"What ordinance is that?" she asked.

"Several years ago, a law was passed in Redbud Grove that all undesirable or vagrant type people were required to be out of the city limits before sundown; specifically, it names all coloreds and Mexicans and migrant workers, such as the broom corn itinerates." My mother's mouth dropped open.

"You can't be serious." Her voice was not much above a whisper.

"Dead serious, Jackie. I'm sure you can guess which neighbor called me."

"Hal?" The sheriff nodded.

"He's a hothead, and it doesn't take much to set him off. You remember what he was like with Frank Thompson, when Sissy was hurt?" Mom nodded. "I'm sure that he watched every move in the park. I had to get the girls out of there before Hal decided that he'd open-fire on the Negroes. Just the coloreds being there made him angry, and seeing you two girls with them made him furious."

"Pat, this is central Illinois, not Mississippi; and the Civil War ended a long time ago. This is a nice little town, and people are friendly and helpful…"

"And prejudiced, Jackie. That's why the ordinance was passed. People are afraid of what they don't understand, and there are more people in this town like Hal Norris than you might think. I did the only thing I could this afternoon. I don't think a colored person has ever stayed overnight in Redbud Grove. As far as I know, there're no klan members here; but that doesn't mean we don't have our share of sympathizers. A lot of people have come here from the southern states, even before the oil boom; and old traditions are hard to let go."

I bit my lip. Lucinda looked at the tabletop.

"Sissy?" I looked at Sheriff Pat Murphy, my friend. He smiled at me, but his eyes were sad. "Do you understand?" I nodded and so did Lucinda.

"But it's not fair, Sheriff; and it's not right. I have never spoken to a colored person before this afternoon, but I wasn't afraid of them. They were just people driving to a funeral in Chicago. They couldn't help it if their bus broke down here. It's just not *right*!"

"No, Sissy, I can't say that it's right; but that's the way it is."

Pat stood up and shook hands with my mother. He touched my head briefly as he passed behind me. "I'm going home." He glanced into the living room, where my dad still slept. "Looks like he's enjoying the ballgame." Mom smiled and walked the sheriff to the door.

"Thanks, Pat."

"You know, most of the time I like my job," he said. "But sometimes it's a real pain in the…rear." He gave a small salute and walked to his car. Before the night was over, Sheriff Murphy wished he had chosen just about any occupation other than law enforcement.

When Dad woke up, we told him what had happened in the park; and he wanted to know why no one had wakened him.

"What good would that have done?" Mom asked. "Besides, you were sleeping like a little baby with that ballgame in your ear." Dad just grunted and went to the garage to get his golf clubs.

"You girls want to hit some balls with me in the park?" Dad called from the backyard. Lucinda and I looked at each other. Simultaneously, we shook our heads. We'd had enough of the park for one day.

"Mom, is it okay if Lucinda and I go to the show?" It was three forty-five and the movie started at four. If we hurried, we could make it just in time for the cartoon.

"I suppose so," my mother answered. She took three quarters from her mad-money cup in the cabinet. "Here's enough for the two of you to go to the show and get a couple of Cokes."

"Thanks, Mom."

The movie wasn't all that great. It was a silly story about two guys trying to get to Jamaica, where one of them had buried a lot of money. Three other guys, who also wanted the money, kept trying to kill the first two. At least it was cool in the theatre, and the Jamaican music and scenery were nice.

After the movie, Lucinda and I made arrangements to meet the next day. Her mother had the weekend off from work, so Lucinda felt safe. She reassured me that she would come to my house, if Al said or did anything to make her uneasy.

I got home just in time to hit a couple of golf balls across the park. Dad and Buddy had been taking turns driving and putting on the little green Dad had marked off on the grass. It was Buddy's job to return the bag of clubs in the garage, the one chore he didn't complain about, as he did most others. Dad had scolded him several times for leaving an iron outside overnight; but that didn't keep Buddy from slipping one out now and then. He always intended to put it back.

I had my bath early that evening. It was hot and muggy, like early August nights can be in the Midwest. Heat lightning flashed in the distant skies, but there was no thunder or real threat of rain. I stretched out on my bed and positioned the small table fan to blow directly on me. The portable radio, which I had received the previous Christmas, was tuned to a popular music station; and Nat King Cole sang soulfully to Mona Lisa. I dozed.

A noise at the attic window woke me. I opened my eyes to darkness. My mother had turned off the light and the radio; but the fan was still blowing, and the room was much cooler. The door to Buddy's room was closed. I could hear his fan running. The rest of the house was quiet. I sat up and looked out the window. Lucinda stood on the front sidewalk, with her arm raised, preparing to toss another pebble, when she saw me and motioned for me to come down.

Silently I slipped downstairs and went out the back, being careful to close the screened door without a sound. The dewy grass was cool to my bare feet. Lucinda joined me at the side of the house, and we crept across the lane to the park.

"What are you doing here so late?" I whispered. "Where did you leave your bike?"

"I walked," Lucinda murmured. I looked at her feet. She was barefooted, like me.

"With no shoes?" I forgot to whisper.

"Shhhh. Someone will hear you." I looked at her more closely, and what I saw scared me. She was crying. Her pajama top was torn and hung by one strap. I took her chin in my hand and lifted her face, staring at the cut on one cheek, visible even in the faint light from the street lamp.

"Lucinda, what happened to you?"

"Al hit me. His ring cut my face." Her voice was muffled. It looked like her lip was swollen, too.

"What? Why? What happened!" Lucinda shook her head.

"Someone got sick, so they called Mom to work. Al drove her in and said that he wouldn't be back for awhile, that he was going to a bar with some friends." Lucinda's voice broke and she sobbed quietly for a moment. "But he lied. All the bars are closed on Sundays. I thought I had time to take a bath and lock myself in my room, or maybe come here before he got back. But when I came out of the bathroom he was sitting on the couch, waiting for me. Sissy, he...he..." Lucinda covered her face with both hands and sobbed. I put my arms around her.

"Let's go get my mom."

"No! No, I can't let anyone see me! They'll blame me!"

"But you're hurt! Lucinda, did he, um, you know, did he...?"

"You mean did he rape me? No, but he would have! He grabbed me and tore my clothes and threw me down on the couch and said that he was going to show me how to be a woman and how to please a man and that I was going to like it and that I was prettier than my mother and for me to be still and not to scream but I did and he put his hand over my mouth and I couldn't breathe and I bit him and that's when he hit me…" Lucinda drew in a deep breath, then another. "…and I slipped out from under him and ran and he chased me to the street and I kept running and hid in the bushes at Mrs. Murphy's house."

"You ran all the way to Mrs. Murphy's?" At any other time, the thought of Lucinda in Mrs. Murphy's yard would have made me laugh.

"I saw Al's car go by a couple of times, and then he turned toward Route Forty-five. He was driving really fast. I think maybe he left, I mean for good. There's no way my mom will let him stay now." Lucinda's chin lifted and she seemed calmer. "If Al is gone, this was almost worth it." She touched the cut on her cheek and winced.

"Why don't you come in with me, and we'll get you cleaned up and put something on your face," I suggested. Lucinda shook her head.

"No, we'd wake your mom. Can I borrow a shirt and maybe some shoes to go home?"

"Are you sure Al is gone? What if he comes back before your mom gets home?"

"I'll be careful. I won't go in if he's there."

"Ok, but I still think…"

"I'll be all right, Sissy."

We tiptoed quietly to my house; but as we rounded the corner to the kitchen door, I tripped on something, and barely stopped the yelp that formed in my mouth. I bent down to rub my toe and found one of Dad's golf clubs, compliments of Buddy, in the wet grass. I picked it up and leaned it against the house, promising myself the satisfaction of doing great bodily harm to my brother the next day.

Holding my breath, I inched my way upstairs, grabbed a blouse and a pair of sandals for Lucinda, and slipped back down. She was waiting at the kitchen door. She took the items from my hands as I opened the screen.

"Don't come out," she whispered. "I'll be fine. You go on back to bed, before your mom catches you."

I nodded and waved silently. When I was halfway up the stairs, Mom called.

"Sissy? What are you doing?"

I froze and swallowed hard.

"Just going to the bathroom, Mom."

"OK, Honey. Goodnight."

Sleep was a long time coming. I kept looking out the window, half expecting to see Lucinda again. I finally dozed...

It is Friday afternoon.

I am walking alone, not slowly, not fast, thinking about the day.

My arms swing freely, unencumbered by books, because Mrs. Sylvester has given no homework today. I think about the evening ahead. I can play outdoors after supper or listen to the radio, or read. I am happy.

I skip a few paces just because it feels good. I like the way the muscles bunch in my legs and the sound my shoes make on the brick walks. A warm autumn breeze rustles through the brilliant oak and maple trees that line the street. It stirs my long blond hair, and I toss the wispy stands away from my face.

In front of Mrs. Montgomery's house, a brown van is parked beside the curb. It faces me, and I wonder who is inside. On the front of the van is a white emblem, a circle with the letters V and W inside. I glance through the open window and see a man looking at a map, spread across the steering wheel. He does not look at me.

Down the next block I see Mr. Arnold, the old man who walks his dog, McDuff, every afternoon. I love McDuff. I quicken my steps, eager to wrap my arms around the gentle dog and let him wash my face with Irish setter kisses.

I am almost past the van, when I hear a door open. I stop and turn around, curious to see who else is inside.

"Hey, Sweet Little Girl." The voice is musical, unlike any I have ever heard before. There are three men sitting inside the open door. They are looking at me. The man who called to me has black skin, and he is smiling. His hair is long and curly, falling along each side of his face onto his shoulders. He beckons.

"Come, Little Sweetheart. Come to Jamaica Jack. He will make you so-o-o-o happy." When he says his name, the sounds are strange, seductive, like Zsamaica Zsack.

I stare at him, unable to look away from his twinkling, smiling black eyes. I have never seen a black man up close before. He is beautiful. Slowly he unfolds himself from the van. He is very tall and slender. He is dressed in black and a long, white scarf hangs loosely around his neck.

"Yes-s-s, yes-s-s," he says. His voice is lilting, soft, seductive. "Jamaica Jack loves your pretty blond hair. Like gold, it is, like honey in the sunshine. Jamaica Jack thinks it will feel like silk." He is moving slowly toward me. I take a step away. The other two men are standing and seem much closer to me when I look at them.

One has a brown beard and a long braid hanging down the front of his shirt. He is very big. The other is bald, but is not old. I am confused. I am beginning to be frightened.

"Look at me, Pretty Girl, look only at Jamaica Jack." The beautiful black man is much closer to me. His white teeth flash in a reassuring smile. "You come with him. He will show you wonderful things, yes-s-s-s. Come, Pretty Girl." He stretches his arms, extending an open hand, reaching for me.

Inside my head, I hear my mother's voice. Run! Run! Don't look at him! Run! Adrenalin surges through my body in a painful rush. I lift my feet to run away.

"Grab her!" The growling voice from the van is angry.

My heart is pounding. Ahead I see McDuff and Mr. Arnold. I want to go to them, but my movements are slow and heavy. My feet seem stuck to the sidewalk. I am moving, but going nowhere. I hear the black man's steps right behind me. I am filled with terror.

McDuff is running toward me. I see his shiny coat, rippling in the sunlight; and he is mad. It shows in the force of his lunges. I hear the growl in his throat, as he comes nearer. I cannot move. My legs are leaden, useless sticks. My heart is beating so hard I think it is going to suffocate me. A hand closes around my upper arm.

I look up and over my shoulder into the face of Jamaica Jack. His hands are like steel claws around my arms, as he drags me toward the van. His black, black eyes glitter with the cold hardness of broken ebony glass. There is a long, thin scar beside his mouth. He is no longer beautiful. His is the face of a nightmare.

I stare into his eyes. His face is no longer black. It is the face of Uncle Al, and I am no longer myself. I am Lucinda Barnes and Lucinda is me, but we are one person.

I look back at McDuff. He is straining to reach me, but he is moving in slow motion; and Jack/Uncle Al is lifting me into the van, where other arms grab me.

I call for McDuff to hurry, to save me; but no sound comes from my mouth. He is almost here. Hurry, McDuff, hurry! Hurry!

The van door slams shut, with the solid thud of finality; and I know that I am lost. There is the sound of a motor running and the pressure of fingers on my lips, replaced by the white scarf wound tightly around my head; and the ends are stuffed into my mouth. Brutal hands pull at me and I hear cloth rip.

Silently I scream and scream...

"Mom! Mommy-y-y-y-y-!"

I sat up. The sheet was twisted around me, and I struggled to be free of it. My pajamas were wet with perspiration, and my hair clung to my neck in sweaty strands.

"Sissy? Sissy, what is it?" My dad came running up the stairs, followed closely by my mother.

"Sissy, Honey, what's wrong?" Dad turned the light on and peered into every corner of the attic, even the unfinished part, while Mom sat beside me and pulled me into her arms. Buddy's door flew open. With wide eyes, he stared at us.

"What happened?" His voice squeaked.

"Mom, it was awful! I couldn't get away!"

"Sh-h-h-h, Sissy, it was only a dream, Honey, only a nightmare."

"But it was so real! There was a colored man and a bald man and McDuff and Uncle Al and I was Lucinda and..."

"Sissy, calm down now. It was just a bad dream." Dad's steady voice fell onto my terror like a soft blanket, and the images from the dream began to fade. While Dad went downstairs, Mom brought fresh pajamas from a drawer and helped me change out of the sweat-soaked clothing.

"Mom, can I get in bed with Bethy? I won't wake her up." Mom smiled.

"Sure, Honey, come on downstairs. You need clean sheets anyway. Buddy, are you okay up here by yourself?"

My brother nodded. "Yeah, I'll be fine." We started down the stairs. "Um, Mom? Can we leave the stair lights on?"

"We can," she answered him. There was a smile in her voice.

So I climbed into bed with my six-year-old sister and wrapped my arms around her little body, drawing comfort from her closeness. When I closed my eyes, the grinning face of terror was still there; but it's name was not Jamaica Jack—it was Uncle Al who lived in Lucinda's house—Uncle Al, who was not an uncle.

Morning brought sunshine and banished my nightmare. Bethy was delighted to find me in her bed. I rewarded her with a story, one I had read in a Jack and Jill magazine, about a little oilcan, who fixed every squeak he heard, even a squeaky mouse, making the mouse go glug-glug instead of squeak-squeak. Bethy never tired of it, and that morning I embellished it dramatically to reward her joy in my presence.

We finished breakfast, which was always cereal in the summer; I washed the dishes while Bethy dried them, a task she had only recently undertaken and one she still enjoyed. Occasionally I spattered her with water, which made us both giggle. Sometimes, having a little sister was not so bad.

It was unusual for the sheriff to come to our house on a Monday morning. I peered out the kitchen window in time to see him get out of his car. He was wearing his uniform, and his face looked grim. Mom met him at the front door. He spoke without preamble.

"Jackie, I need to talk to Sissy."

My mind scurried around, wondering what misdeed I had done to merit another visit from Pat Murphy so soon. I couldn't think of a thing. I dried my hands and went into the living room. The sheriff took off his hat and nodded to me.

"Sissy, have you seen Lucinda Barnes since yesterday afternoon?" he asked. I just looked at him, uncertain what to say. If Lucinda were in trouble, I didn't want to add to it.

"What's wrong, Pat?" My mother's voice was very quiet.

"There's no easy way to say this, Jackie. Joe Bob Brady called me to the Barnes' house early this morning. He says he was passing by, that he sometimes goes for walks down by the river. He says he heard someone in the house, screaming; so he went up on the porch and looked through the screened door, where he saw Mrs. Barnes struggling with someone. That person hit Mrs. Barnes with a club or a stick and then ran out the back. Joe Bob says he went inside and found Mrs. Barnes, dying on the floor, and Al Pitts, dead beside the couch. There was no sign of Lucinda."

Pat looked at me. "Have you seen her, Sissy?" I shook my head, without meeting his eyes. "What about Joe Bob, Sissy? Why would he be at the Barnes' house, at two o'clock in the morning?"

"I think he does go for walks along the river. Lucinda told me she's seen him out there lots of time. He likes Lucinda," I said, "and he wouldn't hurt anyone, especially Lucinda."

"There's some talk about dragging the river, if she doesn't turn up soon."

Nausea swept over me like a cold, prairie wind. I ran from the living room into the bathroom, and closed the door. I sat on the edge of the tub and put my head between my knees, like my mother had always told me. It didn't help. Mom came in, as I was leaning over the stool. She ran cold water over a washcloth and gently wiped my face.

"Are you all right now?" Her voice was very gentle, but her eyes were peering into my face with the sharpness of a mother who knows her child. I nodded. "Sissy, is there anything you want to tell me?" I looked at the familiar, loving face of my mom; and for the first time, I was aware of gratitude to whatever chance of nature had made her mine. And I lied to her.

"No." She opened the door and waited for me to precede her.

"Mom?"

"What, Honey?"

"Does God really care about people? I mean, why doesn't He stop bad things from happening?" Mom silently looked at me for a long moment.

"Sissy, don't you remember what the verse in the Bible says, about how God watches even the little sparrow and knows when it falls?"

"But, Mom?"

"Yes?"

"The sparrow still falls."

My mother put her arms around me and held me tightly.

"Come on, Sweetie. Pat's waiting for us."

The sheriff stood where we had left him. He extended one hand toward me, in supplication, I think, before he let it drop to his side.

"I'm sorry, Sissy," he said. "It's an awful thing." He turned toward the door, put on his hat, turned back. "Hal Norris is already pointing fingers at those two colored boys who were here yesterday. His notion is that they went after Lucinda, that one of them took her, while the other one fought with her mother and then attacked Pitts, when he came in."

"For goodness sake, Pat! They were just kids! And they were gone long before any of this happened!" Mom sounded furious. Pat shook his head.

"I'm not saying it's even possible, Jackie. I'm just telling you what Hal is spreading around, so don't be surprised when you hear it." He looked at me. "And if you hear from Lucinda, or can think of *anything* to help find her, Sissy, you call me." I met his eyes before quickly looking away. "*Anything*, Sissy." I nodded.

The day passed in a blurred haze of fear and dread. I didn't know what to do. I couldn't really believe that Lucinda was dead, as many townspeople were beginning to think; but I had no idea where she would go, besides my house. There was just no sign of her.

Hal Norris came by that evening, and my dad went outside to talk to him. I watched from my bedroom window, as Mr. Norris waved his arms and paced back and forth in front of Dad. I couldn't hear everything, but some of what Mr. Norris said made me cringe.

"I tell you it was those damned *niggers* that sneaked back into town and killed that woman and her boyfriend when they tried to keep 'em from taking that girl! Now that ain't much of a loss, but I hate what they've done to that girl; and I bet they killed her after they got done with her! I *knew* there'd be trouble when I saw Sissy and that Barnes girl in the park with those black bastards! I should have—!"

"That's enough, Hal! Whoever killed Mrs. Barnes and her friend was not among the people in the park. They were gone hours before it happened." Dad put his hand on Mr. Norris's shoulder and pointed him in the direction of his own home.

Long after the house was quiet that night, I slipped downstairs. The linoleum on the kitchen floor felt cool and smooth to my bare feet. I paced aimlessly from the kitchen to the living room and back again, worrying about Lucinda and wondering who had killed her mother and Al Pitts. I knew that it couldn't have been Joe Bob Brady.

I looked out the window of the kitchen door, which normally was left open on hot summer nights, to invite any stray cool breeze through the locked screen door. Tonight the other door was locked.

I thought about the previous day and night, about the busload of colored people from Alabama, about the sadness in the sheriff's eyes after they left, about what Al Pitts had done to Lucinda, about trying to convince her to stay with me, about stumbling on the golf club— the golf club that I had forgotten to tell Buddy to put away.

Carefully, I opened the kitchen door and slipped outside. It was only a few feet to the corner of the house, where I had left the club. I could put it back in the bag inside the garage, and Dad would never know it had been left out for so long. Dad loved those clubs. I was carrying around enough guilt already, without having him heap more onto my head.

The club was gone. I felt along the grass, several yards around the corner of the house; but the club was not there. Buddy or Dad must have moved it, without saying anything. Just to be sure, I went into the garage to count the clubs in the bag. The streetlight on the corner of the park illuminated the garage enough to keep me from stumbling. The old quilt that covered the bag was gone, but all the clubs were there. Buddy probably forgot to re-cover the bag, but that was a minor thing. I turned toward the door.

A shadow moved in the corner. It felt like my heart jumped into my throat, and for a moment I couldn't breathe. I took a slow step, and the shadow moved again. I poised for flight. Thoughts of the nightmare chilled me.

"Sissy. Sissy, help me."

The voice was barely a whisper, but I knew whose it was.

"Lucinda?"

"Sissy, help me."

I hurried to the corner, where the shadow had moved, and found Lucinda, wrapped in the old quilt from the golf bag. She was crouched behind a row of heavy boxes stacked head-high, and she had pulled my bicycle across the space where she was hiding. I moved the bike and took her hand.

"Come on, Lucinda. Let's go inside. Mom and Dad will help you." I expected her to protest, but she did not. She took my hand and let me lead her from the garage, into the house; but she kept the quilt wrapped around her body. I turned on the light above the sink, pulled out a chair beside the kitchen table, and helped her sit down.

"Wait here, Lucinda. I'll get Mom." Lucinda nodded her head. I hurried into my parents' room and shook my mother. "Mom, wake up. Lucinda's here." My mother didn't even ask what I was talking about. She was fully awake and on her feet immediately, grabbed her robe and was in the kitchen before she finished tying the belt.

"Oh, Lucinda." Mom knelt beside the chair and took Lucinda into her arms. I watched as Lucinda buried her head in my mom's shoulder and wept. Great, heaving sobs shook her body; and I felt my own tears run down my cheeks. Lucinda looked terrible. Her face was spattered with blood, and the quilt was bloody in patches where it touched her body. Lucinda's shoulders were bare above the quilt. I couldn't tell if she wore any clothing beneath the cover.

Dad came into the kitchen. He was never given to swearing in front of his family; but words came from his mouth that, under any other circumstances, would have left him so frostbitten from my mother that he would never have thawed out. "I'll call Pat," he said.

The case was never solved.

It was decided that person or persons unknown had broken into the Barnes home, intent on burglarizing the place. Lucinda told the police she woke up and saw someone in her room. When she screamed, someone had attacked her, which had awakened her mother. When Mrs. Barnes appeared, the attacker had gone after her.

Al Pitts had then joined the fracas. Lucinda had run away and hidden among the thickets, along the riverbank, for a long time. Just before dawn, she had come to our house and had hidden in our garage. She was badly beaten and would have scars inside and out.

That coincided with Joe Bob Brady's story that he had come upon a man beating Al Pitts with a club of some kind. There was no reason to doubt either account, especially since several things were missing from the house. The only thing taken of real value, was the heavy gold ring that Al Pitts always wore, a ring with a coiled snake whose eyes were made of rubies.

People kept their doors locked for a long time. The sense of security and peace disappeared from the little town. An outside force of evil and violence had invaded the community of Redbud Grove, and it would never again be quite the same.

Lucinda went back to Oklahoma to live with her grandmother. I missed her.

In September I enrolled in the eighth grade. It was good to be busy and pick up the comforting routine with old friends. We discussed Lucinda at first, but gradually other events captured our interest; less and less, she was the main topic of conversation.

Joe Bob seemed different, older somehow. He had a new group of friends, boys who were in high school. He finally got glasses, with dark frames, that looked good on him; and his hair lay smoother. He combed it differently, too. Joe Bob Brady suddenly looked like James Dean, with glasses, and a nose just slightly crooked. He didn't tease any of the girls, either.

It was several weeks before Dad played golf again. One balmy Indian summer day in October, he brought the bag of clubs from the garage and emptied it, saying that he wanted to evict the mice that habitually took up residence in the bottom of the bag. He stood the clubs along the garage wall and turned the bag upside down. He was right. Several mice scattered in various directions, and something bounced off the sidewalk and skipped into the grass.

"What was that?" Dad asked. I knelt on the grass, expecting to find a rock or a bolt that had probably fallen into the bag from Dad's workbench. There was nothing.

"I can't find anything," I said. I stood up, and at that moment the sun glinted off something in the grass. I bent down again; and there, staring up at me, were the ruby eyes of the snake that still coiled atop the ring that had been taken from Al Pitts's finger.

"Find something?" Dad asked me. I stood up. I covered the ring with my foot and pressed down hard.

"Nope. Nothing."

After he left, I dug up the ring and washed the dirt from it in the bathroom. I took it to my room and studied it for a long time. There was only one person who could answer the questions I had. At morning recess the following Monday I told Joe Bob to meet me at the boat docks on the river after school. He nodded his head and asked no questions.

It was a beautiful day. The October sky was so blue it hurt my eyes to look at it. Ordinarily, I would have enjoyed the long walk through such spectacular colors as the trees were wearing. Most of the streets had at least a few redbud trees, which were all bright yellow. They made a brilliant statement against the multi-hued maple and oak trees.

As I approached the river, I couldn't help but admire the extensive grove of redbud trees that lined the far bank. The river ran slowly, and there was hardly a ripple to mar the perfect yellow reflection.

When I reached the docks, Joe Bob was sitting on a weather-beaten bench. I watched him for a moment before I approached. His arms were crossed loosely across his chest, and his long legs extended in front of him. He looked deceptively relaxed. Joe Bob stared across the river. I slipped my hand into my jacket pocket and clutched the heavy gold ring, then sat down beside him.

"What happened, Joe Bob?" I held out my closed fist and slowly opened my hand. "This was in my dad's golf bag. How did it get there?"

His face paled as he stared at the ring, resting in the palm of my hand. He looked up at me, and I saw what Lucinda had seen all along. Joe Bob was going to be a handsome man, was already well on the way. He snatched the ring from my hand and stood up. He threw the ring as hard as he could into the river, where it disappeared with a tiny plop.

"Why did you do that?" I demanded.

"Because it's an evil thing! That filthy creep cut Lucinda with that ring, and I hope he's rotting in hell!"

"What really happened at Lucinda's house that night?" I asked. Joe Bob looked down at me. He took a deep breath before he sat beside me.

"You know what happened."

"No, I don't. I only know what you and Lucinda *said* happened," I said.

"Mrs. Barnes was killed. Al Pitts was killed."

"Who killed them?" I whispered. He looked at me for what seemed like a long time before he answered.

"It was dark. I couldn't tell who it was."

"But you said..."

"Forget what I said, Sissy! Just leave it alone!" Joe Bob sounded really angry.

"But, Joe Bob..." Joe Bob grabbed my upper arms and shook me, once, twice, hard.

"Sissy, just go home and forget about it!"

"I can't," I wailed. "Lucinda came to me that night, after Al Pitts had beaten her up! If I had told my mom and dad, maybe none of this would have happened! But she didn't want me to tell, so I didn't! And now I've found that ring..." Joe Bob released me and leaned back on the bench. He sighed.

We sat in silence for a long time. I wanted life to be like it was before this ugliness happened. I wanted Lucinda and her mother to be in their little house beside the river, with no Al Pitts to make them miserable. I didn't want to know what I was afraid of knowing. Joe Bob gently touched my shoulder.

"You know there was nobody else in that house, Sissy. So it had to be either me, or Lucinda. Who do you want it to be?" His soft, southern voice could not blunt the hard truth.

I didn't answer him. My heart hurt inside my chest, hurt too much to cry. I shook my head, unable to say anything.

"Go home, Sissy; and we won't ever talk about this again. Okay?" I stood up and looked down at Joe Bob Brady. Was he a murderer or a hero? I didn't know, but I wasn't afraid of him. I did a very strange thing. I leaned down and kissed his cheek. I kissed Joe Bob Brady, and then I turned around and went home to my safe house, my wonderful parents, my little brother and sister, and my warm, cozy bed.

I didn't see or hear from Lucinda Barnes for nearly twenty-five years, but I thought about her.

I thought about her often.

#

Barbara Elliott Carpenter

VICTOR

The chains creaked, sending tiny vibrations through my fingers. I leaned back, pointed my toes skyward, and for a moment my body lay suspended, parallel with the earth, before the drag of gravity brought me swishing backward. The rush of warm, moist air threw my hair away from my face on the upward swing and tossed it forward on the falling arc.

Puffy white clouds chased each other in changing forms across an April sky so blue that it throbbed with intensity. The mournful call of doves and the cheery chirp of redbirds intermingled, while busy robins patrolled the grounds. Barn swallows flew in slow, sweeping patterns, catching warm currents, tossing careless melodies, as they dipped and soared. The air seemed to vibrate with life.

I was enchanted with the gentle shades of spring that touched the trees in the park with different hues: yellow-greens, so soft they were nearly white, rosy-lavender branch tips, lacy green leaves, so tiny and fragile they appeared to be floating upon the limbs. I drank deeply of the warm, moist air that was sweet with the newness of things just beginning, of buds, of blooms and of new grass.

The boy behind me pushed the swing higher and higher. I closed my eyes. I willed this moment to be burned into my mind, an eternal moment that I could take out and re-live when I was old, however ridiculous the thought of my aging seemed.

The boy stopped pushing and held onto the chains, slowing the movement and bringing me back to earth. He placed his hands on my waist. I sat silently on the swing, afraid to move, afraid that the boy would take his hands away, afraid that he would not. His touch melted through the cotton of my blouse and into my skin, drawing the scents, the colors, and the sounds around me into one glorious sensation.

Slowly I turned my head, and my cheek brushed the front of his shirt. The boy drew me backward, until we were face-level. His lips touched my skin, just below my jaw-line, as softly, as briefly, as butterfly wings; and then he let me go. The swing moved lazily back and forth. The boy walked away. I kept the swing barely moving, pushing against the ground with my toes, until I could no longer hear him.

Only then did I stand and half-turn, just enough to catch a brief glimpse of his white tee shirt, before he disappeared from view. I dream-walked toward my house, not knowing where else to go. My heart beat in a new way. The cadence seemed to say the boy's name. Victor. Victor. Victor.

I floated through the kitchen door and found Bethy at the table with her crayons and coloring book, her constant companions. "Look, Sissy. Did I do good?" I glanced at the page she offered for my approval.

"Um-hum." Satisfied, she continued carefully wielding her way within the lines. "Where's Mom?" I asked.

"Across the street. She took some cake to Mrs. Lula." I fell to earth rapidly. The jolt nearly took my breath. If my mother were across the street, she might have seen me in the park with Victor Delacorte. That wouldn't be a good thing! I hadn't seen her leave our house, but my mind hadn't been on anything but Victor.

I'd been at Sharon's earlier that Saturday afternoon. On the way home, I had noticed how lovely the park looked; and the swings had seemed to beckon me. It had been a long time since I'd swung on them—not since Lucinda had gone away the previous summer. No one else had been in the park, and I'd always liked solitude. It had felt good to push with my feet and pump the swing, gaining momentum, recapturing the simple pleasure that felt as good at the age of fourteen, as it had at the age of seven.

I hadn't heard Victor approach. He was just suddenly there.

"Want a push?" he'd asked.

I had nearly swallowed my tongue, before I could give an intelligent, near-adult answer.

"Uh, sure."

The whole thing had been over so quickly. Victor had appeared, he pushed me, he kissed me, and he left. I could almost make myself believe that it hadn't happened. I touched the spot on my throat where his lips had brushed so softly. Oh, yes. My fluttery stomach told me that Victor had not been a fantasy.

"I'm going up to my room," I told Bethy.

"Mom said for you to fold the towels in the basket."

Great. I wanted to sprawl on my bed and daydream romantic scenarios, and now I had to waste time in the washroom with a basket full of towels. How romantic was that?

"Who was pushing you on the swings this afternoon?"

I kept my head down and concentrated on my bowl of soup. Maybe if I pretended not to hear, Mom would not pursue the issue.

"Sissy?"

I looked up and tried to assume an air of surprise, as if I'd just heard her. I don't think she bought it.

"Who were you with in the park?"

"Who, me?"

Mom's lips tightened and her eyes narrowed.

"Oh, that was just a boy passing through the park. He gave me a push on the swing." I looked down at my soup and stirred it briskly.

"It looked like the Delacorte boy." Mom was not going to let it go. I didn't answer. "Sissy, *was* it the Delacorte boy?" I nodded.

"He was walking through the park, Mom, honest. He just walked up and asked if I wanted a push, and I said sure, so he pushed me, and then he went away." I could hear myself talking too fast.

"Is that the kid who was sent here from Chicago? The one living with the Butlers over on Walnut Street?" Dad asked. He refilled his glass with tea from the pitcher and fixed his eyes on me. I shrugged.

"I guess so." Supper was not going well for me. I swallowed a spoonful of Mom's vegetable soup. "May I be excused?" I started to rise.

"No, you may not." Dad sounded awfully calm. "How well do you know this boy?" he asked.

"I don't know him at all, Daddy. He's never even spoken to me, before today. Besides, he's in high school and runs around with older

208

kids." I was telling my father the truth. Dad pinned me with his steely-blue eyes. He pointed his spoon at me.

"You stay away from him, Sissy. He got into trouble in Chicago; and his parents sent him down here, to live with his aunt and uncle. You hear me, Girl." I nodded. Dad motioned with his head that I could leave the table. I went with as much dignity as was possible, while my brother grinned at me and my little sister stared at me with her mouth open. I didn't look at my mother.

I went upstairs to my room and shut the door harder than was necessary. I kicked off my shoes and flopped onto the bed. I hadn't done anything wrong! What was the matter with them? I lay on my stomach with my arms folded under my head and looked out the window, at the deepening lavender of the sky. My face flushed and grew warm at the vivid recollection of Victor's mouth on my skin. What would my mom and dad do if they knew about that? I would just have to make sure they didn't find out.

A few stars were visible. More appeared as I watched. The sky darkened quickly. It lost the faint streaks of rose and amethyst and gold. Darkness formed a velvety backdrop for the nightly display of diamonds. I sighed. It was Saturday night; and I would have loved being somewhere, anywhere, with my friends. No one had called me; and it was getting too late for me to call someone, except maybe Sharon.

Homework waited for me on my desk. I rolled off my bed and dropped sullenly onto the desk chair. I *felt* sullen. That was one of my mom's favorite warnings: "Don't you *sull up*, now!"

I didn't know what was wrong with my mother lately. It seemed that everything I did and everything I said upset her, for instance, my hair. Mom had always cut my hair in a short pageboy style, complete with bangs. The summer I was twelve, I had refused to let her cut it; and now, at fourteen, my hair was long enough to style into a ponytail. All the really glamorous movie stars wore their hair long, and the way their shiny tresses fell over their shoulders appealed to me. But my mother didn't like my long hair, and she repeatedly told me that I looked much better with it short.

For some reason I couldn't fathom, I no longer had the same freedom I had enjoyed. My mother insisted that I tell her where I was going, who I would be with, what we planned to do, and when I was coming home. Actually, she *told* me when I was coming home. It was beginning to be a real drag, but there seemed to be no way around it.

I skimmed through my Civics/History book and half-heartedly glanced down a page of assigned reading. Who cared when the Civil War ended? What did it matter where Lee surrendered to Grant? I slammed the book shut. If I didn't get out of this room and this house, I was going to go crazy! I went downstairs.

Sweet, I thought. Be sweet.

My mother stood at the sink. Great. Tonight was my turn to clean up, and Mom had nearly finished the job. I picked up a dishtowel and began to dry the dishes she had placed in the drainer.

"I'm sorry, Mom. I lost track of time. I'll do double-duty tomorrow." Mom smiled at me, but said nothing. She wiped down the sink and folded the dishrag over the rack inside the cabinet door. "Mom, is it okay if I go up to the Sweet Shoppe for an hour or so? I thought I might call Sharon and see if she can go."

"Sorry, Sissy. Dad and I are going to the Simpson's to play cards this evening. I need you to stay with Bethy."

"Why can't Buddy watch her? I'll only stay an hour or so. Please, Mom?"

My mother stared at me for so long that I got nervous. Automatically, I reached for a strand of my hair that fell over my shoulder. I curled an end around my finger. That was not a smart move.

"I wish you would do something with your hair," Mom began. I dropped my hand and tossed my hair off my shoulder.

"Please, Mom, can I—*may I* go uptown for an hour?"

"I thought you wanted to call Sharon," she reminded me.

"She's probably already there."

Mom contemplated. "You remember what your dad told you this evening?" I nodded. "If you promise to be back here at the house in an hour, and…"

"Thanks, Mom!" I hugged her and ran upstairs to put on a streak of the pale pink lipstick she allowed me to wear, now that I was fourteen. Sharon had a tube of bright red, which I had sampled more than once at school, always being sure to scrub it off with a harsh, brown paper towel before I came home.

I threw off my blouse and pulled a new red boat-necked tee shirt over my head. I turned sideways, both directions, admiring my bosomy silhouette. I tossed my hair over one shoulder and dropped my chin, as I looked into the mirror above the dresser. I sucked my cheeks in, striving for the Lauren Bacall look, and failing miserably. Well, maybe my hair looked a little bit like hers. I wondered what Victor Delacorte would think about the red tee shirt. Maybe he would be at the Sweet Shoppe. I really *needed* a red lipstick!

I straightened the cuffs of my jeans, picked up a white cardigan sweater and ran down the stairs. With any luck, I could be out of the house before Mom changed her mind or issued new instructions.

"One hour, Sissy," Mom called from the living room. "Dad and I will wait for you to come home, before we go to the Simpson's. We've already called them, so don't be late."

"Okay, Mom." I hurried out the kitchen door and jogged to Sharon's house, hoping that she would still be at home. There were streetlights on all the corners now, but I wasn't crazy about walking the four blocks to the Sweet Shoppe alone in the dark. At seven o'clock in April, the sun had disappeared completely.

"Come in, Sissy." Mrs. Bennett opened the front door at my knock. She was a lovely lady with short dark hair, a gentle voice and calm disposition. "Sharon," she called. "Sissy's here."

Sharon emerged from her room. She looked as bored as I had felt.

"Want to go to the Sweet Shoppe for an hour?" I asked. "That's all the time Mom would give me, so we have to hurry."

"Okay, Mother?" Sharon asked.

"Sure, Honey. Have a good time."

I went to Sharon's room with her to get a jacket.

"Bring your red lipstick," I whispered. Sharon's hazel eyes darted at me and she grinned. She picked up the tube from her dresser and tossed it to me. I bent to the mirror and drew a quick outline around my mouth, covering up the nondescript pink.

"Matches your shirt," she said.

The Sweet Shoppe was crowded. The side booths were packed with teen-aged boys and girls, but no couples. From the jukebox in the back room, where dating couples gathered, came the clarion voice of Theresa Brewer belting out Till I Waltz Again With You. Sharon and I picked up cherry Cokes from the soda fountain counter and slowly made our way to the back. There simply was no place to sit up front.

A glittering silver ball spun slowly from the ceiling. The only other light came from the huge jukebox, which stood against the back wall. High school couples swayed to the music, oblivious to everything outside their little circles of movement. Sharon pointed to an empty booth in the far corner; and we hurried to it, hoping not to find a purse or other evidence of staked out territory.

It looked unclaimed. We slid across the seats, facing each other, and turned so that we could watch the dancers. We had practiced dancing with each other and our other friends, but none of us had as yet been asked to dance with a boy. I leaned over the booth-top and whispered.

"You won't believe what happened in the park this morning after I left your house. You know that boy that lives with the Butlers, Victor Delacorte? He pushed me in the swing and when it stopped, he…"

"Shh-h-h-h-h," Sharon whispered.

"Hello, Ladies."

I looked up. My heart started that crazy double-time thump that made me short of breath. Victor Delacorte was standing beside our booth! He held out his hand to me.

"Dance with me," he said. I looked at Sharon.

"Go ahead," she ordered. Mute as the statue in the library, I slid out of the booth. Victor took my hand and led me to the edge of the dance floor. The silky, soft voice of Nat King Cole crooned soulfully through the room, *"Pretend you're happy when you're blue; it isn't very hard to do…"* Victor put his arms around me and drew me close to him."

I was dancing with Victor Delacorte! I was fourteen years old, and Victor Delacorte's right hand gently guided me in the steps of a slow dance in the back room of the Sweet Shoppe! My mom and dad would kill me if they knew—worse, they would lock me in my attic room for the rest of my life! Unless, of course, I died from sheer euphoria right there on the dance floor!

The slowly spinning globe cast silvery streams of light upon the dancers, lending an air of fantasy and mystery. I thought that I must surely be dreaming, but the boy who held me certainly felt real. Neither of us spoke for what seemed like a long time. Victor danced as if he had been dancing all his life, and he made me feel like Ginger Rogers.

"You're a pretty little thing." Victor's low voice murmured in my ear, stirring wisps of my hair. I didn't know what to say, so I kept quiet. "How old are you?" he asked. "Sixteen, seventeen?" I couldn't tell him I was only fourteen and a half! So I just lifted my eyes to his and smiled.

Victor was the most handsome boy I had ever seen. He stood four or five inches taller than I; and his body had the lean, muscular look of someone older than his eighteen years. His black hair curled across his forehead, and it grew a little longer than the boys wore their hair in Redbud Grove. His sideburns were longer, too, and looked dashing above the collar of his denim jacket.

Black eyes framed with black lashes smiled down at me. I couldn't seem to look away from Victor's face. His mouth curved in a tiny smile, revealing incredibly white teeth behind his full lips. He smelled like spearmint gum and something else I couldn't identify. I liked it.

"You don't talk much, do you?" he teased. I could feel the blush that crept into my cheeks, and I was grateful for the dim light. I dropped my lashes. He chuckled, and goose bumps ran up and down my spine at the low rumble so close to my ear. "Why does everyone still call you 'Sissy'? Haven't you outgrown that by now?"

"I like it better than my real name," I replied. I was grateful that I could still find my voice.

"It can't be that bad," Victor said. "What is your name?"

I whispered my name in his ear. Most of my close friends didn't even know what I had just told Victor Delacorte. He chuckled again.

"It's a combination of both my grandmas' names. I never liked it," I explained.

"Okay, we'll keep your nickname, Sissy." The way he said my name made it sound beautiful, not childish. Until today, I was unaware that he even knew my name.

The music stopped and Victor dropped his hand from the back of my waist. He walked me to the booth, where Sharon sat watching us approach.

"See you," Victor said. He left as suddenly as he had appeared.

"*Tell me!*" Sharon ordered. "What did he say? What did you say?" She sounded as breathless as I felt.

"I can't," I whispered. I looked at the illuminated round clock on the wall. It would take me ten or fifteen minutes to walk home, and then my hour would be nearly gone. "I'd better go, Sharon. If I'm not home by eight, my mom will never let me out of the house again."

"I'm coming with you. And you're going to tell me everything Victor said to you! I can't believe it! *You danced with Victor Delacorte!*" Sharon was nearly squealing. I didn't know how to describe the feelings that Victor had stirred inside me, and we hadn't said much. I didn't want to talk about it. I just wanted to go home, lie on my bed, look at the stars from my window, and relive every touch, every sound, and every tingly sensation.

Some things just could not be shared.

I made it home with a few minutes to spare. I thought that would surely earn me points. I was wrong.

"What's that on your mouth?" Mom demanded. I had forgotten to wipe off the red lipstick!

"Oh, Sharon got a new tube and wanted me to try it. Do you think it's too bright for me?" I looked right into my mother's face, and with my dad's guileless gray-blue eyes, I placed the blame for my scarlet mouth upon my friend, Sharon.

"Makes you look cheap."

"I'll wash it off," I promised. "You and dad go ahead to the Simpson's. I'll take care of Bethy." Mom stared hard at me for a moment. There was a puzzled expression on her face, and for a second I thought that she was going to question me about my evening.

I turned away from her and went into the bathroom, where I quickly removed the offending color from my mouth. My face looked a little flushed.

"We'll be back by ten," Mom called from the kitchen.

"Okay. Have a nice time."

By nine o'clock, I had put Bethy to bed. Buddy was in his room, doing whatever he did in there. I was free to retreat to my starlit sanctuary and relive the exciting sensations I had experienced for the very first time in my life. And that is what I did.

Every one of them.

Monday could not come fast enough. I knew there was little chance that I would see Victor at school, since my classroom was not considered a part of the high school. It was tucked into a corner, along with the seventh grade classroom, away from the flow of high school students. We shared the cafeteria, but fraternization between the two grade school classes and senior high was discouraged.

I had never seen Victor inside the building. He had been in Redbud Grove a few months; but until Saturday in the park, I had only caught glimpses of him on campus. It occurred to me that he had no way of knowing that I was not his peer. He was a senior, and he obviously thought that I was a sophomore or junior. We would not necessarily be in any of the same classes. I surmised that Victor had not spoken to anyone about me. I prayed that he would not!

I might be in the throes of a full-blown crush, but I didn't fool myself. Once Victor knew how old, or rather how young, I was, he would not give me another glance.

I didn't see Victor again for several days. I had watched for him at school; and I had stayed within sight of the park the following weekend, hoping that he would stroll across it again. He didn't. Whatever fluke had brought him through the park was not repeated.

I needed to do some research for a report that was due on Monday, so I took Bethy with me to the library the next Saturday afternoon. Bethy, who was approaching the age of eight, was only weeks away from receiving her own library card. She had already developed a love of books and could happily spend hours in the younger children's reading room.

The tables were empty next to the encyclopedias. I arranged my notebook, text, and research materials around me and settled down to work. Ancient Egypt held some interest for me, and it wasn't long before I was immersed in the region of the Nile. I don't know how long it was before I became aware that someone had joined me at the table. I glanced to my left and did a classic double take.

Sitting sideways, facing me, was Victor Delacorte.

"What are you doing here?" I whispered. Miss Ghere was a stickler for silence in the library.

"I was driving by and saw you come in. Thought I'd see if you were still here. Would you like to go get something to drink?" Victor whispered, too.

I looked down at the books and papers in front of me. "I can't," I said. "My little sister is with me, and I have to finish this report by Monday." I couldn't *believe* that Victor had come looking for me! And Bethy was in a room nearby!

"How long will you be?" he asked.

"Probably another half hour, maybe forty-five minutes." Victor wore a navy tee shirt and jeans. He looked dangerous and wonderful! None of the boys in Redbud Grove wore colored tee shirts; but they would never look like Victor, if they wore every color of the rainbow. I was shaking inside.

"I have to get the car back to my uncle's house pretty soon. Want to meet me at the Ritz tonight? There's a Marlon Brando show on— should be pretty good."

I thought quickly. Mom would let me go with my friends. I could call Sharon, Melissa and Shirley. They would go with me, and then I could meet Victor. Just planning it made my heart beat faster.

"Okay," I told him.

"I'll wait for you in the lobby." He smiled and stood up. I watched him walk away; and after he left, I sat staring at the door until Miss Ghere caught my eye from the checkout counter. The look she leveled upon me was similar to the one my mother would have used, under the same circumstances. I could only pray that Miss Ghere would say nothing to Mom that would result in my being terminally grounded.

I smiled at Miss Ghere and turned my attention back to my report. Egypt had lost its appeal. Quickly I finished my notes and returned the research volumes to the shelves. Bethy had chosen a book to check out, so within minutes we were out the door and on our way home.

"Why do we have to hurry?" Bethy asked.

"I have a lot to do." I walked fast, and Bethy nearly had to run to keep up with me.

It took a lot of time to get ready. After my bath, I gave myself a liberal dusting of Evening in Paris powder, a birthday gift from one of my aunts. I chose a flared, dark print skirt and tucked a white peasant blouse into the waistband. I could pull the elastic neckline onto my shoulders, after I left the house. My mother would never allow me to wear it that way, but she would never know.

I brushed my hair until it shone, and I tucked the ends into a wavy pageboy. I coaxed a strand into a long curl and pulled it onto the front of my left shoulder, just like the movie stars wore their long hair. I bit my lips until they were reddened, but Mom could not complain if the color were natural.

It worked out as I had planned. Shirley came by my house, and together we picked up Sharon. Melissa met us at the theater. We stood in the lobby for several minutes, visiting with other friends. My eyes kept straying to the door, but there was no sign of Victor. Disappointment settled upon me like a dark mist.

"Come on, the show is starting." I followed the girls into the darkened theater, and we found seats mid-way from the back. Unseeing, I stared at the screen, as previews of coming attractions and then a cartoon paraded across the front.

"Where's Victor?" Sharon whispered in my ear. I shrugged. "Maybe something happened to him."

"He probably found out I'm only fourteen," I whispered back, bitterly. I sat there until I could stand it no longer. "I'm going outside," I told Sharon.

"Do you want me to go with you?"

"No. You guys watch the show. I'll be out front."

I waved my ticket at Mrs. Gordon, the ticket agent, as I left the lobby. It was dusk, and the streetlights had begun to flicker. A silvery, misty moon, just short of full, lolled above the treetops; and there was a heady scent in the air, a mixture of lilacs, and of tulips and poppies that bloomed in pots and planter boxes along the streets. I looked toward the Sweet Shoppe across the street and thought about going in for a soda, but changed my mind. I turned back and nearly ran into Victor Delacorte.

"Hi," he said. He smiled and my heart zig-zagged in my chest. "Sorry I'm late, but I had to pick up some stuff for my aunt. The good news is she let me borrow her car." Victor pointed to the shiny, gray nineteen fifty-three Chevrolet parked across the street. "Did you just get here?"

I shook my head. "No, I was inside. The show has already started."

"Do you want to go back in?" Victor's dark eyes were all over my face. My cheeks grew warm. It felt as if he had touched me. I

217

looked away. I had forgotten to pull the neckline of my blouse onto my shoulders, but right now that seemed like a good thing: less blushing skin exposed. "We could go for a drive," he said. My mind raced. *I could actually sit beside Victor in a car, where no one could see us; and I didn't have to go home, until it was time for the movie to be over!*

"Okay." Everything I had ever been told about getting into a car with someone I barely knew, evaporated from my mind like water on a hot sidewalk. Victor pointed the car west, toward the Amish community; and in no time we had left the limits of Redbud Grove behind us. We rolled the windows down, and the balmy May air felt wonderful blowing through my hair. I laughed with the sheer joy of it.

Victor tuned the radio to a pop station and turned it up loud.

"Come sit close to me," he ordered. I scooted across the seat and sat with my left leg tucked beneath me, not quite touching him. "Listen. I heard this a few days ago. This guy really knows how to sing a song." The sound was different from anything I had heard before. *"Tr-a-a-in, tra-a-a-a-in, Comin' round the be-e-end..."* The singer's voice throbbed with intensity, a breathy, sensual sound that struck a chord inside me. We listened until the song ended.

"Who was that?" I asked.

"His name is Elvis Presley. That beat is really something. I'm going to learn to play like that."

"Do you play a guitar?" I asked. My dad was the only other person I knew who played a guitar, and he didn't play anything like this Elvis person. Dad played old stuff.

"Yeah, I play. Someday I'm going to play with that guy, with Elvis Presley." He sounded very sure of himself. "Would you like a soda?"

"Sure."

We had reached the outskirts of the adjoining town. Victor turned the car into the parking lot of an A & W root beer stand, and I basked in the look of envy the carhop gave me when she took our orders. I felt very grown-up. I flinched a little when Victor reached across me and opened the glove compartment. He grinned at me.

"Did I scare you?"

"No."

"Liar." He took a pack of cigarettes from the compartment and shook one into his hand. He offered one to me, but I shook my head. My dad smoked, and I didn't like the smell of it on him. Victor lit the cigarette and blew a stream of smoke out his window. He had the look of someone who knew exactly what he was doing. I felt a twinge of disappointment.

"This looks like another dopey little hick town, just about like Redbud Grove." There was a note in Victor's voice that I had not heard before. "What do people do for fun here?" The arrival of a very loud car saved me from the embarrassment of stumbling through an answer.

"Hey, Man, what're you doing here?" It was Sonny Shaw, Redbud Grove's resident delinquent, and Betty Mahoney, the only girl in RG High with bleached blond hair. Victor waved at Sonny.

"Not much," Victor replied, "just bummin' around." Sonny revved the engine of his car, and the mufflers rattled.

"Wanna drag back toward the 'Grove?" he asked.

"Why not? Soon as they bring our drinks."

Sonny nodded and backed out of the parking lot, scattering gravel as he went. Victor drummed his fingers on the steering wheel and sang the song we had heard on the radio. He sounded good. He tossed the cigarette butt out the window, as the carhop approached with our frosty mugs of root beer.

"Wish this was the real stuff," Victor muttered. He handed a mug to me. He winked at me and gave me a crooked grin. "Maybe we can find some down the road." I wrapped my hands around the icy glass and took a long drink. I didn't know what to say or do, and there was the nagging certainty that I was in way over my head with Victor Delacorte.

Victor drained his mug and looked meaningfully at mine. I swallowed root beer so fast that it nearly went up my nose. He honked the horn, and the carhop came scurrying. She barely had time to remove the tray before Victor had started the car and begun to back away. I unfolded my leg and moved away from him, but Victor reached for me with his right hand.

"Huh-uh," he said. His fingers closed around my right shoulder, and he tugged me toward him. "I want you right here." Reluctantly, I slid closer to him. He didn't release the pressure on my shoulder until

I was pressed tightly against his side, with his right hand hanging loosely just below my collarbone. I was afraid to breathe. "That's better," he whispered into my ear.

I could feel my heart beating in my fingertips. Being held so closely against Victor felt good. But the sensations I felt were unfamiliar, and more than a little scary. "Relax," Victor chuckled. Embarrassed, I tried to relax against him, but tightened up again when his fingers curled lightly against my throat. I leaned forward and peered at the clock on the dash.

"Victor, I have to be back at the theater by nine." It was a little past eight o'clock, and the moon floated higher in the sky.

"Why?" he demanded. "It's Saturday night."

"My friends will wait for me, and I have to be there."

"Then I guess we'll have to hurry." Victor accelerated, throwing me back against him. He cupped the back of my head with his hand, drew my face to his and kissed my mouth, hard, all without taking his eyes from the road. I didn't know whether to be thrilled, angry, or scared. Somewhere in the mix was the thought that I had just experienced my first kiss; and it had happened so fast, that what I felt most was disappointment.

"Whoo-o-o-o-o! There's Sonny!"

I hadn't seen the car idling beside the road, but Victor saw it. Sonny pulled up beside us and yelled at Victor.

"Ready?"

"Yea-a-a-ah!" Victor put both hands on the steering wheel; and I slid away from him, hugging the passenger door. He pushed the gas pedal to the floor, and the car rushed forward so fast that my head pulled backward. I scooted down enough to rest my head on the back of the seat and brace my feet on the floorboard. The speedometer climbed to sixty-five, seventy, seventy-five, eighty. Sonny drove in the left lane right beside us, and the muffler on his car sounded like a tractor. His laughter mingled with the sound of Betty's squeals, as they gradually pulled away from us.

"Damn!" Victor hit the steering wheel in disgust. "This old man's car won't run!"

"Victor, there's an Amish buggy!" I screamed. Sonny's lights illuminated the horse and buggy coming toward him. There was no place for Sonny to go except the field, and that's where he went.

Victor braked hard. We slowed enough to watch Sonny's car sail over the ditch and bump along the edge of a cornfield, smashing young corn stalks for several yards before coming to a stop. We saw Sonny and Betty get out of the car. They seemed unhurt. The Amish buggy continued on its way, as if nothing had happened.

"That means we won, Baby!" Victor laughed.

"Aren't you going to help them?" I asked.

"Nah, they're okay. Man! I bet Sonny needs clean underwear!" Victor continued to laugh, but I was still shaking and saw nothing funny about the near-accident. I remained silent, while he crowed his victory. I was unprepared for the sudden turn Victor made onto a gravel road that led past several Amish farms.

"Where are you going?" I asked.

"Just a little drive through the country. I'll have you back to town by nine." I looked at the clock. Eight-thirty. Victor turned again, down a narrow lane between two fields. He shut off the lights and drove slowly, a little farther, before turning off the engine. The moon shone so brightly that he didn't need headlights to see. My heart raced.

"Come here." Victor's voice had changed. It held a husky quality, almost a purr. I stayed where I was. "Hard to get, huh? Well, I'll just come to you." He slid close to me and circled my shoulders with one arm, my waist with the other, drawing me against his chest. He buried his face in my hair and nuzzled my neck. Frantically, I tried to think of something, anything, to say.

"Uh, Victor, why did you have to leave Chicago?" *Stupid, stupid, dumb, stupid, idiot, ignorant, stupid...*

Victor raised his head. "What?"

"I'm sorry. I really didn't mean to say that. It just kind of popped out."

"You mean you haven't already heard?" he asked. I shook my head. He tucked the top of my head beneath his chin and locked his hands together around my waist. It felt nice, kind of secure, being held like that.

"I did a stupid thing one night, and my dad decided that it would be better for me to finish school down here. There was just three months of school left, and he wouldn't let me finish with my friends. I really hated him for that." I wouldn't have liked that either, I

221

thought. I couldn't think of anything much worse than leaving all my friends, again.

"What did you do?" I asked.

"I took a ride with a kid I knew. At least, that's what I thought I was doing. He said he needed to stop at a gas station to get some cigarettes, but the idiot pulled out a gun and robbed the station. I didn't know what he'd done until the cops stopped us, several blocks away."

"Were you arrested?" I didn't know whether I should be frightened or not.

"Well, yeah, at first. When we got to the police station, this kid told them that I knew nothing about it. They got my dad out of bed to come get me, so I didn't have to stay in jail or anything. But my dad was so mad at me, he sent me down here, to live with his sister. I guess it's a little better than jail...especially now."

Victor slid one hand under my chin and lifted my face. He kissed the tip of my nose, and then each cheek, and then my forehead. I dropped my head, embarrassed and scared and totally ignorant.

"Victor, I really need to get back to town." I could hear the breathlessness in my own voice.

"In a little while," he murmured. His hand circled my neck, tilting my head up, bracing my chin with his thumb. He slid his mouth along my jaw line and nibbled lightly at my throat. I think I shivered. "Just a little while." And then Victor kissed me, *really* kissed me. He kissed the corners of my mouth, my upper lip, my lower lip, sideways, and diagonally. I tasted the cigarette, but it was only mildly unpleasant.

"Put your arms around me," Victor whispered. Mindlessly, I did as he said. My arms crept around his neck, apparently of their own volition. I don't remember making the decision to put them there. I was so enraptured with his mouth that every other conscious thought disappeared. I shuddered when his tongue touched my lower lip. *Oh, yuk! I could do without that!* I drew back a little and looked into Victor's face. His eyes glittered in the moonlight, and he was breathing hard. He spoke against my mouth.

"Kiss me." Hesitantly, I touched his mouth, drew back, brushed my lips across his mouth again and felt a little braver. I guess I was a fast learner. I kissed him as he had kissed me: corners, upper lip, lower lip, sideways, and diagonally. I even experimented a little. But then something changed.

Victor moaned softly and pulled me tighter against his chest. His mouth opened slightly, and closed over mine; and the intensity of his kiss scared me. I felt younger than fourteen, and I wanted to go home. He nipped my lower lip with his teeth. It didn't really hurt, but I thought he was going to eat me alive!

I brought my arms down and pushed against his shoulders, but he only drew me tighter against him. Somehow the elastic neckline of my peasant blouse had slipped off one shoulder and Victor's mouth seemed to be all over my collarbone, my chest, my shoulder.

"Victor, stop! I want you to stop!"

"You don't mean it," he whispered against my throat. I pushed hard.

"Yes, I mean it! Stop it!" I yelled at him.

Victor grasped my upper arms and shook me. "What are you? Some kind of little tease?" There was real anger in his voice. I shook my head.

"No! I want to go home!"

"You want to go *home*? *Now?*"

"Yes. Take me home. You said you would have me back by nine, and it's nearly that now." I pointed to the clock, it's glow-in-the-dark hands clearly closing in on nine o'clock. I pulled my blouse back where it was supposed to be.

"I thought you would change your mind," he said. I shook my head.

"I've got to go straight home from the movie. My mom will be expecting me."

"Your *mom*? Why would your *mommy* be waiting for a big girl like you at nine o'clock?" Victor asked. I dropped my head.

"Because I'm only fourteen," I muttered.

I didn't look at Victor's face, but I felt his shock as he stared at me.

"Where did a fourteen-year-old learn to kiss like that!" he demanded.

"From you!" I shouted back.

Without another word, Victor slid under the steering wheel and started the car. He backed into a field and turned around quickly. He didn't speak to me until he came to a screeching stop in front of the theater, just as people were coming out the double doors.

I risked one glance at him as I opened the car door.

"I'm sorry," I said. Victor gave me a half-grin.

"Forget it, Kid," he said. I bit my lip. I was back to being a kid. I got out and closed the door. "Sissy," he called. I looked at him. "Maybe I'll look you up when you're eighteen." I thought about the cigarettes, his desire for beer, his lack of concern for Sonny and Betty, his attitude toward the little town I loved.

"Maybe I won't want you to," I answered. Victor laughed.

"You are really going to be something," he said. I felt quite secure, standing outside his car, safely out of reach of his arms.

"I already *am* something," I retorted.

Victor waved and drove away. Sharon, Shirley, and Melissa joined me on the sidewalk.

"Where have you been?" Shirley demanded.

"Let's go to the Sweet Shoppe, and I'll tell you," I said, "but I need to call Mom and tell her where I am, so she won't worry. Do any of you have an extra dime?" Melissa handed me the coin; and as soon as we entered the Sweet Shoppe, I headed for the pay phone on the wall.

"Hello, Mom? I just wanted to tell you that the movie's over, and we're at the Sweet Shoppe, getting something to drink. Would it be okay if I stay here with the girls for a little longer?"

"Sure, Honey. Just be careful, and you come home by ten."

"Okay, Mom. I will. I love you, Mom."

"I love you, too, Sweetie."

"Bye, Mom."

I would be angry with my mother many times during the next few years; but I never again lied to her about a boy.

Well, not exactly.

Eighth grade graduation was held on May twenty-fifth. As one of the top three, scholastically, in my class, I had to memorize and deliver a short speech during the ceremony. Near the end of the saccharin phrases, I caught a glimpse of Victor Delacorte. He stood in the open doorway of the small auditorium, and he looked straight at me. I lost my thoughts for a moment and stammered over a couple of words, before I tore my eyes away from him. I looked back, as I ended my speech. Victor was gone.

One week later, the high school graduation took place in the same auditorium. I attended with my friends. We applauded with the audience, as the graduates filed across the stage and received their diplomas. Something in my heart twisted as I watched Victor shake hands with the superintendent, take the folded parchment, move down the few steps, and take his place in the front row. If he saw me, he gave no indication.

Following the ceremony, I saw Victor with his parents in the hall. His mother was a tall, slim woman with thick, dark hair and eyes as black as Victor's. There was an air of elegance about her, as she stood there in a simple black dress adorned with a single strand of pearls.

Mr. Delacorte, on the other hand, looked like a boxer, with a thick chest, and arms that bulged in the sleeves of his jacket. His thinning, blond hair was streaked with gray; and his face had a florid, beefy look that spoke of too much rich food and too great a fondness for Italian wine. He was no taller than his wife.

They walked away together. I saw Victor pull away from his dad, when Mr. Delacorte threw his arm across his son's shoulders. I couldn't blame Victor for that. Mr. Delacorte had meted out a punishment not fitting Victor's so-called crime. Watching them made me sad. I was sure that I would never see Victor again, because the next day he went back to Chicago with his parents.

I suppose that a girl always remembers the boy who gave her that first kiss, who wakened those feelings that let her know she was well on her way to becoming a woman, even when the boy was not the right one for her. Unfortunately, during my dating years in high school and college, no other boy made me feel the way Victor Delacorte did that one night.

They never even came close.

#

FAREWELL

"Where are you going, Sissy?"

"Nowhere, Mom. Melissa's coming over, and I'm going to wait for her in the park." I stood in the front doorway and listened for whatever do or don't was to be forthcoming. There was only silence from the kitchen for several moments.

"Come in here, Sissy. I need to talk to you." I sighed and closed the door. I hadn't been fast enough. Mom sat at the kitchen table, idly stirring a cup of coffee, which was strange for her to be doing so closely to noon. As a rule, she would be busily making lunch, especially during the summer, when Dad came home to eat.

The glow from graduation still clung to me, a week after it was over. I felt so much older, now that I had left grade school behind; and high school waited just beyond what was sure to be a wonderful summer. I still basked in the knowledge that I was the only girl in my class, who had received her first kiss; and I enjoyed repeating the details to any of my friends who wanted a play-by-play recap.

No matter how grown-up I might feel, I was still just a kid to my mom; and I certainly couldn't tell her what advancements I had made into adulthood. Sometimes maintaining both personas became difficult.

"What, Mom?"

"Sit down, Sissy."

This did not bode well. Mom looked at me for a long time, without saying anything. I began to feel very nervous. I swallowed hard and prayed that word about my date with Victor hadn't reached her.

"Honey, something has happened. I know that you're going to be upset, but there's nothing we can do about that." Dread settled upon me as thick and oppressive as heavy, black smoke. "We decided to wait until after graduation to tell you, but we can't put it off any longer. Sissy, your dad has been transferred; and we'll be moving from Redbud Grove before school starts."

I stared at my mother, wondering what language she was speaking, because she made no sense to me. Transferred? Moving? From Redbud Grove? She had to be playing a bad joke on me. There was no way we could leave Redbud Grove. I was going to high school in September; and I was going to graduate in four years, along with the same boys and girls who had been in grade school with me for nearly eight years. I had a place here, a *position*!

"Honey, did you hear what I said?" Mom asked.

"I don't believe you," I whispered. "Why would Daddy take a job anywhere else in the world? This is our *home!*" I shouted the last word.

"The company is opening a new foundry, and Mr. Jackson wants your dad to be in charge of it. It's really a great promotion, Sissy. The Jacksons are moving, too, and will help your dad find a really nice place to live."

I didn't care about the Jacksons. They had two boys, one older and one younger than I; and it meant nothing to me that they would be moving, too. Except for the fact that Mr. Jackson was my dad's employer, the Jackson's were not a part of my life.

"Just where is this place?" I demanded, not that I cared. Tears filled my mother's blue eyes, which caused answering sorrow to pour down my own cheeks.

"It's a town on the outskirts of Charleston, West Virginia." She may as well have said Jupiter or Mars. I did a mental drawing of the United States and realized that we would have to cross Indiana, Ohio, and maybe a bit of Kentucky. I shook my head.

"No, I'm not going. I'm not leaving Redbud Grove." I folded my arms across my chest, ignoring the tears that dripped onto my shirt. "I'll live with Sharon, or Sheila, or Mrs. East. Mrs. East would keep me." Mom smiled at me through her tears and then wiped them away with her hands.

"Don't be silly," she said. "Of course, you'll go where we go. That's what families do." There was a knock at the front door.

"Hello? Sissy?"

"It's Melissa," I said. I stood up and brushed the tears from my face.

227

"Honey, I'm sorry," Mom whispered. I didn't look at her. I hurried through the living room and out the door before Melissa could come inside.

"What's the matter?" Melissa asked. She ran with me to the park and sat down beside me on the picnic table. Her mass of curly auburn hair formed little tendrils all around her face, and her lovely green eyes peered at me with concern.

"My mom just told me that we're going to move away before school starts this fall." I couldn't believe the words, even when I heard them come out of my own mouth. A piercing memory of how painful the relocation *to* Redbud Grove had been, made my lower lip tremble; but contemplating *leaving* this lovely little town was simply unbearable.

"Sissy, you can't!" Melissa's voice was a soft wail. It was my undoing. I clasped my knees with both arms, dropped my forehead onto my knees, and sobbed. "Oh, Sissy, what can we do?" Melissa cried with me. My disbelief was replaced by anger, followed quickly by sorrow, and that old enemy, fear of the unknown. Now I knew exactly what Victor Delacorte meant about hating his father. At the moment, I certainly had no good feelings about my own. How could he *do* this to me! To all of us!

Melissa put her arms around me, and we rocked back and forth in our sorrow. Eventually I stopped crying. You can only cry for so long. I wiped my face on my shirt and gazed around the park. I knew every tree, every bush, every picnic table and fountain. Every swing had held me, and I knew the sounds of each cable and chain.

In the northwest corner could be seen the lasting imprint of the circle in the grass, made by Mr. Spanhook's palomino pony. Every summer, Mr. Spanhook stood in the center of the circle and guided the pony with a long lead rope. He allowed the smaller neighborhood children to take turns riding the pony, whose name was Blondie. After the rides ended, the track made a great place to run or race bicycles.

There was the section of broken sidewalk, from which we had extracted pieces of pink quartz that had been in the gravel mix. I had made "jewels" from the glittering rocks I found there when I was a little girl. Some of the really shiny pieces remained in a small chest in my room.

I had learned to roller skate on that same sidewalk, wearing the skates I had received for Christmas the year I was eight. I had worn the metal skate key on a long string hung round my neck, guarding it carefully, because no other key would fit my skates. That key was used to tighten and loosen the metal tabs that held the skates to my shoes.

After I had finally mastered the technique of remaining upright, I had skated along that sidewalk fast enough to make the key swing from side to side against my chest, fast enough to make my hair stream behind me. I had loved the swoosh, swoosh sound of the skate's wheels upon the concrete.

For seven summers my brother and I had considered the park our own personal playground, and now my little sister played here with her friends. Although I no longer participated in childhood games, I treasured the solitude I found in the park; and I enjoyed observing the changes in the foliage, as the world turned.

"I don't understand," I said. "How can they do this? How can my dad even consider leaving here? We *belong* here! They have friends, too! So what if my dad would make more money in West Virginia? He could run the foundry here and we would do just fine!" I beat my thighs with my fists.

"You're moving to *West Virginia?*" Melissa's voice squeaked. "That's a long way from here! I thought maybe you were just moving to another town, not far away!"

"Well, I'm going to talk to my dad," I declared. "Maybe I can change his mind."

"I hope you can, Sissy. I'll really miss you if you go." She was silent for a moment. "I guess you don't feel like doing anything, huh?" I shook my head. "Okay. I'll call you later." Melissa waved and walked away.

I stretched out on the table. A warm summer wind moved through the branches, and I thought about all the times I had lain on this table and watched the limbs swing and sway above me. Now I knew the meaning of the word, dismay.

In spite of my brave words about talking to my dad, I knew that the decision to leave Redbud Grove had already been made. Mom would not have told me, had there been the slightest chance the relocation would not take place. I thought about her tears. She had her own circle of friends and acquaintances that were just as dear to her as mine were to me.

No one seemed hungry at supper that night. Mom had told Buddy and Bethy that we'd be leaving Redbud Grove. Buddy seemed as unhappy as I, and Bethy was very quiet. She would be entering third grade in the fall, and Buddy would be in the seventh grade. We were all sad.

Dad finally put down his fork and pushed his chair back from the table. He sighed loudly. "Look, I know that no one is happy about leaving Redbud Grove. I don't want to go, either; but at the new foundry I'll be making nearly twice the money I do here. We can get a bigger house, and Mom can have her own car. Won't that be nice?"

No one answered. We stared at our plates. Then, in a very small voice, Bethy said, "I like this house. I like my school. I like my friends. Daddy, I don't wanna move away!" Her words ended in a wail, and then all of us were crying. In desperation or self-defense, Dad stood up and walked out the back door.

"I suppose he's running away to the pool hall," I said, bitterly. "Who's he going to play pool with in West Virginia?"

"That's enough, Sissy." Mom brushed the tears from her face. "We're going to get through this. We'll find a nice house, and all three of you will make new friends. So will your dad and I. It won't be easy at first; but you'll like your new schools, too. Remember how you didn't want to move here, Sissy?"

"Yeah, I remember. I didn't know anyone and it was really hard!"

"But look what happened," Mom went on. "Just look at all the friends you have, that you would never have known, if we hadn't come here. There are people in the new town who will become just as close as your friends here." I didn't believe her. Not for a minute. I would *never* have other friends like Sharon or Cathy or Shirley or Sheila or Leah or Melissa. And there had been Lucinda.

"I know something else," I said. "Your friends forget you after you move away. I bet Becky Jeffries and Jerry Davis and Jackie Duncan don't even remember my name! I bet they never thought about me again after we moved away! And no one here will remember either! I'll just be that kid in the pictures, whose name everybody forgot!"

Like my dad, I rushed out the back door. I ran along Alley St. toward Sharon's house. My tears had dried. Anger had replaced the sadness, at least for the moment.

The next few weeks went by quickly. Each day seemed to gain momentum and pass more quickly than the day before, until they spun away like thread unwinding near the end of the spool. Dad went to Dixon, West Virginia, and was gone for two weeks. During that time, Mom collected boxes and started packing bed linens and winter clothing and canned goods. My brother, sister, and I had our own boxes to fill with nonessentials: mementoes, books, things we had collected and wanted to keep, school papers and the like. I still wanted to believe that it was just a bad dream, and that I would awaken to find everything back to normal.

I spent as much time as possible with my friends. They were sympathetic and seemed as sad at my departure as I was. I visited with all the widows, who were very encouraging and assured me that I would like my new life and make lots of new friends. I didn't believe them.

Dad returned from West Virginia with black and white pictures of several houses. In spite of myself, I was curious; and I examined each one as it was passed to me. Only one piqued my interest. The house was two-storied, with two dormer windows in front. A covered porch stretched across the front of the house and wrapped around one side. Tall evergreen trees grew along one property line. The yard sloped upwards sharply behind the house and was dotted with lots of leafy trees and evergreens.

"What color is this house?" I asked my dad.

"It's white, Sissy, with a red roof. It's a big house, with a bedroom for each of you kids. There's a bathroom and two bedrooms downstairs, and two bedrooms, with a bathroom between them, upstairs. Wouldn't two bathrooms in the house be nice?" He pointed to a window on the lower floor. "This is where the dining room is, and there's a big kitchen behind it. Across the hall from the dining room, is a long living room with a fireplace at one end."

A white house with a red roof, like Grandpa Bannister's house, where I was born! A fireplace! A tiny little spark of excitement tingled down to my fingers and toes. A fireplace would be wonderful at Christmas. There would be a mantel to decorate, and the room would look so cozy with a huge tree…except that none of my friends would be there to share it with me. The tingling stopped.

Mom liked the house. She told Dad to take it, that she would be happy with it, if he liked it. So Dad went back to Dixon, leaving Mom to make arrangements with movers and a realtor to sell our house. I couldn't believe how quickly my life was being rearranged, and that I had no say in the matter.

I walked along every sidewalk and street in Redbud Grove, from the north to the south, from the east to the west, and along the riverbank. I rode my bicycle through the rural countryside and looked at every farmhouse and field.

At the Thompson place, I stopped for several minutes, remembering the winter night Frank brought me home. The dogs barked at me, but didn't seem as vicious to me as they once had. On a whim I waved to Mr. Thompson, who sat in his usual place on the porch. There was no response.

I stopped beside the fence of Juliana Kitchener's house. Juliana had been my friend. Mr. Cunningham had removed the gate and refurbished the house. It now held his insurance offices and was an asset to the neighborhood.

One afternoon I went to the East Side Grade School and sat in a swing on the playground. July was already half gone, and soon preparations would begin for the new school year. As I gazed at the jungle gym, the monkey bars, the teeter-totters, I remembered learning to play on all of them. I thought about all my teachers, beginning with the beautiful Miss Kate, Mrs. Erickson, and Miss Covalt, the stately third-grade teacher, who insisted that her students learn beautiful penmanship.

During the fourth and fifth grades, my classrooms had been on the second floor. Although it was against the rules, someone slid down the worn banister daily; and I did my share of sliding, without once getting caught. Mrs. Cox had been my fourth grade teacher, an older, soft-spoken woman with gentle eyes and salt and pepper gray hair.

Mr. Brehm, my first male teacher, taught fifth grade. He was a tall, handsome man with dark hair, parted in the middle and combed into deep waves on each side, blue eyes, and a terrific sense of humor. He had made school a delightful place to be.

Tears spilled down my cheeks at the thought that I might not ever return to this place, and that my brother and little sister would not have the privilege of finishing grade school in Redbud Grove. At least I had been allowed that.

I rode my bike to West Side and sat on the front steps of the building. I thought about some of the boys and girls from the sixth grade, who became and still were my friends; Nellie, Charles, John, Doretta, Linda, Margaret, Ellen Kaye, Lyle, Connie, and Leah, my see-saw buddy.

And I cried.

"Sissy, our friends and neighbors want to have a going-away party for us in the park this Friday evening. I was told not to bring anything but my children." Mom sounded pleased. *A going-away party! Just the thing to make a person really feel missed! Here's your hat, what's your hurry?* "Isn't that nice of them?"

"Sure, Mom. Nice." So I was entitled to a little bitterness.

I didn't know that so many people could gather in the park at one time. They seemed to come from everywhere. They moved the picnic tables together and formed a long buffet, which was filled with every conceivable finger food and beverage. All the widows and every neighbor from the surrounding blocks brought something.

As the evening drew to a close, we received tearful hugs and good wishes from those whose lives had been a part of ours. My dad would be home the next day; and our last day in Redbud Grove would be Sunday, the following day. This night would be the last time we would see most of these people. How good it was to discover that so many cared about us, many whom I had not seen nor thought about for a long time.

Like dark chocolate on my tongue, the bittersweet evening lingered in my heart.

There remained one more dreaded task to complete. Dad had told us that we could not take Juliet, my big, longhaired, neutered cat with us; so Mrs. Lula had agreed to take him back and care for him. Toasty, Bethy's cat, had disappeared. We never knew what happened to him. Juliet was a non-partisan kitty, who accepted devotion from all of us.

233

Bethy walked with me through the evening twilight to Mrs. Lula's house. I held Juliet in my arms; and he completely relaxed against me, purring and talking to me, as he had always done.

He had visited Mrs. Lula's house often on his neighborhood prowls. I knew that he would be safe and happy with her, but I still cried as Bethy and I walked home without him.

Before I went to bed that night, I slipped quietly out the back door to make one last visit to Pup's grave. Buddy was already there, kneeling on the damp grass beside the little flower-covered plot.

"The new owners won't even know he's here," Buddy said. I knelt beside him.

"But we'll know; and we won't ever forget him," I promised. I heard a tiny sniffle, so I stood up and left Buddy to say his goodbyes in private.

The next day the house was packed up and impersonal looking. Dad got in really late, long after everyone, except my mother, had gone to bed in this house for the last time. I wasn't asleep when he parked outside the garage. I was awake a long time after they went to bed. I listened, but they didn't talk. They must have been too tired.

I lay in my bed and looked out the window at the stars. It was a beautiful night. The stars were brilliant and seemed closer than usual. Without a moon, they seemed to form a near-solid mass across the blackness. This was my last night to lie in this room and wonder what lay beyond the stars. I hurt too much to cry.

Seasonal images stole across the easel in my mind, creating colorful landscapes that I seemed to see all at once. There was the crystal iciness of winter, the gentle pastels of spring, the many green hues of summer, and the riotous, rambunctious joy of autumn. I would see none of them here, again.

I remembered the day that Mom and Dad had planted the two elm trees in our yard, one on the northeast side of the house, and one on the south. I had been eight years old, and the trees had not been much taller than I that day. Six years later, they were taller than the house and had begun to branch enough to offer a modicum of shade.

My throat tightened. It ached with unshed tears. There was a thump from Buddy's room across the little hall, and I knew that he felt as awful as I did. Sometime during the early morning hours, I slept.

"Get up, Sissy, Buddy. We have to get going," Dad called from the bottom of the stairs. I dressed, dragged the sheets off my bed and stuffed every loose item into a big duffel bag. Except for the furniture, which the movers would pick up the following day, my room was empty.

My brother and I entered the hall at the same time. He looked at me, and I could see the remnants of tears on his face. "I hate this," he said. "I'd have been on the junior varsity basketball team this year." I put my hand on his shoulder, briefly; and he didn't shrug it away. That was abnormal for both of us.

Breakfast consisted of milk from paper cups and rolls we ate from our hands. Everything else had been removed from the refrigerator. Nothing personal remained in the house.

"Everybody make a trip to the bathroom," Dad instructed. "And one more thing—I don't want any trouble in the back seat from any of you; no fussing, or arguing, or complaining. It's a long drive, and we're not having any nonsense. Understand?" I rolled my eyes. I supposed that I still loved him, but I didn't like the decision he had made. It was ruining all our lives. I just knew it.

Dad put suitcases into the trunk. Buddy and I each carried a stack of our favorite magazines, and Bethy was armed with a small case full of crayons and coloring books. As we walked out of our little house on Pine Street for the last time, I looked with longing at the park. Sitting on the nearest picnic table were Sharon, Shirley, Cathy, and Melissa.

"We brought you something," Sharon called as they came into the yard. She handed me a small, floral box. "Open it," she commanded. I put the magazines on the hood of the car, and pulled off the top of the box. Inside was a stack of envelopes, stamped, and addressed with their names. Underneath were sheets of paper and a couple of pens.

"So you won't have an excuse not to write," Melissa explained.

"You write as soon as you get there, and let us know all about your new house, and how far away it is from a park," Sharon instructed.

"I will," I promised.

"We've got to go, Sissy," Dad said. I hugged each of my friends individually, and then jointly. All of us had tears running down our cheeks, as I climbed into the car. Dad already had the engine running. He turned north onto Pine Street. My brother, my sister, and I looked back at our house and waved to my friends, until Dad headed east on Route One-thirty-three, past Mrs. Murphy's old house, past Mullikin's Café, across the river bridge, and quickly out of the city limits.

I thought my heart would break.

The trip was horrible.

It began to rain somewhere in Indiana, and it rained all the way across Ohio and into West Virginia. Dad pulled off the highway several times, unable to see through the downpour. During one of those stops, my brother made an announcement.

"I don't want to be called 'Buddy' any more. At the new school I'm going to tell them my name is 'Bill', short for William; and that's what I want you to call me." His tone said it all. At the age of twelve, he had issued a proclamation of emancipation from his childhood name.

"Me, too." Bethy declared. "I don't like my baby name. I'm eight years old, and my name is Beth." Mom and Dad looked at each other. Dad grinned.

"You mean I can't call you 'Wiz-bet', ever again?"

"Well, *you* can, Daddy; but no one else!"

"What about you, Sissy? Are you going to change your name, too?" Dad asked.

"Nope."

So not only were we leaving our old home, we were leaving "Buddy" and "Bethy" behind, too. It would take some conscious effort, but it would be done.

After that break and a long three hours of driving with no stops, Dad finally pulled into a big truck stop in Cincinnati. He ordered everyone out to use the restrooms, while he had the gas tank filled. It was the largest gas station I had ever seen. A convoy of National Guard trucks was parked behind the station, and the place was crawling with young men wearing army green fatigue uniforms. They ran back and forth from the trucks to the station.

"Sissy, you go inside and find the restrooms. Bring the umbrella back and Bud—*Bill* can go next. Then I'll take Beth. Hurry, now," Mom told me. She handed the big umbrella to me, and I opened it as I got out of the car. The rain hit the pavement so hard that it splashed upwards.

Inside the huge building, I saw a sign that pointed to restrooms toward the back. I wound my way through aisles filled with uniformed young men, until I reached the door that said RESTROOMS. No one stood near the door, for which I was thankful. It opened into a hall, where I slipped into the closest door.

There were four stalls inside. I found the first stall empty, and went inside, quickly took care of business and shook the water from the umbrella. The outer door opened, and someone pushed against the door of my stall. I started to announce my presence, but I caught a glimpse of the feet of the new entrant. I clamped my mouth shut. A pair of big, black, army boots rested just inches from my size seven sandals, with only a swinging metal door between them and mine.

"Sorry, Fella'," came the apology from a decidedly masculine voice.

Ohmigosh! I thought. *I'm in the men's restroom! How do I get out, without someone knowing how stupid I am?* I listened closely. I wanted to make certain that only one man had come inside. Carefully I flipped the latch and opened the stall door a crack, then wider. I heard the other stool flush. As quickly and quietly as I could, I opened the outer door and slipped through...and ran headlong into a group of soldiers, gathered in front of the door.

"Whoa, Little Lady." Two hands grasped my upper arms and held me upright. Another soldier picked up my umbrella, which had clattered to the floor.

"Are you lost?"

"Or do you always use the men's john?"

"Hey, she can use it with *me*!"

Face flaming, I grabbed the umbrella and ran for the door. I didn't open the umbrella. I just ran as fast as I could to the car and crawled inside.

"Sissy, for heaven's sake! You're getting the whole car wet!" Mom scolded. "What's wrong with you?" I didn't answer. I was glad

237

when everyone had taken a trip to the restrooms and we were on our
way again, even if it meant leaving Redbud Grove farther behind.

It was early evening when Dad announced that Dixon was only a
few miles away. Inexplicably, the rain stopped; and the sun appeared
in the west behind us, throwing streaks of gold and dark violet onto
the cumulus clouds in the east.

"There's a rainbow!" Mom exclaimed. As one, the three of us in
the back seat peered around our parents, trying to see. She was right.
A bow of brilliant color stretched from one mountaintop to another,
forming a perfect arch with the highway centered beneath it. It
looked as if we could drive right under it.

"Would you say that's a good sign?" Dad asked. No one
answered. "Is anyone interested in seeing our house before we go to
the hotel?"

"Yes, Will, I'd like to see the house," Mom answered.

"Me, too," Beth echoed.

Dad turned off the highway onto another paved road, which led
through the hills and valleys to yet another road, before we
approached the city limits of Dixon, where a sign stated the
population as ten thousand five hundred. I blinked in disbelief a
couple of times. That was nearly five times the size of Redbud
Grove! On the hills and green mountainsides sprang houses, all the
way to the tops of the slopes. Streets snaked along, forming
switchback after switchback, connecting the houses.

"Dad, is our house on the side of a hill?" Bill asked.

"Just about all the houses are on the side or on top of a hill in this
country," Dad answered. I stared in amazement as Dad drove through
the center of the town. It seemed so big! There were stoplights
instead of signs, and department stores and large grocery stores, and
shops of every description.

Dad turned right at a light. He made many more turns down
winding streets, and I knew that I would never be able to find my way
back to the center of town. He finally pulled into a driveway that
sloped upward sharply for fifty feet or so, before leveling onto a well-
kept lawn.

The house looked just like the picture, except that it seemed much
bigger. A four feet tall rock wall bordered the front yard, which was
no more than fifteen feet deep. Below the wall was a rock en-crusted

drop to the street. The lawn on the west side of the house was wide and dotted with lots of trees, while the area behind the house was level for about twenty feet, before sloping upward to another rock wall that hid the street above us.

"What do you think, Jackie?" Dad sounded surprisingly vulnerable. Mom didn't say a word for several moments, and then her words came slowly.

"I think that the house is beautiful, Will. The whole area is beautiful." Mom seemed pleasantly impressed.

"Kids?" Dad looked at us.

"Wow," said Bill.

"Can we get out, Daddy?" Beth asked, and there was excitement in her voice. I didn't say anything.

"Sissy?" Dad pinned me with his eyes. I looked at my dad. Although I was his daughter, I knew that he was a handsome man. He was tall and slender, to the point of thinness.

Although he was only thirty-five, there were lots of lines around his eyes; and lines formed parenthesis on each side of his wide mouth. He combed his hair straight back from his forehead; and it had begun to thin a little, just above his temples, where a few silver strands could be seen. Dad's face was thin, too, with high, pronounced cheekbones. Blue-gray eyes, that could sparkle with laughter or flash with anger, had been his main genetic legacy to me. His handsome face was so familiar to me that I had never seen him as a person.

My strong father, who made decisions for us, who demanded respect and obedience from us, and who supported us, was silently asking for my approval; and I knew it. It was within my power to hurt him, and I knew that, too. The icy lump that had been inside my chest for several weeks, began to melt; and I felt compassion for my dad. I couldn't knowingly hurt him.

"It's a nice house, Dad. It has a roof just like the house where Grandpa Bannister lived, doesn't it?" Dad smiled and released his breath in a long sigh.

"Yes, it does." He looked back at the house. "Grandpa's house had a big front porch, too." He cleared his throat. "Well, we'd better find that hotel and see if we can rustle up something to eat. I'm sure most of the restaurants are closed on Sunday nights, but we can probably find an A & W."

239

"Gee, Dad, do you suppose they have an A & W in these hills?" I asked.

"That's really funny, Sissy. You're a regular Lucille Ball." Dad was smiling.

Our furniture came four days later. Dad couldn't take time off work; so Mom had to instruct the movers and oversee the placement of every piece, some of which got placed and replaced several times, before she gave final approval.

Beth was thrilled with her room, which had a window that opened onto the wide side-yard. My brother and I drew straws for first choice of the upstairs bedrooms, and he won, choosing the room above Beth's. That left me with a window that opened onto the evergreen border on the short side of the lawn, but that was okay with me. I still had a view of the sky above the hillside.

The rooms in the house were large. Our furniture looked sparse, although the pieces had been crowded in our other home. The only item in the dining room was my big ebony upright piano. The movers had groaned and grunted and complained as they brought it in, and I remembered the day my dad had brought it home.

Three of his friends had helped him maneuver it through the front door of the living room, and roll it against the south wall. I had been ecstatic. I was ten years old at the time; and I had been begging for a piano, since the first day I saw the grand piano in Sheila's house. Mine was a beautiful thing, solid, shiny black, with panels of carved vines and flowers on the front. The bench was so heavy that I had not been able to move it; and when I had sat upon it, my feet dangled above the floor.

I must have driven my mother crazy that first day, because I tried to pick out melodies for hours. By evening I had found the notes of The Tennessee Waltz and How Much Is That Doggie In The Window, two tunes of the day sung by The Singing Rage, Miss Patti Page. Mrs. Wilson, my music teacher, had discouraged playing the piano by ear; so I hadn't let her know that I could and did play by ear every day. By incorporating the two methods, I was able to play just about any melody I heard.

I sat down on the stool and touched middle C, the only key missing an ivory. The tone sounded much different in a room without furniture. I played some chords and listened to them bounce off the bare walls; and then I swung into the seductive fingering of <u>In The Mood</u>, followed by <u>Chattanooga Choo-Choo</u>. I ended with a slide from the highest keys to middle C.

Applause shocked me. I looked up to see the four movers, standing just inside the dining room, clapping their hands enthusiastically. Embarrassed, I slid from the stool and made a hasty retreat through the living room and out the front door. I hurried down the front steps and crossed the narrow expanse of grass to the rock retaining wall. I climbed onto the wall and sat with my knees up to my chin.

I looked down the slope to the layers of houses below. Our house was about halfway to the top of the hill. The view from here was quite lovely, completely different from anything I had ever seen before. I wished that my friends could see it. Tall pines and spruces dotted the hillside lawns; and I could imagine that, in the winter, it would look like a scene on a Christmas card.

"Hello-o-o!" I looked around me, but could not locate the voice. "Up here!" I looked up the hill and saw a girl standing on a wall, just above the road that wound above our house. She waved and I waved back. "My name is Karen! What's yours?" I stood up and faced her.

"Sissy! Sissy Bannister!" I shouted.

"Hi, Sissy Bannister! Is it okay if I come down?"

"Sure!" I yelled back. And come down Karen did. She jumped from the wall, crossed the street, jumped upon the wall above our house; and within minutes she had scooted down the slope of our backyard. I waited for her on our wall, excited and a little nervous before she appeared around the corner of the house.

"Hi," Karen said again. She was slim and pretty and only a little taller than I. Soft brown eyes, with lashes that reminded me of Bambi, sparkled with good will. "I saw the moving truck pull in this morning, and I just wanted to welcome y'all to Dixon. I'm Karen Courtney, and I live in the first white house above y'all." I smiled.

"I love your accent," I said. Karen laughed.

"Honey, down here, y'all are the one with the accent, and it's pure Yankee." She laughed and so did I. We sat on the wall and let our legs dangle over the side as we talked. She was fourteen and was going to be a freshman. Karen told me about the school from which she had graduated in the spring, and about the high school we would be attending.

I told her about Redbud Grove and about the park. She told me that there was a small, hilly park a few streets away and offered to take me, anytime I wanted. A warm feeling of welcome emanated from her, and I couldn't help but bask in it.

"Tell you what," Karen continued. "I'll get some of my friends together one night this week, and y'all come up to my house and meet them."

"I'll have to check with my mom," I told her. Karen laughed again.

"Actually, so will I," she said. "Is your phone hooked up yet?"

"I think so."

"Good. Call me after you ask your mom. It's in the phone book under David Courtney. I'd better get back home. I didn't tell my mother I was leaving the yard. 'Bye."

I watched Karen Courtney climb like a mountain goat back up the slope and disappear over the wall. Quickly I found my mother and told her about Karen and the invitation to her house all in one breath.

"Do you think I can go?" I asked.

"Probably," Mom answered, "but right now it would be nice if you finished up your room."

As we did a few evenings before, my brother, *Bill*, and I, slept in our upstairs bedrooms; but now a nice bathroom separated the rooms, which were larger and more comfortable. I had placed my bed so that I could look out the window at the night sky. In Redbud Grove, my window had opened to the east. The exposure in my new room was to the west, and my first night in it I caught the last remaining glow of the sun, as it disappeared behind the mountain. Hovering above the hill was a huge, single star, one that I had not been able to see from my attic window in Redbud Grove. In the darkened room a pleasant sense of anticipation filled me.

Perhaps life in Dixon, West Virginia, would not be so bad, after all.

Karen invited me to her house to meet her friends the following Saturday. Mom was not too thrilled that I planned to go to Karen's via the back slope; but I convinced her that I would be careful, and that Karen would walk me back to our yard. My stomach quivered with a mixture of excitement and fear, as I attempted to climb the slope as gracefully as Karen had climbed it. I found that it would take a lot more practice before that would happen.

Karen met me at the door and led me through her house to the back yard, which seemed crowded with boys and girls, but actually held no more than ten or twelve. She introduced me to Judy, a tall girl with long blond hair and big brown eyes and a voice as soft and slow as cold molasses; to Beverly, whose Indian heritage was apparent in her dark eyes and high, wonderful cheek bones; to Gary, who cocked his head to one side a bit, as he looked at me. His big, round blue eyes looked huge beneath a thatch of curly brown hair. Jimmy, a cousin to Judy, gave me a shy smile that crinkled the skin around his merry brown eyes. Rowena, another brown-haired girl, welcomed me with a quiet voice and sweet demeanor. Oren, who looked like a very young Gary Cooper, sent a small wave my way, but except for a little smile, extended no other welcome. Hmmmm, I thought. We'll just see about that.

"Where's Jerry?" Karen asked her friends.

"He went back inside to get some more sodas," someone said. "Here he comes." I watched a boy exit the back door of Karen's house and approach the group.

"Jerry, come meet my new neighbor," Karen called. At fourteen, the boy was not much taller than I. His hair was very blond and his eyes, very blue. There was a deep dimple in one cheek. He reminded me of someone, but I couldn't remember who it was.

"Sissy, this is Jerry Davis. Jerry, Sissy Bannister." I blinked. I blinked again. Jerry frowned, grinned, and shook his head.

"Nahhh," he said, "it couldn't be." He shook his head again. "You aren't from Illinois, are you?" he asked. I nodded.

"Are you?" He nodded.

"Was Mrs. Freeman your first grade teacher?" I asked. He nodded. And then we both started talking at once. "You gave me a black eye!"

"I gave you a black eye!"

"What are you doing here?"

"What are you doing here?"

243

We were talking in unison, asking the same questions, laughing, joking, grinning, and trading insults as if the separation of the last seven years had not happened.

"I read faster than you did," I bragged.

"Not really. Mrs. Freeman just let you think you did. Actually, I beat *you.*"

"Did not!"

"Did!"

"Did not!"

"Did!"

"You guys *know* each other?" Karen demanded. We both nodded.

"We started first grade together and then I moved to Redbud Grove," I explained.

"She couldn't stand the competition," Jerry quipped. And we were at it again.

"You have a Southern accent," I accused. "How did you get it?"

"I do not!" he denied.

"Do too!"

"Do not!"

"When did you come here?" I asked.

"We moved here right after I got out of first grade," he explained.

"You mean you moved away not long after I did?"

"Yep."

Jerry and I spent most of that evening catching up, and I didn't talk much with Karen's other friends. It was so great knowing that someone in this bigger, new world, into which I had just arrived, already knew me, and that I was not totally alone, as I had been when we moved to Redbud Grove. There would be one familiar face from my past, however distant, a kind of cushion, a buffer against the crowds of people I would meet in the next few weeks.

I forgave my dad. I loved the new house, although I missed my old friends, the ones who had become a part of my life and with whom I would always have a bond. I wished they could come to Dixon and see the big high school where I would spend the next four years.

Often my dreams put me back in Redbud Grove, and when I woke there was a period of disorientation. However, it is amazing how quickly the young adapt to changes and new surroundings. I accepted the challenge of making a new life, making new friends, and forming alliances that would be a part of my life forever. How bad could it be? I already had the most important things:

My family.

A new friend.

An old friend.

It just doesn't get any better than that.

#

Barbara Elliott Carpenter

EPILOGUE

There are places I'll remember all my life,
Though some have changed,
Some forever, not for better;
Some have gone, and some remain.
All these places had their moments
With lovers and friends
I still can recall.
Some are dead and some are living,
In my life, I've loved them all.

ALL MY LIFE
Words and music by John Lennon and Paul McCartney

ABOUT THE AUTHOR

Barbara Elliott Carpenter grew up in a small Midwest town, much like the fictional town of Redbud Grove, Illinois. Her love of writing began in the fourth grade and is now a passion, taking precedence over oil painting, which she also enjoys.

Barbara has received awards and prizes for her poems and short stories, some of which are currently included in the curriculum of a California high school Literature class. A prolific writer, she has been published in *Reader's Digest* and other periodicals, as well as various online publications. Barbara was a member of the Cedarhurst Writer's Roundtable for many years. She is currently working on a sequel to *STAR LIGHT, STAR BRIGHT...*, which is entitled, *I WISH I MAY, I WISH I MIGHT...*, and has three more novels in progress. She has two children, four grandchildren, and a lazy male cat, named Juliet. Barbara and her husband, Glenn, live in south central Illinois. They have been married for forty-four years, many of them, quite happily.

Printed in the United States
1162500003B/175-225